Also by James Oswald

The Inspector McLean Mysteries

Natural Causes

The Book of Souls

The Ballad of Sir Benfro

Dreamwalker

The Rose Cord

The Golden Cage

Other Novels

Running Away

Jacob

Head

Abundance

One Good Deed

Travel Writing

Pedalling Uphill Slowly

The Book of Souls

JAMES OSWALD

PENGUIN BOOKS

PENGUIN BOOKS

Published by the Penguin Group
Penguin Books Ltd, 80 Strand, London WC2R ORL, England
Penguin Group (USA) Inc., 375 Hudson Street, New York, New York 10014, USA
Penguin Group (Canada), 90 Eglinton Avenue East, Suite 700, Toronto, Ontario, Canada M4P 2Y3
(a division of Pearson Penguin Canada Inc.)
Penguin Ireland, 25 St Stephen's Green, Dublin 2, Ireland (a division of Penguin Books Ltd)
Penguin Group (Australia), 707 Collins Street, Melbourne, Victoria 3008, Australia
(a division of Pearson Australia Group Pty Ltd)
Penguin Books India Pvt Ltd, 11 Community Centre, Panchsheel Park, New Delhi – 110 017, India
Penguin Group (NZ), 67 Apollo Drive, Rosedale, Auckland 0632, New Zealand
(a division of Pearson New Zealand Ltd)
Penguin Books (South Africa) (Pty) Ltd, Block D, Rosebank Office Park,
181 Jan Smuts Avenue, Parktown North, Gauteng 2193, South Africa

Penguin Books Ltd, Registered Offices: 80 Strand, London WC2R ORL, England

www.penguin.com

Published in electronic edition by Penguin Books 2012
Published in this edition 2013
001

Set in 12.5/14.75pt Garamond MT Std
Typeset by Jouve (UK), Milton Keynes
Printed in Great Britain by Clays Ltd, St Ives plc

A CIP catalogue record for this book is available from the British Library

ISBN: 978-1-405-91316-4

www.greenpenguin.co.uk

Penguin Books is committed to a sustainable
future for our business, our readers and our planet.
This book is made from Forest Stewardship
Council™ certified paper.

ALWAYS LEARNING   **PEARSON**

For Barbara

I

The streets are empty. An unnatural quiet spreads over the north end of the city as if all the sound has been sucked out of it by the festivities on Princes Street. Only the occasional taxi breaks the calm as he follows his feet who knows where. Away from the crowds, away from the excitement, away from the joy.

He has been wandering for hours now, searching, though in his heart he knows he is too late. Has he been here before? There is a terrible familiarity about it all: the clock-tower arms reaching towards midnight and the opening of a new millennium; the cobbled streets glistening with slippery rain; the orange glow against warm sandstone painting everything with a demonic light. His feet take him downwards, through the nine circles, despair growing with each muffled footfall.

What is it that stops him on the bridge? An impossible sound, perhaps. The echo of a scream uttered years ago. Or maybe it's the sudden hush of the city holding its breath, counting down those last seconds to a new dawn. He can't share their enthusiasm, can't find it in himself to care. If he could stop time, turn it backwards, he would do things so differently. But this is just a moment, and it will be followed by another. Another after that. Onwards to infinity.

He leans on the cold stone parapet, looks down on the

dark rushing water below. Something has brought him here, away from the world of celebrations and festive cheer.

A loud explosion marks the end of the old and the start of the new. Fireworks come in quick succession, rising over the tall buildings and lighting the sky. A million new stars fill the heavens, chasing away the shadows, reflecting in the black water, revealing its dread secret.

Flash, and the water sparkles with strange shapes, fading away like afterglow on the back of the eye.

Flash, and startled fish dart from the floating fingers they have been nibbling away.

Flash, and long black hair tugs glossily in the flow, like seaweed on the tide.

Flash, and the pent-up force of a week's rain pushes past the latest obstacle, moving it slowly down towards the sea, rolling it over and over as it goes.

Flash, and a ghostly white face stares up at him with pleading, dead eyes.

Flash . . .

2

'Argh! Jesus! Is that a rat?'

'Keep it down, constable.'

'But sarge, it crawled over my foot. Must've been the size of a bloody badger.'

'I don't care if it was as big as my shiny arse. Keep it quiet until we get the signal.'

A grumbling silence fell over the dark street as the small group of police officers crouched among uncollected rubbish sacks outside a lifeless tenement. The constant quiet roar of the city around them underlined the stillness, the insufficient glow of the one functional street light casting everything in twilight shadow. Early morning and you could rely on the natives of this part of town to be asleep, or stoned out of sensibility.

Two clicks on an airwave set, then a tinny voice through an earpiece. 'All clear round the back. You're good to go.'

The bodies shuffled around, hemmed in by the rubbish on either side. 'OK people. On my mark. Three . . . Two . . . One . . .'

A crash of splintering wood split the air, followed closely by a scream.

'Argh! Bastard wasn't even locked.' Then, 'Jesus Christ! There's shit all over the floor.'

Detective Inspector Anthony McLean sighed and switched on his torch. In front of him he could just make out the black-clad figure of PC Jones struggling to extricate himself from a pile of rubbish sacks inside the tenement hallway.

'Did they not teach you in Tulliallan to check that first?'

He pushed past the struggling constable and into the dank building, sniffing the air and trying not to gag. Rotting garbage mixed with stale piss and mould, the favoured aroma of the Edinburgh slum. It wasn't usually this ripe though, and that didn't bode well for why he was here.

'Bob, you take the ground floor. Jones, help him.' McLean turned to the final member of their party, a baby-faced young detective constable who'd been unlucky enough to be in the canteen at the station an hour earlier looking like he had nothing better to do. That's what you got for being keen. 'Come on then, MacBride. Let's see if there's anything here worth breaking down an unlocked door for.'

There were three storeys to the tenement, two tiny flats on each floor. None of the doors were locked, and the graffiti liberally scrawled over every available surface was at least two generations of squatter out of date. McLean stepped carefully from room to room, the beam of his torchlight playing over broken furniture, ripped-out electrical fittings and the occasional dead rat. DC MacBride never left his side, hovering like an obedient labrador, almost too close for comfort. Or maybe it was just that he didn't want to brush up against anything. Couldn't blame him, really. The smell of the place would take weeks to wash out.

'Looks like yet another complete bloody waste of time,' McLean said as they left the last flat and stood on the landing at the top of the stairs. All the glass had long since gone from the window looking out over the gardens behind. At least that meant a cold wind could blow away the worst of the smell.

'Um. Why did we come here, sir?' The question choked in MacBride's throat, as if he had tried to stop himself asking it at the last minute.

'That's a very good question, constable.' McLean shone his torch down into the empty stairwell, then up at the ceiling with its high-angled roofline and reinforced glass light well. That was out of reach of the vandals, and tough enough to withstand thrown missiles, but even so a couple of panes were crazed and sagging. 'An informant. A snitch. What is it they like to call them these days? A Covert Human Intelligence Source?' He made little bunny ear inverted commas with his fingers, bouncing the light from his torch up and down as he did. 'Bugger that. Mine's a stoner called Izzy and he's a useless tosser. Spun me a load of old crap just to get me out of his hair, I've no doubt. Told me this place was used as a distribution hub. My own fault for believing him, I guess.'

More lights flickering in the darkness downstairs were Detective Sergeant Bob Laird and Police Constable Taffy Jones stumbling through the rubbish sacks in the entrance hall. If they'd found anything they'd have shouted, so it looked like the whole episode was a complete waste of time. Just like every other bloody raid. Wonderful. Dagwood was going to be so pleased.

'Come on then. It's probably best if we don't make Grumpy Bob climb all the way up here. Let's get back to the nice warm canteen.' McLean set off down the stairs, only realising he wasn't being followed when he was half-way to the next floor. He looked back and saw MacBride's torch pointed at a space above the fanlight over one of the flat doors. A small hatch gave entry to the building's loft space. It looked almost completely unremarkable, except for the shiny new padlock hasp screwed into it.

'D'you think there might be something up there, sir?' MacBride asked as McLean rejoined him on the landing.

'Only one way to find out. Give us a leg-up.'

McLean shoved his torch in his mouth, then trod gently in the cup made by the constable's interlocked fingers. There was nothing to hold onto except a small lip below the hatch, and he had to stretch his other leg out to the wobbly banister before he could reach up with one hand and unclip the hasp. It gleamed where until recently a padlock had swung.

'Hold steady.' McLean pushed against the hatch. It resisted slightly, then swung in on well-used hinges. Beyond was a different darkness, and a sweet musk quite at odds with the rank odour wafting up from below. He swung his head around until his torch pointed in through the hatchway, seeing aluminium foil over the rafters, low wooden benches, fluorescent lighting.

'I can't hold on much longer, sir.' MacBride's voice shook with the effort of holding twelve stone of detective inspector. Well, maybe thirteen. McLean transferred as much of his weight as he dared to the banister, then swung around and dropped back down to the stone landing. The constable looked at him with a worried expression, as if expecting to be shouted at for his weakness. McLean just smiled.

'Get on your airwave set,' he said. 'I think we're going to need a SOC team here as soon as possible.'

Removing the rubbish bags had helped clear the air, but the flagstone floor they had covered was sticky and slippery with fluids best not thought about too deeply. McLean watched the stream of white-suited SOC officers as they trooped from their van, along the corridor and up the stairs, lugging battered aluminium cases of expensive equipment.

'Pity the poor bastard who's going to have to go through all that.' Grumpy Bob nodded at the pile of rubbish bags each now sporting a 'Police Evidence' tag and waiting in the middle of the road for a truck to come and take them away.

'That would be me, as it happens. Who's the officer in charge here?' A white-suited figure stopped mid-corridor, pulling off a hood to reveal an unruly mop of spiky black hair. Emma Baird either was or wasn't going out with McLean, depending on which station gossip you spoke to. He'd not seen her in a couple of weeks; something about a training course up north. As she scowled in the half-light, he wished their reunion could have been in better circumstances. He looked at Grumpy Bob, who shrugged back at him an eloquent refusal to take any responsibility.

'Hi, Em.' McLean stepped out of the shadows so he could be seen. 'I thought you were still up in Aberdeen.'

'I'm beginning to wish I'd stayed there.' She looked at the growing pile of rubbish. 'You know that attic's not been disturbed in months, right?'

'Shite.' Another dead end. And it had all been looking so promising.

'Exactly, shite. Twenty-three stinking black bin bags of it, to be precise. And I'm going to have to go through every last one of them knowing there's going to be bugger all in there of any use to your investigation. Unless you decide it's unnecessary. . .' She trailed off, looked at the two of them, eyes flicking between them as if unsure who she should be addressing.

'If I could, I would, Em.' McLean tried a smile, knowing it would just look like a grimace. 'But you know Dagwood.'

'Oh crap. He's no' in charge, is he?' Emma scrunched her hood in her gloved hands, shoved it in a pocket of her overalls, turned and shouted to the assembled SOC crowd. 'Come on you lot. Quicker we get started, quicker we can hit the shower.' And she stalked off without another word.

3

An icy rain whips around the cemetery, turning the winter snow into salt-grey slush. The sky is leaden, clouds settling down over the small party like a drowning wave. He stands at the edge of the grave, staring down into blackness as nearby a minister mutters meaningless platitudes.

Movement now, and strong men grasp the sash cords slipped under the coffin. She is inside it, lying still and cold in his mother's favourite dress. Her favourite dress. No good to anyone now. He wants to break open the lid and look on her face just one more time. He wants to cradle her in his arms and will the past to melt away. For the bad things to have never happened. What would he give to go back just a couple of months? His soul? Of course. Bring on the contract and the blood-tipped quill. He has no need of a soul now that she's gone.

But he doesn't move. Can't move. He should be helping the strong men lower her into the earth, but he can't. It's all he can do to stay standing.

A hand on his arm. He turns to see a woman dressed all in black. Tears run down her white-painted face, but her eyes are full of an angry hatred. They stare at him full of accusation. It's his fault that all this has happened. His fault that her baby girl, her only joy, is slowly being covered with shovels of earth. Food for the worms. Dead.

He can't deny those eyes. They're right. He is to blame.

Better she push him in the grave now. He won't stop her. He'd be happy to lie on that coffin while they threw the dirt on top of him. Anything would be better than trying to live without her.

But he knows that's what he will do.

4

Noon had scarcely passed and the late autumn sun was already heading for bed. McLean stared up at the clouds hanging in mackerel strips high above Salisbury Crags and shivered at the thought of impending winter. The concrete hulk of the station would swallow him into a world of artificial light and tinted windows soon enough. For now he just wanted to feel the wind on his face. Be anywhere but inside.

'You going to stand out here all day, sir? Only there's a cup of tea with my name on it in there.' Grumpy Bob slammed shut the door of the pool car and set across the car park towards the back door of the station. He'd not gone more than a half dozen paces when a blaring of horns made him jump back in alarm. Brakes squealed and a shiny new Jaguar estate ground to a halt on the ramp that led down to the secure storage under the station. A tall figure pushed open the driver's door before struggling out and limping around the front of the car.

'Sorry about that, Bob. Didn't see you in the sunlight.'

'Jesus, Needy. You nearly had me there.' Grumpy Bob put a theatrical hand over his chest, the other patting the car's bonnet. 'Nice motor, mind. I must have missed the news about sergeants' pay.'

'Now, now, Bob. Just because you spend all your money on beer and loose women.' McLean looked over at Needy,

Sergeant John Needham to those who didn't know him well. King of the subterranean depths of the station, the evidence locker and labyrinthine warren of archives and stores. Normally he could be relied on to bring a touch of humour to any situation. Now though, he looked strained, grey-faced and tired.

'Afternoon, sir.' Needy moved stiffly to address McLean, his damaged leg obviously giving him more gyp than usual. McLean remembered the athletic detective sergeant who'd taken him under his wing all those years ago. If not for an unfortunate encounter with a drunken, bottle-wielding thug, it would have more likely been Needy running the investigation and McLean calling him sir.

'Afternoon, Needy.' McLean nodded at Grumpy Bob. 'He's right though. It's a nice motor. You decided to treat yourself to a retirement present? Can't be long now.'

'February.' Needy didn't look altogether happy about the prospect. 'Just need to get Christmas and Hogmanay behind us, then it's goodbye to all this.' He held up his hands as if praying to the courtyard and looming walls. Or taking applause from the silent windows. 'There were Needhams working out of the old station before they even built this place. Reckon about a hundred years of service, all told. And I'm the last.'

'How is the old man, by the way?' McLean asked. Tom Needham, beat copper for forty years, man and boy. It'd been a while since he'd last visited the station, wandering around as if he owned the place and poking his knobbly walking stick into everyone's business. No matter that he was long retired and didn't have clearance; there wasn't a senior officer in the district would dare tell him to go home.

A shadow passed over Needy's face and he began the laborious process of lowering himself back into his car.

'He's in the hospital again. I was on my way over to see him.'

'Well give him my best,' McLean said. 'And don't let us keep you.'

'Aye, I'll not at that,' Needy said. 'I want to be as far away from here as possible when Dagwood hears about your raid this morning.'

'How could you possibly know anything about that?' McLean asked, but Needy just smiled, pulled the door closed and drove off.

The tension grew as you climbed the stairs from the back foyer towards the dark heart of the station. McLean could feel it as a stillness in the air, a heavy weight on his shoulders, a pressure in his sinuses. And then there was the smell of fear that pervaded the corridors. Either that or some of the junior constables were in need of a wash.

The largest incident room in the building took up a good proportion of the front of the first storey, its long windows overlooking the busy commuter route funnelling traffic from the Borders into the city centre. McLean hovered in the double doorway, surveying a study in busy-ness. Uniformed constables and sergeants scurried back and forth between a bank of computer screens, a whiteboard the length of the room and a map of the city that took up one whole end wall. Two dozen different voices chattered into headpieces as yet more manpower disappeared into the ever-swelling overtime budget. And all for what? A crappy tip-off that had led them to a long-abandoned site that probably had nothing whatso-ever to do with their current investigation.

'Well, well, well. Look what the cat dragged in. I was beginning to wonder what had happened to you.'

McLean faced his accuser, grateful at least that he'd be able to break the news to someone who might not chew him up and spit him out. Detective Inspector Langley was all right really, as far as drug-squad detectives went. Tech-nically speaking, this whole investigation was meant to be under his command, with McLean giving logistical sup-port, whatever that meant. But they had both been forced into a different role by the constant interference of a cer-tain detective chief inspector who, thankfully for McLean, didn't appear to be around right now.

'So how'd it go then?' Langley asked, with a look on his face that almost convinced McLean he didn't already know.

He shrugged. 'Too early to tell. Forensics might come up with something. We certainly left them enough to work through.'

'Aye, I heard.' Langley scratched at his nose and then peered at the tip of his finger as if pondering whether or not to stick it in his mouth. Deciding eventually to rub it on the side of his jacket instead. 'So's the boss.' And he flicked his gaze past McLean's shoulder towards the open door behind at the same time as McLean felt the tempera-ture drop and the hubbub fall to silence.

'Where the bloody hell have you been, McLean? I've been looking for you all day.'

McLean turned to see the tall figure of his least-favourite colleague stride through the doors. Detective Chief Inspector Charles Duguid, or Dagwood to anyone not within earshot. It must have been a brown suit week, and the faded polyester mix of this particular number had frayed at the cuffs, gone shiny at the elbows. He looked more like a schoolteacher than a detective, the kind of schoolteacher who takes great pleasure in picking on the slow kids, and whose whole demeanour just encourages his pupils to be insubordinate. From his thinning, ginger-grey scraggle of hair, to his blotchy white face that could turn red with anger at the slightest hint of an excuse, to his gangly frame and over-large hands with their long fingers and bulbous bony knuckles, he put McLean in mind of an orangutan in a suit, only less friendly.

Try to be reasonable. At least at first. 'If you remember, sir, I told you I was going to follow up a potential lead from one of my informants. You know how hard it's been to pin this lot down. I thought I'd hit the place fast, get there before they scarpered.'

'So the investigation's winding down now? We've got the felons stewing in the cells as I speak, and the city is once more free of the menace that is farmed cannabis,' Duguid sneered. 'Weren't you just a sergeant last month?'

'It's been almost a year, and I hardly see what that's got to do with —'

'Some of us have just a little more experience running an investigation than you, McLean. Even Langley here's put a few dealers away in his time. And you know what the single most important facet of any investigative team is, eh? You remember that from your training, eh?'

With each 'eh?' Duguid came closer and closer, looming over McLean, making full use of his extra height.

'It's that little word, McLean.' And now Duguid jabbed

him with a bony finger, the nail cracked and yellowing from a lifetime's proximity to cigarettes. 'Team. T-E-A-M. You don't go swanning off on some dawn raid without co-ordinating it with everyone else first. What did you do? Grab the first uniforms you could lay your hands on and go in all guns blazing?'

McLean was going to protest, even got as far as opening his mouth just a fraction, but shut it again when he recognised the irritating nugget of truth in the chief inspector's words. He hadn't completely forgotten the team structure – DI Langley had been in on the short briefing he'd arranged at six that morning. Nice of the man to come to his aid now, instead of sloping off towards the computers lined up in the centre of the room, pretending to be very interested in the latest useless actions they were churning out.

'Well, what have you got to show for yourself?' Duguid asked, shoving impatient hands into his jacket pockets, guddling about a bit and coming up with a slightly yellowing mint imperial. He rubbed a few crumbs of what McLean hoped was rolling tobacco off it before popping it into his mouth.

'We found high-power lights and hydroponics gear in the loft of the tenement my informant named,' he said, then went on to fill in the chief inspector about the morning's activities. For once Duguid didn't interrupt, possibly because he was too busy enjoying his nicotine-infused mint.

Finally he picked at his yellow teeth, peered at whatever he'd found, now lodged under a cracked, yellow nail. 'So now SOC are going through two dozen rotten bin bags full of shit for us, and you say this place looked like it hadn't been used in a while?'

McLean grimaced. 'At least we know they were there.'

'We know where they've been, McLean. We've got a half dozen sites across the city where they've been.' Duguid wafted an over-large hand towards the computers and the hard-working constables poking at keyboards, peering myopically at screens. 'We've no end of work finding out all about where they've been. I need to know where they are now.'

'I know sir. But —'

'I don't want to hear it. I really don't. It's bad enough having to listen to bloody Langley bleating all day like some constipated sheep. I brought you in on this investigation because Chief Superintendent McIntyre thought it was a good idea.' Duguid grimaced as he mentioned his superior, as if the thought of her was enough to put him in a foul mood. 'She was obviously fooled by your winning smile, but it doesn't work on me.'

'If you don't want my help, sir, I've plenty other things to be getting on with. We still don't know who's been setting fire to those old buildings, for one.' McLean could hear the petulant schoolboy in his voice, but it was too late to take the words back. Duguid bristled, his face reddening like a startled octopus.

'Get out, McLean.' His voice was rising in pitch and volume. 'Go chase your little arsonist. Leave the real police work to those of us who know what we're doing.'

5

'Christ almighty. This is some gaff!'

He stands in the enormous hallway of a palatial mansion and looks up at the wide staircase climbing around three walls towards a vast skylight high overhead. Coming down the drive, he assumed that the house was split into apartments, but now it seems the whole thing belongs to just one man.

'Takes a bit of getting used to, doesn't it lad.' Detective Inspector Malcolm 'Mac' Duff is shrugging off his coat. Detective Sergeant Needham has already thrown his down onto an old chair sitting by the door.

'Welcome to my not-so-humble home,' Needham says. 'Or should I say my father's home.'

'I didn't think they paid duty sergeants that much.'

Needham laughs. 'Don't go getting any ideas, constable. They don't. This place has been in the family for generations. Here, let me give you the two-cents tour.'

It reminds him of his grandmother's house, up in Braid Hills, though in truth it makes that place look small by comparison. Still, there's that air of a home waiting to be filled. Most of the rooms are cold, damp, unused. Only the kitchen, with its vast range oven and long wooden table, has any real warmth to it. The tour ends there with the inevitable mugs of tea.

'You'll be wondering why we've all come out here, lad.'

Duff has taken the head of the table, even though it's not his house. 'Needy's got the space, and no wife or children to go upsetting. You know how the station can get; so busy you can't hardly hear yourself think sometimes. So we use this place as a sort of unofficial incident room.'

'For what?' He asks the question even though he suspects he knows the answer.

'The Christmas Killer's what, lad.' Needham stares at him with an unusual intensity. 'Eight years we've been trying to catch the bastard. You impressed everyone with the way you solved the Probert case. Now's your chance to have a crack at something really difficult.'

6

The sound of laughter echoed out of the propped-open door to the CIB room. McLean paused outside, his ears still ringing from the bollocking he'd got from Duguid. It was always worse when you knew you'd fucked up and deserved the rant. Hard to ever accept that the DCI was right. Jovial company wasn't what he needed right now, but neither was the prospect of folding himself into his tiny office and getting to work on the overtime rosters or whatever else the duty sergeant had chosen to heap on the most junior DI in the station. He glanced at his watch; too early to call it a day? Probably, even if it had started long before dawn. Well, there were plenty of other cases demanding his attention, that at least had been the truth. And what better place to start than down in the archives, far away from anyone who might remind him of his failings.

The station was an architectural monstrosity, designed by a committee and thrown up in the seventies when the fashion for unadorned concrete was all the rage. Like much of Edinburgh, it had been built on top of something else, in this case an earlier, Victorian police station, and the basement levels were a different place altogether. Descending the old stone steps, worn in the middle by countless criminal feet, was like passing into another world. The walls were brick, painted with countless layers of thick white and laid in perfect vaulted arches by master craftsmen who had obviously taken pride in their work. The rooms down here were small, windowless. Cells from an earlier age. No longer deemed safe for housing prisoners, they had been co-opted into storage space for evidence and old files. One had been converted into an office, and it was from here that Sergeant John Needham ruled his underground realm.

McLean approached the doorway quietly, not out of any desire for stealth so much as because the place demanded silence, a bit like a cathedral, or a crypt. As he came closer, he saw that the office door was open, the light on, and from inside came the unmistakable noise of a man trying very hard not to cry. McLean peered around the doorway to see the sergeant hunched over his desk, back to the door, shaking gently.

'Needy?'

The sobbing stopped as if a switch had been flipped. Sergeant Needham looked up, rubbing at his cheeks as he tried to focus through raw-red eyes.

'Who –? Oh, Inspector McLean, sir.'

McLean recalled the conversation earlier, asking about old man Needham. They'd been close, father and son, in that curious, reserved way of a family robbed of female influence. There was only really one thing that could account for this.

'Your dad?'

Needy nodded. 'Aye. About two hours ago.' He sniffed, produced a tangled white handkerchief from his trouser pocket and blew his nose, then used a corner to dab at his eyes. 'Poor bugger. They were going to operate on his cancer today, but when the doctor opened him up . . . Well, there wasn't much point.'

'I'm sorry, Needy. I really am. He was a good copper.'

'Aye, he was that. Right crabbit bastard at times too.' Needy gave a grimacing smile and glanced past McLean, who followed his gaze to a clock on the far wall. Half-past five, Edinburgh time. 'So what brings you down here this evening?' he asked.

McLean looked at Needham and remembered the detective sergeant who had in turns bossed him around and shown him the ropes, all those years ago when he'd first joined CID. Needy had been a good detective, solid and thorough. Some might have even called him obsessive, but not McLean. They had been friends after a fashion, though never close. So what was it friends were meant to do at a time like this?

'It wasn't important. Just some background stuff, but it can wait. Why don't we get out of here? Go get a pint? I reckon we've both earned one, eh?'

'Funny. I had you as more a real-ale man.'

Needy sat on the cheap vinyl bench in an alcove that looked like an escapee from a bad gangster movie, his hands folded together on the cheap fake-wood Formica table. McLean put down the two pints of ice-cold fizzy keg beer that was the closest the place came to something drinkable, and squeezed his way onto the opposite bench.

'Not much choice, really.' He pushed one of the glasses across the table, noticing as he did that neither of them were what would pass for clean. The pub was close to the station, and that was about all it had going for it.

22

Needy took his pint, studiously ignoring the grimy ring around its middle, and raised it into the air.

'To Esther McLean.'

'Aye, and Tom Needham,' McLean added, raising his own glass. They both drank, then fell silent for an awkward, long moment. It was Needy who broke first.

'How long was it, mind? That your gran was . . . You know? Before she . . .'

'Eighteen months, give or take a day or two.'

'Jesus. That long? How'd you cope with that?'

'I don't know. You just have to, I guess. Nothing else you can do.'

'Yeah, I think I know what you mean.' Needy took another long drink. 'Doesn't mean it's easy though. Watching someone die in front of you, bit by bit.'

The silence was even longer this time. McLean tried to hurry it along, but his pint was too gassy to gulp.

'You thought about what you're going to do?' Stupid question. Of course not. Old man Needham's not cold yet. His gran had been dead half a year now, and he'd still not begun to sort out her affairs

'Christ no. One day at a time, I guess.'

McLean raised his glass again. 'I'll drink to that.'

Needy took a sip, then slumped back against the wall. 'You know, this is almost like old times. The two of us in a god-awful pub somewhere, moaning about the bitterness of life. We just need Bob Laird and Mac Duff, and we'd have the whole team.'

'I can give Grumpy Bob a call, if you want.' McLean fished his mobile phone out of his pocket. 'Duff, though . . .'

'I heard he was in a home somewhere in the Borders. Alzheimer's.'

That killed off the conversation for another long pause. Needy studied his pint, nervous fingers caressing the sides of the glass. He didn't look up when he finally spoke again.

'I've always wondered, Tony. How'd you do it? How did you find him?'

And this is why the old team never got back together. McLean didn't need to ask Needy who he was talking about. Donald Anderson, the Christmas Killer, was never far from his thoughts. Least of all when the nights were long and dark and cold.

'I got lucky.' McLean laughed like a man who's been knifed in the gut. 'Hah, lucky. Don't know why I went into his shop. Can't remember much from back then. But he kept mementoes. You know as well as I do. And he had that piece of her dress.'

Needy looked up then and McLean saw the grief in his eyes, realised the deep bond that had formed between the sergeant and his father. How many years was it now since his own parents had died? Too many to count, and he'd been too young to really understand.

'I still don't know how you did it, though. After what he'd done to you. Christ knows, I'd have beaten him to death if it was me'd found him.' Needy flexed his hands, claw-like and liver-spotted. 'I'd have throttled him there and then.'

McLean reached for his beer, knocked back as much as he dared without disturbing the crusty bits milling around the bottom of the glass. He glanced at his watch.

'I thought about it. I still do. Look, I've got to go. I'm supposed to be preparing Dagwood's briefing at six and it'd be nice to get home and have a shower.'

'Aye, you're right.' Needy picked up his glass, swirled around the beer left in it. 'Think I might have another one of these though. Maybe something to help with the taste.'

'You'll be all right getting home?'

'Don't you worry about me, inspector. We Needhams survive. Always have, always will.'

Oily puddles shivered on the pavement when McLean stepped out of the time-warp pub and back into the real world. The rain had stopped, but a lazy wind blew in off the sea; too idle to go round, it cut through everything in its path, stealing any spare heat it could find. He hunched his shoulders against it, pulled up the collar of his overcoat and started out on the long walk home. In this weather, he could see the sense in owning a car. Or perhaps he should say owning a proper car. Not the impractical classic Alfa Romeo his gran had left him. It would be nice to be warm, dry. But then again, the traffic was crawling more slowly than he could walk, and if he owned a car there'd be nowhere to park at the other end, and a massive annual charge from the council for the privilege. A taxi was the answer, of course, but there weren't any to be seen. Not here, not now.

The phone buzzed against his hand, thrust deep into his coat pocket. McLean pulled both out, peering at the screen to see who was calling him. It was the station, no doubt Dagwood wanting to make his life a misery again.

'Tony? You at home?'

Not Dagwood. 'Oh, chief superintendent, ma'am. Um . . . No, I'm out walking. It's . . .' He didn't really know what to say. He'd got the impression from Needy that few people knew, and the sergeant would prefer it to stay that way as long as possible. On the other hand, there wasn't much got past Jayne McIntyre. 'I took Needy to the pub.'

The silence at the other end of the line was the chief superintendent working out what that meant. To her credit, it didn't take long.

'Damn. That's going to be hard for him.'

'He'll be OK, ma'am. Those Needhams are tough old bastards.'

'Aye, you're right there. But still.' The line went silent again.

'I take it that's not why you called me though.' McLean assumed that word of his morning cock-up had made it to the top of the pile, no doubt suitably embellished by Duguid to make him look even more stupid than he felt. He'd be expected in first thing for a professional bollocking.

'No. Something else.' McIntyre paused once more, as if she was trying to find the right words. Christ, he hadn't screwed up that badly had he?

'I thought you needed to hear this from me first. Before you got it second hand. It's about Anderson.'

McLean felt a chill in his gut that had nothing to do with the wind. 'Oh, aye? They letting him out for good behaviour are they?'

'Not exactly, Tony. I've just had a message from Peterhead. Seems someone took a knife to him in the kitchens. He's dead.'

7

'"In the midst of life we are in death: of whom may we seek for succour, but of thee, O Lord, who for our sins art justly displeased?"'

McLean stared out over the ranks of headstones towards a small knot of people clustered around a grave in the spattering rain. A sharp November wind blew off the North Sea, tugging at the thin grey hair of the priest, his head down in his prayer book. A brace of uniformed police officers shifted uncomfortably, like they would rather be anywhere else. A slim, red-haired woman struggled with her useless umbrella, rain darkening the grey of her tailored trouser suit. Two scowling men dressed in the dirty green overalls of Aberdeen City Parks Department waited impatiently to one side. No family, of course. Not much of a turn-out for the deceased at all.

'"Yet, O Lord God most holy, O Lord most mighty, O holy and most merciful Saviour, deliver us not into the bitter pains of eternal death."'

McLean dug his hands deep into the pockets of his heavy overcoat and huddled against the cold that seeped into his bones. Low clouds scudded across the sky, blanking out what little weak afternoon sun could hope to reach this far north. Dreich was the word. It matched his mood.

'"Thou knowest, Lord, the secrets of our hearts; shut not thy merciful ears to our prayer."'

He tuned out the words, looking around the cemetery. Flowers dotted here and there, even the odd photograph. The headstones glistened wetly, granite grey like the city that spawned them. Just the occasional angel to break the monotony. What the hell was he doing here?

'"Suffer us not, at our last hour, through any pains of death, to fall from thee."'

The council workers hoisted the heavy coffin up on thick canvas straps, kicking aside the scaffold planks it had been resting on, before dropping it clumsily into the hole. No elegant sashes and six young men to lower the bastard to his last resting place. He deserved nothing more than he was getting.

'"In sure and certain hope of the resurrection to eternal life through our Lord Jesus Christ, we commend to Almighty God our brother —"' The priest paused, then scrabbled around in his prayer book, coming up with a small scrap of paper. He peered at it myopically before the wind whipped it from his arthritic fingers and away over the graveyard. 'Our brother Donald Anderson and we commit his body to the ground; earth to earth, ashes to ashes, dust to dust."'

McLean couldn't suppress the smile that slid across his face at the priest's mistake, but it was short-lived. He felt no satisfaction, no closure. Turning away from the scene, he walked to his car. It was a long drive back to Edinburgh; might as well get started. Not like there was going to be a wake or anything.

'Might I ask what your interest in Anderson is?'

McLean turned at the voice, seeing the woman with the useless umbrella standing a couple of paces away. She was

28

slightly shorter than him, her face pale and freckled, its elfin shape exaggerated by the way the rain had plastered her short red hair across her scalp.

'Might I ask yours?'

'Detective Sergeant Ritchie, Grampian Police.' She fumbled in the large canvas bag slung over one shoulder and pulled out her warrant card. McLean didn't even bother looking at it. He probably should have told Aberdeen headquarters he was coming, but then they'd have escorted him everywhere, dragged him down the pub to celebrate Anderson's death.

'McLean,' he said. 'Lothian and Borders.'

'You're a fair bit off your patch, inspector.' So she knew of him, even if she hadn't recognised his face.

'I put Anderson away. Just wanted to make sure he was gone for good.'

'Aye, well. I can understand that.'

The two uniformed officers trudged past, the collars of their black fleeces turned up, yellow fluorescent jackets pulled tight against the wind. Behind them, the priest looked as if he was going to hang around and say something, then thought better of it. McLean stared back towards the grave where a mini digger was dumping heavy earth onto the coffin. 'How does a piece of shit like Anderson end up being buried in a place like this?'

'Plot was bought and paid for, apparently. Some solicitor from Edinburgh sorted it all out. Seems Anderson had money. Plots here aren't cheap.'

'What about the man who killed him?'

Ritchie didn't answer straight away. McLean didn't know her, couldn't read the expression on her face. She looked young for a DS, boyish even, with her short-cropped hair and business-like suit, but she held his gaze as if to say his seniority didn't intimidate her.

'Harry Rugg. Anderson's cell-mate in Peterhead. They were both on kitchen duty. Rugg took a carving knife and stabbed Anderson in the heart.'

'So I heard. Any chance of having a word with him?'

Ritchie wiped wet hair out of her eyes. 'I could talk to DCI Reid for you. He's in charge. But I doubt he'd let another force anywhere near. What do you want to ask him anyway?'

'Ask? Nothing. I just wanted to say thanks.'

The phone rang as he was crossing the Forth Road Bridge, and he fumbled with the buttons as he coasted to a slow stop in the traffic. Sudden rain squalls made angry red stars of the brake lights ahead of him; welcoming him home. He cradled the receiver to his ear, hoping there weren't any traffic cops around. It would be embarrassing to be pulled over on his day off.

'McLean.'

'You back from Aberdeen yet?' Duguid didn't bother with any conversational niceties.

'On the bridge, sir. But—'

'Well get yourself over to Sciennes. There's another fire.'

McLean was about to complain that he was off duty, but Duguid gave him the street name, then cut the call. There was no point arguing, anyway. It never did any good.

The traffic grew steadily worse as he approached the scene; exhausted office workers fighting to get home down unfamiliar roads. At least the uniforms had cordoned off the whole street, which meant he could abandon his car and walk the last couple of hundred yards. Smoke drifted down between the tenements in choking swirls, ash falling like black snow. Everything smelled of childhood bonfires, and high overhead the dark sky reflected rippling orange.

The fire was in an old factory, built well over a hundred years ago, its stone façade dark and grimy. The redevelopment signs had appeared several months back; just before the credit crunch had set in. Nothing much seemed to have changed since then. Until now. Six fire engines clustered around the site, two of them hosing down the adjoining tenement blocks to try and stop them catching. The factory itself was past saving. Flame roared from shattered windows, and as McLean watched, the roof began to buckle and collapse. Firemen sprinted away; uniforms pushed the security cordon further back; onlookers gasped with excitement.

'Enjoy the funeral did you, sir?' Grumpy Bob strolled up cradling a mug of tea in his large hands, oblivious to the chaos unfolding around him.

'Where the hell did you . . . ?' McLean pointed at the steaming cuppa. 'No, don't bother. Just bring me up to speed, Bob.'

'It looks like another one of ours. But we won't really know until it's out and the fire investigation team have had a crack.'

'Christ, that's just what we need.'

'Aye. Place is boarded up like Fort Knox. There's plate steel over the downstairs windows and all the doors. Took the first fire crew twenty minutes to cut their way in. Too late by then.'

McLean stared up at the roaring fire, feeling the heat radiating from the old stones. It seeped into his body, making him drowsy despite the noise and hubbub around.

'Inspector McLean.' A light tap on his shoulder. He turned, then cursed. Short and scruffy in a grubby old leather coat, Joanne Dalgliesh might have been mistaken for someone's mum, but she had a nose for a good story, and the newspaper she wrote for wasn't known for pulling its punches, especially where Lothian and Borders Police were concerned.

'This is the ninth fire at a redevelopment site in the city in two months. Are you any closer to catching the arsonist?'

'Who the hell let you in here?' McLean looked around for the nearest uniformed officer. 'Constable!'

'Come on, inspector.' Dalgliesh glanced over her shoulder as the constable hurried towards them. 'Just a word. Anything. Surely this isn't coincidence, all these buildings burning down?'

'You know I can't comment until the fire investigation team has been inside, Ms Dalgliesh.'

'But you're treating all the fires as connected.'

'We're not ruling out anything at this stage.'

'Which means you haven't got a clue.'

McLean ignored her. 'Constable, escort Ms Dalgliesh back behind the security cordon. And make sure no one else gets through. We don't want anyone getting hurt.'

'We can help you, inspector. If you let us,' the reporter protested as she was led away.

'Aye, right,' McLean muttered under his breath.

'She's got a point,' Grumpy Bob said.

'Yes, well, thanks for the support, sergeant. That's really helpful. So what's the situation here? You doing any actual policing, or just drinking tea?'

Grumpy Bob downed the dregs, then looked for somewhere to put the empty mug. 'I've had Constable MacBride working the crowd. You never know, we could get lucky. There's good CCTV coverage. We'll pull the tapes, see if anyone's lurking.'

Long hours of staring at grainy television images, trying to see if the same faces turned up at more than one fire. Wonderful.

'Inspector? Sir?'

McLean looked up to see MacBride winding his way through the abandoned cars and dodging the milling fire crews. He had an airwave set in one hand, his notebook in the other, a look of excitement flushing his face. Either that or he'd been too close to the fire.

'What is it, constable?'

'Call just came in . . . they've found a body.'

McLean rubbed his face, trying to get the tired dryness out of his eyes. The firemen had moved back towards the burning building now, but as far as he could tell no one had gone inside.

'What, in the fire? How?'

MacBride looked momentarily confused. Then held up his radio.

'No, sir. South of the city. Looks like a murder.'

'I'm supposed to be off duty. Can't they give it to anyone else?'

'Dagwood's gone to some important society dinner.'

Grumpy Bob bent his knee, miming the rolling up of his trouser leg. 'Langley and his crowd won't want to be first in if there's no obvious drugs connection.'

'What about Randall?'

'Off with the flu.'

'Oh Christ.' McLean shook his head to try and scare away the fatigue of a long day about to get even longer. 'Give us the details then.'

MacBride consulted his notebook. 'It's out near Gladhouse. Young woman, naked in the water. Sergeant Thoms said something about her throat being cut.'

Despite the heat from the fire, McLean's insides were as cold as the wind in an Aberdeenshire graveyard. Beside him, Grumpy Bob went suddenly very still.

'The Christmas Killer?'

McLean shook his head. 'It can't be, Bob. He's dead. I watched them bury him just this morning.'

But in his mind, he wasn't so sure.

8

A circle of bright white light hovered over the crime scene like some strange alien spaceship. Or maybe the Star of Bethlehem, given the time of year. That made McLean either a shepherd or a wise man, but he couldn't decide which. Whatever he was, he was tired. He stifled a yawn as he clambered out of the car, then remembered he was supposed to get it back to the hire company by seven. Even driving like a maniac he'd miss that by an hour. Well, it wouldn't be the first time his one-day hire had turned into two.

A line of squad cars and a couple of battered old white Transit vans meant he had to walk a short distance to the fluttering crime-scene tape. Closer in, the arc lights set up by the SOC team washed out an area of rough ground below the road. Fat drops of rainwater glistened on the spiky tips of the thick gorse bushes and splashed down from the bare, black, twisted branches of scraggy birch trees. Through it all ran a deep-culverted stream, gurgling loudly with recent rain. It was a while since he'd been out this way. But if memory served, it was part of the reservoir system that fed the city. Just the sort of place you wanted to find a body.

'I'm sorry, sir, this is a crime scene. You can't—'

McLean cut off the young uniformed constable who had tried to block his way, wearily pulling out his warrant card for inspection. It wasn't surprising the lad didn't recognise him; this was Penicuik's patch, after all.

'Who's the officer in charge?' McLean asked once the constable had finished apologising.

'Sergeant Price, sir. He's down there with the pathologist.'

'Already? That was quick.' McLean looked up the line of cars; sure enough, parked at the far end Angus Cadwallader's British Racing Green and mud-coloured Bentley poked one salt-encrusted headlight out from behind a SOC van.

'Dunno about that, sir. I've been here over two hours already. Call came in about four o'clock.'

Long before Dagwood had set out for his masonic knees-up. Bloody marvellous.

Knee-high grass and gorse bushes soaked his trousers and shoes long before he made it to the edge of the culvert. A group of people clustered around an improbable Heath-Robinson arrangement of scaffolding poles, light stands and other paraphernalia. Steam rose off the hot lights, adding to the already surreal, hellish feel of the place.

'Sergeant Price?' McLean waited while a large, white-haired, uniformed officer turned slowly around, trying not to slip on the wet concrete edge of the culvert. The drop was about ten feet, spate-swelled waters running noisily below, so McLean couldn't really blame him.

'About bloody time someone senior showed up,' was all the greeting the old sergeant gave. That and a cursory nod. McLean tried not to rise to the bait.

'It's my day off, OK? I spent the morning in Aberdeen burying Donald fucking Anderson. So cut the small talk and tell me the story.'

If Sergeant Price was impressed by McLean's sacrifice, he didn't show it.

'Couple of lads out on their mountain bikes saw her first,' he said. 'What they were doing down here is anyone's guess.'

'They still about?'

'No. They called in from Temple. You can't get a mobile signal here. I've got names and addresses.'

'OK. What about the body?'

Price shrugged. 'See for yersel'. Crime scene's a' yours.'

McLean inched slowly to the edge, giving the two SOCOs holding the arc lamps time to shuffle aside. A ladder dropped down to a makeshift platform rigged up over the flowing water, two people kneeling together like penitent sinners, praying before a third. He recognised the balding pate of Angus Cadwallader, city pathologist, and the shiny black bob of his assistant Tracy, but the other person in the threesome was a stranger to him.

It looked like the water had carried her downstream until she had been pinned against a rusty iron grating. Her arms were splayed wide, her legs twisted back underneath her body as if she were posing for some arty erotic photograph. Wisps of green-black pondweed trailed across skin so white it could have been porcelain, and only the ugly dark welt across her neck stopped him from thinking she was merely sleeping.

'Tony. Good God, could they not have given this to someone else?' Angus Cadwallader looked up, shuffling carefully off his knees and upright before helping his assistant do the same. Only when he was safely out of the culvert did he finally give McLean a quizzical raise of the eyebrow and add: 'I thought you were in Aberdeen today. Christ, talk about timing.'

'I was,' McLean said, remembering the windswept cemetery as if it had been a lifetime ago. 'So, what's the score here?'

Cadwallader pulled off his latex gloves and ran a hand over his wet hair. 'It's difficult to say much from where she is. Rain's washed her down from somewhere upstream, I'm fairly sure. She's also very clean. Not been in the water too long, though.'

'Cause of death? Time of death?'

'Ah, Tony. You always ask, and I always tell you I can't say. Not now. It looks like she's had her throat cut, but that might have been post-mortem. As to time, well, it's cold here, and she's been in the water. But unless she was kept on ice, I'd say somewhere between twelve and twenty-four hours. Thirty-six tops.'

'What about bruising? Any ligature marks?'

'She's ten feet down in a concrete culvert that's barely wide enough for the two of us, Tony. Let me get her back to the mortuary, then I'll tell you what happened to the poor wee lass.' Cadwallader put a damp hand on McLean's shoulder. 'We're not going to find anything here.'

'You're right, Angus. I just. Well . . .' McLean tailed off, unsure what he wanted to say. He needed answers, but even he could tell he wasn't going to get any here. 'I guess you'd better get her out of there then.'

Cadwallader nodded to one of the SOC officers, who scurried off to get help. They followed him back up through the gorse to the roadside, just in time for another squall of rain. The pathologist hurried to his car, Tracy leaping into the passenger seat without even bothering to remove her white overalls. McLean quickly got into the back seat.

'It's not the same, Tony,' Cadwallader said. 'This isn't another Christmas Killer victim.'

'You sure of that, Angus? It looks pretty close to me.'

'I'll get the PM scheduled as soon as possible, but you know what I mean. He's been locked up since the start of the millennium. And now he's dead. This is something else. Someone else.'

McLean shivered, though whether it was the cold he couldn't be certain. 'I hope you're right, Angus.'

The lumpy beat of an engine at tick-over and a spiral of steam in the damp darkness gave away Sergeant Price's position, sitting in the warmth of one of the squad cars. When McLean tapped on the misted-up windscreen, he wound it down with obvious reluctance.

'It's your lucky night,' McLean said.

'Aye?'

'I want this road closed for a quarter mile either side of the crime scene. First light, a search team's going to be back to go over the whole area, and I don't want anyone to have disturbed it in my absence. OK?'

'But my shift ends in an hour. I've got stuff to do—'

'I don't want to hear it, sergeant. This is a murder enquiry, so you're good for the overtime. I'll be back at dawn, and I'll expect to see your smiling face here to greet me.'

9

He wanders the streets in a daze, feet following the familiar path they know from when he was on the beat. The steady rhythm of leather on pavement helps to dull his mind, stop the feelings that threaten to overwhelm him at every turn. Thinking is too painful, so he marches instead.

What brings him to this place? He doesn't really know. There must be some reason, but teasing it out might dislodge something else. Better just to go with the flow. It's a second-hand bookshop, smelling of dust and libraries. The aisles between the shelves are narrow, towering over him, lined with countless ranks of words. He runs his fingers over uneven spines as he walks towards the desk at the back. There was a reason for coming in here. Something he needed to say.

No one about. A few old paperbacks lie abandoned on the counter, a ledger open as if the shop owner were called away whilst in the middle of cataloguing them. Beyond the counter, a door opens to a small office. Not quite sure why, he goes through.

Still no one. A pair of old filing cabinets stand against one wall, a low shelf of books under the large window that looks out onto a scruffy courtyard behind the shop. An antique desk fills most of the space, its top empty save for a reading lamp and a large, old, leather-bound book.

There's something about the book that sends a shiver

through him. Has he seen it before? He doesn't know, doesn't want to think. Thoughts are too painful now. But it won't let him go, drags him towards it like a magnet, whispers to him to open it up, to read.

He is reaching out to it when he notices the marker. A thin strip of fabric slipped between heavy vellum pages, drooping out over the edge of the desk like a wilted flower. His hand moves towards the cloth, takes it between finger and thumb, slides it out of the book. Something like a far-off scream of rage and frustration echoes in the silence, but he pays it no heed. There is only this piece of cloth, this hem torn from a dress. At that touch he knows it.

He knows everything.

10

Early morning, and a steady stream of buses blocked the flow of traffic as McLean walked briskly across North Bridge towards Princes Street. Heads down, breath steaming in the cold November air, the first wave of commuters spilled out into the dark and onto the wide pavement, desperately trying to avoid eye contact with their fellow condemned.

What would it be like to have a normal job, with regular working hours? It might be nice to have the occasional evening off, some time to spend with his friends. Except that with far too few exceptions, all his friends were either police, or inextricably linked to the job.

He was so busy working his way through the knot of bodies that at first he didn't notice the person ahead of him. But something about the shape and size, the pattern of wispy hair on the back of the man's head, registered enough to grab his attention. He couldn't think why he felt a frisson of discomfort at the figure, but neither could he get closer through the throng. Then the man turned side on, heading round the corner of the North British Balmoral Hotel, and McLean's heart nearly stopped.

'Anderson.' The word came out as a hoarse whisper, ignored by the people all around him. Someone bumped his shoulder and he realised he'd stopped walking. His knees felt weak; the blood rushing in his head sounded like the London train far beneath his feet, out of control and speeding through Waverley station. And the impossible figure was getting further away.

'Anderson!' This time it was a shout, and the noise propelled McLean into action. No longer caring about the sensibilities of Edinburgh commuters, he pushed through the crowd, trying to make up the distance. The man he was chasing, seemingly deaf and oblivious, disappeared down Princes Street.

'Oi! Watch what yer doing.' An angry pedestrian turned as McLean tried to jostle past, his face red with quick anger.

'Police. Get out of the way.' McLean thrust him aside, breaking into a run as he cleared the throng, then slowing down as the next crowd gathered by the crossing. He hugged the wall of the hotel, managing to squeeze past an old lady with a tartan shopping trolley, and a couple of lost tourists, their backpacks lethal to everyone around as they turned to see what the commotion was all about. Round the corner, seeing the flow of sleepy humanity pouring up Waverley steps and onto Princes Street, McLean scanned the crowd, looking for his quarry. Donald Anderson was nowhere to be seen.

By the time he reached his tiny office, tucked away at the back of the station and the end of the queue for the heating, McLean had almost convinced himself that he'd been mistaken. It couldn't possibly have been Anderson; he'd watched the man's coffin being lowered into the ground less than twenty-four hours ago. And there was no way that Peterhead jail could have made a mistake about the identity of one of their more notorious inmates.

'You all right, Tony? You look like you've seen a ghost.'

McLean started at the voice, realising he'd been staring into space. Hovering in the open doorway, Chief Superintendent Jayne McIntyre looked like she'd only just stepped out of the shower; face scrubbed pink, hair still wet, uniform as yet unrumpled by a long day in the office.

'Didn't get much sleep, ma'am. We found a body last night. There's some nasty similarities to Anderson's MO.'

'Aye, I heard from Grumpy Bob. That's what I wanted to talk to you about.' McIntyre looked around the room for a spare seat, then propped herself on the edge of the desk.

McLean's heart dropped. 'You're giving the investigation to someone else.'

'I thought about it. God only knows, you've enough on your plate right now with Anderson being killed.'

'With respect, ma'am, I don't see what that's got to do with anything.'

'Oh don't be so pompous, Tony. We both know what he did to you, and he's going to be all over the papers for the next few weeks at least. Jo Dalgliesh'll have a new edition of her book out before the end of the month, you can count on that. You might think you've buried the past and moved on, but it's going to come back with a vengeance now.'

'So that's it then. Who do I hand over to, Dagwood? You do want us to catch whoever did this, don't you?'

'What is it with you two? Charles is an experienced detective with a very good clear-up rate. And yes, he will be in overall charge of this investigation. But I know you well enough, Tony. You'll just go sticking your nose in it anyway. Make a bloody nuisance of yourself. And we're not exactly overburdened with detectives right now, so you're going to be leading things on the ground.' She smiled, but McLean knew she was only half joking. 'Talking of short staff, I've put the word out around the other forces. See if anyone fancies a transfer to sunny Edinburgh. Do it that way and we can squeeze a couple of detective constables out of the budget. Maybe even a sergeant.'

'We could certainly do with the help.' McLean looked at the pile of case files strewn across his untidy desk; enough work to keep him busy for months. Just a pity the city kept on throwing up new crimes for him to solve.

'I know you like to work with just a small team, Tony, but this is high profile. Like you said, nasty similarities to the Christmas Killer. We need to be seen to be doing everything we can.' McIntyre stood up, smoothing imaginary creases from her suit. 'We all know what Anderson did to you. Are you sure you want to rake over all that again?'

McLean tried to read the superintendent's expression. Was it pity, or worry? He wasn't sure he wanted either.

'This isn't Anderson, ma'am. He's dead. I watched them bury him yesterday.'

Gladhouse Reservoir wasn't much better in the early morning light. Snow clung to the flanks of the Moorfoot Hills, a chill wind bringing a taste of deep winter. McLean looked at the unenthusiastic gaggle of uniforms that were all he'd been able to rustle up from Penicuik and Mortonhall. He couldn't really blame them; it was very unlikely they'd find anything after last night's weather.

'OK ladies, you know the drill.' Grumpy Bob directed officers away in various directions, then stuffed his hands deep into his coat pockets. 'Bloody hell but it's cold, sir.'

McLean shivered in agreement. 'Let's get out of this wind, Bob.' He nodded in the direction of the culvert. 'I want to start where we found the body.'

It was much the same as the evening before, only without the star attraction, removed to the mortuary to await the attentions of the pathologists. McLean clambered down the rickety staging that had been jury-rigged out of the bits and bobs lurking in the back of the SOC van, then inched out onto the platform above the water. More rain overnight had swollen the flow, threatening to flood the boarding and soak his feet, but he squatted down anyway, trying to remember the scene as it had been.

'She was splayed out like this,' he began to say, then realised that he was alone on the platform. Looking around and up, he saw Grumpy Bob's face peering back down at him from the safety of the bank.

'If you think I'm coming down there, sir . . .'

McLean shook his head, then grabbed at the ladder as the platform swayed dangerously. He waited for the motion to steady, watching waves slop over the wooden board, tried to imagine the scene as it had been the night before. Where the girl had lain, water gurgled down the grating into some dark underworld.

'You reckon it's worth getting divers in, sir?' Grumpy Bob asked from above. 'Maybe see if anything's stuck down there?'

McLean took one last look around, then clambered back up the ladder. 'There's no point, Bob. She was naked when she was dumped. And if the killer did drop anything, it's in the Firth of Forth by now. Still . . .' He looked around at the woods, back up towards the roadside, hidden by the bank, and through the bushes. And then he saw the bridge.

'What is it, sir?' Bob asked, but McLean was already off, pushing his way through the sodden undergrowth, slipping on the muddy ground as he scrabbled up the steep slope towards the road. Stupid. The culvert took the water from the reservoir on the other side. There had to be a bridge. Why the hell hadn't he thought of it before?

By the time Grumpy Bob had caught up with him, McLean was under the road, perching on a thin strip of concrete beside the rushing water. He fished around in his pocket for a torch, playing the narrow beam first over the far bank, then around his feet, and finally into the flow itself.

'Jesus, I'm soaked through. What the hell are you up to, sir?' Grumpy Bob wheezed into the narrow space, running a hand through his thinning hair as if that would make it any drier. McLean ignored him, trying to see the shapes distorted by the roiling flow. There was definitely something down there.

'Grab my hand, Bob.' He poked the end of the torch into his mouth and reached out for the old sergeant. Then he took the torch out again and added: 'And hold onto something secure with your other one?'

The water was icy cold, tugging at his trouser bottoms and filling his shoes. McLean ignored it, leaning as far forward as he dared before plunging his arm in. His fingers numbed almost instantly, but he could feel the rough

47

outline of the concrete sloping away from him. Then an iron loop, rusted chain links caked in green weed, and finally, the flash of white his torch had illuminated.

'You got that pocket knife of yours, Bob?'

'Aye.'

'Well pass it over then.'

'Ah. That would mean letting go of the bridge, sir.'

'Trust me, Bob. It's not going anywhere.'

Grumpy Bob grumbled something McLean couldn't quite make out over the echoing roar of the culvert. There was a heart-stopping moment when he thought he was going to pitch head-first into the flow, and then the knife was passed over.

'Grab my coat. I'm going to need both hands.'

'You know we could have a diver out here in half an hour, sir,' Bob said, but McLean felt the reassuring pressure around his chest. He leant forward again, this time putting both hands into the water. It took a moment to find what he was looking for, longer still to get the knife to cut through. The water was flowing so strongly he nearly dropped his prize, grabbing at it with sausage fingers and hauling it out like a tickled trout. Taken by surprise, Grumpy Bob fell over and in the confined space they both ended up on their backsides.

'Ah, bastard. I've got a damp arse now. What the hell was that all about?'

McLean sat on the wet concrete, his back against the arch of the bridge and said nothing. Just looked at the white plastic strap lying in his hand. Fresh and clean, not covered in green algae like everything else. A heavy duty cable tie not unlike the ones that were replacing handcuffs these days. He handed it to the old sergeant to shut up his grumbling.

'I'll lay good odds there's another one like that on the other side,' he said after a while, and pulled an evidence bag out of his damp pocket. Grumpy Bob dropped the cable tie in and took the bag, sealing it up as he stood stiffly.

'You'll no' mind if I phone that diver now.'

11

McLean left Grumpy Bob to oversee the rest of the search and hitched a lift back into town in a squad car. Even with the heating up full and blowing into the foot-well, his feet were still sodden by the time he made it to the station. He squelched uncomfortably up to his cold office, wondering whether he could spare the time to go home and change. The stack of reports piled up on his desk answered that question.

He banged on the radiator a couple of times in the vain hope that abuse might make it do the job it was supposed to. Come summer no doubt it would be blasting out heat, but now it remained in a cold sulk.

'Sod you then.' He squeezed around his desk and sunk into the creaky chair, checking the stack of reports in case they were ones he had already dealt with. Well, it was worth a try. The top one was a summary of last night's fire, pre-pared by Constable MacBride. A green Post-it note stuck to it read: 'No joy with Mis-Per. Dr C phoned. PM at 4.30.' It had originally been '4.30 pm' but for some reason the con-stable had crossed the pm out. Probably reasoning that it was unnecessary. McLean looked at his watch: a quarter to ten and there was bugger all he could do about the dead girl. They didn't know who she was, where she'd come from, when she'd gone missing. Nothing. Just a cold sensa-tion in the pit of his stomach matching the chill in his feet.

He picked up his phone and dialled the CID room. After eight rings he accepted that no one was going to answer, grabbed the fire report off his desk and went in search of a detective the old-fashioned way.

Detective Constable Peter Robertson, newly arrived from Fife Constabulary, was not given much to idle chatter. This suited McLean just fine as they drove south out of town towards the Loanhead offices of Randolph Developments, owners of the site of the previous night's fire. More of a problem was his lack of familiarity with the suburbs and dormitory villages surrounding the capital; he had to be redirected several times before they made it out to Burdiehouse and then on under the bypass.

'You're in bandit country now, constable,' McLean said as he pointed to the turning they needed to take.

'Sir?'

'You never heard of the Border Reivers? Cattle thieves and thugs to a man. They'd cut your throat if you so much as looked at them in a funny way.'

Robertson looked at him with an expression that was hard to read, but which might have been worry. They were spared a more awkward moment by their arrival at the compound where Randolph Developments had their offices. A high wire fence surrounded a desolate wasteland, with a huge old stone building set towards the back of it. The McMerry Ironworks hadn't produced a single ingot in almost half a century; now it was surrounded by portacabins waiting to be taken to other building sites in the city, heavy machinery and stacks of pallet-loaded concrete blocks. All around it, the old industrial land was slowly being reclaimed for modern offices, small factory units and housing.

Set closer to the edge of the compound and the gate they had just entered, the headquarters of the company was an architectural melange of glass and steel, surrounded on three sides by ornamental ponds and exotic shrubs. Edinburgh's economic miracle might have stumbled a bit of late, but it had obviously paid handsomely for some.

An attractive young receptionist took their names, then went off to fetch them coffee whilst they waited in a spacious atrium. After what seemed like only seconds, the far door banged open and a vast man bounced out. He wore red braces over his blue-striped shirt, but the thing that was most noticeable about him was the way his body tapered from the enormous girth of his stomach up to the flat top of his head in an almost straight line. He put McLean in mind of a toy from his childhood: Weebles wobble but they don't fall down.

'Inspector McLean? Hi, I'm William Randolph.' He held out a surprisingly small hand to be shaken. 'Come through to my office, won't you?'

He led them through an open-plan area where draughts-men worked at large flat-screen monitors, no doubt drawing the future shape of the city. At the back, a glass wall partitioned off a smaller area dominated by a large desk. Randolph offered them seats on one side before making his way around to the executive chair on the other and dropping himself into it. Leather squealed and springs protested, and for a moment McLean thought the fat man was going to crash to the floor in a tangle of broken office furniture.

'I take it you've come to see me about last night's fire.' Randolph didn't wait to be asked questions. 'Terrible business. I'm just glad no one was hurt. And those poor people turfed out of their homes so late at night. I've put my PA onto sorting out some kind of recompense for them. Christmas presents for the kiddies, something a bit warmer for the grown-ups. You know the kind of thing.'

'That's very decent of you, Mr Randolph.'

'Decent, nothing. It's self-preservation, inspector. There were enough complaints about that development without all this to compound things.'

'Complaints? Do you think anyone was angry enough to set fire to the place?'

Randolph did a passing impression of looking aghast, as if the thought had never occurred to him before. 'I don't know. I guess so. But why? Burning the place down's not going to help. I've seen the damage and frankly the best we can do is demolish the place. Start from scratch.'

'And is that what you wanted all along, Mr Randolph?'

'Ah. I see where you're coming from.' Randolph hauled himself out of his chair and McLean wondered whether he imagined the sigh of relief coming from the crushed leather. He motioned for McLean and Peterson to follow as he left the office they'd just entered and walked across the open-plan office to the far end. Here a series of detailed models was laid out on separate tables, each showing a Randolph Developments project.

'These are our current works,' Randolph said. 'There's a half dozen in Edinburgh city, these two in Peebles and Biggar, and three sites awaiting planning in Glasgow. Not to mention the ironworks out there. I've got great plans for that. But this . . .' He reached out and carefully removed the roof from the model of the building McLean had watched burn the night before. Inside were detailed layouts of a couple of large apartments filling the roof space. Beneath that were two further storeys of living space and on the ground floor a swimming pool and gym, all lovingly recreated in miniature. There were even Matchbox Porsches, BMWs and Mercedes parked in the tree-lined yard at the back, but no Alfa Romeos, McLean noticed.

'This was our flagship project, inspector. The site alone cost me two million. I was planning on having the rear penthouse for my own city home. Do you think I'd really want to burn it all down and shove some cheap boxes on the site?'

'I really don't know, Mr Randolph. That's why I'm here. It could all be a dreadful accident, but we've been seeing rather a lot of those in the city these past few months. Two of your other sites included. And I've heard property development's gone tits-up recently. Insurance money'd be very useful for a man with cash-flow problems.'

'I can see where you're coming from, inspector, but you're wrong. Yes, we had insurance, and I dare say the money will help. But we're not a fly-by-night operation here. We deal in prestigious, luxury developments. Our customer base hasn't really been affected by the credit crunch and our bottom line is healthy. I'm quite happy to let you see our accounts, if it helps.' Randolph slowly put the pieces of the model back together, his tiny fingers caressing the top floor apartment with its steel gantry balcony looking out over the car park towards Arthur's Seat. It was clear to McLean that he hadn't torched his own building for the insurance money.

'How far down the line were you with the project then?' he asked.

'We'd done all the preparations, stabilising the foundations and stonework, sorting out the drainage, that sort of stuff. We were about to start taking the floors out. A pity we hadn't done it already, really.'

'Why's that, sir?' Robertson asked. McLean noticed he'd been taking notes.

'Because then there'd have been nothing in the place to burn. It's got a concrete ground floor and stone walls. But the floorboards and roof joists are all hundred-and-fifty-year-old timber.'

'It was empty last night?' McLean remembered the smoke and angry orange flames. Could all that have come from just floorboards and joists?

'Completely stripped. I went round it in the afternoon with a couple of the lads.' Randolph pointed to two young men working at their computer screens, raising his voice as he added, 'Pat, Gary, the Woodbury building. The clear-out was finished when we went round yesterday, wasn't it?'

Pat, or possibly Gary, looked up and nodded.

'That's right. Should have been some plant being delivered in the morning, but they called to say it wouldn't be til today. Damn, I hope someone's cancelled.' He reached for the phone and began dialling.

'Did anyone else have access to the place yesterday? After you were there?' McLean asked.

'Only old George McGregor. He's the caretaker. Apparently he used to work there when it was still a furniture factory. Mad as a coot, but reliable. You should hear the stories he tells about the place.'

'I will,' McLean said. 'If you'll just tell me where I can find him.'

George McGregor lived in a tiny basement flat not far from the burned-out Woodbury building. He opened the door a crack when DC Robertson knocked, then spent long minutes peering through manky, scratched spectacles at both detectives' warrant cards before letting them in with obvious grudging. They entered a low-ceilinged, narrow hallway and followed the old man down it to a door that stood open on the right. The sitting-room beyond gained what little light it could from a grimy window that looked out onto a grey concrete wall, street level just visible if you craned your neck. A bare light bulb hung from a short flex in the ceiling, but the old man made no move to switch it on. He shuffled across the room, weaving through piles of books and taped-up cardboard boxes that littered the floor, before dropping himself into a tired, old armchair. Clouds of dust puffed out of the worn cloth, bringing with them an odour of long-departed cat.

'So what's it you're wanting?' McGregor didn't offer them a seat, and looking around the room McLean realised he would have been hard put to do so. There was a sofa, wedged into one corner, but it was covered in piles of old newspapers.

'The fire last night,' he said. 'William Randolph tells me you're the caretaker on the site.'

'I didnae torch it.'

'I never said you did, Mr McGregor. I can't see how doing so would help you in any way. I just wanted to ask what time you locked up.'

'Burnt itself. Jes' like all those others.'

'I'm sorry?'

'Was twelve years old when I went tae work in that factory. Proudest day've my life. Old Man Woodbury himself welcomed me. Shook me by the hand an' give me my card. Six years, I was apprentice there. Six years, ye ken. Aye, we learnt our trade back then. No' like today. It's nae wonder the country's goin' tae pot.'

McLean sighed. He knew where this was going. 'Mr McGregor, you were telling us what time you locked up last night.'

'No I wisnae. Do I look stupit?'

McLean didn't answer that. 'Well, what time was it, then?'

'Back of four. Maybe half-past.'

'Why so early?'

'There's nae work going on there the noo. Would've stayed later, if there'd been a delivery or anything. But they postponed.'

'And what time did Mr Randolph leave?'

'Four, mebbe a wee bit earlier. No' much, mind.'

'So you didn't hang around.'

'No, no. It's no' a nice place to be after dark. Too many memories. Too many ghosts.'

'Ghosts?'

'Aye, ghosts.' McGregor was warming to his tune now. 'D'ye ken they built that factory in 1842. 'Fore that there was a wee close there, wi' a dozen workshops. Folk've been working on that site for more'n five hundred years. It's got history. There's blood in the ground.'

'So you think a ghost set fire to the place, sir?' DC Robertson's question was asked without any hint of sarcasm, but even so McLean winced. He'd met too many crabbit old men like McGregor before.

'Don't be daft, son. There's no such thing as ghosts. No' like you see on the telly.' McGregor nodded towards an ancient wood-veneer box with what looked like a shiny glass bowl on the front of it. Late sixties black and white Rediffusion, if McLean wasn't mistaken, and probably worth a bit to a collector. Most likely the old man had owned it from new.

'But you said—' Robertson started to say, but was cut off by an angry tirade.

'Don't you tell me what I said, son. I'm eighty-four years old an' never took a day off sick in my life, you know. I fought in the war.'

'I'm sorry, sir, I didn't mean to upset you. We're just trying to understand—'

'You're a Fifer, aren't you laddie. I can tell by your accent. East Neuk if I'm no' wrong.'

'Pittenweem, sir.'

'My Esme was frae Struther,' McGregor said, and his face changed, his eyes looked haunted and lost behind his thick, grease-smeared lenses. McLean wondered how long it had been since his wife had died; wondered too if social services were even aware of this half-mad old man living alone in his squalor.

'Mr McGregor.' He hunkered down in the middle of

the room so as to be on the same eye-level. 'How do you think the Woodbury building was set alight? You were the last person in there. Could you have left a light on or something?'

'There were nae lights in there. Took the 'lectrics out a week past. That's why I didnae much like staying there after dark.'

McLean sniffed the air, then wished he hadn't. There were many unpleasant aromas best left unidentified in the flat, but tobacco smoke wasn't one of them. 'You don't smoke, do you, Mr McGregor.'

'No' since Esme died. Was the cancer that took her.'

'I'm sorry to hear that, sir. What about Mr Randolph? Or the electricians?'

'There's no smoking on site. It's a workplace, see. That's the law. Had yon fire chappie round about a few days past, tellin' us all aboot it.'

'So there was no electricity in the place, and no stray cigarettes.' McLean looked around at DC Robertson. This case was starting to bear an uncomfortable similarity to the nine other fires, with equally little hope of ever being solved. 'Christ, how does an empty warehouse, locked up like a bank and with no wiring in it spontaneously catch on fire?'

'I told you. The building did it tae itself.' McGregor leant forward in his saggy armchair, gnarled hands clenching the faded and ripped covers on the arms as if he were about to have a heart attack. McLean rocked back on his heels, bashing against a box that clinked as if it were full of china.

'I'm afraid I don't understand you, Mr McGregor.'

'No, I don't suppose you do. You young lads're all the same. No idea of place, you dinnae ken whit history's all aboot. It's no' kings and queens an' dates and shite like that. It's folk living an' working an' dying. That's what the Woodbury was. A place of work, a factory for all those years. Centre of the community like the kirk and the pubs. Then they went and turned it into a warehouse. That was bad enough, but this – expensive flats for rich folk, a swimming pool. Jings, the building couldnae take that. All those memories. All those lives. The sweat and blood. I could feel it coming. Feel something coming. I wasnae surprised when they telt me it had gone. It wanted to die, y'see. It burned itself.'

The cold air outside Mr McGregor's flat was a welcome relief when they finally escaped ten minutes later. DC Robertson started to walk back to the car, but McLean stopped him.

'Leave it where it is, constable. You don't want to lose a parking space round here. They're like gold dust.'

'Are we no' going back to the station?' Robertson looked at his watch.

'Not just now, no. We're only a few minutes' walk from the Woodbury. Might as well drop by. See if the fire investigation team have had a chance to look at it yet.'

A temporary traffic-light system was doing its best to ease the congestion when they reached the burnt-out hulk of the building. A large fire investigation truck took up the southbound lane, and high metal barriers had been erected all around the front to protect idiots from falling masonry. The street wasn't a major thoroughfare, but it was busy. Chances were it was going to be blocked for quite some time. Judging by the sounding of horns, and the air of barely constrained rage, the city's travelling public weren't very happy about that.

The investigation truck housed all manner of arcane equipment, but most of it was turned over to a temporary command centre. A harassed-looking fireman greeted them with what might have been a smile but looked more like a grimace. He had a phone tucked between his head and hunched shoulder and was juggling with several sheets of paper.

'Aye?'

'DI McLean.' McLean held out his warrant card but didn't say any more.

'You'll need to speak to Jim. Jim Burrows. He's inside. Follow the path and you'll find him.'

'Thanks.' McLean made to leave but before he reached the door the man shouted back.

'Wait a mo. You'll need these.' He held up a couple of hard hats which McLean took, handing one on to DC Robertson.

'Not that they'll do you much good,' the fireman added. 'If a wall comes down or summat.'

Suitably hatted, the two detectives ventured through the front doors of the building, into an image from World War II London. The fire had been completely extinguished, but it hadn't left much behind. Most of the detritus was made up of broken roof tiles, with here and there a charred piece of roof truss or floorboard. A path had been cleared in a wide circle, picking its way past the biggest piles of rubble towards the middle of the vast space. Looking up, McLean could see the cold grey clouds rushing past with the wind. For a moment, framed against the stark, blackened stone walls, it felt as if the whole building were hurtling along at great speed. He quickly looked back down again, staggering slightly as his sense of motion caught up with him. Ahead, DC Robertson didn't seem to have noticed.

They found two fire investigators busy conferring over a folded paper floor plan in a small patch of clear ground at the heart of the old building. One of them looked up at their approach, eyes narrowing.

'Jim Burrows?' McLean asked.

'Aye. And you'd be?'

McLean made the introductions. 'I was just talking to the caretaker. Thought I'd check in and see how you're getting on. I know you won't have much for me yet.'

'Well, you're right enough there. We're still trying to work out where the damn thing started. I'm thinking it's somewhere round about where we're standing, but that doesn't explain why she went up the way she did.'

'What do you mean?'

'Well, by the look of the floor here, this is where the fire burned hottest.' Burrows pointed at the charred and blackened concrete. 'But according to these plans, we're nowhere near a pillar or anything. Even if there'd been a big pile of pallets or something here, it shouldn't have set the whole building off like that.'

'Any sign of accelerants?'

'Not the usual, anyway. You'd smell it even after all this. Careful, laddie. You don't want that lot coming down on top of you.'

McLean looked to where Burrows had directed his warning, seeing DC Robertson staring up at a precariously balanced roof beam sitting on a heap of broken tiles as tall as him. Then there was a sudden crack, and the constable disappeared.

13

January 27th 2000 saw the close of a dark chapter in Edinburgh history. For that was the day Lothian and Borders Police raided the house and shop of Donald Anderson, an antiquarian book dealer. It wasn't dogged investigation that brought them to this place; not the application of sound procedure; but more the random hand of fate. It was by chance that Anderson had chosen the fiancée of a young detective constable as his victim. It was by chance that same detective came to his shop looking for a book, and found instead a memento of his murdered bride-to-be. That single, simple clue, that strip torn from the hem of a hand-me-down dress, was enough to bring to an end the longest manhunt in the history of the city. For when they entered the basement of that innocuous-looking bookshop, the true identity of the Christmas Killer was finally revealed.

A tutting noise brings him to his senses, and he notices the shop assistant standing by the stack that has such prominence at the front of the shop. He looks at his hands and realises that he has dropped the book to the floor.

He should have known this would happen. Part of him did. He's changed his phone number twice to try and stop the calls, the endless requests for interviews and banal questions about how he feels. He feels nothing. He feels everything.

And then there is this.

The table holds hundreds of copies of the book, each bearing that hated face on its cover. The windows of the bookshop are filled with posters, each six foot high and showing the same dreadful figure. Donald Anderson is famous; the monster who has terrorised the winter city streets for a decade, now made flesh. Immortalised by this book, this bestseller he can't even bear to hold. *The Christmas Killer* is in every bookshop in town. It's plastered on the sides of buses trawling up and down Princes Street, thrust upon the poor unwary traveller in a thousand different hoardings, bus stops, magazines and newspapers. A number-one bestseller, its author will be doing the circuit, pressing the flesh, appearing on daytime TV, raking in the cash. Donald Anderson has been good to Joanne Dalgliesh. Very good indeed.

There are ten grieving families who can't say the same.

He turns away from the stand, blind to the shop assistant as she picks up the fallen book, wipes it with her hand as if it is a thing of beauty, puts it back with all the others. He cannot see the world around him, the seething masses seeking titillation in the sensationalist deeds of terrible evil. All he can see is the cold dirt shovelled onto a dark wooden coffin in the icy rain.

14

'What the hell were you doing in there anyway? Shouldn't you be trying to identify your dead body? '

Chief Superintendent McIntyre stood with her hands on her hips. Head thrust slightly forward and legs apart as she shouted, she looked like a fishwife berating her drunken husband. McLean had barely managed to stand up from the uncomfortable plastic chair in the hospital waiting room before she had started to tear him off a strip.

'The PM wasn't til half four.' He glanced at his watch, shifted uncomfortably, wanting to take a step back, knowing that if he did so she would just move closer again until he was pinned against the far wall. 'Guess I'm going to miss it now.'

'Oh?' McIntyre's eyebrows arched. 'Why's that? It's not as if you're doing any good here.'

'Well . . . I . . .' McLean stopped talking. There was nothing he could usefully do from a hospital waiting room but assuage his guilt at almost getting one of his junior officers killed.

'How's Robertson, anyway?' The chief superintendent leaned back, her angry expression softening.

'He's in surgery right now. They reckon he's fractured his pelvis and broken his back. His spinal cord's not severed though; they're hoping he'll be able to walk again.'

'Thank Christ for small mercies. What the hell happened?' McIntyre sat down, the bollocking over at least for now. McLean took the chair next to her.

'He fell through the floor. Well, it collapsed underneath him. The fire investigator said the concrete had probably all blown away from the underside with the heat. It's so bloody stupid. McGregor told us they'd built the place on top of an old close, but the plans didn't say anything about a cellar. I guess they must have just forgotten all about it. Poor bloody Peter. He's only just started. This'll kill his career; even if he does make a full recovery it's going to take months. Years even.'

'He'll be all right, Tony.' McIntyre put her hand on McLean's, a brief, comforting contact. 'We look after our own.'

'Shit, I'm sorry, ma'am. It's not as if we can spare the manpower, is it?'

'No.' McIntyre looked thoughtful for a moment, a half smile coming to her face as she thought of something. 'We'll just have to see about promoting someone to CID on a temporary basis. Same as happened to you, if I remember right. That turned out more or less OK, I suppose.'

'Inspector McLean?' A woman, too young surely to be a doctor, stood before them wearing a long white coat, a stethoscope and a weary expression.

'Any news?' McLean stood up.

'They've just finished working on him. It's . . . well, it could have been a lot worse.'

'He'll be able to walk again?'

'There's hope. He's got some inflammation around the break in his back. That's putting pressure on the nerve

68

right now, but it's still intact. We won't know for sure until he comes round, and we're keeping him sedated for now.'

'How long, before you know?'

'Tomorrow. Maybe.'

'Please, doctor, keep me informed.' McIntyre stood up and handed over her card. The doctor looked at it, her eyes widening with surprise as she read. 'There's work and private numbers on there. Call any time. Day or night. As soon as you have any news.' Then she turned on McLean. 'And you can get over to the mortuary. We need an ID on this dead girl. And fast.'

'Ah, Tony. I was beginning to think you'd stood me up. Did you not get my message?'

McLean let the door to the examination theatre swing closed behind him and tried not to breathe in the stench of death. Across the small room, Angus Cadwallader was up to his elbows in the dead young woman, aided as ever by his shadow, Tracy. She smiled at McLean as she held up a stainless-steel specimen tray ready to receive some no-longer-required internal organ. The scowling form of Dr Bairnsfather lurked a few feet behind the table, necessary witness to the proceedings.

'I knew you'd start without me, Angus.' McLean stepped closer, getting his first look at the woman's face since it had been covered up at the scene. She was young; couldn't have been more than twenty. Long black hair, striking, angular cheekbones, perfect lips palest blue against alabaster white skin. How could it be that no one had reported her missing?

'Any idea who she is?'

'Ah, now, that's your department. Or so I'm led to believe.' Cadwallader ploiped something suspiciously liverish down on the tray and Tracy placed it on the scales, noting something on her worksheet.

'What about cause of death?'

'That I can help you with. Poor girl bled to death from that gash across the throat. Blade went right through to the bone. She'd have died quite quickly.'

'Some small blessing, I suppose.'

'Yes, well, you might want to reserve judgement on that.' Cadwallader picked up one of the dead woman's hands, twisting the arm so that McLean could see the livid bruising and scratching around the wrist. 'She was shackled for a considerable time before death. Arms and legs.'

'There were cable ties. Under the bridge upstream from where she was found,' McLean said.

Cadwallader frowned, then pulled the overhead light closer, bending down to peer at the mottled skin. 'That would have been after she was dead. These marks are more like handcuffs.' He put the arm back down, stepped back from the table. 'Her stomach was completely empty, which would suggest she'd not eaten anything for several days. And she's been repeatedly raped. I take it you're seeing a pattern emerging here?'

'Abducted, kept locked up somewhere for anything up to a week, raped and then finally murdered by a sharp knife to the throat. Body washed and placed under a bridge in flowing water.' McLean heard the words as if someone else were speaking them. He was far, far away, on a dark night with fireworks exploding overhead.

*

70

His phone rang as he was walking back to the station an hour later. Darkness had already fallen over the city, and the offices had begun to vomit their workers back out onto the street. He peered at the caller ID, not recognising the number. Decided he might as well answer it. Not as if the day could get any worse.

'Yes?'

'Inspector McLean? Jo Dalgliesh here.'

McLean cursed under his breath. Cheeky bitch had got herself a new number. Most of the city's more persistent reporters were already in his phonebook precisely so he could avoid talking to them, and Dalgliesh was right there at the top of his list. He thought about hanging up, but before he could do so, the reporter started up again.

'Body found out at Gladhouse. Young woman. Killing bears some similarities to your old friend Donald Anderson.'

'Goodbye, Ms Dalgliesh.' McLean took the phone from his ear, hearing the tinny voice recede as his thumb hovered over the off switch.

'Her name's Audrey—'

He lost the rest in his hurry to clamp the phone back where it had been. 'What did you say?'

'Ah. I thought that might get your attention. You've been treating her as a Jane Doe, haven't you.'

'How the hell could you know who she is? You haven't even seen her.'

'Actually, I have. Your young Constable MacBride circulated an e-fit around all the papers about half an hour ago. The news editor just sent it to my phone. Lucky I bothered looking at it.'

'Lucky?' McLean could think of other adjectives. 'So who is she then? How come you know her?'

'Ah now, inspector. You know how it goes. I show you mine, you show me yours. What's in it for me?'

McLean shuddered at the thought. There was nothing about Joanne Dalgliesh he imagined ever wanting to see not covered by her manky old coat.

'Do I need to remind you that we're investigating a murder here, Ms Dalgliesh?'

'Please, call me Jo. And aye, I'm just teasing. She's a wanderer. A vagrant. That's why nobody bothered to report her missing. Well, not round here, anyways.'

McLean pictured the dead body in his mind, recalled the post-mortem he'd just witnessed. She'd been thin, sure, but not emaciated. In overall good health, Angus had said. Apart from the lack of blood and being dead bit.

'You sure about this?' he asked. 'I've just been at her post-mortem and there was no sign of drug abuse.'

'Aye, well, there wouldn't be. Strongest stuff Aud ever touched was a bit of blow. She wasn't living on the street because she had to, she was there because she wanted to. Told me she was going to write a book about it some day.'

'Told you? When did you last see her?'

'\'bout a week back. Supposed to meet her again last Tuesday, but she never showed.'

'And you didn't think to report her missing?'

Dalgliesh laughed. 'Jings, no. If I called the polis every time one of my sources didn't turn up you'd have no time for real work.'

McLean realised he'd stopped walking. 'Look, why were you meeting with this Audrey . . .'

'Carpenter. Audrey Carpenter. I was going to do one of those in-depth profiles for the Sunday supplement. Probably still will, but I'll need to change things a bit now. Do a bit more background. See, Carpenter wasn't the name she was christened with. No, that was her mum's name. Aud took it to get away from her father.'

'And this is leading somewhere?' McLean fumbled for his notebook, dropped it into the gutter, then realised he wouldn't have been able to write anything down anyway.

'Does the name Jim MacDougal mean anything to you?'

'What, Razors MacDougal?'

'Aye, that's him. When he wasn't busy carving out his wee empire in Tongland he married his childhood sweetheart, Jenny Carpenter. They had a daughter, Violet Audrey. Seems old Jim was rather too fond of sitting young Audrey on his knee, if you know what I'm saying. She did a runner about two years back. Been living in squats ever since.'

'Shit.' McLean rubbed at his face with his free hand. The last thing he needed was a link to a Glasgow crime lord. But there was potential motive there, and he at least had an ID to work with.

'Look, Ms Dalgliesh, I really need you to come down to the station and make a statement. Anything you can tell us about Audrey's movements before she went missing could be crucial in catching her killer.'

'Aye, well it'll have tae wait til tomorrow. My train's jest coming into Dundee.'

'Dundee? What're you doing there?'

'That's for me to know and you to ask, inspector. And since I've given you a solid lead, maybe you could answer me a few questions.'

'Such as?'

'You're heading up this investigation, right?'

McLean admitted that he was. At least for now.

'They're suggesting it bears all the hallmarks of the Christmas Killer. Is that right?'

'I don't know, Ms Dalgliesh. You'll have to tell me who "they" are.'

'C'mon, inspector. You of all people ought to see the similarities.'

'We're not ruling anything out at this stage. Neither are we going to jump to any conclusions.'

'So you're considering the possibility that this might be the Christmas Killer come back. That Anderson might have been the wrong man after all?'

15

'You deny abducting and murdering Kirsty Summers, Mr Anderson, and yet the police found forensic evidence in your cellar proving that she was held there against her will. That she was killed there.'

He sits in the gallery, staring down at the old man in the dock. White hair shaved close to the scalp in an almost monastic tonsure; tweed suit hanging elegantly off a slim frame; horn-rimmed spectacles perched on the end of a long, tapering nose; dark, pin-prick eyes fixed intently on the counsel for the defence. He should really hate Donald Anderson; should burn with an almost unstoppable urge to leap down into the court, vault over the low rail and throttle the life out of this evil man. But all he can feel is despair and helplessness. Nothing he can do will bring her back, and nothing this court can do will make it all unhappen.

'I didn't kill her.' Anderson's voice is calm. The patient tones of a teacher long used to explaining things to those less intelligent than he. 'My body may have done these terrible things, but I was not in control of it. The book was in control. It made me kill her.'

'This would be the so-called *Liber animarum* you claim to have found in a house clearance sale.' The advocate makes a show of consulting his notes. 'The Book of Souls.'

'Precisely.' Anderson's smile is like a slash in the face of hell.

'And this same book forced you to abduct and murder all those other women? Laura Fenton, Diane Kinnear, Rosie Buckley, Joss Evans. You must have had it a long time, Mr Anderson.'

'No, no, no. That wasn't me. That was the book. It takes control of you, you see. So that it can feed.'

'Feed?'

'On their souls, sir. That's what it does. It feeds on their souls.'

16

Jim MacDougal, known to most as Razors, lived in an ex-council semi in one of the better parts of Calton, which was to say right on the very edge of the place, pretending to be somewhere else. Over the years there had been some attempts at gentrification, but it pretty much remained the shit-hole that had been the battleground of the Tongs in the sixties and seventies. Only the crime had become more sophisticated; now the prostitutes spoke with Eastern European accents and the drugs came in designer packaging. The thugs running the show were just the same.

McLean sat in the driver's seat of the CID pool car, glad that it was one of the older models and generally not worth stealing. Beside him, Detective Constable MacBride fidgeted with the edge of his too-shiny suit. Still new to plain clothes, there was no worry anyone would think he wasn't a copper.

'You phoned Strathclyde, told them we needed some local back-up, right?' McLean peered through the grubby windscreen, surveying the streets for anything remotely resembling a squad car.

'Of course, sir. I spoke to a Detective Sergeant Coombes. Told him we'd be here at six. He said he'd have someone meet us.'

McLean looked at the clock on the dashboard. Half-past, and they'd been sitting here for forty minutes waiting.

'You want I should call him again?' MacBride pulled his bulky airwave set out of his pocket.

'No. I've got better things to do than wait on some daft Weegie to get his arse in gear. Come on. Let's get this over with.'

The front door opened almost before MacBride had knocked. The man standing in front of them looked like he'd have to turn sideways to fit through the frame. His chest was enormous, his forearms the size of a body-builder's biceps, and he must have been six foot seven if he was an inch.

'Um, Mr MacDougal?' MacBride asked. McLean didn't have the heart to correct him.

'Who the fuck are youse?'

'Detective Inspector McLean, Lothian and Borders.' McLean held up his warrant card. 'And this is Detective Constable MacBride.'

'Thought I smelled pork. Why've you been watching us?'

'I was waiting for my colleagues from Strathclyde Region to join us, but they seem to have been delayed. Look, this isn't what you think it is. It's about Mr MacDougal's daughter, Audrey.'

Something that sounded like a small animal being flayed alive escaped from the hallway behind the huge minder. He was elbowed aside and a thin, pale woman darted out of the house.

'My Audrey! You've found her? Is she . . . ?' Jenny Mac-Dougal's eyes darted from MacBride to McLean and back again, her hands wringing together as if in prayer. But no more words escaped from her and the minder put a surprisingly gentle hand on her shoulder, steered her back into the house.

'You'd better come in then.'

'Please forgive my wife. These past two years haven't been easy on her.'

Razors MacDougal was smaller than his police photograph and reputation suggested. Or maybe it was just that he surrounded himself with such enormous muscle that any normal man was going to look small in comparison. Besides the heavy who had shown them in, there were three more equally large men in the house, which turned out to be both halves of the semi knocked through. Looking around the large living room into which he had been shown, McLean saw a number of professional portrait photographs of a strikingly beautiful woman and could only agree that Mrs MacDougal had taken the disappearance of her daughter hard. He could also see the unmistakable similarity between mother and child, which didn't really make his job any easier.

'I'm very sorry, sir, madam,' McLean nodded at Jenny MacDougal who had curled herself almost foetally into an oversized armchair. 'There's no easy way to say this, really. But we think your daughter may be dead. We also think that her death was not an accident.'

'Is this some kind of sick joke, Inspector McLean? Only I don't find it fucking funny.' MacDougal's low growl reminded McLean of how he'd got his nickname.

'I can assure you, sir. This is no joke.'

'What do you mean, you think Violet might have been killed?'

The question threw McLean, both because of the unfamiliar name, and the fact that it was Jenny MacDougal who had voiced it. Her face had drained of all colour so that she looked even more like her daughter laid out on the slab. McLean nodded to MacBride. 'The photographs please, constable.'

A4 glossies, fresh from the colour printer that afternoon. It was difficult to make a corpse's head look anything other than what it was, but the pathology photographer had tried.

'This young woman was found in a stream near Gladhouse Reservoir on Monday evening.' McLean handed the photographs to Razors MacDougal, trying not to notice the shake in the gangster's hands as he took them, avoiding the man's eyes. MacDougal looked at them for less than a second before dropping them to the floor, cupping his face in his hands and running his fingers through his straggly, greying hair.

'In the water, you say. She drowned?'

'No, sir. She was put there after she died.'

Suddenly MacDougal was on his feet, and he didn't look so small now. His face was bright red with anger, veins straining through skin, eyes wide. He was too close. McLean could feel the gangster's breath on his own face, but he stood his ground. There were two ways this could go, and one of them wasn't at all appealing.

'What're you saying, inspector? She was murdered?'

McLean was about to answer when a screeching wail rose up from the floor. He looked down to see Jenny MacDougal sprawled out on the carpet, clutching the discarded photographs, screaming incoherently. He bent down to help her, but Razors pushed him roughly aside, stooped, picked up his wife.

'Get her out of here,' he said to one of the bodyguards. Jenny fought and kicked as she was hauled bodily from the room, but it was a weak effort, worn down by two years of worry.

'Jesus, but you've got a nerve.' MacDougal paced back and forth, flexing his over-large hands into fists. 'What the fuck do you think you're doing, bringing this in here?' He swept an arm in the direction of the crumpled photographs.

'I take it that is your daughter, Mr MacDougal?'

'Aye, it's her.' For the first time he looked like he might actually be grieving, a rime of tears forming in his eyes. He sniffed hard, wiping his face with a sleeve. 'So what happened? And why's it taken this long for youse lot to come and tell us?'

'When we found her she was naked, no personal effects. Missing Persons didn't come up with a match. I'm sorry about that, they really should have done. It wasn't until we put an e-fit out that a name came up. She was calling herself Audrey Carpenter.'

McLean could see that MacDougal wasn't really listening. He'd gone to the sideboard, poured himself a large scotch from a hideous crystal decanter. Why did villains always decant their whisky? Probably because it was cheap and they wanted to pretend it wasn't.

'Audrey was living in a squat somewhere in Edinburgh,' McLean continued. 'She'd been talking to a reporter at the *Scotsman*, mostly about life on the streets, I think.'

MacDougal might have been a thug, but he wasn't

stupid. Two quick steps brought him face to face with McLean, staring at him with those wild eyes.

'Who? This reporter. I want his name.'

'You know I can't tell you that, sir. I can pass on your request for a meeting though.'

'Don't give me that shit, inspector. The name.' MacDougal prodded McLean in the chest with a stubby finger. The whisky in his other hand sloshed around in its glass, giving off an unmistakable Islay peat aroma. So much for that theory.

'When was the last time you saw your daughter, Mr MacDougal?'

For a moment, the words just hung in the air, echoing in the silence as the colour in MacDougal's face darkened. Then he pointed at the door and growled like an angry bear.

'Get out!'

McLean held the gangster's gaze for a couple of seconds more, then nodded his head. 'Constable,' he said without turning. MacBride scurried out of the room like a frightened mouse.

'We'll speak again, Mr MacDougal,' McLean said, and then he walked slowly to the door.

'You'll be wanting to keep your head down, sir. Old Dagwood's looking for you and I don't think it's to give you a medal.' The duty sergeant smiled from behind his glass barrier as he buzzed McLean back into the station.

'What have I done this time, Pete?'

'No idea, but he's been tearing a strip off anyone who gets in his way. Right foul mood he's in.'

'No change there, then. You know where he's looking right now? So I can avoid him.'

'Haven't got a clue. Just keep your ears open and you'll be fine.'

McLean wasn't so sure as he made his way down into the bowels of the station. Those few officers he passed on the way seemed to be giving him a wary look, as if he were bad luck walking. The CID room was almost empty, just one lone figure slumped in a chair with his feet up on the desk. McLean looked around the room with a faint nostalgia. It was only a few months since he'd moved out and into his cubbyhole of an inspector's office, but he already missed the place.

'You up for some work this evening, Bob?' he asked. Detective Sergeant Laird did a good impression of a man waking from a deep sleep, almost falling off his chair in the process.

'Shit, you gave me a fright there, sir. You seen Dagwood yet?'

'No, and the longer I can put it off the better. Any idea why he wants to see me?'

'No, but I can tell you this much. He's not a happy bunny.'

'My heart bleeds for him. Did you get the PM report on Audrey Carpenter yet?'

'Who?' Grumpy Bob's face was a mask of confusion.

'The dead lass we found out at Gladhouse. Audrey Carpenter. Or Violet Audrey MacDougal if you prefer.'

'I didn't think we had an ID for her yet. When did this come in?'

McLean slumped against one of the desks. 'Just after

the PM. Jo Dalgliesh made the ID, of all people. I could do without having to be grateful to her.'

'Does Dagwood know?'

'He should do. I left a message on his phone and a report on his desk before I went. I thought he'd have told you.' And slowly the pieces began to fall into place. 'Shit. He's not been into his office, and he's not listened to his messages, has he.'

'At a guess, I'd say no. And that's probably why he's on the warpath right now.'

'Well, I'd better go and find him before he does something even more stupid than usual. Meantime I need you to get the ball rolling on this one. Put a team together. Set up an incident room.'

'Erm, this is it,' Grumpy Bob said, adding as an afterthought: 'sir.'

'What? There's no spare rooms we can use right now?'

'Nope.'

'Not even that cupboard we used for the Smythe case?'

'Tech boys have got it while the basement's being damp-proofed again.'

'Nothing on the first floor?'

'All taken up with the drugs investigation.'

'Fucking marvellous. How the hell can we be short-staffed and not have enough room? No, don't answer that, Bob. Just set it up, OK. I'll go see what's got up Dagwood's skirt, and then I think I'm going to need a drink.'

17

McLean found DCI Duguid in his office on the second floor. It was warm, three times the size of McLean's tiny cupboard, and in the daytime would have a commanding view of Arthur's Seat. The privileges of seniority, no doubt.

'I believe you were looking for me, sir?'

Duguid grunted something from his desk, leafing through a file of papers. McLean couldn't help but notice that his preliminary report on Audrey Carpenter had been carefully laid to one side.

'You've identified the dead girl, I see,' Duguid said after a long pause. 'Even been to see her parents.'

'We needed confirmation, sir. And—'

'Didn't anyone tell you that it's both polite and a good idea to consult with another force if you're conducting an investigation on their patch?' Duguid's tone was neutral, which never boded well.

'We did contact Strathclyde, sir. Spoke to a DS Coombes who said he'd send some support round to meet us.'

'Is that so? Then why, tell me, have I just spent an hour on the fucking phone apologising to some tosspot detective superintendent from SOCA with an impenetrable Weegie accent because one of my officers seriously fucked-up his ongoing investigation?'

'Investigation?'

'What? You thought it'd be OK to just go and have a wee chat with one of Glasgow's most notorious hard men? Thought it would be fine to accuse him of murdering his own daughter?'

'I never—'

'Don't interrupt me when I'm speaking, McLean.' Duguid rose up out of his chair like a volcano, hands smashing on the desk. Now he was angry, and that was much easier to deal with. 'You went to see MacDougal without any back-up, right?'

'I had Constable MacBride with me.'

'Brilliant idea. Why not endanger the life of yet another new recruit. No wonder we've no bloody staff. You keep on trying to get them killed.'

Remain calm. Don't rise to the bait. Take the bollocking and move on.

'What were you even doing there, for Christ's sake? You could have faxed the photographs through to the nearest station and let them deal with it.'

Aye, and wait a week for a reply. 'I needed to speak to Mr MacDougal myself, sir.'

'Why? So you could make wild allegations about him to his face? You do know why they call him Razors, don't you?'

'The man abused his daughter. That's why she ran away. That's why she was living on the streets. But she was talking to the press. It was only a matter of time before it all came out. I don't know about you, sir, but I think that's motive enough for a man like MacDougal.'

Duguid slumped back down into his seat, his expression changing from anger to something more like excitement. He glanced sideways at the report, then back at McLean.

'You shouldn't have gone in there without someone from SOCA. Or at least Strathclyde CID. MacDougal's a career criminal; he knows how to play the system. There's already been a formal complaint lodged about your behaviour.'

'If Professional Standards want to talk to me, I'm always available, sir. I've done nothing wrong here.'

'Aye, I've heard that about you. Go on, get out McLean. We'll pick this up at tomorrow's briefing. If we've got a suspect, that's something to keep the press off our backs at least.'

'Sir, I really don't—'

'Tomorrow, McLean.' Duguid waved him quiet. 'Right now I've got to make some calls to Glasgow.'

Christmas shoppers thronged the lamp-lit pavements of Princes Street and the upper end of Leith Walk like some vast, unpredictable beast. At least McLean assumed they were Christmas shoppers, even if it was only just December. Getting on for nine and the shops really ought to have been closed by now, but the St James's Centre was bursting at the seams. So much for the age of austerity.

He hunched his shoulders against the throng and tried to fight his way up towards North Bridge. It had been a long, crap day and he really needed a drink.

Deep in thought, it took a moment for McLean to register that he'd seen something through the glass doors of John Lewis. He couldn't quite say what, but whatever it was, it stopped him in mid-stride, forcing muttered curses from the other pedestrians as they had to adapt to a sudden rock in their stream. He took a step back, peering through the glass at the shoppers inside, the staff in their uniforms, the mind-boggling variety of Christmas decorations and assorted seasonal tat.

And then he saw him; three-quarters turned away. Wearing a jeans and leather bomber jacket combination that was atypical for the man. But otherwise unmistakable.

'Anderson!'

McLean pushed his way through the crowd, not caring who he knocked aside. The shop doors were slow, motorised rotating panes of glass that stopped whenever one of the mindless crowd bumped too close. And in his rush to get inside, they were all mindless now. He wasted long seconds shuffling impatiently, trying to peer over heads and into the shop, desperate not to lose his quarry. Finally the wheel opened, spilling people out into the warmth. McLean pushed past them, ignoring the scowls and half-muttered comments, hurrying to the stand where he had seen Anderson.

'Can I help you with anything, sir? Only we're closing in ten minutes.' McLean looked around to see a young shop assistant giving him an uncertain smile.

'Actually I'm looking for someone. An old man, about so high.' He raised his hand somewhere between the top of the assistant's head and his chin. 'Wearing jeans and a brown leather jacket. Grey hair, but not much of it.'

'I'm sorry, sir. I really couldn't say. We're very busy, and it's been like that all evening.'

'What about CCTV?' McLean scanned the upper reaches of the atrium and saw several, all pointed at the revolving doors.

'I'm not sure it would be appropriate—'

'I'm a police officer.' McLean dug out his warrant card and noticed an immediate change in the young woman. Her eyes flicked nervously away from him and towards the tills.

'I'll just get the departmental manager,' she said, and fled.

'There. Stop there. Can you zoom in?'

McLean sat in the darkened viewing room somewhere in the depths of the department store and peered at the slightly fuzzy images on a bank of flickering screens. It was a far more sophisticated set-up than the makeshift viewing room back at the station, but not a patch on the city's Central Monitoring Facility, where the surveillance culture really started. The security manager stifled a yawn as he fiddled with buttons, focusing the image down to just one man. The picture deteriorated to a series of flesh-coloured blobs, but even then McLean could tell.

'No, sorry. That's not him. Go back a bit will you.'

'Is this going to take a lot longer, sir?' the manager asked. 'Only I was due to clock off an hour ago.'

McLean looked at his watch. Half-past ten and they'd scarcely made a dent in the available footage. The shop seemed to be awash with cameras, all of them showing an endless bustle of desperate shoppers just slightly out of focus. It was a mammoth task, and the rational part of his brain was already telling him he was being an idiot. It wasn't Anderson, just someone who happened to look a bit like him. Perhaps he was just over-reacting because of the burial. And the dead girl.

'You're right. Sorry.' McLean rubbed at his aching eyes.

He needed to do something, but perhaps staring at a flickering screen for yet more hours wasn't it. 'Look, is there any way I could get a copy of this evening's footage? Just a couple of hours leading up to closing?' Or a few minutes. He'd already seen his own hurried entry into the building immortalised on tape or hard disk or whatever it was they used these days.

'I'm not sure. I'd have thought so, but I'll have to run it past the senior manager. Did you want it now?' The security manager gave him a look of such utter desperation that McLean had to relent.

'No, you're all right.' He fished in his jacket for a card, handed it over. 'It's not that urgent, but if I could get it in the next couple of days.'

The security manager took the card like it was a winning lottery ticket. 'Aye, well, I'll see what I can do.'

18

McLean thumbed the number as he stepped out of the staff door into the cold night air. He should probably have programmed it into the phone's memory, but it was imprinted in his brain just fine. What he needed now was a drink anyway, not a half hour fight with some irritating but essential technology.

'Hello?' Female voice at the end of the line. Rachel. Damn, he'd been hoping not to have to talk to her.

'Hi Rae, Tony here. How's things?'

'Oh, you know, same old. Got some samples through for the bridesmaids dresses, and I need to finalise the menu. The band's mucking us about, too. I don't suppose you could, oh I don't know, give them a parking ticket or something?'

McLean laughed. 'Rae, the wedding's not for another six months.'

'Six months is nothing, Tony. It'll be gone like that. I have to have it planned.'

'You'll be fine. And anyway, I thought Phil was going to spirit you off to Vegas, get you hitched by an Elvis impersonator.'

'Don't you even start. I suppose you want to talk to him.'

'Actually, I was hoping I might be able to borrow him for the evening.' He glanced at the dark clouds, the empty, lamp-lit back street. 'What's left of it.'

'Please, take him. He's only getting in the way here. Just promise to bring him back.'

'OK, Rae. It's a deal. Tell him I'll be in The Arms in half an hour.'

Putting his phone away, McLean voiced an unheard thanks that he'd caught Rachel in a good mood. Lately, as the impending wedding loomed slightly closer, she'd taken to calling him at the oddest of times to ask him stupid questions. Had he organised the stag night? Did he have a partner for the wedding? What was she going to wear? He could only pity Phil. His ex-flatmate and best friend was surely having to endure ten times worse.

Even allowing the time it took to grab a kebab and eat it in the steamy warmth of the shop, McLean still made it to the pub first. He was halfway down his pint before the swinging doors drew in a blast of chill air and the gangly, unkempt figure he'd been expecting.

'You're late.' McLean held up the full glass that had once been twin to his own. Phil took it, draining enough to match in one long gulp.

'Cheers, I needed that.' He wiped foam from his upper lip and smiled. McLean thought he looked tired, the creases round his eyes less from laughter than from lack of sleep. 'Christ, sometimes I wonder what possessed me.'

'Rachel getting that bad, eh? She sounded all right on the phone.'

'No, not Rae. Sure she's a bit obsessed, but she makes up for that in other ways.' Phil smirked, something of his old self showing through. 'No, it's the lab. I thought being a professor meant sitting in my office all day reading papers, making life miserable for undergrads and waiting for the invitations to international conferences to come in.'

'And it's not?'

'Hell, no. I've got a budget the size of a small banana republic, a staff of overpaid academic prima donnas, each of whom needs their ego massaging at least once a day, and that's not to mention the committees. Health and safety, public relations, ethics. I can't remember the last time I actually picked up a test tube. What's so funny?'

'You.' McLean slapped his old friend on the back. 'You sound almost grown up.'

'Yeah, well, I guess. People depend on me.'

'Tell me about it. Sounds a lot like being an inspector. Technically I'm a detective, but half the time all I'm doing is telling sergeants and constables what to do.'

'At least it's only half the time. Here, let me get another one in.' Phil had finished his pint, and McLean drained what was left of his, waiting patiently whilst it was replaced. They took their bounty to a table far away from the noisy jukebox blaring out old eighties' tunes.

'So, you've got your best man speech sorted, I take it?' Phil asked.

'Can't I just wing it?'

'Depends on whether or not you want to live out the day, mate. You've not seen Rachel when she's roused.'

'Perhaps I'd better do something about that then. And I guess there's your stag night, too. Any idea what you want to do?'

'As long as it doesn't involve too many of your police friends.'

McLean feigned a hurt look. 'What's wrong with them?'

'Individually? Nothing at all. Bob's a good laugh. That young lad, Mac-whatsit – a bit earnest, but he's got promise. Big Andy's useful in a pub quiz team. But you know, get them all together at once and it can get a bit out of hand. I used to think undergrads drank too much.'

McLean remembered Big Andy Houseman's stag night, and knew what Phil was talking about. Put a bunch of off-duty policemen together in the same place as large quantities of alcohol and it was never likely to be pretty.

'I'll keep the uniform count down, Phil. You can trust me on that.'

'What're you planning then. Ten-pin bowling and curry? Skating at Murrayfield? A lap-dancing club down in Leith?'

'And you wish.' McLean made a mental note to get started on organising something. It was only six months since Phil had asked him to be his best man, after all. 'Rachel will kill me if I do anything involving women, you know.'

'Of course. But she doesn't need to know. Anyway, Jenny's got something outrageous organised for the hens. She was asking, by the way. Wanted to know if she should ask Emma along, to get to know some of the other girls, you know. So she's not completely lost come the day.'

'I don't know.' McLean took a long sip of his beer, uncomfortable at the way the conversation had turned and not quite sure why. 'I'll have to ask her.'

'What? You mean you haven't asked her already? You have asked her, haven't you? Tell me you have. Rae'll have a fit if she thinks the best man's coming single.'

'I will, Phil. I promise.'

'I don't know, Tony. What is it with you two anyway? You seemed right pally for a while back there. Then . . . what?'

'Shifts, the job. I don't know, Phil. Maybe I've just got used to being single.'

'You're a fool, Detective Inspector McLean.' Phil levered himself off his bench and grabbed the two empty glasses that had mysteriously replaced the full ones they'd sat down with.

'My shout.' McLean reached for his wallet.

'Nah, you can get the next one. I need the loo anyway.' Phil set off, leaving him to ponder exactly why it was he hadn't tried harder with Emma Baird, SOC officer and the only person to have slept in his bed other than himself in ten years or more. Even if she had climbed in drunk and passed out when he was already asleep.

'You know I really could have done with this yesterday,' Phil said once he'd returned with their third pint.

'You should have called.'

'I did, but you weren't answering. No point leaving a message on that stupid machine of yours. You never listen to it.'

'Oh yes, that's right. I was in Aberdeen. Didn't get back til late. Then there was that fire at the Woodbury building. Must've been after two before I got in.'

'The fire, aye, I saw that on the news. Place went up quick, didn't it? I guess they'll rip it down and stick a block of flats in its place now. Not sure what's worse, that or turning a factory into posh apartments for people with too much money.'

McLean frowned. 'Why'd you say that?'

'Well, it's just sad to see these great old buildings being snapped up by greedy developers. The men who built them were entrepreneurs. They generated wealth and life in the city. These places, I don't know. It's all security cameras and razor wire. Gated communities. They just suck all the life out of the town.'

'It's funny, you're the second person to say that today.'

'Oh aye?'

'I spoke to the caretaker, mad old bugger he was. Reckoned the building burnt itself down rather than be converted. Sort of committed suicide.'

Phil choked on his beer, spluttering foam out of his mouth and nose. McLean slapped him on the back a couple of times until his coughing subsided and he could breathe clearly again.

'Still got the drinking problem, I see.'

'Ah, that's priceless. Buildings committing suicide. You really know how to pick them, don't you, Tony.'

'I guess I do.'

'So what took you up to Aberdeen then?' Phil's voice was a half octave higher than normal still. McLean frowned; he'd hoped that the conversation wouldn't have reached this topic, but that was wishful thinking really. The news would be out soon enough, and his best friend had more right to know than most.

'Anderson's dead,' he said, and then he told Phil all about it.

Much later. The city was as near silent as it ever got as he walked home from the pub. Just the occasional taxi gliding across the Meadows; a snatch of drunken shouting;

the distant roar of three quarters of a million people simply existing. McLean breathed the cold air in deep and tried hard not to think about Donald Anderson or Audrey Carpenter. But still the earth clattered down on the coffin lid in a windswept Aberdeenshire cemetery. Still the dead, pale face peered up at him from the mortuary slab. And the beer made it harder to hold onto those thin porcelain features, moulded them into another face, another time.

It wasn't until he was fishing around in his pocket for his keys that the thing that had been bothering him all the way up the street finally hit home. McLean sniffed the air; something was burning with a familiar, pungent, illegal smell. He looked around, seeing nobody else. A late bus passed by the end of the street, and in the wake of its noise he heard the distant, muffled crackling of flames. He stepped back from the front door, looking up to the windows of his own tenement flat. They were blank, reflecting the dull orange of the clouds overhead. But movement in the corner of his eye dragged his attention down a floor, and across the building.

It was the student flat; never the same faces from one month to the next it seemed. At least this latest lot didn't prop the street door open with rocks. They did have a tendency to play loud music late at night, and they kept the old wooden shutters closed on the windows almost all the time. They were shut now, but a tiny gap down the middle showed light, dancing and flickering behind.

He was all fingers and thumbs as he grappled with the heavy keyring, searching for the right one for the front door. The keys for his grandmother's house over the other side of the city were on there too, and their combined weight conspired to make him drop the lot of them. Cursing the drink, McLean finally managed to fumble the front door open and stepped into darkness.

It was warm, far too warm for December, and the smell of burning stuck in the back of his throat as soon as he breathed in. Looking up, he could see pale grey smoke hugging the ceiling. At the back of the hallway it snaked down the stairs and through the cast-iron banisters. He pulled out his phone, dialling 999 as he made his way upwards.

'Emergency helpline, which service did you require?' The woman on the other end of the phone sounded bored. One too many crank calls to really care any more.

'Fire, ambulance, police.' McLean went for the triad. He gave the address as he reached the landing. Two doors: the student flat and the merchant banker, who was working overseas at the moment if memory served. The glass fanlight above one flat was dark, the other rippling with orange dancing light and boiling black smoke. It oozed through the keyhole and under the door.

He took the rest of the stairs in leaps, covering his mouth and nose with the sleeve of his coat as the smoke began to thicken. Ignoring his own front door, he went straight to the flat opposite and hammered on the wood.

'Mr Sheen? Can you hear me? Mr Sheen? It's Tony McLean. You have to wake up. There's a fire.' Even as he said the words, choking as oddly sweet smoke bit at the back of his throat, he could hear how stupid he sounded. He stepped back, looking up at the fanlight, waiting for the bulb in the inner hall to come on. Nothing. Or was there? Light flickering?

Not waiting to be certain, McLean kicked at the door with all his might. It cracked, but held. He kicked it again, sending one panel flying back into the flat beyond. Looking through he could see only smoke swirling around; in moments it had begun to billow out through this new gap. He reached inside, feeling for the latch, hoping that his neighbour didn't have a deadbolt. Luck was on his side.

The heat pressed around him as he opened the door, smoke flooding out onto the landing. He took a breath of the relatively fresh air and stepped carefully in. The floor creaked under his weight, seeming to sag inwards, and he was suddenly all too aware of the raging inferno beneath. He should really leave this to the firemen, but what if they got here too late?

He opened the door to what he hoped was the bedroom. Smoke billowed about the room and across the narrow hall; Mr Sheen was not one to sleep with his window open. McLean wanted to shout, but he was afraid of breathing in deep enough to do so. He hurried as fast as he dared to the bed, reaching for the sleeping figure, shaking him hard by the shoulder. Nothing.

Bending down close, he tried to see if the man was breathing, but it was too dark, too full of smoke. Tears blurred his vision. Smoke burned at his throat. He was dimly aware of more noise, the roaring of flames finally breaking free. There was no time. He dragged back the covers, pulled Mr Sheen out of bed and threw him over his shoulder. As he gasped for breath, staggering back out into the hall, McLean was glad that his neighbour was a thin old man. Even so, the weight made him stagger, and the heat was more unbearable still. The living-room door burst into flame in front of his eyes, like something from a cheap horror movie. The light it cast over the inner hallway showed polished floorboards blackened and twisting. Flames underneath were eating away at the ceiling and joists in the flat below. Soon the whole lot would come crashing down. If he didn't make it out in time, he'd be going with them.

Hefting Mr Sheen's pyjama'd form onto his back more squarely, McLean staggered forwards. He could hear the floorboards groaning under his weight, feel the whole floor shifting and buckling like a sinister bouncy castle as he took the mad option and ran for it. He sprang forward at the last, crashing through the open doorway and onto the relative safety of the stone landing as the floor finally collapsed.

A great gout of flame billowed out over his head, singeing his hair and catching Mr Sheen's pyjamas alight. He fell to his knees. For a moment he was too exhausted to move, his mind too confused by the lack of oxygen. All he could do was stare at the tiny flames eating away at the cotton. And beyond them, just out of focus, the door to his own apartment. His whole life. He needed to get in there, to save those few things he might be able to carry out. Those last reminders of the life that had been stolen from him.

Something exploded down below. The noise cut through the fog in his mind, and McLean woke enough to realise what had been happening. He slapped at the flames on Mr Sheen's pyjamas, then staggered to his feet, dragging the old man up with him. Leaning heavily against the stone wall, he inched his way carefully down the stairs to the next landing. The door to the student flat was ablaze, flames licking at the underside of the stone landing he'd been lying on just moments earlier. Through the fanlight over the other door, he could see that the merchant banker's flat was going strong now. His own place upstairs would catch soon.

The heat boiling out of the student flat was almost unbearable, but he had to pass close to the blazing door to get to the stairs. Gritting his teeth against it, he hurried past, shielding the unconscious form from the worst of it and praying his coat wouldn't catch. Once past, he could feel the wind on his face as the blaze sucked air in through the open front door and up the stone stairwell. It was a welcome relief and gave him the strength to stagger down the last flights, dragging Mr Sheen along with him.

The wail of sirens echoed off the other tenements as McLean collapsed onto the pavement across the road. He gulped down sweet, cold Edinburgh air, too shell-shocked to pay attention to the still form beside him. All about the street, lights were flicking on like will-o'-the-wisps from a nursery rhyme. Tiny faerie faces stared from windows. A fire engine screeched round the corner before coming to a halt. It had scarcely disgorged its crew of yellow men before another joined it. McLean struggled to his feet and headed back across the road as a familiar figure came running up. Jim Burrows, the fire investigator, obviously didn't recognise him.

'Is anyone else in there?'

'Ground floor.' McLean pointed at the nearest bay window. 'Old Mrs McCutcheon. Lives alone. Watch out for the cats.'

'Bloody hell! Are you all right, sir?'

McLean looked around to see two uniformed officers approaching at speed. He was pleased to see that one of them was Sergeant Houseman, but before he could say anything more, a deafening explosion slammed through the night. Glass and bits of window frame rained down on them, tinkling on the roofs of the parked cars. Then something heavier landed at McLean's feet, charred and blackened but giving off that oddly sweet smell as it smoked.

'Secure the street, Andy. And get as many bodies here as possible. We're going to have to evacuate everyone in the next two tenements. And round the back, too.' He bent down and prodded the lump of smoking material, noticing as he did that his hand was blackened with soot. Sometime soon, he was going to go into shock; maybe he already had.

'How's Mr Sheen?'

'Who?' Houseman asked.

'My neighbour.' McLean picked up the lump of material, brushing off the charred mess on the outside. It was cool and unburnt beneath a thin layer. He crumbled it in his fingers as he turned back towards the far pavement where he had left the old man, a horrible thought beginning to form in his mind.

A group of people had gathered on the pavement, and a couple of paramedics were hunched down beside the prone figure. Big Andy followed McLean over, moving the gawpers aside to give them some room, but McLean could tell that it was no use. The paramedics weren't fighting to save Mr Sheen's life and their slumped shoulders gave everything away.

'He's dead, isn't he.' McLean hunkered down beside the nearest paramedic, still rubbing the charred lump of material in his hand.

'There was nothing we could do,' the paramedic said without looking around. 'He was gone before we got here.'

McLean stood up, catching hold of a nearby car to steady himself as the world started to spin. The street was chaos now: fire engines lined up, too many to count; ladders and hoses and noise; the smell of steam, charred wood, burning plastic and flesh.

'Are you all right, sir?' It was the paramedic, McLean realised in a tiny part of his brain. Mostly his concentration was on the lump of burned something that had blown out of the student flat. He knew what it was now, finally understood what had happened.

'Andy?' he said, looking around for the large policeman.

'I think we need to get you checked over, sir.' The paramedic put a hand on McLean's arm. He shrugged it off.

'I'm a police officer.'

'You're a police officer going into shock, by the look of things.'

'I'm OK. Just a bit woozy is all. A bit too much smoke.'

A large figure hove into view, and it took McLean a while to realise it was Sergeant Houseman.

'Andy? There you are. Get onto the station. Get Dagwood down here.'

'It's two in the morning, sir. I don't think he'll be there.'

'Well, wake him up. No, on second thoughts that's not such a good idea. But tell him anyway.'

'Tell him what, sir? Don't you think you ought to go with the paramedics?'

'I'm fine, Andy.' McLean held up the lump of charred something, flaking a corner off with his thumb. All around him was chaos, his whole life had just gone up in flames, and yet he was struck by how ridiculous everything was.

'It's hash, Andy. The stuff we've been trying to track down for months now. Little bastards were growing it right under my nose.'

And then he couldn't help it. The laughter bubbled out of him like vomit. He choked and gasped for air, his lungs protesting at the smoke they had inhaled, but he just couldn't stop. Even when the paramedic slipped an oxygen mask over his head.

19

'You know what you are, Tony McLean? A selfish bastard, that's what.'

He sits at the kitchen table, coffee mug held between his hands, trying hard to find a way to protest. But even as he mouths the familiar response, he can't help admitting, deep down, that she's right.

'Look, Kirsty. It's not as if I had any choice in the matter—'

'Don't you give me that. Don't you even start on that.' She's standing in the doorway, hands on hips, long black hair loose today, trailing down her back. The skirt he gave her for her birthday looks good, goes well with the green of her eyes. Even in her anger, he can't help but notice them and smile, just a little.

'Are you even listening to me? God, it's like talking to a child. We've been planning this weekend for months.'

That wipes the smile off his face. 'I know, K. I was looking forward to it too. And it's been in the leave sheets since July. But you know what Duff's like.'

She throws herself into one of the kitchen chairs. He's never seen someone do that before, but there's no other way of describing it.

'I know what you're like. Spineless. You don't stand up to these bullies soon, they're not going to have any respect for you, you know.'

'Duff's a detective inspector, K. You know how hard I've worked to get into CID, and it's only a temporary posting whilst Keen's off with his broken leg. If I don't make a good impression now, when am I going to get another chance?'

'So that's it then?' The chair topples backwards to the floor as she leaps up, just as violently as she had sat. 'Drop everything at his master's whistle? Roll over and have your tummy tickled.'

'Kirsty, I—'

'Forget it. Just . . . Forget it.' She grabs her coat from the rack in the hallway, slams the door so hard on the way out that it bounces back open again. He hurries after her, out onto the landing where their elderly neighbour stares at him with an embarrassed, surprised look.

'Kirsty! Where are you going?'

But all the answer he gets is her long black hair, billowing out behind her as she hurtles down the stairs.

20

'Come in. I'll just be a moment.' Chief Superintendent McIntyre didn't look up from her desk as she furiously annotated some important report. McLean had made it from the open door, upon whose frame he had knocked, to a point right in front of the vast, busy desk before she finished with a flourish of signature. 'What can I do for you— Tony! What the hell are you doing here? And what is that suit you're wearing?'

'I'm fine, thank you, ma'am. How are you?' McLean smiled. It wasn't often he managed to catch the superintendent off-guard.

'Sorry.' McIntyre nodded her head at him. 'It's just, well, that's a very striking pinstripe.'

McLean pulled at a gaudy sleeve. 'I believe it was fashionable in the 1920s. It's my grandfather's. The only thing I could find that came even close to fitting. If you don't count some of my gran's old dresses, that is.'

'A wise choice, I think. Have you been . . . you know . . . back?'

'Not yet, no. I assume they put the fire out. Looked like they had it under control when I went off last night.'

'Yes, Big Andy told me all about that. You really shouldn't be here, you know. I'm surprised the doctors let you out of hospital. They reckoned you'd breathed in a lot of smoke.'

McLean tried to suppress the urge to cough, but couldn't quite manage. 'What else could I do? Sit around moping about the unfairness of life?'

'Well, you could have gone shopping, I suppose.' McIntyre smiled.

'Don't worry, I'll be requesting some time off. But I needed to know what happened.'

'Give us a chance. They only secured the building a couple of hours ago. Charles is champing at the bit to get in there, but the firemen won't let him.'

'Ah, so he got my message then. How's he feeling about that?'

'You can ask him yourself. He wants to interview you about the flat where the fire started.'

'What's to say? I've never met the owner, it's just rented out to a continuous stream of students. This last lot were better than most. I guess I didn't pay them all that much attention.'

'You're a detective, Tony. You're trained to pay attention. How long ago did they move in?'

'I don't know. End of the summer? After the Festival.'

'So they've been running some kind of drugs operation right under our noses for at least four months. Christ, the press are going to have a field day.'

McLean's heart sank. Of course the press would get their grubby little hands on this story. And it wouldn't take long for them to work out that at the same tenement block in which a drug factory had been set up there also lived a detective inspector.

'It doesn't look very good, does it, ma'am.'

'No, it doesn't. And DC Robertson's accident doesn't

help either.' McIntyre rubbed at her eyes. 'Professional Standards want to talk to you,' she said after a while.

'I'd expected as much,' McLean said, though his heart fell even so.

'It's informal at this stage, Tony. No one's made an official complaint.' McIntyre put on her serious face. The one she used when frightening the new constables. 'I'll do what I can to keep it that way. I'm on your side on this. But I can't make any promises. For now, though, I want you to keep as low a profile as possible. Go and talk to Duguid, then I don't want to see you back in the station until the hearing.'

'But I'm in the middle of a murder investigation, I can't—'

'Until the hearing, Tony. Or I'll have you suspended. DS Laird can take on your case-load whilst you're away. It'll do him some good to actually work for his wage. Go do some shopping. Go home.' McIntyre paused, some of the colour leaching out of her face. 'Shit, that was insensitive. Sorry.'

'It's all right, ma'am. I know what you meant.'

'Where are you staying, by the way? Not Grumpy Bob's I hope.'

'No. I'm at my gran's old place. Up Braid Hills way.'

'Well, make sure we've got a phone number where we can reach you.'

McLean nodded, turned to go, then stopped. 'Any news about DC Robertson?'

'He'll walk again.' McIntyre rubbed at her eyes again. 'But they reckon he's going to be off sick for at least a year.'

'Bloody hell. We're short enough staffed as it is. Any chance of pinching a few more from uniform?'

'I'm working on it, Tony, but believe it or not, not everyone wants to be a detective these days.' McIntyre scratched at her face absentmindedly. 'Still, Aberdeen have come to our rescue; they're sending one of theirs down on secondment, with a possibility of transfer.'

'Oh aye. Anyone I know?'

McIntyre pulled a sheet of paper from her out-tray and peered at it for a moment.

'DS Ritchie,' she said. 'She'll be here in a fortnight. You can show her around. If you're still with us.'

McLean didn't much fancy getting into a shouting match with Duguid, certainly not with his throat still as sore as it was. So instead he set off in search of Grumpy Bob. The detective sergeant found him first.

'Didn't expect to see you today, sir. How the hell are you?'

'I'm fine, Bob, thanks.' McLean coughed and his lungs spasmed in pain. 'Well, near enough. Can't say the same for my neighbour though.'

'Aye, I heard about that. Poor bastard. Still, the doctors reckon he just died in his sleep. I guess that's better than being burned to death.'

'Have you been to the site?'

'I was there this morning, soon as I got in. It's a mess all right. Tried your mobile, but it's going straight to message.'

McLean slapped the pockets of his grandfather's suit, trying to remember which one he'd put his phone in. He found it, pulled it out and peered at the screen. Something inside appeared to have melted, and now he thought about it, he couldn't actually remember using the thing since he'd called the emergency services the night before.

'Looks like I'm due an upgrade, Bob. Just one more thing to add to the shopping list. Listen, do you know where Dagwood is right now?'

'Up in the main incident room, I think. He's got everyone working on tracking down the tenants, but they're having a hard enough time finding out who the landlord is.'

'So he's not on site. What about SOC? They been allowed in yet?'

'I'm not sure. We could always go and find out.'

'Just what I was thinking. Grab us a pool car. I'll meet you out front in ten minutes. Need a cup of tea first; my throat's killing me.'

'Ha! That's a tenner the lad owes me.' Grumpy Bob grinned as they both set off along the corridor. 'He didn't reckon you'd show up today at all.'

The canteen didn't serve the best tea in the world, but right then, McLean didn't much care. He just needed something to soothe the burning sensation in his throat. Perhaps he'd been wrong to ignore the doctor's pleading and sign himself out.

'There you are, McLean. Don't you ever answer your bloody phone?'

McLean swung around lazily in his seat, and didn't bother to stand. Duguid wasn't worth the effort on a good day, and this wasn't remotely that.

'I'm afraid my phone's buggered, sir. Something melted in last night's fire and I haven't had a chance to get a replacement yet.'

'Yes, well,' Duguid pulled out a chair and dropped himself into it. 'About that. It's a serious business, you know. There we are searching the whole of the city like we haven't got a clue, and all the time they're right on your bloody doorstep.'

'Thank you, sir, I'm fine. Apart from a bit of a sore throat and the fact that all my worldly goods and possessions have just gone up in smoke.'

Duguid looked momentarily embarrassed before his natural anger swelled to the fore, reddening the pale, freckled skin under his wiry hair.

'You're obviously fit to work, or you wouldn't be here. What I'd like to know is what you're doing sitting here drinking tea when Chief Superintendent McIntyre quite clearly told you I wanted to see you.'

'I'm sorry, sir. She didn't tell me it was urgent. She did tell me I should take some time off, but I thought I'd have a cup of tea and grab a few things before heading out.'

'You know what they're saying, McLean?' Duguid's anger was never a good thing to provoke, but right then McLean really didn't care.

'No, sir, please enlighten me.'

'They're saying you knew damn well what was going on next door. You were protecting them.'

McLean put down his mug, pushing it away from him and towards the DCI. He got up, scraping his chair legs on the floor as he placed it carefully back under the table. Duguid looked at him, as if expecting him to reply, so McLean leant down, settling his knuckles onto the Formica either side of the mug and bending close, whispering so that only Duguid could hear him.

'You really are an idiot, sir,' he said. Then walked away.

21

Grumpy Bob wasn't the only one in the pool car as McLean clambered into the passenger seat; DC MacBride was sitting behind the wheel and the old sergeant had taken up residence in the back.

'Nice suit, sir,' MacBride said as he piloted the car into the afternoon traffic flow.

'Don't you start, constable. It was my grandfather's. And very fashionable in its time.'

'And today, sir. Mate of mine's just had something similar made up. Cost him a fortune.'

'Well, if he can get into this one, he can have it as a spare. It's bloody uncomfortable.' McLean shifted in his seat, trying not to think about the seam that was wearing away at his privates. No wonder his grandad had only managed to father the one child.

It took a long time to reach the area where his flat had been, and as they approached it, McLean could see why. The whole street had been cordoned off, blocking a major route out of the city. Not far away, traffic was backed up by the one-way system still in place after the Woodbury building had burned down. One more fire and the whole south city would grind to a halt.

'They're going to have to get this sorted soon.' DC MacBride showed his warrant card to a uniform standing at the blue and white tape, then inched slowly forward into the street. Two fire engines were still in attendance, though their hoses were stored away. The fire investigation team's truck was there too, across the street where McLean had laid Mr Sheen down on the pavement the night before. A half a dozen cars sat more abandoned than parked. Closer in, the battered old white Transit van of the SOC team stood with its rear doors wide open. Beside it, a large flatbed truck was slowly being denuded of its load of scaffolding.

They parked as far away from the action as possible, and as McLean got out of the car, he looked up at what had, for the past fifteen years, been his home. The façade of the building was still intact, but none of the windows remained. Black streaks of soot ran from each opening like upside-down tears. From a distance, he could see that the roof had partly collapsed in, the stark shapes of the chimney stacks silhouetted against the darkening evening sky.

'Fuck me. I mean . . . Sorry, sir.' DC MacBride looked down at his shoes.

'No, I think you're right, Stuart. Fuck me just about sums it up.' McLean stared up at what had been his living-room window as an aeroplane flew over in the distance, sinking down on its way to Ingliston. For a surreal moment, he could see it through the window and the missing ceiling beyond. Then it passed out of view.

'What're we here for then, sir?' Grumpy Bob had come out without a coat, and paced around, rubbing his hands together and occasionally stamping his feet. Of the three of them, he hadn't looked up at the building, and seemed to be avoiding doing so.

'I'm not really sure, Bob,' McLean said. 'I just wanted to see what had survived. Looks like not much.'

He walked over to the SOC van, looking for a familiar face. It appeared in a rush of squealing that sounded almost like a pig being strangled. Before he could tell what was happening, he had been enveloped in a huge, crushing hug that made his lungs burn, his throat scream.

'Please, Emma. I can't breathe.' McLean extricated himself from the SOC officer's embrace and she stepped back, suddenly self-conscious.

'When I heard . . . the address . . . I thought . . .'

McLean took her hands in his. 'It's OK, Emma. I wasn't in there when it started.'

'But they said you were in the hospital.'

'I got a bit of smoke in my lungs trying to get someone out.' He coughed as if to emphasise the point. 'Look, don't worry about it. I'll be fine. Tell me what's going on. Have you found anything yet?'

'We can't get inside. They're still trying to stabilise the building.'

McLean walked past the SOC van and picked his way through the detritus lying about the street until he reached the pavement. A crew had begun assembling scaffolding up the entire front of the building, working with much greater delicacy than he had ever seen it done before. Looking up, it felt like the whole sandstone wall was swaying outwards, but it was just the clouds passing by high above. The front door was strangely still intact, propped open with a bit of broken pavement the way the previous students had always left it, and beyond, lit by powerful arc lights, all he could see was a narrow tunnel.

Something brushed past his legs. McLean almost jumped, then looked down to see a black cat nuzzling his trousers with the side of its soot-smeared face. He bent down and offered his hand, then scratched the animal behind its ears. Turning back to the tenement, he could see through the bay window at the front where old Mrs McCutcheon had used to sit of an evening, watching the world go by. Looking around for someone to ask, he spotted a fireman coming out of the front door tunnel.

'The old lady who lived downstairs,' he said, getting the fireman's attention. 'Did she get out all right?'

'Couldn't tell you, pal. Nobody in there now, mind. Have a word wi' Jim. He'll know.'

McLean thanked the man then headed off for the fire investigation truck, trailed by the cat. Jim Burrows looked up from his desk as he knocked on the door.

'Inspector. Good to see you up and about. You didn't look in such good shape last night.'

'A bit too much smoke. I don't know how you guys cope with it.'

'We wear breathing apparatus. And we don't generally go running into a burning building without working out a plan first. You know you're lucky to be alive.'

'I know.' McLean suppressed a shudder. 'And I should've known better. I've had basic training in fires.'

'What were you doing in there anyway? Just walking past and decided to play hero?'

'Nobody told you?' McLean was surprised. But then there was probably no reason why anybody would have done. 'I live there. Top flat on the end. Well, I used to live there, I suppose.'

Burrows looked at him with an unreadable expression. 'Ach, I'm sorry. So the old man—'

'Mr Sheen. He'd been there more than fifteen years. I never did know what his first name was.'

'We found other bodies. Four in the right-hand side, second floor. All badly burned. Two in each of the first-floor flats. And there was one in the main door. Small, that one was, buried under a lot of stuff, so probably the ground floor, maybe the first.'

'First-floor flats were both professional couples. Renting, I think. The small one . . .' McLean slumped down onto a nearby chair, drained of all energy. The cat which had followed him into the mobile office now leapt into his lap and pushed its head against his hand until he started stroking it.

'You know who it was.' Burrows' voice was soft, concerned.

'Mrs McCutcheon. Christ, she was old. Probably born in that flat. She was a nosey old bat, but she didn't deserve that. None of them did.'

They sat together in silence for a while. He was still stroking the cat when Grumpy Bob and DC MacBride found him.

'Wondered where you got to, sir.' Grumpy Bob climbed up into the tiny space, then noticed the cat. 'Who's your new friend? Oh.'

'Everyone who lived in that tenement died last night, Bob. Ten people dead. Except me.'

'No' everyone, sir. Yon cat's still got at least one of its lives left.'

McLean held the purring beast up, staring into its eyes

and wondering what he was going to do with it. He should probably call the SSPCA warden, have it taken away. But that seemed somehow disrespectful.

'What's the status of the building, Mr Burrows?' He asked, finally.

'We've got all the bodies out. Pretty sure of that. Scaffold work'll take a few hours yet, but they'll go through the night. We can't open the street until it's done and I've had traffic control screaming at me all afternoon to get it sorted.'

'What about the SOC team. When can they get in there?'

'For what? They'll no' find anything much.'

'They have to try.'

'Well it'll no' be til tomorrow, that's for sure.'

'OK.' McLean put the cat back down on the floor and stood up. It twined itself around his legs again, purring all the while. 'And thanks, for trying.'

'Don't mention it. It's my job.'

The air outside smelled of damp and charred wood. McLean hadn't noticed it before; he'd been too caught up in the strangeness of the whole scene. Now, as if he were slowly awakening from a dream, he started to see more of the details. The cars that had been parked in the street in front of the tenement were all being removed by a series of trucks. Shiny and clean down one side, their paint was blistered and cracked by the heat of the fire on the other. One had caught fire itself, its tyres melted like chocolate left on a sunny windowsill. They'd be taken back to the SOC lab for tests before being released to their owners.

With luck, one or more of them might have belonged to the drug dealers; it might even be that elusive clue that opened up the whole case.

But it wasn't his case. It was Duguid's. He'd already pissed off the DCI once today, best not to make it a brace.

'MacBride, I'm afraid you've drawn the short straw here, since you've only just joined the hallowed ranks of CID.' McLean told the detective constable all that he had learned from Burrows, then suggested he might like to find a subtle way of passing the information on. 'Just don't tell him I was here. You know what he's like. Oh, and you'll have to walk back to the station.' He held his hand out for the pool-car keys.

MacBride looked like he was going to complain, but stopped himself. No doubt reasoning that in the time it took to get there, Duguid might well have gone home. Or even decided to visit the scene himself.

'What're you going to do, sir?' He handed over the keys and McLean passed them on to Grumpy Bob.

'Me? I'm meant to be on compassionate leave today, and for the rest of the week at least. So Bob here's going to take me home. Then he's going to start reviewing all of the cases I'm currently working on. Come on, Bob.'

He started walking back to the car, not surprised to find that the cat had decided to follow him. Grumpy Bob took a bit longer to catch up.

'What do you mean, review the cases?'

'What I said, Bob. I'm on leave. And then Professional Standards are going to give me a grilling. Someone's got to pick up the work. The chief superintendent said you were man enough to step into my shoes.'

They reached the car and McLean climbed into the front passenger seat. Before he could close the door, the cat had leapt up onto his lap. It turned around once, then curled up into a black, furry ball as Grumpy Bob opened his door and got in.

'You know anything about cats, Bob?' McLean asked.

'Don't even ask, sir.'

'Then it looks like this one's coming home with me.'

Just then McLean heard the patter of running feet. Before he could turn to look, the rear door had been wrenched open and someone jumped in.

'Hope you don't mind.' Emma was a little breathless, but no longer wore her SOC overalls.

'Um, what are you doing, Emma?' McLean asked.

'What are you doing?'

'I'm going home. Well, to my gran's place, but I guess it's home now. Then I'm going to head into town and buy myself some fresh clothes.'

'Exactly.' Emma grinned. 'And if that suit's anything to go by, you're going to need all the help you can get.'

22

'Just wait outside the office, Tony. This shouldn't take long.'

The words rang in McLean's ears as he sat in his moulded plastic chair. He felt like a naughty schoolboy sent to see the headmistress, but if that was the case, he didn't know what Sergeant Dunstone beside him had done. The union rep couldn't stop fidgeting, constantly playing with his hands, looking up at the clock, opening his mouth as if to say something, then closing it again with a loud pop. Behind Superintendent McIntyre's door, closed for once, the unmistakable sounds of argument could be heard, voices rising and falling like waves. The words were unintelligible; the emotions behind them all too clear.

Sergeant Dunstone snapped to his feet so suddenly it took McLean a moment to realise that the office door had opened. Before he could even begin to stand up, Chief Inspector Callard marched out of the room and was gone. By the thunderous look on his face, things hadn't gone entirely his way.

'It's all right, John.' McIntyre addressed Sergeant Dunstone before he could ask. 'There's not going to be any disciplinary procedure.'

McLean watched the relief spread across the sergeant's face. No disciplinary procedure meant no tiresome paperwork. No shuffling the work rotas. No breaking in a brand-new, wet-behind-the-ears detective inspector. For himself he was surprised to find a level of disappointment mixed in with his relief, but it was short-lived. Perhaps he could get back to work now. Perhaps he could get back to finding who had killed Audrey Carpenter.

'I need a quick word.' McIntyre gestured towards her now-open office door and retreated inside. He looked at Dunstone, giving him a nod of thanks and saying, 'I'll see you in the canteen', then followed the superintendent into her den.

'It'd be a good idea if you didn't do anything to piss off Professional Standards in the next, I don't know, lifetime?' McIntyre sat herself at her desk, not motioning for McLean to take the other seat. He stood instead, hoping this meant whatever she had to say would be short.

'I don't know how you talked them around, ma'am, but—'

'I went out on a limb for you, Tony. That's how. Chief Inspector Callard wanted you demoted back to sergeant and taken out of CID. Quite frankly I'm short enough staffed as it is, without losing a seasoned detective to traffic.'

McLean fought back the urge to say anything about Callard's rather extreme sanction, but something of what he felt must have shown on his face.

'Rab Callard's been a friend of Charles Duguid since they were both at Tulliallan, Tony. That would probably explain some of the more daft allegations he made against you.'

'You can't believe I actually knew about the drugs operation. I—'

'Of course not. But you did call Duguid an idiot to his face. And you all-but accused a very powerful Glasgow gangster of murdering his own daughter.' McIntyre smiled a weary smile. 'Callard has the ear of important people, including the Deputy Chief Constable. Best you keep under his radar as much as possible. OK?'

'I understand, ma'am.' McLean started to leave.

'There's one more thing, Tony.'

He stopped, turned back again. It was never going to be that easy. 'Yes?'

'I had to give them something, you know that. Otherwise Callard would have insisted on a full enquiry. You'd have been on gardening leave at least until Charles's investigation was over, and we both know how long that's likely to be. You're going to have to take another week off. Technically you're on suspension pending internal enquiries, but we're calling it medical leave just to keep the media at bay.'

It could have been worse. Grumpy Bob had already been making regular visits to the house to keep him up to speed on the investigations. No reason why that shouldn't continue.

'And I had to agree to you undergoing psychiatric counselling.'

'You what?' McLean rocked on the balls of his feet as if he'd been punched. 'Why?'

'Stress, Tony. Why else?'

'But I'm—'

'This is always a hard time of year for you. Doubly so with Anderson's death in the news. Don't think I haven't noticed your work patterns. Add to that the loss of your home and everything that means to you, it's hardly surprising if you start making small mistakes.'

'But I—'

McIntyre held up her hand. 'I know, I know. But like I said, I had to throw PS a bone. There's no harm in going to a few counselling sessions. Might even do you some good.'

Mrs McCutcheon's cat sat on the counter beside the old Aga, licking at its paws and occasionally treating him to an imperious stare. McLean slouched in a wooden chair in front of the vast kitchen table, a mug of tea in one hand and a thick report in the other, staring off into the distance as he tried to take in the details of his late grandmother's estate. Police work was one thing; he relished ferreting out the tiniest details, piecing the puzzle together, forcing the chaos of everyday life into some kind of order. But this was a different beast altogether. Even months after her death it showed no sign of coming together. Accounts, share certificates, IHT and trust funds. Somewhere in among all the dancing figures there was a bottom line, he was sure. He just needed to summon up the energy to find it.

The doorbell was a welcome distraction. No doubt Grumpy Bob dropping round to bring him up to speed on everything. He drained the last of the tea, almost choking on the sludgy mess of biscuit at the bottom, then padded out across the hallway in his socks to the front door.

A six-foot-four mass of muscle and tattoo blocked the light. Not Grumpy Bob.

'Mr MacDougal wants to speak to you.'

McLean went to shut the door in the man's face. 'I'm on leave. He'll have to talk to DCI Duguid.'

The door slammed open again and the big man stepped inside. 'Mr MacDougal wants to speak to you. Now.'

McLean looked up into the over-large face. Eyes set just too far apart to convey any sign of intelligence.

'I'll get my coat.'

'No need.' The big man pushed the door even further open, then stood to one side. Razors MacDougal stood on the gravel driveway, looking up at the house. He treated McLean to an evil grin.

'I guess there's no' much point trying to bribe youse, then.'

'Well, this is all very grand now, isn't it. I like what you've done with the decorations, too.'

MacDougal turned on the spot, looking around the large drawing room at the front of the house where McLean had directed him and his gargantuan minder. All the furniture was hiding under dustsheets and the shutters had been closed for longer than he could remember in an attempt to stop the hideous flock wallpaper fading. It was about as inviting as a disused crypt, which suited him just fine.

'What do you want, Mr MacDougal?' McLean whipped a sheet off an ancient, squashy sofa and indicated for his uninvited guest to sit.

'Ah, that famous Edinburgh hospitality.' MacDougal settled himself down gently. 'As it happens, I have had my tea.'

'The point?'

'You asked me when last I saw my daughter, inspector. You and I both know what that was all about. But you've got me wrong. I loved Violet.'

McLean suppressed the urge to mutter, aye, that's what I heard too. Instead he leant back against the mantelpiece and crossed his arms.

'I've been doing a bit of digging, you know,' the gangster continued, 'since your visit. Seems you've lost someone close to you, too. Turned up much the same as my wee girl, I heard. Was that why they put you on this case? Figured you'd have a special insight?'

McLean gritted his teeth, pushing down the anger that flushed hot in his cheeks. He looked up at the minder with his piggy little eyes and tree-trunk biceps. No point even thinking about getting physical.

'You should know that I can't discuss an ongoing investigation, even with a relative of the victim.'

'Oh come on, inspector. Get real. I can find out anything I want to about your investigation wi' a single phone call. But that's my wee girl lying there in the mortuary. Some bastard locked her away and raped her, then cut her throat and tossed her in a burn. You'll ken I'm no' happy about that.'

So that was why he was here; a none too subtle way of letting McLean know just how well-connected he was.

'What do you want from me, Mr MacDougal? Or are you just here to finish the interview I started a week ago. Because if that's the case you'll need to speak to Detective Sergeant Laird down at the station. I can give him a call if you want.' McLean pulled his mobile phone out of his pocket, but before he could do anything, MacDougal was on his feet, reaching out a hand to stop him, grasping his arm with a grip that was more desperate than violent.

'I want you to catch him, inspector. I want you to find him and put him away.' MacDougal's voice was quiet, but edged with steel. 'I'll take care of it after that.'

23

Two weeks on from the fire, and Sunday afternoon should have been peaceful before plunging back in to the maelstrom that was work. He'd found some coal down in the basement, and after a couple of false starts had managed to conjure up a fire in the library. Now it was just him, a book and Mrs McCutcheon's cat, which seemed to have taken a liking to its new home. What had become of the other half dozen or more the old lady had kept, he had no idea. It was enough to be looking after this one.

There were still moments when McLean felt the world spinning out of control beneath him. The house was too big, for one thing, and every corner held memories of his grandmother. Going through the empty rooms was a reminder of all that had passed, all the people who had left him. All the people he'd failed. That was why he'd been avoiding the place all those months since she'd died, why he'd ignored it for the eighteen months she'd been in a coma. Always putting off doing anything about it. And now his hand was forced.

The phone ringing brought McLean back out of his self-indulgent musing. He put the book down, stepped around the cat and managed to reach the elegant writing desk before the answering machine switched on.

'McLean,' he said to the silence on the other end.

'Ah, sir. I was hoping you'd be in.' Grumpy Bob sounded like he meant the exact opposite.

'I am supposed to be on leave, Bob. What's up?'

'I think we've got another one.'

'Another what?'

'Another Christmas Killer victim. They've found a body out in the Pentlands. Near the Flotterstone.'

'It can't be the Christmas Killer, Bob. He only kills once a year. And anyway, he's dead.' McLean stuck the heel of his hand into his eye socket and rubbed hard. This wasn't what he wanted to deal with on his first day back at the office. And that wasn't supposed to be for another sixteen hours. He looked out the window. Dusk would be falling soon, and fast this close to Christmas. Someone wasn't going to have much of a festive time of it.

'Who's out there now?'

'The lad's on site, liaising with Penicuik.'

'No one more senior?'

'Dagwood's away at some conference, DI Randall's got the flu again. Everyone else is suddenly busy. I was at home, but when I heard the details I thought I'd better let you know. I'm just about to head out myself.'

'OK, Bob. I'll see you there.' McLean scribbled down where he was supposed to be going and hung up. The hall was cold after the warmth of the library fire, but something else entirely made him shiver as he pulled on his coat and checked the pocket for his notebook and keys. Only then did he realise that he couldn't exactly nip down to the station and grab a car. And a taxi would take for ever to arrive this late on a Sunday afternoon. There was only one thing for it; he'd have to take his grandmother's car.

*

In the summer, the Flotterstone Inn was busy with tourists, some of whom had even intended visiting it, rather than just ending up there after getting lost in the maze of tiny B-roads that criss-crossed the high Midlothian plain and washed up on the flanks of the Pentland Hills. A hundred yards further up the glen, on the single-track road leading to the Glencorse Reservoir and some serious mountain biking, a second, larger car park catered for the day trippers and casual hikers from the city. This close to Christmas, and with snow sticking to the upper faces of Scald Law, it was pretty much deserted. Unless you counted the three squad cars, SOC van and ambulance huddled together at the far end for warmth. A young uniformed constable marched up as McLean pulled into the car park, a local he assumed, since he didn't recognise him.

'I'm afraid you can't park here, sir,' the PC said as McLean opened the door and started to get out. 'Police business.'

McLean fished out his warrant card and held it up. 'It's OK, constable. I'm supposed to be here.'

'Sorry, sir.' The constable looked from the warrant card to McLean's face and then to the bright red sports car. 'I didn't think . . .'

'Fair enough, it's not your average detective inspector's car.'

'Erm, what is it?' the constable asked, then added: 'Sir?'

'This is a 1969 Alfa Romeo GTV, and it really doesn't like salted roads.' But needs must, even if he could hear his gran tutting her disapproval from her grave.

'She's a beauty, sir. Had her long?'

'She?' McLean raised an eyebrow. He'd not really

thought of the car in such terms, but it seemed oddly appropriate. 'My father bought it in sixty-nine, so you could say it's been in the family a while. Now I believe there was something about a body?'

The constable's face darkened. 'Yes, of course, sir. Up the burn a ways.'

McLean followed him across the car park then along a short path that ran parallel to the road. He could hear the water babbling over rocks some way below the path, and up ahead, through a gap in the spindly winter trees, narrow concrete and steel bridged the water. Just before it, someone had broken a rough path through the undergrowth and marked it off with blue and white police tape.

'Down there, sir. I'll stay up here.'

'That bad is it?'

'It's . . . well . . . there's not a lot of room.'

McLean nodded his understanding. The young constable couldn't have been long out of training college, so there was every chance that this was his first body. Based in a quiet station like Penicuik, it was unlikely he'd ever encounter many. Lucky sod.

The path was slick with recent rain. McLean had to hold onto branches overhead to stop himself tumbling down and into the cold brown water. His new shoes might have been comfortable, but they had no grip on their soles to speak of. Through the scrub, he saw a small group of people and recognised Detective Constable MacBride amongst them. And there, at their feet, the victim.

She lay on her back, face staring sightless at the darkening sky, hair waving like seaweed in the flow, arms outstretched in parody of crucifixion. His eyes transfixed by the familiar, horrifying sight, it was a while before McLean noticed the neat slash across her throat that had almost certainly been the cause of her death.

'Not the most pleasant way to spend the afternoon, Tony.' Angus Cadwallader shifted around slightly, affording him a better view. 'But that's the price we pay for our professions.'

'Who found her?' McLean asked.

'A fisherman, headed up for the loch,' MacBride said.

'What? On a Sunday?'

'Aye, well. They've got him up at the car park if you want a word.'

'You've interviewed him?'

MacBride nodded.

'Then you can let him go. Just make sure we can get back in touch. And ask him to come into the station tomorrow to give us a full statement.'

The detective constable hurried away with obvious relief, and McLean stepped carefully into the position on the bank he had been occupying. Cadwallader sported a pair of fishing waders, Tracy thigh-length galoshes that were just about adequate for standing in the flow. They both looked chilled to the bone, but nothing like as bad as the dead woman.

'How long have you been here?' McLean asked.

'About half an hour. I don't think the call's long in.' Cadwallader bent down, the better to examine his subject, then stood up again. 'Where're those bloody lights. I can hardly see a thing here.'

As if in reply, twin arc lamps banged into life directly overhead and a voice called down: 'That better, doc?'

McLean didn't hear what Cadwallader muttered in reply; his attention was on the young woman. Like long-gone fireworks overhead, the details came to him in flashes. Plastic cable ties fixed her wrists to two rusty metal poles bashed into the riverbed. A third, at her feet, wobbled dangerously in the flow. Water bubbled up between her white legs and that neatly trimmed dark triangle. Washed over her flat stomach and barely noticeable breasts. Gurgled around the raw gaping wound that was her throat. Billowed her hair out around her head like an auburn halo.

'I can't tell you anything here, Tony.' Cadwallader levered himself out of the water and helped his assistant join him on the bank. 'She's been in the water too long to give you an accurate time of death, but it's at least twelve hours ago.'

24

He sits towards the front of the courtroom; media attention has waned and the public have lost their appetite for the spectacle. No doubt they'll be back for the verdict and sentence, but for now this farcical drama is played out to judge, jury and few else. Donald Anderson sits in the dock, his face impassive. Two burly constables stand behind him, but it's inconceivable that this slight, mild-mannered man would do anything untoward. Would never abduct women, one a year for ten years, rape and torture them in the basement underneath his respectable antiquarian bookshop, then murder them when he had grown tired of them. Never wash down their battered bodies and stake them out in fast-flowing water, under a bridge where they would be easily found.

'The psychosis is not that unusual, though of course not often seen in such an extreme example.'

He focuses on the man in the witness box. Professor Matthew Hilton. A psychiatrist occasionally used by the police to create profiles of murderers. If memory serves, Hilton originally suggested that the Christmas Killer would be in his mid-forties, a frustrated underachiever with below-average intelligence either living with an elderly, domineering parent or abused by one who had subsequently died. Somehow that doesn't quite tally with the sixty-plus, wealthy bookshop owner standing in the dock.

'The trigger for the behaviour is often obscure, hidden deep in the subconscious. Perhaps a traumatic event in childhood, long suppressed, is brought out by a chance occurrence in later life. The violence is compartmentalised along with that suppressed memory, and so the patient genuinely feels that those acts are perpetrated by another person.'

The patient. Hah. Murdering rapist bastard, more like. Or is it all part of Hilton's act? Label the accused as a loony and you're halfway towards persuading the jury that's what he is.

'Faced with the realisation of what he has done, the true horror of his crimes, he constructs a false reality around him, based on his life and work. Thus we have a fixation with an ancient book, somehow possessing the soul of any man who reads it and forcing them to do unspeakable things. It's quite a wonder how inventive the human mind can be.'

He slumps back in his hard plastic chair, looking from the smug face of Hilton, to Anderson, to the judge and then the jury. Are they buying into this bullshit? Will they acquit on grounds of diminished responsibility?

'So in your opinion, Professor Hilton, Donald Anderson cannot be held responsible for his actions. He is, in short, insane.' This from the counsel for the defence. Sneaky little shit of an advocate. How can he sleep at night, knowing he's defending a monster?

'He's psychotic and delusional. I'd say classic schizophrenic.' Hilton turns to face the jury, letting a smile play across his features. 'I don't like the word, but it is one which most lay-people understand, so yes, I'd say Donald Anderson is insane.'

25

'You seem very tense, inspector. Could it be that my profession puts you on your guard?'

McLean sat in Chief Superintendent McIntyre's office, on one of the comfy-looking but surprisingly hard armchairs in the informal side of the room. The chief superintendent herself had gone to a meeting at Force HQ, and her door, normally open to all, was firmly closed. In the other chair, smiling with his mouth but not his eyes, Professor Matt Hilton tapped an idle pencil against his hand.

'I don't know if you're aware,' McLean said. 'But we found a body out in the Pentland Hills last night. Young woman, throat cut, staked out in a running burn, under a bridge.'

'Yes, I had heard. And you found another one a fortnight ago.' Hilton had chubbed-up a bit since last they had met. His hair was unfashionably long, tied in a greying ponytail that snaked down his back and seemed to be sucking everything from the front, as if it had been pulled too often by the school bullies.

'And yet you wonder why I seem a little tense?'

'Ah. You see the actions of a copycat, aping Donald Anderson. I can imagine that brings back all sorts of unhappy memories. How does that make you feel, inspector? Or may I call you Tony?'

'No, inspector works fine for me.' McLean forced himself to relax, though every instinct in his body screamed for him to get up and leave the room.

'So it makes you feel isolated. Persecuted.'

'I think the word you're looking for is frustrated, Hilton. I'm supposed to be investigating a double murder. I don't even know the identity of the second victim yet, and I'm stuck in here with you because my superiors think I might be under intolerable stress. I've been on enforced leave for two weeks. That's two weeks during which time I might have been able to catch this sick bastard. Then it would have just been the one set of distraught parents I needed to explain myself to. That's your stress right there. Not being able to do my job.'

'And you don't think Sergeant . . .' Hilton shuffled through his notes for a moment '. . . Sergeant Laird is up to the job? I understand you've worked well with him in the past.'

'Bob's a good detective, but I like to think two pairs of hands are better than one. Besides, he didn't work on the Anderson case. I did.'

'Neither did he lose his fiancée to the Christmas Killer. But you did.' Hilton's pencil stopped its tapping. 'And now, just a few days after Anderson dies, someone starts killing using his methods. I ask you again, Tony. How does that make you feel?'

'It makes me bloody angry that people can publish books telling the world in great detail what those methods are. How do you think this new killer knew how Anderson killed and disposed of the bodies? How do you think he knew what Anderson did to his victims before he killed them? That bloody book which you and Jo bloody Dalgliesh cobbled together.'

'Anger. Good.' Hilton hitched his smile up a little higher, but it still couldn't reach his eyes. 'And then the day after the first victim is found, you start seeing Anderson in crowds. This despite knowing that he's dead. You went to his funeral, I understand.'

'His burial. There's a difference.'

'Indeed. Tell me, why did you go to Anderson's . . . ah, burial?'

'Maybe I just wanted to make sure the bastard was dead. I think you psychobabblers call it looking for closure.'

'Hm. And did you find closure? I'd suggest not, given your rather irrational behaviour in a department store the other night.'

McLean suppressed the urge to scream. Tried to remind himself that these sessions were meant to help. And that if he didn't play along, they'd continue for a very long time.

'What do you think you'd do?' he asked. 'You've just found out that someone's been murdered using exactly the same MO as a notorious serial killer who's recently died. Then you see someone in the street who looks exactly like that serial killer. Wouldn't you give chase?'

'In the street? Give chase?' Hilton flipped through his papers again. 'I thought you said you saw him in John Lewis. In the Christmas decorations department. Seems very apt, really.'

McLean ground his teeth to stop himself from saying any more. He'd completely forgotten that he'd not mentioned the first Anderson sighting to anyone.

'Anyway,' Hilton added, 'on top of all this, your tenement then burns down. I'm told the fire started in a neighbouring apartment that was being used as a cannabis farm. That must be a bit embarrassing, mustn't it.'

'Very.'

'There's no suggestion that you knew about the operation, of course. In some ways it might have been better if you had.'

'Is this relevant?' McLean choked back the rest of what he wanted to say.

'I don't know. Is it? I'm trying to assess your state of mind here, Tony. Are you fit for work?'

'Well I'm at work. Or at least I would be if I wasn't in here with you.'

'So about the fire. You lost everything. That must have been very traumatic. Like losing a loved one.'

'It was a place to sleep, eat and shower. I spend more of my time here, or out in the city catching criminals than I ever did there.'

'And yet it was full of memories. I'm told you've lived there since you were a student. That's a long time to be in one place. And of course that's where you and Kirsty made your home together.'

A light tap at the door was the only thing that saved Hilton's life. Or at least his nose. The professor scowled slightly, glancing at his watch before saying: 'Goodness, we've been here over an hour already.' It gave McLean time to compose himself, count to ten, and stand up. Jayne McIntyre poked her head around the door.

'I'm so sorry, Matt,' she said, 'but you said an hour, and we've got a briefing scheduled for fifteen minutes' time.'

'Of course, Jayne,' Hilton said, not looking at McLean

as he added: 'I think we're making very good progress, too. But there's a way to go. Might need to make these sessions bi-weekly.'

'And you'll pass Tony fit to work?'

'For now, yes.' Hilton said, and McLean felt very much like a child being talked about by two adults who really don't care that he can hear them. 'I'll be able to keep an eye on him anyway. Since I'm going to be working with the team on profiling your serial killer.'

'The careful attention to detail suggests a ritualistic approach to death. Our killer is most likely reliving some facet of his early life that both traumatised him and brought him comfort.'

McLean sat in the corner of the CID room, letting the meaningless words wash over him as he watched the performance. Matt Hilton looked like he was in his element, standing in front of the wall-sized whiteboard as if he was delivering a lecture to first-year psychology undergrads. The word cocksure sprang to mind, along with another beginning with cock. Just cock would do, actually.

'Our killer works alone, probably in a job that minimises social contact. I'm thinking night watchman, security guard, that sort of thing.'

He'd not slept well. Hardly at all, to be honest. And what sleep he had managed had been filled with dreams of Kirsty, her long black hair billowing out in the stream. That and the early morning psychoanalysis had left him drained. McLean made no effort to stifle the yawn that shuddered through his whole body as the professor droned on. He'd heard that there were profilers out there who could pinpoint their subjects down to their choice of clothes, favourite foods and the kind of pets they kept, but Hilton wasn't one of them. Much of what he had said already was so hedged with qualifications as to be meaningless.

'Well, I think I've talked quite enough.' Hilton began to wind up. 'Of course it's early days yet, and I'll be working on refining the profile as more information comes in. In the meantime I'll hand you back to the chief superintendent.'

McIntyre stood to take his place, and Hilton looked momentarily confused, as if he had been expecting applause and couldn't quite understand why his audience didn't appreciate his genius. Looking around the team they had managed to cobble together, it wasn't hard to see why. A dozen uniform constables who made McLean feel like he must surely be due to retire soon; a couple of civilian support officers who would probably be able to make a cup of tea if they really had to; DC MacBride looking pink and freshly scrubbed; Grumpy Bob looking anything but; and sitting nervously in the chair next to the one just vacated by the chief superintendent, newly arrived from Aberdeen, Detective Sergeant Ritchie. Of DCI Duguid, nominally in charge of the whole operation, there was no sign. McLean couldn't help thinking this was a good thing.

'Thank you, Matt,' McIntyre said without a trace of irony. 'I'm sure that's helped to sharpen the picture. Now I know this is a small team for a double murder enquiry, but rest assured you'll be getting more help as soon as I can lay my hands on it. So, any questions?'

'We're definitely treating the deaths as linked, then?' DC MacBride asked. McIntyre nodded to McLean, who reluctantly levered himself out of his chair and went to the front.

'For now, yes. The MOs are too similar not to. And the victims are both female, early twenties. Similar size, build, hair colour.'

'What about the similarities to the Christmas Killer?' one of the infant constables asked.

'We're going to look into that, of course,' McLean said. 'Our killer is certainly copying Anderson's methods quite closely. It doesn't help that there's a bestselling book about him out there. Pretty much any Tom, Dick or Harry knows what Anderson did and how.'

'I think we can rule out most of Jo's readership, inspector.' Hilton gave a little simpering smile that reminded McLean just who had co-written Anderson's hagiography. 'Stick to the profile I've drawn up, we'll narrow it down pretty damn quickly. And the more information comes in, the better the profile.'

'Thank you, professor, but I'd rather not wait for another dead body to turn up before you can tell us what kind of toothpaste the killer prefers.'

26

Heavy rain battered against the window, making his office feel even colder than it actually was. McLean felt a moment's guilt that Grumpy Bob was out in it, organising the search of the area around the Flotterstone car park. Then he realised who he was thinking about. Grumpy Bob would be tucked up warm inside the van, directing things from behind a mug of hot tea. It was the poor bastard uniforms who deserved his sympathy.

Sitting in the middle of his desk, a large cardboard file box awaited his attention. The old case files from the Anderson investigation. They called to him with a siren song. And like a siren, he knew that what lay inside was heartache and sorrow, photographs he really didn't need to see ever again. It was a part of his life he would dearly like to leave behind, and yet every time he thought it was past, it reared up its ugly, spiteful head. Sank ice-cold talons into his heart.

He took a deep breath, started to open the box. Only then did he notice the Post-it, perched precariously on top of another pile of papers awaiting his immediate attention. Scooping it up, he tried to read the oddly neat but spidery scrawl, not recognising the handwriting: '*Mort cld PM @ 2 PM. GN 4 Cof – KR*'.

It took him a while, but eventually McLean worked it out. First morning of her first day in the new job, and already DS Ritchie was taking his calls. He picked up the styrofoam cup on his desk, peeled off the lid and peered at the scummy muck within. It was cold and uninviting, as was the congealed, half-eaten bacon buttie that had come with it. Dropping the buttie in the bin, he went off with the cup in search of a refill.

Grumpy Bob's expletive-laden entrance interrupted McLean as he was heading back to his office, cradling a cup of something that approximated coffee. Water dripped from his police-issue macintosh as, head down, the old sergeant crossed towards the locker room, oblivious to anyone else in the building.

'Bastard, bastard rain. I swear the countryside hates me.'

'Afternoon, Bob. Aren't you supposed to be somewhere else?'

Grumpy Bob looked around, startled. 'Oh, sir. I didn't see you there.'

'That much is obvious. What's the situation up at Flotterstone?'

'Bloody miserable is what.' Bob dragged off his coat and shook it out on the grey-blue carpet tiles. 'It's been lashing it down since about five this morning, and now there's a mist so thick you could use it to smother an old-age pensioner. Did I mention that it was bloody freezing, too? Brass monkeys. Jesus.'

'And the search?'

'Not a bloody thing. I've had twenty constables moaning away at me all bloody morning, and all for what? There was never going to be anything. There never was before.'

'We still had to look, Bob. And we didn't know. This

isn't Anderson doing this. He's dead. Has been for over a month.'

'Well, whatever. There's nothing suspicious within a couple of hundred metres of where we found the body. The usual garbage has been bagged and given to the SOC labs to play with. It's just fag packets and shite like that. No' even a used bloody condom.'

'You finished then?'

'Too bloody right. No way we're going to find anything else in this weather. And even if we did it'd be useless. You know it, too, sir. Waste of manpower keeping those constables out there any longer. And bloody cruel, too.'

'You're right, Bob. Still, thanks for doing it. I know you hate the countryside, but MacBride's not senior enough to run a search and I don't trust Penicuik to find their way about a crime scene.'

'What about the new lass?'

'Should be down in the CID room right now, putting some flesh on the bones of MacBride's report. Where is he, by the way?'

'Last I heard he was wringing out his heid.' Grumpy Bob ran a hand through his sparse, greying hair, coming up with a good spray of water. 'I'm no' kidding, sir. It's pishing it doon out there.'

McLean went to the back door, peering through the misted-up glass at the crowded car park beyond. Sure enough the rain was coming down in stair rods. And over on the other side, his bright red Alfa was scarcely visible in the haze of rebounding water. Ah well. At least it should keep it clean. And wash away all the salt on the roads.

'OK, Bob. You go get yourself a cuppa. DS Ritchie and I'll be going to the PM in . . .' He looked at his watch. 'About an hour. Meantime, get on to Mis-Per and see if they've got anyone matching our description.'

'We going to set up an incident room now, sir?'

'You know if anywhere's free? Last I heard Dagwood'd taken all the big rooms.'

'Shite, I don't want tae be stuck down in that damp wee cupboard by the bogs.'

'Well, keep using the CID room for now,' McLean said, clutching at straws. 'We've that few detectives it's not like we'll be getting in anyone's way.'

The rain had eased off considerably an hour later, but it was still persistent. Consequently when McLean and a strangely silent DS Ritchie tried to find a pool car to take down to the mortuary, they had all been signed out.

'You got a car?' He asked Ritchie. She shook her head.

'Sorry, sir. I walked this morning. It's not far and I didn't expect this rain.'

Faced with the options of walking and getting wet, or taking his own car and having to explain to Traffic why he'd parked it on a yellow line, McLean opted for the latter. Traffic owed him a favour anyway.

'Come on then.' He pushed open the back door and held it for Ritchie. 'Far side. Red thing.'

By the time he'd reached the car, unlocked both doors and opened the driver's side, she was standing in the middle of the car park, stock still and staring. The rain spattered off her hair onto the shoulders of her long black coat, but she didn't seem to notice.

'Hurry up. I don't want to get the seats wet.'

McLean got in and started up the engine, setting the heater to full demist and the fan on high. A few moments later, DS Ritchie delicately opened the passenger door, climbed in and closed it again with barely a clunk.

'Is this . . . ? I never thought . . .' She looked at him with utter bewilderment.

'That manky thing I brought up to Aberdeen was a hire car.'

'But this?' Ritchie was obviously searching for words. 'It's like Inspector Morse. Don't you get the piss taken out of you? Sir?' she added as an afterthought.

'Actually this is the first time I've brought it in.' McLean peered through the slowly clearing windscreen, flicked on the wipers and decided it was clear enough to proceed. 'I've never had to drive to work before. I kind of inherited it about a year ago and it's the only car I own.'

'It's beautiful. Alfa Romeo, GT Veloce, 105 series. This would be the 1750?'

'You know your cars, Detective Sergeant Ritchie.' McLean inched carefully out of the car park and into the street beyond.

'Aye, well. It was either that or football if I wanted to be taken seriously in the job. Never really saw the point of football.' Ritchie leaned back into her seat, ran a finger lightly over the dashboard. 'And it's Kirsty, by the way.'

McLean jabbed the brakes rather harder than he'd intended, juddering the car to a halt and throwing them both forward, eliciting an angry beep of the horn from a following car.

'Sorry. What?'

'Kirsty. My name. Or you can call me Ritchie. I don't mind. "Detective Sergeant" just seems so formal, don't you think?'

McLean didn't respond. It was only a name, after all. Shouldn't be a problem. Just why did she have to pronounce it that way?

27

Angus Cadwallader was already prepped and eager to start when McLean showed DS Ritchie into the autopsy theatre. They were both drenched from the short walk from the car to the mortuary, the cold December rain soaking through the thin fabric of McLean's new coat. His old one would have been a bit more robust, of course. But his old one was just ashes now.

'You're late, Tony,' the pathologist said. 'That's getting to be a bit of a habit.'

'We had to find somewhere to park.' McLean wiped at his face with a handkerchief.

'Raining again, is it?' Cadwallader ran his eyes over the two of them, lingering perhaps a little longer than was polite over DS Ritchie before breaking into a broad, welcoming smile and adding, 'Since the rude detective inspector isn't going to introduce us, please allow me. Angus Cadwallader, city pathologist.'

'Um, Detective Sergeant Ritchie,' she said, slightly uncertainly.

'Detective Sergeant?' Cadwallader looked at McLean. 'Have you been keeping secrets from me, Tony?'

'That depends, Angus. DS Ritchie only started work here this morning. Before that she was up in Aberdeen.'

'Aberdeen,' Cadwallader echoed. 'Well, I'm afraid my humble mortuary isn't a patch on your facilities up there, but I'll try to live up to your high standards. Shall we begin?'

The dead woman's body lay on the cold stainless-steel examination table like some narcissistic sunbather, basking under the harsh rays of the overhead lamp. Dried and cleaned after her time in the river, she looked younger than McLean had first assumed, and tragically pretty. Her body was well-toned, despite its death pallor and yellowing-grey bruises. In life she would have been both fit and attractive.

'I'd estimate age at very early twenties.' Cadwallader began his detailed exploration of the victim's body. McLean had watched his friend work far more times than he would care to admit. Mostly he'd been alone, left to the gruesome task by a superior officer. Occasionally he'd been accompanied by Grumpy Bob or another colleague. But now, with DS Ritchie standing beside him, he felt oddly self-conscious. Perhaps it was because the dead woman was young, naked, and, well, a woman, but this time the post-mortem examination felt like more of a violation than normal.

He glanced across at Ritchie, who was studying the procedure with an intense glare. Apart from that obvious concentration, her expression was impossible to read. Rocking back onto his heels, McLean folded his arms over his chest and settled down for an uncomfortable show.

Too long later and Tracy was busy sewing their Jane Doe back together. McLean and Ritchie followed Cadwallader as he walked towards the little office off the main examination theatre, peeling off his scrubs and dumping them into a laundry bin on the way.

'Cause of death is definitely the wound to the throat,' he said. 'Happened somewhere between twenty-four hours and two days before we found her. I'd estimate she'd been in the water not more than six hours and she was washed with some kind of soap before that. She's got bruising around her ankles and wrists consistent with being tied up for at least a few days. And she's had sexual intercourse. Unwillingly, judging by the bruising and tearing. About a day before she died. Her stomach's empty, too, so she hadn't eaten anything in at least two days before her death. Possibly more.'

'What about toxicology? Anything useful there?'

'We're still waiting on results of the last body. I'm guessing we're not going to have much more luck with this one. She's been starved, and then bled almost dry. We've got very little to work with.'

'No chance it's not the same person who killed Audrey Carpenter?' McLean knew the answer, but he still asked anyway.

Cadwallader shook his head. 'There's always a chance, Tony. But it's vanishingly small.'

By the time they reached the station, McLean had almost convinced himself.

'It can't be Anderson,' he said. 'Anderson's dead.'

'What about Dalgliesh?'

McLean stopped walking so abruptly that DS Ritchie kept on for a couple of paces before she noticed.

'You think it could be her? But why?'

'No, I didn't mean her murdering the girl. What I meant was, what about her book? Does that give out as much detail as our killer seems to know about? If not, then we've got an angle to work on.'

'I don't know,' McLean said. 'I've never read it.'

'You haven't? I'd have thought—'

'What? That I'd want to be reminded all about what happened? I was there, detective sergeant. I witnessed it first-hand. I found my own fiancée floating face-up in the Water of Leith on fucking Hogmanay. Some party that turned out to be.'

'I . . . I'm sorry, sir.' DS Ritchie looked down at her feet and McLean felt a little stupid for snapping at her.

'Look . . . Ritchie.' He realised he wasn't sure what to call her. 'We've not got off to a very good start. Today should have been about orientation, introducing you to the team. It's just bad luck you arrived at the same time as all this.'

'I understand, sir.' Ritchie stopped at the back door to the station. 'Truth be told, I'd far rather be straight in to serious work than pissing about for a month on training and familiarisation courses. And, as I said, it's Kirsty.'

'What?' McLean's stomach clenched again at the mention of the name.

'My name. Kirsty. But Ritchie's fine. That's what most of Aberdeen CID used to call me. I don't mind.'

McLean stared at her, unable to think of anything to say. The awkward pause was interrupted only when DC MacBride caught up with them. He was clutching a sheet of paper and looked like he'd run all the way from the CID room.

'Sir. I think we've found her.' He shoved the paper in McLean's direction. It was a fax from Missing Persons over at Force HQ, most of the page taken up with a grainy black and white photograph of a young woman's face. McLean read the name and details before handing it over to Ritchie for her opinion. He didn't need it; even though the picture quality was poor, there was no mistaking their victim. And now she had a name.

Kate McKenzie.

28

The tenement was eerily like his own, only without the extensive fire damage. Edinburgh was full of these streets: housing built for the growing middle classes in Victorian and Edwardian times, they defined the city as much as did Princes Street or the castle. A vast social experiment where people lived cheek by jowl, it somehow worked here. Unlike the slum tenements in Glasgow or that more modern take on the concept, the great tower blocks of Craigmillar, Trinity and the like.

Kate McKenzie had lived near Jock's Lodge, sharing a neat little one-bedroom apartment with Debbie Wright, who had reported her flatmate missing almost a week ago. The two young women could not have been more different. Whereas Kate had been slim, fit and dark-haired, Debbie was round, short, rosy of cheek and with an unruly mop of bleach-blonde curls cascading from her head. She took one look at McLean's warrant card and burst into tears.

'It's Katie, isn't it. I knew something was wrong when she didn't come home.'

'I'm very sorry, Miss Wright. Could we maybe come in?' McLean let DS Ritchie lead the way as Debbie showed them to the living room. He peered about the hallway in passing, seeing open doors leading to a bedroom, bathroom and kitchen, along with a closed one for what he assumed was a press cupboard. It was all very tidy, very domesticated.

'Is she . . . is she dead?' Debbie's voice trembled. She stood in the middle of the room as if she didn't quite know what to do with herself. McLean sat down on the low, leather sofa that ranged along one wall.

'Why don't you sit down, Debbie.' He turned to DS Ritchie. 'Perhaps you could rustle up a cup of tea, sergeant?'

Ritchie gave him what might have been an old-fashioned stare. Debbie started to move, going to help her, but Ritchie stopped her with a light hand placed on her chubby arm.

'You stay here, OK? Sit down. I'll find my way.' She gently pushed Debbie into an armchair, then left the room.

McLean pulled a photo out of his pocket, hesitating slightly before passing it over to the distraught young woman. The killer hadn't touched Kate's face, but there was no denying that it was a picture of a dead person.

'Is this Kate?' He didn't really need her answer. There were photographs on the walls and mantelpiece of the two of them together in all manner of places. Always smiling, holding hands, hugging. Best of friends. Alive.

'She looks so peaceful.' Debbie sniffed, then rubbed her nose with the scrumpled-up end of her sleeve. 'I should never have argued with her. It was so stupid.'

'You had a row?' McLean tried to keep his voice neutral despite the sudden chill.

'It was daft. She just wanted rid of all the stuff. Couldn't care less what it was worth. Said she didn't want anything from the miserable old git.'

'Slow down a bit, Debbie. What stuff? Who's a miserable old git.'

'Her dad, that's who.'

McLean took out his notebook, wishing things could, just for once, be simple.

'Where does he live, her dad?' He wondered if he could persuade someone else to go and break the bad news. Debbie looked up at him as if he were mad.

'He's dead, isn't he. That's what it was all about. He left her everything, but she didn't want none of it. He'd only ever given her grief when he was alive.'

'What about her mother?'

'Nonna died when Katie was just ten.' Debbie looked up at McLean, her eyes red-rimmed and filled with tears. 'How's that fair, inspector? To lose someone like that and be left with your drunken bastard of a father to raise you?'

'Did she . . . did Kate have any other family?'

'I'm her family. We were going to get married.' Debbie held up a shaking hand to show a slim silver band on her ring finger. 'We needed to save up for the wedding. That's why I was so angry with her throwing out her dad's stuff. He had some valuable things, but she just gave them away.'

McLean supposed he should have seen it. One-bedroom flat, no sign of a fold-down bed anywhere. But what did he know about modern relationships? Nothing at all, it would seem. He sighed, pulling the other photograph out of his pocket.

'Listen, Debbie. I know this is hard. But could I ask you to look at something?' He handed the picture over, all too aware of how similar Audrey Carpenter was to Kate McKenzie. And how different. 'Do you know this woman at all?'

Debbie sniffed loudly, wiping her nose with the back of her hand whilst she looked at the photograph. Her eyes were already red and puffy, and now new tears filled them to overflowing. But McLean saw no glint of recognition in them. She shook her head once, before handing the picture back.

'She's . . . she's dead too?'

McLean nodded.

'Oh my God. Was it the same person? Oh God. Katie.' Then DS Ritchie arrived with tea and Debbie burst into tears.

An orange-red gloaming had filled the sky by the time a family liaison officer arrived to escort a white-faced Debbie Wright to the mortuary for a formal identification. Rush-hour traffic already clogged the roads, and McLean could only watch in frustration as the temperature gauge on the Alfa Romeo climbed past the one hundred mark and on towards the red. So much for the romantic image of the detective in the classic sports car. A line of unmoving vehicles snaked away from them towards the gates to Holyrood Park, brake lights blazing angrily.

'What do you reckon to Debbie Wright then, sergeant?'

Beside him, uncomfortably upright in the passenger seat and looking like she was terrified she might break something, Ritchie didn't answer at once.

'She's either genuinely distraught or a very good actress,' she said after a while. 'But she does have a copy of Dalgliesh's book.'

'You had a snoop around while you were making the tea?'

'No. Well, yes. But it was in the living room. She had quite a collection of true-crime books, and some novels, too.'

'So you reckon it was a crime of passion covered up to look like the return of a famous monster?'

'It's always possible.' Ritchie didn't sound as if she meant it.

'No, not really. Kate McKenzie was raped. That kind of rules out Debbie. And there's no sign she was accidentally pushed down the stairs, or even stabbed in a fight. Whoever abducted her planned the whole thing in minute detail. He knew what he was going to do, and how he was going to get rid of the body afterwards.'

'So we're not much further along with the investigation than we were first thing this morning.'

'On the contrary,' McLean said. 'We know our victim's name and we know the address where she was most likely staying. We've got a timeframe for her abduction. Now all we have to do is work out where it happened and who did it.'

'You make it sound easy, sir.' Ritchie's voice dripped sarcasm.

'It's never easy, sergeant. But we have to keep trying. And we know more about Kate McKenzie than we've managed to find out about Audrey Carpenter in over two weeks.'

The traffic freed up as they entered the park. McLean increased his speed a little, hoping some airflow over the radiator would stop the engine from blowing up.

'This isn't the way back to the station,' DS Ritchie said after a while.

'Top marks for observation. We're not finished yet.' McLean negotiated a set of double miniature rounda-bouts outside Holyrood Palace, and then ground to a halt in the next snaking queue of traffic.

'Where're we going, then?'

'Gracemount,' McLean said. 'Just off the top of Liber-ton Brae, if memory serves. That's where Kate McKenzie's father lived, and that's where she most likely went after she ran out on her girlfriend.'

'Don't we need a warrant to get in?'

'Who're we going to serve it against? Father and daugh-ter are both dead.'

'Well then? How're we going to get in?'

McLean smiled, keeping his eyes on the road as the traffic lurched forward again. 'I really have no idea.'

29

Lifford Road was a fairly nondescript suburban street, perched on the east side of Liberton Brae; a rat run for commuter traffic making its way to Moredun and Gilmerton. No. 31, home of the late Donald McKenzie, had the look of neglect empty houses soon acquire. The front lawn was little more than a few square yards of overgrown scrubby grass and dead bedding plants, strewn with litter blown in on the constant wind that howled off the Firth of Forth across the city. McLean parked over the road from it, next to a wet patch of parkland, empty save for an old man walking an arthritic Westie.

'That it, then?' DS Ritchie peered through the quickly fogging car window.

'If Debbie's telling us the truth, aye. That's it.' McLean didn't move from his seat, nor undo his seat belt. Instead he watched the houses to either side of No. 31.

'So what are we waiting for?' Ritchie started to open her door, but McLean leant over and stopped her.

'Just a minute. Watch.' He pointed to the left-hand house, and sure enough there was a twitch of the curtain. An elderly Honda Civic stood on the short driveway in front of the house. A sensible car, probably bought new and used no more than once a week for the trip to the shops. 'OK, let's go.'

Ritchie headed for No. 31, but McLean called her over

as he walked up the driveway to the neighbour's house: No. 29, even though there were no houses on the other side of the road. Or 'Dunroamin', if you believed the cast-iron plaque attached to the wall beside the frosted glass front door. He pressed the doorbell, half expecting it to sound the tune of some dreadful musical, but it just sang a plaintive 'ding-dong' in the hall beyond. Somewhere deep within the house, a terrier began to yip.

'Why here, sir?' DS Ritchie looked uncertain as to what was going on.

'We go snooping around next door, she'll only call the police.'

'How d'you know it's a she?'

'Call it intuition. Unless you want to put money on it.'

The noise of bolts being clacked back interrupted any chance of making the bet. Through the frosted glass, McLean could make out a short figure bending down. Then the door opened a fraction on a slim golden chain. An old lady's blue-rinsed head peered through the gap at shoulder height, a black and tan hairy-nosed face at ankle level. The latter yapped and growled.

'I'm no' buying anything. My Barry told me not to trust nobody.'

'Your Barry is very wise, madam. My name is Detective Inspector McLean and this is Detective Sergeant Ritchie.' McLean showed his warrant card, which the old lady peered at with surprisingly keen eyes. 'I wonder if I might ask you a few questions?'

'Of course, of course.' The old lady closed the door on them and unhooked the chain. Through the glass they could see her bend down and scoop up the wee dog, then she opened the door wide. 'Why don't you come in. Don't mind Archie. He tries to bite but he's no' teeth any more.'

McLean let DS Ritchie go first, then followed the two women through into the front room with the net curtains. It was spotlessly clean and every available surface was covered in what could only be described as tartan tat. There were little figurines of pipers and dancers, Westie dogs and Skye terriers. The walls were heavy with picture frames holding up quotes from Burns and cheap reproductions of Landseer paintings.

'Would you maybe like a cup of tea?' The little old lady pointed to the immaculate red sofa, indicating that they should sit. McLean considered the cup he'd just recently drunk at Debbie Wright's flat.

'That would be lovely, Mrs . . . ?'

'Stokes. Doris Stokes. Like the famous medium, you know. Please, inspector. Sit you down. I won't be a moment.' And before he could say anything more, she had scuttled out of the room, terrier still under her arm.

McLean had a poke around, peering at the few photographs on the mantelpiece. There were two of dogs and one of a balding man, his last few strands of hair swept over his pate, Bobby Charlton style.

'Just what are we doing here, sir?' DS Ritchie stood directly behind him so that when he turned to face her he nearly fell over. She stepped back and narrowly missed crashing into the coffee table.

'Trying not to wreck the place?' McLean smiled at her sudden blush. 'We're here because the curtain twitched. Mrs Stokes knows everything that happens in this street

I'll wager. She'll have seen Kate coming and going and I reckon she'll remember exactly when it was.'

'Couldn't we just ask her, sir?'

'We could, yes. But we wouldn't get very far. Trust me, I know the type. She needs to feel involved.'

It was a few minutes before Mrs Stokes came back into the room, bearing a tray with tea things on it. The little terrier trotted in behind her, then went to sniff at DS Ritchie's ankles. Absent-mindedly she put down a hand to be licked and began to pat the dog on its head. McLean took the tray from the old lady, placing it on the table as she sat herself down in a particularly hideous armchair close by. As she bent herself to the task of pouring tea, he turned back to the mantelpiece.

'Is this your Barry, Mrs Stokes?'

'Och, no. That's Norman. God rest his soul. He passed, oh, gone five years ago. Barry's my wee nephew. Norman's brother's boy. He's a good lad is Barry. Keeps an eye on his old auntie.'

'You're lucky to have someone like that. And I'm sorry, about your husband.'

'That's kind of you to say, inspector.' Mrs Stokes poured the tea, handing a cup to DS Ritchie. 'There you go, lass. Biscuit?'

McLean took his own cup and retreated to the sofa beside the sergeant; keeping the coffee table as a barricade between him and the old lady. A plate on the tray offered chocolate Hobnobs so he took one, sneaking a guilty bite. It was soggy, stale and on close inspection the chocolate bore a white, crazed coating that he hoped wasn't mould. He balanced the rest precariously on the edge of his saucer, chewing the mouthful he'd already taken and swallowing it with great difficulty.

'Well now, inspector. I can't say it's not nice to see a policeman round here from time to time, but I don't suppose you just stopped in for tea. I've no' done anything wrong, have I?'

'Of course not, Mrs Stokes. It's about next door.' McLean nodded towards no. 31.

'Oh aye. Donnie McKenzie's place? Such a shame when he died. Used to keep his garden lovely. But that was months ago. Has something happened?'

'Have you seen his daughter lately?'

'Wee Katherine? Aye, she was in and out for a while about a week ago. There's a poor wee lassie, growing up without her mum. I know Donnie tried his best with her, but she was always a handful. Sich a temper when she was a bairn.'

'Was she staying at the house? You know, overnight?'

'A couple of nights, aye.' Mrs Stokes put her own cup and saucer back down on the tray, got up and went to the other side of the room. For a moment McLean thought she was going to bring back a diary with all Kate McKenzie's movements listed in it, but instead she unfolded a copy of the *Radio Times* onto her lap, then pulled a pair of spectacles up from where they had been tucked neatly down her cardigan front on a chain around her neck.

'Let me see now.' She leafed through the pages. 'I was watching that programme about the polar bears the first night she came in. Aye, that was Tuesday. She was there on Wednesday afternoon. I heard the vacuum cleaner going. Yes, that's right. She went out about seven o'clock that evening and that's the last time I saw her.'

Mrs Stokes thumbed quickly through the rest of the pages, as if Kate McKenzie might suddenly appear from the middle of them, then dropped the magazine into her lap all of a sudden.

'Oh me. She's gone missing, hasn't she.'

'I'm afraid it's worse than that, Mrs Stokes. Kate . . . Katherine is dead.'

The little terrier ceased its snuffling around DS Ritchie's feet almost as soon as McLean had said the words. Silently it returned to its owner and leapt with surprising grace into her lap. She started to stroke its head with long, rhythmic motions of her hand, saying nothing for what felt like hours but was probably only a minute.

'Was it . . . was it an accident?' She asked eventually. 'I know the roads can be dreadful these days.'

'I'm afraid she was murdered, Mrs Stokes.'

'Murdered? Crivens. Who could do such a thing?'

'That's what we're trying to find out.'

'Here? It didn't happen around here, did it?'

'No, I don't think so. We found her . . . outside the city. What I'm trying to do now is put together her last movements. See what she was doing, where she was going.'

'Oh, I see.' Mrs Stokes put the terrier back down on the floor and once more levered herself out of her chair. She headed back to the corner of the room where the *Radio Times* had come from. 'You know she has her own flat on the other side of town. Shares it with a nice young girl. So much safer sharing like that. Not like these student places where there's boys and girls all cooped up together. I've got the number here somewhere.'

McLean put his cup down on the tray, got up and walked over to where the old lady was rifling through an address book.

'It's all right, Mrs Stokes. We've already spoken to Debbie. She was the one who told us Kate was missing.'

'Oh, right.' Unable to be any more help, she looked rather lost, her eyes slowly sweeping over the room as if it represented the sum total of her existence. Their visit that afternoon had quite possibly been the most exciting thing to happen to her in years.

'Well, I think we've taken up quite enough of your time, Mrs Stokes.' McLean took out a business card from his pocket and handed it over. 'Thank you so much for the tea. And biscuits. If you think of anything else, please, give me a call.'

'Och, that's nothing, really. It's nice to have a wee bit of company from time to time.'

'Will you be all right?' McLean stepped out of the living room into the hallway, almost tripping over the dog as it decided to play a game with his feet. 'I know this must be quite a shock. I can have a constable pop round for a while if you'd like.'

He could see in her eyes that it was a tempting offer, but eventually she declined. 'No, no. Barry'll be round for his tea in an hour or so. I'll maybe just take Archie here for his walkies before that.'

'Well, thank you again, Mrs Stokes. You've really been very helpful.' McLean had made it outside now, DS Ritchie ahead of him. The street lights were on in the road, blackening the falling dusk and giving everything an oddly heavy feel. The old lady watched them from the open front door as they walked down the short driveway, then started up the garden path of no. 31. Only then did she tell them.

'If you're wanting inside, I've got a key.'

30

No. 31 Lifford Road was a marked contrast to its neighbour. The house was tidy enough, but it hadn't been decorated in many a year. The furniture was old, worn out like the greying carpets. Mould had begun to form in the bay window of the front room and the Formica on the kitchen units had been peeling off for quite some time. It smelled like a house that hadn't been lived in for months.

'We looking for anything in particular?' DS Ritchie asked, picking up a folded copy of the *Scotsman* from the kitchen table.

'I don't know. What's the date on that paper?'

'Last Wednesday.' She stooped down, bringing up a bin from beside the sink unit. 'There's another in here. Tuesday. Takeaway burger box. Couple of Coke cans.'

'She was here when the old biddy said, then.' McLean jangled the key ring that he'd finally managed to get from Mrs Stokes without having her come over and get in the way. It was unlikely that they'd find anything here that would point to whoever had abducted Kate; he was fairly sure she'd not been taken from the house. But he didn't want a well-meaning member of the public who'd watched too many episodes of *Miss Marple* mucking up what might turn out to be a crime scene.

'Sir, through here.' DS Ritchie called from the utility room beyond the kitchen. A laundry basket sat in front of the washing machine, which was filled with clean washing. The cycle had finished but the machine was still switched on.

'Might as well check it,' McLean said. Ritchie bent down and opened the door, pulling out a small collection of clothes. They smelled slightly fusty, left too long damp in the machine.

Upstairs revealed three bedrooms and a bathroom. The smallest bedroom was decorated in shades of baby pink, like a nursery, though the bed was plenty big enough for an adult. It was the only one that looked like it had been slept in. A small wash bag lay on the dressing table, its contents strewn haphazardly in front of the mirror. Lipstick, foundation, deodorant, hairbrush, a bottle of Chanel No. 5. Beside them, a small silver photo frame held a picture of Kate and Debbie, hugging each other cheek-to-cheek and grinning like idiots. At the end of the bed, a small grey suitcase with wheels and an extendable handle lay open, clothes spread about in an untidy mess. McLean looked on as Ritchie picked up items of underwear he had no names for. He left the bedroom, worried she might find something even more intimate. That wasn't something he'd be comfortable sharing.

The bathroom yielded more secrets. A toothbrush and toothpaste, the latter a new tube, its uncapped end hardly dry at all. Well, it was likely less than a week since it had last been used. In the bath, a Lady shaver and tube of shaving gel propped up against the taps. It all started to fall together in his mind. He stepped back out onto the landing where DS Ritchie was waiting.

'Are we done here then?'

'I reckon.' McLean clumped down the steps, stopping only briefly in the hall before going back outside into the darkness. The house was as dead as its owners.

McLean let DS Ritchie lock up. He wandered over the road to his car, staring out across the park towards Liberton Brae. Not far beyond was Mortonhall Crematorium and the garden of remembrance where he'd laid his grandmother's ashes to rest alongside those of his parents.

'Back to the station then, sir?'

McLean turned to see DS Ritchie standing by the still-locked passenger door.

'No, not yet,' he said. 'Now we're going to go to the pub.'

Early on in the evening, the Balm Well was almost empty; just a couple of old men nursing their half pints and grudges in the corner; a fat man tucking into a burger and chips at a table by the window. Across from the bar, a huge flat-screen TV was mercifully blank, the only noise in the bar the occasional electronic chirrup as the one-armed bandit had another epileptic fit.

McLean approached the barman, who was polishing glasses with a towel, holding them up to the light to check for smears. He stopped as soon as he saw the two police officers.

'Evening, sir, madam. What can I get you?'

McLean looked at the hand pumps, considering a pint of Deuchars. Then he remembered that he'd driven here. Still, the clock said six, and that was surely late enough.

'You fancy a drink?' he asked DS Ritchie. Startled, she took a moment to answer.

'Am I no' still on duty?'

'Nope. Technically your shift ended at five.'

'In that case I'll have a white-wine spritzer.'

McLean did the ordering, agonising over the pint before settling for a fresh orange instead. They took their drinks and a couple of bags of crisps over to a quiet table away in the corner.

'Well, here's to my first day with Lothian and Borders.' Ritchie lifted her glass in a mock toast. McLean did the same.

'It's not over yet,' he said as she took a sip.

'No?' She eyed her drink nervously.

'What did you reckon to the house?' McLean nodded towards the window looking out onto the park over which they had just walked.

'Well. She's obviously been there. Makes sense if she had keys. She'd not packed much, hence the washing. My guess is that she was probably planning to spend a few days there before going back. If it was me I'd probably have kipped on a friend's floor.'

'Broken up often have you?'

'I . . . No.' Ritchie's face flushed again, her freckles darkening across her cheeks. McLean just grinned at her.

'Sorry, that was uncalled for. Wouldn't want to be accused of sexual harassment.'

'What about you, sir?' Ritchie asked, then hurriedly added: 'What did you make of the house?'

'Like you said, she was there. It was her bolt-hole after their argument. I don't know if she would have gone back and patched things up or whether it was the last straw in a troubled relationship. What I do know is that she got herself dolled-up on Wednesday night and went out to some party she never made it home from.'

'How d'you reckon that?'

'She'd shaved her legs, made herself up and was wearing some fairly risqué underwear. That doesn't sound like a girl popping down the shops for a microwave burger and a bottle of Coke. And wherever she went must have been close by, too. She'd only left Debbie on Monday and her mobile's not been used since Tuesday evening. The phone in the house was disconnected, so she didn't arrange to meet a friend, and she didn't call a taxi.'

'And that's why we're in the pub?'

'Exactly. It's the only place within easy walking distance. And Wednesday night was cold and wet, if I remember right.'

'Shame. I thought you were being nice to me because it's my first day on the job.'

McLean ignored the jibe, finished his orange and took the glass back to the bar.

'Can I get you another, sir?' The barman asked.

'Actually, I was wondering if you might be able to help me.' McLean took out his warrant card and the photograph of Kate McKenzie. 'We're trying to track down this young woman's movements last week. Was she maybe in here on Wednesday night?'

'I don't know, let me see.' The barman picked up the photograph and looked at it closely. 'It gets pretty hectic in here on a Wednesday, what with the Women's rugby club coming in and all.'

'She'd have been dressed up for the night. You know what young women are like these days.'

'Hang on a mo. I'll ask Sian.' The barman stuck his head through an open doorway at the back of the bar and yelled. After a few moments a dark-haired woman came through.

'What is it, Mike?'

The barman showed her the picture. 'She in here Wednesday last?'

Sian studied the picture for a while. 'Yeah, I think so. She had a yellow top on. Spent the night talking to those rugby lasses.'

'Any idea what time she left?' McLean asked.

'Late, that's for sure. Maybe after midnight.'

'Was she alone? With someone?'

'I couldn't rightly say. Wednesdays are always busy with the rugby crowd. So many faces, it's difficult to know who's who.'

McLean thanked them both, taking back the photograph. DS Ritchie had finished her spritzer and brought the glass back to the bar. He told her what he had found as they were walking out.

'What about CCTV footage?' She asked. 'Any chance we might pick her up on that?'

'There's no cameras in here, I checked.'

Ritchie smiled a triumphant little grin. 'Aye, but they've one in the car park looks out onto the road. And we're right next door to Howdenhall nick.'

31

An anxious Grumpy Bob was waiting for them when McLean and DS Ritchie returned to the station some while later, laden with long-play video tapes.

'Where've you been, sir? We've been trying to get in touch for hours.'

'What's the matter, Bob?'

'It's the press. They've been hassling us all bloody afternoon. Dan in the liaison office is spitting chunks. Says he had to go on the half-six news bulletin without any briefing.'

McLean dug out his phone, remembering that he'd switched it off before going to see Debbie Wright. He'd completely forgotten to switch it back on again.

'Bugger. What did Dan do, the usual waiting-to-talk-to-next-of-kin bit?'

'Not even that much. We didn't know whether you'd confirmed her identity or not.'

'Shite, so all he could do was say we'd found a body. Oh great. I guess I'd better go see him, try and calm him down.'

'It's not him you need to worry about, sir. It's the chief superintendent.'

McLean stopped walking. 'How did she get involved?'

'She was mobbed, sir. You should have seen it here earlier. There were camera crews blocking the street outside the front door.'

'Christ, why?'

Grumpy Bob looked very uncomfortable. 'They're playing the Anderson angle, sir.'

'Anderson's dead, Bob.'

'Aye, I know. But bloody Jo Dalgliesh's got hold of detailed info about both murders. She's been harping on about Anderson being fitted up and us not knowing our arses from a hole in the ground. You can bet it's going to be all over the papers tomorrow.'

McLean looked down at the handful of video tapes. He'd been planning on handing them over to DC Mac-Bride to sit through, but right now the thought of hiding himself in a dark viewing room was extremely tempting. Better still if he could go in there and not come out until spring. He looked at his watch; it was almost eight. Thirteen hours since he'd started that morning. Grumpy Bob had been up just as long, if not longer. Well, it wouldn't be the first time they'd pulled long shifts.

'OK then, Bob, let's go and see the super. Might as well get the bollocking over and done with.'

Mrs McCutcheon's cat stared at him from the kitchen table when he let himself in the back door many hours later. McLean shooed it off, but all it did was twist itself around his legs, waiting to be fed. He dug a scoop of dried food out of the bag in the larder, ladled it into the bowl on the floor and then went to check the litter box. There was a cat flap in the back door, but he'd kept it shut for the few weeks since he'd adopted the beast; someone somewhere had told him once that you needed to keep cats locked up in their new homes for a while, otherwise they'd just wander back to the old one. For the life of him he couldn't remember how long it was you were supposed to confine them, but looking at the diary pinned up by the phone in the kitchen, he saw to his dismay both that it was three weeks since his flat had burned down, and that it was only three days to Christmas.

He supposed he should have realised. It wasn't as if the shops weren't full of tinsel and tat, and the street decorations had been up for at least six weeks. Perhaps he could lie to himself and say he'd been so wrapped up in his work that he'd just let time pass him by, but the truth of the matter was that he always hid from the festive season.

The cat twined around his legs again as he stood staring at the diary. There was nothing written in it, just a blank accumulation of days almost finished. He'd have to pick up one for next year soon.

'You wanting out then?' McLean opened the back door onto darkness and cold wind. The cat looked out, sniffed the air a little, then turned back to the warmth of the kitchen.

'Smart thinking.' He closed the door, then bent down and removed the cover over the cat flap. At least it could come and go if it wanted to. If it knew how to use one, of course. He didn't recall Mrs McCutcheon ever having one; her cats just used an open window. Ah well, he'd show it how or it would work it out for itself.

The fridge yielded little in the way of food, but there was a half bottle of Riesling that clearly needed finishing. He poured himself a glass, and was about to phone the pizza delivery place when the front doorbell rang.

McLean froze. There was no reason for anyone to

come and see him. Not that many people at work knew where he lived now anyway. Grumpy Bob and MacBride had been here, and Emma of course. Guilt warmed his cheeks as he thought about her. Thought about the way he'd treated her. He'd not exactly been cruel so much as unresponsive, and for the life of him he couldn't think why. Except that she was friendly and warm, obviously liked him enough to put up with his many failings, and he really didn't want to go getting close to someone like that again.

The doorbell rang again and for a moment he considered hiding, pretending not to be in. It was daft, he knew. The kitchen lights would be painting a wide distorted square over the driveway outside; it would be obvious to anyone approaching the house that someone was home. And what if it was something important?

Sighing, he put down his unfilled glass and set off across the hall, flicking on the light over the porch as he did so. No sooner had he opened the front door than a dozen or more lusty voices burst into song.

> Good King Wenceslas looked out
> On the feast of Stephen
> When the snow lay round about
> Deep and crisp and even . . .

And on they went, through all the verses whilst he stood there, mouth open like a half-wit. Carol singers. He hadn't heard them in years. Not since he'd been a boy at school. Looking at the heavily coated mob, he thought he recognised some of his grandmother's neighbours. It was possible that some of the younger ones were people he'd known as a child.

The carol came to an end with more or less everyone finishing at the same time, and only then did McLean remember that he was supposed to give them something. His wallet was back in the kitchen, in his jacket pocket hanging over a chair.

'Um, that was . . . great,' he said, mustering as much enthusiasm as he could in the howling, icy wind that whistled around the garden and in through the door. 'Look, it's freezing out here. Why don't you come in. I'm sure I can find something to warm you all up.'

The words were out before he'd really considered the implications of what he was offering. The carol singers murmured desperate thanks anyway, and all trooped into the hall. McLean went back to the kitchen, fished out his wallet and then fetched a bottle of malt whisky from the cupboard. By the time he'd found enough glasses, filled a jug with water and carried the whole lot through on a tray, most of his unexpected guests were staring at the pictures and trying hard not to look like they were being nosey.

They were an odd assortment of people, he discovered as he handed over restorative drams. Only one person declined the offer, an elderly gentleman with a rather pinched expression, thinning white hair and a profuse white beard. He wore a long overcoat and thick gloves, and kept himself pretty much to himself. McLean would probably have tried harder to make conversation, but there were others clamouring for his attention, eager hands reaching for the generously filled whisky glasses.

By the time he came to the last of the carol singers, she had loosened off her overcoat to reveal a black shirt and the inset dog collar of the Episcopalian Church. She was perhaps in her late forties, though it was hard to tell; her face had that lived-in look of someone who's seen a lot, and her shoulder-length straight black hair was shot with grey. But there were few lines around her eyes and mouth.

'I don't believe we've met.' She held out her hand. 'Mary Currie.'

'Tony McLean. Have you been in the parish long, Ms Currie?'

'Mary, please. Long enough to have known your grandmother. I was sorry to hear when she passed away. We had a few good arguments, Esther and I. She didn't really see God in quite the same way as me.'

McLean wondered why his grandmother had never mentioned that the local vicar was a woman. Maybe she had and he'd forgotten.

'Still, I'm glad you decided to move in,' Mary carried on.

'I don't think I'm likely to swell the numbers of your congregation. Religion's not really my thing.'

'Well, there's always room for improvement.' She smiled, then knocked back the last of her whisky. 'Thank you for that, it's not many remember the old traditions of hospitality. Though you might want to put up a few decorations, brighten the place up a bit.'

McLean was uncomfortably aware that there was absolutely nothing festive about the house whatsoever. If you didn't include the usual round of seasonal circulars, he hadn't even received any Christmas cards, which was hardly surprising, as he never sent any out.

The vicar called her choir together; they gave a quick rendition of 'In the Bleak Midwinter' and then filed out into the cold night. He watched them troop back down the gravel path and disappear into the street. They talked amongst each other, laughing and joking, revitalised by their unexpected drink. Except the white-haired old man, who hung back a bit and stared up the drive until McLean closed the door. When he had collected all the empty glasses from their various hiding places in the hall, the house felt suddenly very large and empty.

32

He couldn't quite put his finger on it, but there was something about a sea of journalists that was the stuff of nightmares. Perhaps it was the eager heads straining forward on stretched necks towards him that reminded him of the horror comics he had read as a child. Or maybe it was the smell of them, part fear, part feeding-frenzy testosterone. Whatever it was, McLean hated press conferences perhaps more than anything in his job. And that included breaking bad news to the recently bereaved.

As penance for his disappearance the day before, he had agreed to attend this particular briefing and answer questions about the investigation. If anything could have made it worse, it was the fact that he was flanked on one side by the station's press-liaison officer, Sergeant Dan Hwei and on the other by Chief Superintendent McIntyre. He didn't need his degree in psychology to tell that neither of them was particularly well disposed towards him at that moment. DCI Duguid was lurking at the back with a mischievous grin on his face.

'Ladies and gentlemen,' McIntyre started, 'thank you for coming. I'm sure you're all aware of the terrible nature of this crime. Last night we were unable to give out too many details. However, in the light of some fairly lurid speculation, I think it only fair that we bring you up to speed on the investigation so far.'

'Chief superintendent, can you confirm—' A voice from the back: female, English. McLean felt the air beside him go still, and possibly drop in temperature by a few degrees.

McIntyre cut the journalist off with a withering stare. 'There will be time for questions later. Right now I'd like to introduce the principal officer conducting this investigation, Detective Inspector McLean.'

The hubbub that arose from the crowd was in some way gratifying, since it meant that his name was known. But it was also a touch depressing to think that those people murmuring to each other at the back had not recognised him when he'd first taken his place at the podium. McLean leant forward and tapped his microphone a couple of times before speaking.

'I'm sure you're all aware that we found the body of a young woman out near the Flotterstone Inn late on Sunday afternoon. I can confirm that we have now identified the victim as a Miss Katherine McKenzie, a resident of Jock's Lodge. And I can also confirm that post-mortem examination of her body, er . . . confirms that she was murdered. We have established her movements up until around midnight of last Wednesday.'

Thanks to DS Ritchie and DC MacBride, who had stayed up late to watch a fascinating movie, finally spotting Kate, leaving alone and walking back down Liberton Brae towards her home.

'We have reason to believe she was picked up somewhere near Mortonhall at that time. Our major line of enquiry at the moment is trying to establish where she went after that, though of course we're pursuing other avenues as well.

'There has been some speculation already as to a connection between this murder and that two weeks ago of Audrey Carpenter. Whilst there are superficial similarities between the two, there are also significant differences. We are progressing both investigations in parallel, with close liaison between the investigating teams.'

Because they're the same bloody people. McLean sat back, waiting for the onslaught. It didn't take long for the sea of faces to become a forest of arms. That was when Sergeant Hwei stepped in, picking the first questions from those local reporters he already knew.

'Inspector McLean, the word is the young woman's throat was cut. Is this true?'

'It was a violent attack,' McLean said, 'but I don't wish to confirm any details that might jeopardise either our investigation or any subsequent prosecution.'

'Inspector, is it true that the victim was killed somewhere other than Flotterstone and then moved to the reservoir to be dumped?'

'Again, I can't really say. The body was found just beyond the tourist car park at the south end of the reservoir.'

'Have Miss McKenzie's family been informed?'

'Miss McKenzie's parents are both dead, and she had no other family. We've been working with her . . . fiancée.'

'Do you have any clue as to who might have done this?'

'We have several lines of investigation open, and it's early days yet. If I've got any suspects in mind, I hope you'll appreciate it if I don't share that information with you.'

'Inspector McLean, does it bother you that there are so many similarities between both these deaths and that of Miss Kirsty Summers in the winter of 1999? I believe you were the detective who eventually brought that killer to justice.'

'Thank you, Ms Dalgliesh. We're all aware of your theories here.' Chief Superintendent McIntyre stepped in before McLean could answer. If he could answer. The question had quite literally knocked him back in his seat, even as he had recognised the voice of the woman asking it.

'But surely it's an important line of investigation, is it not?' Dalgliesh persisted. 'If there's the slightest possibility that Anderson didn't—'

'Anderson killed her. And the others before her. He killed them all.' McLean was surprised at the vehemence in his voice, the anger behind it. How dare this scrawny wee shite come in and even suggest that he'd got the wrong man? And why now?

'And yet here we are, nine years later, and two young women's bodies are found placed exactly the same way as all those others before. Killed exactly the same way. Will you at least be reviewing the old case files?'

McLean pictured the unopened cardboard box on his desk. He could feel McIntyre beside him gearing herself up to end the press conference. Her anger was like a wall growing between him and the collected journalists. But before the superintendent could speak, he leant forward, focusing solely on the scruffy woman in her leather coat as she sat a few rows from the front.

'Ms Dalgliesh, Donald Anderson was guilty. A jury

found him guilty. We had incontrovertible evidence of his guilt. He even confessed, though that was just an attempt to get off on an insanity plea.

'But you're right, there are disturbing similarities between these murders and Anderson's. I'll be investigating those similarities very thoroughly.' He looked straight at Joanne Dalgliesh. 'Of course, my job would be a lot easier if his methods hadn't been made public in quite such intimate detail.'

McLean watched from the relative safety of the corridor as the reporters filed out of the briefing room. Only visitors with passes could find him here, peering through the wire-mesh toughened-glass window. And, of course, serving police officers.

'I think that went as well as could be expected.'

He turned around to see McIntyre standing behind him, her uniform serving only to emphasise her seniority.

'You do? I was just about ready to strangle Dalgliesh in there. What the hell was she doing, dragging Kirsty's name into all this?'

McIntyre leant against the wall, perhaps trying to inject a little informality into the conversation. 'You know as well as I do that she's only trying to sell more papers. And there's a new edition of that book of hers, of course. Now Anderson's dead. She doesn't care whose feelings get trampled as long as she gets paid.'

'But you heard her, ma'am. She as good as said we framed an innocent man.'

McIntyre fixed McLean with an oddly puzzled stare, staying silent for a moment as if she was trying to make a decision. McLean could only seethe, glancing back to see the last of the journalists depart. No doubt some of them would be doing pieces to camera out in the street, but at least he'd been spared the added worry of TV recording the actual press conference.

'Come with me, Tony,' McIntyre said finally. He had to hurry to keep up as she led him back up to her office. Once there, he expected her to go straight to her chair on the far side of the desk, but instead she went to the book-case in the 'informal' corner with the uncomfortable armchairs and the coffee machine. She made a good impression of a person trying to decide what to read in the bath that evening, then finally pulled out a fat, hard-bound book that McLean recognised with a heavy heart. The cover bore a chilling photograph of Donald Anderson, and above it the legend 'The Christmas Killer', subtitled 'Donald Anderson and the Book of Souls'.

'You really don't know what Dalgliesh is on about.' McIntyre clutched the book to her bosom. 'And I can understand that, Tony. From a personal point of view. But you're a policeman. A detective. I know that it's painful. Christ, I can't begin to imagine just how painful, losing your fiancée like that. But you can't go on sticking your head in the sand. There's more than one opinion where Anderson's concerned.'

'Ma'am, Anderson is guilty. He killed all of those women. Not just my—'

'I know, Tony. I saw the evidence, and I trust your skills as a detective.' McIntyre pulled the book away from her and held it out for him to take. 'But not everyone else in the world does.'

McLean made no move to accept the book, so McIntyre forced it on him.

'Take it, Tony. Read it. I know it's going to hurt, and I know it's going to make you angry. But you need to understand where people like Jo Dalgliesh are coming from.'

33

McLean had never really liked Joanne Dalgliesh as a person. Fifty pages into *The Christmas Killer*, he felt utterly justified in his contempt of her as a writer too.

For some unfathomable reason, the reporter had taken it upon herself to defend Anderson, seeing him as some victim of both a terrible miscarriage of justice and mental illness brought on by his upbringing. She didn't deny that he had killed Kirsty Summers in the winter of 1999, but the bulk of the book was a detailed exploration of the possibility that he might not have killed the other nine Christmas Killer victims.

The book glossed neatly over the hard forensic evidence that had put Anderson away and focused instead on the mementos he had kept from his victims. Dalgliesh seemed to think that because none of these were individually conclusive, Anderson must have been fitted up for the earlier murders; Lothian and Borders taking the opportunity of Anderson's arrest to clear an embarrassing backlog of unsolved crimes. McLean knew himself that none of the mementos on their own meant anything; Laura Fenton's St Christopher was a mass-produced piece that could have belonged to anyone. Rosie Buckley's ring had been a cheap piece of shit from Ratners, one of millions. And so on with all the other items found in the office behind the shop.

Even the strip of fabric from his fiancée's dress could have come from anywhere – the rest of her clothes had never been found. But he'd recognised it, slipped between the pages of that old book in Anderson's shop. It had been enough for a search warrant, and what the team had found in the basement had brought to a close the longest man-hunt in the history of Lothian and Borders Police. That should have been the end of it, but for Jo Dalgliesh it was only the beginning.

Flicking through the book, McLean was struck by how little respect the reporter seemed to have for the victims and their families. She concentrated on the minutiae of the first nine murders, painting quick portraits of the victims that almost suggested it was their fault they were abducted and then describing their ordeals and fates as if writing a script for a slasher movie. No detail gleaned from the post-mortem reports went unmentioned, each cut and bruise lovingly teased out into a horrific scenario. It sickened him to read it, and sickened him more to know that many thousands of people, maybe millions, thought of such descriptions as entertainment.

Then he arrived at 1999 and the tenth abduction. Curiously Dalgliesh glossed over the forensic detail this time; either because she'd not been able to get hold of the post-mortem report or because Anderson's guilt was unquestionable in this final case. Kirsty's blood had been all over his basement, after all. Instead she concentrated on Anderson himself. It was nothing McLean didn't already know: the lonely boy orphaned in the Blitz; the evacuation to Wales and a cruel upbringing at the hands of a strict Methodist minister; the National Service in the

Far East and unspeakable horrors witnessed; the retreat to a monastery in the Western Isles that then mysteriously burned to the ground; and finally the antiquarian bookshop in Edinburgh's Canongate.

At this point the book stopped even being reportage and strayed into hagiography, as if Dalgliesh were slightly in awe of her subject. When she finally described in lurid, fabricated detail the impossible scene where Anderson plucked an innocent young Kirsty Summers from the streets and subjected her to a week of torture and abuse before callously cutting her throat, McLean slammed shut the book and threw it across the room. His hands were shaking, his whole body tingling as if he had a fever. He got up, paced about the tiny office. Looked out the window at the encroaching winter darkness, back at the book lying on the floor.

McIntyre was right; he had needed to read it. But that didn't make it any easier.

From the look of the whiteboard in the CID room, DS Ritchie had been far more successful piecing together Kate McKenzie's life than Audrey Carpenter's. Several different lines of enquiry spidered from the death-mask photograph towards neatly boxed handwritten notes. McLean peered at the one labelled 'Work', seeing a list of names, presumably colleagues. Another box read 'Gym', a third 'College' and a fourth had the title 'Gay Activism'. Underneath each was a series of names. It was going to be a bugger interviewing them all.

'You've been busy,' he said to Ritchie as she hung up the phone.

'It wasn't all me, sir. DC MacBride's been on the phone all afternoon chasing up names. We've arranged to go to her workplace tomorrow and start talking to her colleagues.'

'College?' McLean pointed at the other list.

'Yeah, she was studying law at evening classes. I spoke to her tutor, Dr McGillivray. He seemed quite distraught when he heard about her. Reckoned she'd have gone far. Very dedicated.'

'So I see.' McLean surveyed the board again, trying to work out what was missing. 'You spoken to Debbie again?'

'That was her on the phone,' Ritchie said. 'I left a message earlier. She's gone to stay with her parents in Balerno. I said I'd pop out and see her tomorrow.'

'You know where you're going?'

'Oh, aye. I did my degree at Heriot Watt. Spent six months living in a nasty old council flat in Currie.'

'Ah, I did wonder how an Aberdeen girl could know her way around Edinburgh so well.'

'Five years of working in bars and living in the cheapest student digs I could find. You get to see a different side of the city.'

'Five years? What went wrong?'

'Wrong? An honours degree and an MSc? What's wrong with that?' Ritchie looked at him with a hurt expression, then added, 'Oh, I get it, you thought I flunked a year and had to re-sit. Well, thank you very much.'

'That's not—' McLean stopped, he had to admit that was what he had thought. 'So what was your subject, then?'

'Sociology and anthropology. I was going to go to

Borneo to study a tribe out there, but the money fell through. I was back home living with my folks, wondering what to do with my life. Dad was a beat sergeant, suggested I go in for the fast track.'

'And the rest, as they say, is history.' McLean motioned towards the whiteboard with an open hand. 'Well, anthropology's loss is our gain, I guess. But it's going to take us weeks to speak to all these people. Didn't you say MacBride was about?'

'Oh, he was here a couple of minutes ago. We've pretty much contacted everyone we can today. Had quite a team working here.'

'So where is everyone then?'

Ritchie nodded in the direction of the clock hanging over the doorway. 'Shift change. Grumpy Bob muttered something about going for a pint. I've never seen a room empty so quickly.'

'And you didn't go with them?' McLean raised a sceptical eyebrow. Ritchie treated him to an elfin smile.

'Oh, I'll be joining them all right. Just as soon as I've let the lead investigator know where we're all going.'

McLean was just walking out the back door of the station when a familiar face trotted up behind him. Emma Baird had a large canvas bag slung over one shoulder, weighing her down as if it contained all her worldly possessions.

'Anyone might think you liked us more than SOC.' He held open the door for her. 'You seem to spend that much time here.'

'I think it's because I'm the new girl,' she said. 'I always seem to get the job of carting stuff to the archives. Helps that I live nearby, I guess.'

'Well, I'm sure it makes Needy's day to see a pretty face every once in a while.'

Emma smiled cheekily. 'Why thank you, Inspector McLean. I do believe that was a guarded compliment.'

McLean was about to say something about the stand-ard of WPCs in the station, then realised the joke would have been neither true nor funny. 'You off home then?' he asked instead.

They had walked as far across the car park as an elderly blue Peugeot, parked between two squad cars, and Emma was even now guddling around in her voluminous bag for her keys.

'Well I was,' she said, giving up the search. 'But if you're making me a better offer.'

34

'Jayne tells me you've read Jo's book, Tony. So what did you think?'

McLean sat in the uncomfortable armchair in McIntyre's office. Another grim day, another pointless counselling session. Neither of them helped by the hangover threatening to engulf him at any moment. It had been a good evening in the pub – better by far than going home and brooding over the book he'd finally read – but his head wasn't thanking him right now.

He looked straight at Hilton. 'To be honest, I don't understand how you could want to be associated with it in any way. But at least you thought Anderson was merely mad. She seems to think that we fitted him up for nine murders he didn't commit. It's a load of old rubbish, but worse it's a load of dangerous rubbish.'

'Dangerous? How so?'

'It describes in excruciating detail exactly what Anderson did to his victims.'

The silence that followed was a long one. McLean was content to sit and stare at the bookcase behind Hilton's chair, scanning the collection that McIntyre had amassed. Biographies mostly, but there were a few management handbooks and policing manuals in amongst them. And the occasional work of fiction. A gap showed where Dalgliesh's book had been shelved, in between a dog-eared copy of *The Dilbert Principle* and the 1985 edition of the *Police Training Manual,* Scottish Edition. He was trying to work out if that meant something deep when Hilton finally broke and filled the void.

'Tell me, Tony. How's the investigation going?'

McLean reluctantly switched his attention back to the psychologist. 'Which one?'

Hilton smiled. 'You know which one. The Christmas Killer.'

'You see. There you go again leaping to conclusions.' McLean knew that it had been a taunt, but couldn't help himself from responding. 'And I thought you were meant to be an open-minded sifter of the facts.'

'Well then, what are the facts?'

'We've got two young women dead, probably killed by the same person. Certainly killed in mimicry of Anderson's methods. Except that Anderson only killed once a year.'

'Anderson was . . . unique, let us say.' Hilton tapped his pen against his cheek, making a hollow popping sound. 'But the trauma of his formative years gives a good foundation for his psychosis.'

'And yet your profile of the Christmas Killer couldn't have been more different. Some help it turned out to be, eh?'

'You know as well as I do that profiling is an inexact science, Tony.' Hilton fixed him with a schoolboy smirk that almost begged to be hit. 'I think if you review the case, you'll find that my work on the Christmas Killer wasn't all that far off the mark. All the pointers were there, I just underestimated his age and intelligence.'

'OK, then. What about this new case? How are you getting on with profiling this new Christmas Killer, since that's what you seem determined to call him.'

'Him? And here you were the one accusing me of being narrow-minded. What's to say we're not looking for a woman? As I understand it, the second victim was a lesbian. Have you enquired as to the sexual orientation of the first?'

'They were both raped, repeatedly,' McLean said. 'Now I'll admit that you're the expert on sexual dysfunction, but that suggests a man to me.'

Hilton tilted his head in a condescending manner. 'As it happens, I agree, though not for that reason. There are very few female serial killers, and in the main they've tended to direct their violence at men.'

'So we're agreed then. We're looking for a man. And one who can read, up to a point.'

'Touché, inspector.' Hilton smiled that annoying little smirk of his again. 'Now let's set aside the investigation for a moment, and concentrate on you. That's why we're here, after all. It can't be easy raking over these coals.'

'It would be a lot easier if you and the chief superintendent and the press and everyone else with an opinion didn't keep reminding me of it.'

'That's a lot of hostility for someone who's come to terms with his loss and moved on.'

'Moved on?' McLean could feel his anger beginning to rise again. 'Who says I've moved on? This isn't something you can just leave behind, Hilton. The sort of person who could leave this behind is precisely the sort of person who could abduct, rape and murder two women without remorse. Me, I have to live with Kirsty's death every day. It's a huge chunk of my life. It colours who I am. But I know that. I cope with that. I can't move on. Not in the way you mean. But I can cope.'

'By throwing yourself into your work? By refusing to engage in anything but the most superficial of relationships? Is that coping, Tony? Or is that putting your head in the sand?'

'I don't know what you're talking about.' McLean crossed his legs, sat up in his uncomfortable armchair, even though he knew it was showing himself off as being on the defensive.

'Listen to yourself, Tony.' Hilton's smug smile was back. 'I've seen your personal file. You're rapidly approaching forty and yet you're not married, don't have children. I've asked around, and as far as I can tell you're not gay. So why no romantic interest? Good-looking chap like you, I'd have thought you'd be fighting them off with a stick.'

'I really don't think my private life has anything to do with you, Hilton. As I understand it you're here to assess my fitness for work. Is there something wrong with my performance?'

'Well, you did take one of your junior officers into a dangerous situation, leading directly to his serious injury.' Hilton peered down at his notebook as he spoke. 'And you trampled unannounced into an ongoing SOCA investigation.'

'And Professional Standards were quite happy that I hadn't acted improperly in either case. Strathclyde were warned we were coming, they just chose not to do anything about it. And as for the accident, the fire officer had secured the site. He was as surprised as I was when the floor collapsed.'

'And when was the last time you visited Detective Sergeant Robertson? I understand he's still in the Western General.' Hilton looked up from his notebook and fixed McLean with an unflinching stare. He wasn't smiling now.

'I . . . I've been busy.'

'Busy? You were on leave for three weeks, Tony. And yet you never once made the effort to visit your colleague. What do you think that says about you?'

The canteen had an air of festive bonhomie about it quite at odds with his own mood. The catering staff had strung tinsel and paper decorations all around the room, and the PA speakers trickled out a tinny collection of kitsch Christmas tunes. McLean ignored it all, trying hard to shake the jitteriness that filled him after Hilton's counselling session. It was bad enough that he thought the man a waste of space; worse still when he was right about so many things.

'Thought you might end up in here, sir. I kept a spot warm for you,' Grumpy Bob called from a table over by the radiators. McLean paid for his coffee and bacon buttie, then went to join the sergeant.

'Christ I needed that,' he said after tearing a couple of bites and washing them down.

'Hilton that bad is he?'

'Worse. And no, I don't want to talk about it.'

Grumpy Bob held up his hands in mock horror. 'Nothing could be further from my mind, sir. That's strictly for late-night sessions fuelled by curry, beer and fine single-malt whisky.'

McLean smiled, letting some of the morning's pent-up tension leach out of him. Soon he'd be finished with the sessions, he promised himself. Soon.

'So where are we with the investigation then, Bob?'

'Well, we could do with more officers, but that's not going to happen right now. Top brass are screaming for results, but as soon as you mention manpower shortages, they start spouting gibberish about budget cuts.'

'Bloody marvellous.'

'Aye, that's about what I said.' Grumpy Bob raised an eyebrow. 'Anyway, we've got pretty much all we're going to get from forensics. Our man knew a thing or two, putting the bodies in running water.'

'But he didn't kill them there, did he? Anderson didn't, anyway. And if our man had done, there'd be something for the SOC boys to find.'

'I guess so.'

'So where did he take them? Where did he kill them?'

'I don't know. Could be anywhere, I suppose.' Grumpy Bob thumbed the edge of his mug.

'Well where were they last seen? Kate McKenzie was up Liberton Brae, near Mortonhall. Audrey was living rough in the Grassmarket area. Too much to hope that there'd be a pattern, I suppose.'

'There never was with Anderson, either. He took his victims from all over the city.'

'But he took them back to his shop in the Canongate.' McLean shuddered as he remembered the place. 'What happened to it? Last I saw it was boarded up.'

'Still is, far as I know. We've probably still got the keys. It's not as if Anderson had any family to hand all his stuff over to. Needy's likely got it all stored away down in his wee kingdom under the ground.'

McLean considered the remains of his bacon roll, the thin slick of grease on the top of what was left of his coffee. He found he'd lost his appetite for both.

'Do us a favour, Bob. Go see if you can find those keys, will you. God alone knows I've been trying to avoid it, but if our killer's obsessed with Anderson, then I'm going to have to reacquaint myself with the sick bastard. Might as well start at home.'

35

Eighteen years ago, when Donald Anderson had bought his shop, this had been a seedy, derelict part of the city. That was before Donald Dewar had decided to build the new parliament just across the road. Now flats around the Canongate were fetching stupid money and most of the run-down shops had been turned into trendy coffee houses, wine bars and delicatessens. But there had always been antiquarian book dealers here, publishers too, and a few still hung on against the onslaught of yuppification sweeping this corner of the city. Even so, the boarded-up shop where Donald Anderson had plied both his trades looked like something from another era.

In the early days, not long after the trial, the place had been a mecca for troublemakers, but between the heavy plywood boarding and the thick metal bars McLean knew were on the insides of the windows, no one had managed to get in. Frustrated, they had taken to daubing obscene and threatening graffiti all over the frontage, as if the target of their fury was ever going to see what they had written. Over time, the public had more or less forgotten about Donald Anderson, and now the graffiti was covered over by many skins of bill posters advertising obscure touring rock bands and long-forgotten Fringe acts.

'Just what are we doing here, sir?' Grumpy Bob asked, stamping his feet against the cold.

'I'm not entirely sure.' McLean sorted through the bunch of keys, looking for one that would fit the large padlock attached to the front door with a heavy-duty hasp. He found it, then had to search again for another key to fit the lock in the door as well. It turned easily, recently oiled, and the door swung open silently. Inside, McLean had been expecting the place to smell of damp and mould, but it was dry. He tried the lights and was surprised to find that they worked, casting skeletal shadows from the lines of empty bookshelves. According to Needy, a firm of auctioneers had been in not long after Anderson's death and cleared out all the stock that wasn't sitting in the basement of the police station. They'd be along for that just as soon as someone made the decision that it was no longer needed.

The shop seemed strange, robbed of all the ancient leather and dusty cloth bindings. Still it was eerily familiar, sending an involuntary shudder through him as he stepped over the threshold.

Beyond the shop itself, the small office that connected with the back hall and the stairs up to the flat above looked somewhat more like a room abandoned for ten years should. The old desk was there, and the chair. Two filing cabinets stood in the corner by a window that would have looked out onto the concrete courtyard behind the building, had it not also been boarded up. Everything here was covered in a thin layer of dust, undisturbed by recent passage. McLean opened a couple of desk drawers, but they were empty. Anything that might conceivably have been evidence had been taken away during the investigation.

Through the office, McLean peered up the wooden

stairs with their threadbare carpet to the landing above. The windows on the first floor hadn't been boarded up, but neither had anyone cleaned them since Anderson had been taken away in a Black Maria all those years ago. Now they were encrusted with muck on the outside, thick with spider webs and dangling fly carcasses on the inside. He climbed up, going from room to room, not really knowing what to expect. He'd searched this place before, and nothing much had changed since then. Only the smell was different; where once it had been heavy with leather oil and glue, cooking odours and cheap aftershave, now it was just empty, dusty, slightly mouldy.

Grumpy Bob hadn't come upstairs. He was still standing in the small hallway, looking back out to the shop when McLean came down. It was odd; if anyone should have been freaked out by this place, it was him, not the old sergeant. But he felt only a heavy sadness as he looked around.

'You're going down there, aren't you.' Grumpy Bob nodded towards the closed door under the stairs. By way of reply, McLean twisted the handle. It was locked, and even though he tried all the keys he'd been given, none of them fitted. He knelt down, feeling the wooden floorboards at his feet. In the edges, near the skirting boards, they were thick with dust. But in the middle, where people might walk, there was none. A path had been worn from the back door to the basement, and recently.

'Give me a hand here, Bob.' McLean put his shoulder to the door; it was only a flimsy thing with a single mortice lock. It shouldn't have put up much of a challenge, but there wasn't a lot of room to manoeuvre in the narrow corridor. In the end it took their combined weight to crack the frame.

The smell hit as soon as the door swung open. McLean gagged a little, covering his nose and mouth with his hand as he looked for the light switch. It hung on a cord by the door and he was about to reach for it when his brain finally caught up with him. He fished around in his pocket for a pair of latex gloves. Beside him, Grumpy Bob did the same. Then he gripped the cord close to the top and pulled.

Light flooded the basement below, but all they could see from where they were standing was a small patch of flagstone floor and the stairs. McLean knelt down once more, checking the treads for dust, finding them disturbingly clean.

'You OK with this, Bob?'

'Shouldn't I be the one asking?'

'Yeah, well. Wait up here until I've got to the bottom. We don't want these stairs collapsing under both of us.'

The stairs creaked under his tread, but no more than might be expected. He reached the bottom without accident, then motioned for Grumpy Bob to follow. The memories were flooding back now. Here was the small space, flagstone floors and the low, white-painted, brick arch ceiling; then, through a wide opening, a bigger vault that ran the length of the shop above and out a ways under the courtyard behind. This was the room were Anderson had brought his victims, where he had done unspeakable things to them before finally killing them. One a year, every Christmas, for ten terrible years.

Like the flat upstairs, the room was largely unchanged

from how it had been left by the forensic team all those years ago. They had removed the tin bath, but the taps and drain were still there. A stiff brush on a long pole leaned up against the wall beside them, a bucket with a plastic bottle of cheap supermarket floor cleaner in it nearby. The bed frame still sat across the room, lit by the single bare bulb fixed close to the apex of the central brick arch, but there was something wrong. Ten years ago, the mattress had been taken away for forensic analysis, but now there was another in its place, covered up with a thick, coarse blanket, dark brown and stained. A coil of rope looped over the bedstead, one end fallen to the floor. It dragged McLean's attention down to the flagstones, which was when he saw the blood. And as his perceptions adjusted to take in the scene, he realised that the blanket wasn't dark brown at all. Or at least it hadn't started out that way.

'Out!' he said to Grumpy Bob, his hand still clamped over his mouth and pointing with his other to the stairs they had just come down. The sergeant didn't need to be told twice. They both retraced their steps, all worries about the stairs forgotten in their anxiety to get away without disturbing any crucial evidence. Only when they were back in the hallway and the relatively fresh air, did McLean take his hand from over his nose and mouth.

'We need a SOC team here as soon as possible.' He pulled out his mobile phone as a fat, lazy bluebottle buzzed up the stairs from the hidden depths below and bumbled out into the hall.

36

'You do realise they all hate you, Tony.'

'Eh? What?' McLean woke from his stupor to see the diminutive form of Emma Baird standing in front of him. She at least didn't seem to be suffering from the ill-effects of the previous night in the pub. Her white paper overalls, overboots and hat contrasted strongly with the black and expensive-looking camera hanging from her neck on a thick strap.

They were standing in Anderson's shop, where a couple of similarly pale technicians were dusting for fingerprints and finding loads. Hopefully DS Ritchie was even now speaking to the firm of auctioneers to get a list of all their employees who had been involved in moving Anderson's books. He doubted any of them would turn out to be his murderer; that would have been far too easy. But they needed to be eliminated from enquiries anyway. As did the lawyers who had been in charge of the place whilst Anderson was in prison. And anyone else who might have had access in the past decade.

'Are you listening to me?'

'Sorry, Em. I'm just trying to get my head around this.' He thought back to what she'd said. 'Why do they hate me?'

'Because it's Christmas Eve. You're not supposed to uncover any crimes over Christmas. It's an unwritten rule.'

'Yeah, well. Sorry about that. But just think about the overtime.'

Emma let out a small harrumph and headed towards the door.

'You done upstairs already?' McLean asked.

'Upstairs?' The question echoed between Emma and the senior SOC officer, who had just emerged from the basement door, his feet clacking on the metal walkway his team had laid down to avoid disturbing McLean and Grumpy Bob's footprints. The two fingerprint technicians stopped their dusting and stared at him too. No one was smiling.

'What? You think someone was using the basement as their torture chamber and never went upstairs?'

The SOC officer gave a weary sigh and trudged back down into the basement, shouting instructions to his team. Emma stalked past him, fuming.

'Now I hate you, too,' she said. He hoped she was only joking.

A last-minute frenzy had the city in its grip, as if the previous three months of advertising had been just practise for the main event. People bustled around like ants disturbed by some giant, invisible echidna, each carrying their own body weight in bags, some also leading small, screaming children. It was as close to a vision of hell as he could imagine. Even coming from the carnage of Anderson's basement.

McLean had arranged to meet DS Ritchie outside the offices of Carstairs Weddell, Solicitors and Notaries Public. She was waiting for him at the door, five minutes early, long overcoat drawn tight against the cold.

'Afternoon, sir.' She stamped her feet. 'And I thought Aberdeen was cold.'

'You think this is bad? Wait til there's snow in the Pentlands, then you'll know what cold is. How'd you get on with the auctioneer's?'

'Most of them are off for the fortnight, but I've got a list of names and addresses for the team that cleared the shop out. Spoke to their antiquarian book guy. He was with them most of the time, says he didn't see anyone go into the house. They pretty much cleared the shop into a truck and left.'

'And the keys?'

'From these guys.' Ritchie nodded at the doorway.

'Well, I guess we'd better go and talk to them.'

The receptionist's smile looked tired; perhaps she'd been a little overenthusiastic at the office party. She showed them through into the elegantly furnished office where a dark-suited man waited for them, surely far too young to be the senior partner of one of the city's oldest law firms.

'Detective Inspector McLean? Jonathan Weddell.' He held out a hand to be shaken. 'And you must be Detective Sergeant Ritchie. I'd wish you the blessings of the season, but given the reason you're here, that might seem a little inappropriate. Exactly how may I help you?'

'We're trying to track down anyone who might have had access to Donald Anderson's shop and house in the last few months. I understand you've been holding the keys?'

'Yes, of course, detective sergeant. We were charged with looking after Mr Anderson's estate whilst he was in prison, and with dealing with his will when he died.'

'Can you tell me what will happen to his estate?'

'Everything is to be sold. As you know, the auctioneer's have already been into the shop. Everything is to be sold and the proceeds given to the Children's Hospital. A bit of a double-edged gift, but I dare say they'll take it.'

Nothing for the ten bereaved families, though. Not even a death-bed apology.

'Well, it's something I suppose. He didn't get to take it with him.'

'None of us do, detective inspector, as I'm sure you're aware.'

'Yes, well. About Anderson's shop. I need to see every-one who had access to it, or the keys.'

Weddell picked up a slim folder from his desk. 'I sus-pected as much, so I've had a list prepared. Would you like to interview them here?'

Darkness had fallen across the city by the time they left the offices of Carstairs Weddell. They'd only managed to interview about twenty people; half of the practice seemed to have taken a fortnight off for the festive season and many of the admin staff had gone home after lunch. Still, it was a start.

'I don't suppose we've much chance of getting round to the rest for a few days,' DS Ritchie said as they walked back along Princes Street towards the last hurrah of the shopping crowds. Her breath misted in the orange glow of the street lights, and she pulled her coat tight around her.

'What, you don't fancy working the Christmas shift?'

'Oh, I don't mind that. But you're not going to get very co-operative answers if you turn up on people's doorsteps when they're carving the turkey.'

'Or listening to the Queen's speech. So you're not much of a Christmas person, then?'

'No. Can't see what all the fuss is about, really. Sure, when I was a kid I loved it. Well, when Mum and Dad were still together. After he fucked off things got a bit less cheery.'

'How so?'

'Well, Mum didn't have much spare cash for one thing. Then good old "Uncle" Derek turned up.' Ritchie made the inverted commas with her black-leather-gloved fingers.

'Abusive?'

'Nah, not really. Just wanted Mum, not the kids.'

'Kids plural? So there's more of you?'

'Aye, I've a wee brother, Jamie.'

McLean stored the information away, realising how little he knew about the latest addition to his team. 'So where's he then? Not visiting his big sister?'

'He's a ski-bum. No, that's unfair. He's an instructor. He follows the snow. Right now he's in Canada. Whistler, I think.'

'And your mum?'

'Tucked up at home with Uncle Derek and a bottle of whisky.'

'Dad?'

Ritchie stopped mid-stride. 'Am I being interrogated here, sir?'

McLean felt a bit foolish for being so insensitive. Truth was he was out of practise with the whole idle chit-chat thing.

'Sorry. Force of habit.'

'I guess that's how you get to be an inspector.' Ritchie smiled and they continued walking back towards the station.

McLean couldn't help but notice she hadn't answered the question.

'So, what's the next step then?' she asked. 'More interviews with lawyers? At least they don't need to have a lawyer present.'

'I'm not sure that seeing them at work's going to help, anyway. We're looking for someone who's obsessed with Anderson enough to take his victim down into that basement and kill her there. That kind of person might seem quite sane and normal in everyday life. I'd need to see where they lived to get a better idea of them.'

'So you reckon it could be someone from the law firm?'

'They're the ones who had the keys. And anyway, where else can we start?'

'It's not going to be easy, interviewing that many people at home.'

'I know, which is why I'm going to need all the detectives I can get my hands on, and then hit the list hard. With luck we can do everyone in a day. But it needs to be soon. I don't really want them all talking to each other.'

'So you do want to do it tomorrow then. Strike while the iron's hot.'

'Yeah, I guess so.' Apart from the fact he'd have to justify the overtime to the chief superintendent, and persuade quite a few people to give up their Christmas, it made perfect sense.

'Where are you going to get the manpower?' Ritchie put her finger on the knotty problem that had been facing

McLean ever since he saw the size of Carstairs Weddell's payroll.

'God help me, I'm going to have to ask Dagwood,' he said. 'And after that, I'm going to need a drink.'

The pub closed early. Well, it was Christmas Eve after all. He couldn't expect the bar staff to work all night. Not quite thrown out into the cold night, a hard core of drinkers stood around debating what they should do next before all deciding to call it a night. Grumpy Bob somehow managed to hail down a taxi, and he, Ritchie and two detective constables piled in.

'You wanting a lift, sir?' Bob asked.

McLean looked at the four of them, and realised that he wanted to be alone.

'No, thanks. I think I'll walk. I'll see you guys tomorrow morning. Briefing at nine, remember?'

He watched the taxi chug off up the hill, then turned for home, hunching his shoulders against the chill. It was a dark night, the clouds low overhead and moving swiftly with the breeze. Perhaps there'd be rain later, maybe even snow, but all McLean could think of as his feet marked out a none-too-steady rhythm on the pavement was the tangled knot of circumstance linking the deaths of Audrey Carpenter and Kate McKenzie back to Donald Anderson; of Jo Dalgliesh's book and its mad theories; of Matt Hilton and all the comfortably suppressed thoughts the counsellor was winkling out of him.

Sighing at the complication of it all, McLean reached into his pocket for his keys as he turned the corner at the top of his street. And then stopped in his tracks. He shook his head, trying to feel the fuzziness of too much alcohol, but it was no more than the usual buzz he'd expect from a relatively quiet session after work.

And yet somehow he'd managed to walk back to the burned-out shell of his Newington tenement flat.

37

The street was quiet, but not empty. A few people walked past him as he stood gawping; mostly couples arm-in-arm. All around him, light flickered and shimmered from windows filled with Christmas decorations, or just glowed behind curtains pulled to shut out the winter cold. All, that was, except the one block directly in front of him.

Scaffolding clung to it like ivy on a diseased tree; warning tape flapped in the breeze. The windows at ground-floor level had been boarded up, but on the top floor, his old living room, he could still see through the eyeless sockets and out into the night sky beyond. It was the first time he'd been anywhere near the place since the day after the fire; nothing of his worldly goods and chattels had survived in any state to be worth recovering.

He crossed the road, approaching the front door with its blistered paintwork. The entry intercom panel still hung from the stonework, but the lights were no longer on behind the buttons. By the diffracted glow of the street lamps he could just make out the names, from top to bottom: McLean/Summers; Sheen; Polson; a cracked and scratched button where a decade of students had tried to replace the little paper insert; two empty buzzers for the rented flats; McCutcheon. Not quite sure why he did it, he put his key in the lock. He was surprised that there wasn't a large padlock on the door, even more so when it swung open on the latch. Beyond that, it was like stepping into another world.

The builders had been busy, securing the structure and clearing out the remaining debris. The old heavy flagstones of the entrance hallway were familiar under his feet, but looking up, McLean could see clouds high overhead. As he let the door close behind him, it shut out the noise of the street, cutting him off from reality.

He walked to the end of the hall, where the stone staircase still climbed upwards in its wide spiral. The iron railing had been removed, but he wasn't too bothered. For the first time in as long as he could remember, the place didn't stink of cat piss, just a damp mixture of charcoal and mildew. He climbed up to the first landing, staying close to the wall. At the top, the stone slabs still held, secured by the walls that defined the entrance hall below. This was the core of the building, unaffected by the fire. To either side, where the individual flats had been, everything had gone.

More stairs, and now he was standing outside his own front door. Only there was nothing left of the wood he remembered sanding down and painting with such pride. Just an empty hole opening up onto a suicidal leap. Ceiling height was now open air, and up here the wind whistled around, bringing in the faintest sounds of life outside. He ignored them, just standing on his threshold, unable to enter, imagining the familiar sights.

There were the polished floorboards, slightly warped and creaky. There the coat rack beside the bathroom door, the box room with its curious arrangement for getting natural light. The kitchen was off to the right, at the back of the flat and overlooking the scruffy wee square of garden below. Next to it, his bedroom with all his clothes and shoes; the cufflinks that had been his father's; his mother's wedding portrait in a silver frame on the dresser. To the front of the flat, three rooms. The spare bedroom, where Grumpy Bob had crashed in the dark days after his divorce, and before that, his best friend and one-time flatmate Phil. Next, his study, full of useless correspondence and rubbish in filing cabinets, a computer he hardly ever used, shelves of books he'd never read again.

And then finally the living room, with its ornate plaster cornice, its open fireplace and deep bay window. The press cupboard with the door taken off where his extensive collection of records was filed alphabetically. The comfy leather armchair he'd picked up for a song in that old furniture salvage yard. His fantastically expensive Linn sound system.

The memories came alive, the happy times he'd spent in this place. His home. He could hear Phil singing out of tune in the bath; see the kitchen full of students drinking red wine and talking pretentiously about Cognitive Behavioural Therapy or whether or not Morrissey had sold out when The Smiths broke up. He watched as Kirsty stepped out of his bedroom, wrapped in a large towel, and padded barefoot across to the living room to put on some music. Something classical he didn't immediately recognise, then she padded back again. At the door, she took off the towel, dropping it to the floor before going naked into the darkness beyond.

And then he could see her lying on the bed. No sheets, no blankets, just a stained old mattress with sharp metal springs poking out from threadbare corners. She was spread-eagled, her arms cuffed to the bedstead above her head in an awkward, uncomfortable position, legs wide apart like some disgusting old pornographer's wet dream. Her breasts flattened and lifeless, skin as pale as the winter moon. Her hair splayed out as if it were a halo of darkness.

A wave of vertigo almost sent him toppling into the abyss. McLean clutched at the burnt remains of the doorframe, felt it crumble and give. Instinct threw him backwards; he tumbled over, crashing hard on the stone floor of the landing and rolling perilously close to the edge where the railings had been removed. He scrabbled about until his back was pressed up against the safe, stone wall, hugged his knees to his chest and tried to squeeze the terrible image out of his mind.

Somewhere in the distance he could hear a young boy sobbing. It was a long time before he realised that the boy was him.

38

The station was as quiet as a church at prayer when McLean arrived none too early on Christmas morning. He felt slightly sick, though whether that was from too much beer or the shock of seeing his burnt-out flat he couldn't tell. Either way, it wasn't enough to keep him from work.

If he thought he felt bad, then DC MacBride looked ten times worse. McLean found the detective constable slumped at his desk, staring bleary-eyed at the screen of his laptop.

'Morning, constable. Happy Christmas.' McLean kept his voice reasonably quiet, but still the young man winced at the noise.

'What's so happy about it, sir?'

McLean considered this for a moment, then said: 'Good point.' He pulled up a chair from the next desk and sat down beside the detective constable.

'I thought you were going home after the pub last night.'

MacBride turned his head slowly, his pale forehead sheened with sweat. 'So did I, sir, but Kir . . . Detective Sergeant Ritchie invited us back to her place. Said she had a bottle of tequila needed finishing. I didn't realise she hadn't actually started it yet.'

McLean didn't know whether to feel aggrieved or

grateful at being left out of the impromptu party, but before he had time to mull it over much, the door to the CID room banged open and the object of his indecision walked in carrying a tray of coffees. As ever, she was neatly presented; if she'd been on the slammers herself it didn't show.

'Oh, sir, you're in already. Happy Christmas.' Ritchie smiled and put the tray down on her desk. There was a greasy paper bag too, and McLean wondered where on earth she'd found a place open to buy breakfast. Or had she made them herself and brought them in? When she opened it up, filling the air with the smell of recently fried bacon, he didn't really much care.

'Please tell me you brought enough of those for everyone,' he said.

'It's all right, sir. You can have mine.' MacBride paled as Ritchie approached bearing bag and coffee.

'Thanks.' McLean took the proffered booty, turning away from MacBride so as to ease the lad's discomfort. 'Is Grumpy Bob in yet?'

'Aye, he's down in the canteen rounding up constables with DC Johnson. Thought we'd better make a start.' Ritchie went back to her desk and picked up a sheaf of papers. 'I've broken the list up into two. Those who would have had regular access to the file store where the keys were held, and those who just work in the office.'

McLean scanned the first list, grateful that it wasn't as long as he'd expected.

'OK,' he said. 'We'll split up into teams. One detective and one uniform to each. With a bit of luck, we should be able to get through them all before lunch.'

'What if they're not in?' Ritchie asked.

'Then we'll try again tomorrow.'

'And if they're pissed off at us for spoiling their Christmas?' This time it was MacBride, clutching a cup of steaming coffee and breathing in the fumes.

'Tell them they're not the ones having to work.'

By the time they'd reached the second on his short list of five addresses, McLean was beginning to wish he'd come out on his own. He couldn't quite believe that PC Sandra Gregg, or Sandy as she insisted he call her, had actually passed her driving test, let alone attended any of the advanced-driving courses that were supposed to be mandatory before you could sign out a pool car. It helped that the roads were relatively quiet, but she kept up a constant stream of chatter as she drove, frequently taking her eye off the road to look at him, and occasionally her hands off the wheel to gesticulate. He'd have called it a conversation, only that would have implied that it was a two-way exchange.

Most of PC Gregg's breathless monologue seemed to be fuelled by outrage at having to work the Christmas Day shift, even though she had to admit that the overtime was handy, what with her Kevin not being in work right at the moment, and with all those mouths to feed and the mortgage not getting any cheaper. McLean tried his best to tune it out as he prepared himself for yet another confrontation with festive cheer.

It was odd, really. This was what, the tenth, eleventh Christmas in a row that he'd worked the day? And Boxing Day afterwards to boot. He was used to spending the time on his own, or with one or two work colleagues, ploughing through the paperwork that had built up over the previous months. Sometimes there was an investigation ongoing that needed urgent input, like today. But usually that was visiting a fresh crime scene. Today he had five homes to visit; five families celebrating whatever it was Christmas was meant to be about these days. And to each one he was bringing a little bit of bleakness, even if they had nothing to do with Donald Anderson, Audrey Carpenter or Kate McKenzie. It was enough to have a policeman turn up on your doorstep to cast a shadow over the rest of the day. Especially today. He felt a bit like the anti-Santa.

The family man they'd just interviewed, Matthew Power, was definitely not what he was looking for; far too wrapped up in his young children and beautiful wife. Maybe the next one on the list, Mike Ayre, would be a better match. If their killer was working for Carstairs Weddell at all.

The door to No. 15 Maiden Avenue was opened by a plump, middle-aged woman with greying hair and a florid complexion. She wore a green-striped apron around her middle and clutched a wooden spoon like it was an offensive weapon. When she saw Constable Gregg's uniform, her shoulders sagged.

'What's he done now?' Her voice was a mixture of resignation and anger.

'Um, Mrs Ayre?' McLean tried not to let his surprise show. This wasn't how he had expected the interview to start.

'Aye?'

'I was hoping I might have a quick word with Michael Ayre.'

Mrs Ayre's expression changed to one of bemusement. 'Mike? No' Peter?'

'Mike Ayre. Works for Carstairs Weddell, the solicitors?'

'So Peter's no' done anything?'

'Not that I'm aware of, Mrs Ayre. Is Mike in?'

'Aye, come on in then. I'll gie him a shout.' She stood aside, letting them into a narrow hallway carpeted in a hallucinogenic pattern of purple swirls and wallpapered with a migraine-inducing splash motif that must have been an escapee from the early 1980s.

'Sit yersel's doon in there.' She pointed to what turned out to be the living-room door. 'You'll no' be long, will you? Only I've Christmas dinner tae cook.'

McLean was about to assure Mrs Ayre that they wouldn't be long at all, but she turned away from them, peered up the stairs and bellowed, 'Michael? Michael! It's the polis want tae speak to you.' Only then did she turn back and ask, 'Would youse two like a cup of tea?'

A few moments later, a young man in scruffy jeans and a torn T-shirt bearing the logo of a band McLean had never heard of appeared down the stairs. He was barefoot and his hair looked like he'd been dragged backwards through a gorse bush. Sleep crinkled the corners of his eyes as he looked at the two police officers.

'Oh, aye? What's Pete done now?'

'Pete would be your brother, I take it.' McLean motioned for the young man to lead them into the living room, following behind. A cream leather three-piece suite dominated the small room, angled towards a large flat-screen television. Mike dropped himself into an armchair, ran his hands through his hair and said, 'Aye. He's a lazy wee shite too.'

'Often in trouble, is he?' Constable Gregg asked, much to McLean's annoyance. He didn't need an untrained interviewer butting in.

'You tell me, officer. Last time youse lot picked him up for shoplifting, but the crowd he's been hanging out with I'd no' be surprised if it weren't something worse.'

'Actually, it was you I wanted to talk to.' McLean made a mental note to check out Peter Ayre when he got back to the station. 'About Carstairs Weddell.'

Mike Ayre sat upright in his chair, his back straight, his bare feet pressed down into the thick, orange carpet. 'Oh, aye?'

'You work in the filing room, is that right?' McLean asked.

'Mostly, aye. I do the mail run and stuff too.'

'They ever ask you to check out the old bookshop down on the Canongate?'

'The Anderson place? No. I don't much fancy it either. Creepy, eh?'

'But you knew where the keys were.'

'In the file, sure. I had to fetch it for Mr Weddell just yesterday morning. Why?'

'It's not important,' McLean said, though he wasn't so sure Ayre was telling the truth about Anderson's bookshop. 'How long have you been working for Carstairs Weddell?'

'About six months now, I guess. Finished school in the summer and they took me on. Money's no' exactly brilliant, but it's a job, eh?'

'And in all those months, you never went with someone else in the office to collect mail from Anderson's shop? They never sent you to do that?'

'No.' Ayre clasped his hands together, intertwining nervous fingers.

'Then how do you know the place is creepy?'

'Look, what's this all about? I've no' done anything wrong.'

'I never said you had, Mr Ayre.' McLean fixed the young man with an uncomfortable stare; he in turn looked away, looked at his feet, across to the television, then fixed on the carpet as if it were the most fascinating thing he had ever seen.

'You have been there, haven't you Mike?' McLean kept his voice level, quiet. 'What was it, a dare?'

'You'll no tell Mr Weddell, will you?' Ayre looked up at McLean with a desperate pleading in his eyes. He was suddenly very young, not a man at all, just a boy not long out of school. He might have something to hide, but it wasn't the murder of Kate McKenzie.

'If it's nothing illegal, I don't see why I should.'

'It was, I dunno . . . like you said, a dare. I knew about the keys; everyone did. Mr Barnes usually checks on the place. But there's this girl, see. Shanna. She's into weird stuff. Goth stuff, you know. I told her about Anderson and she thought it was, like, way cool.'

Having overcome his initial reticence, Mike Ayre proceeded to tell McLean all of his short life history, from first getting a job at Carstairs Weddell all those long months ago, to his awkward infatuation with one of the admin staff in the property department. He told about drunken bravado and stealing the keys one Friday afternoon. Going round that evening together, both of them freaking out before they'd managed to, like, do anything, y'know.

McLean only half listened, waiting for an opportune moment to bring the interview to a close. One more name crossed off the list of suspects. He looked around the hideously decorated living room, taking in the cheap glass-fronted cabinets stuffed with DVDs and CDs; the coffee table strewn with gossip magazines; the overly ornate plaster fireplace with its naff faux-Victorian flame-effect electric fire; the mantelpiece with two large portrait photos, one of Mike, the other of a young man who must be Peter.

Dimly aware that Mike was still talking, McLean stood up and went to the mantelpiece, taking up the picture, staring at it. The face was unmistakable, for all that it was younger than the last time he had seen it, and cleaner.

'This is Peter, right?' McLean said, seeing that Mike had stopped talking.

'Aye, that's him.'

'You seen him lately?'

'Couple weeks ago.' Mike Ayre's shrug showed how little he thought of his older brother. But a couple of weeks was soon enough.

'You know where he is?'

'Somewhere down in Leith, last I heard. I've given up asking.'

McLean fished in his pocket, pulling out a business

card. 'Well, do us a favour, will you? Might even help your brother. But if he gets in touch, comes round, anything. Don't tell him we were here. Just give me a call, eh?'

'What about, you know, the keys and stuff?'

'Your secret's safe with me, Mike.' McLean tried a smile. It seemed to work.

'Aye, OK then.' Mike tapped the card against his hand. 'We done?'

McLean nodded. 'Yeah. I'll phone if there's anything else.' He waited for Constable Gregg to haul herself out of the too-soft sofa, resisting the urge to give her a hand. 'We'll see ourselves out. Happy Christmas.'

It was only once they were back in the pool car that McLean realised Mrs Ayre had never returned with tea. It didn't really matter. He was satisfied that Mike Ayre wasn't a murderer; but his brother Peter, well, that was a different matter.

'What was that about, sir?' Constable Gregg asked. 'You didn't even ask him where he was the week Kate McKenzie was abducted. And that stuff about the girl. You believe that? He didn't even tell us when it happened.'

'What? Oh yes, constable, I do. And it's not important. But I want you to get on to control. Put a search out for the brother. If he's got form then we should have a more recent photo of him.'

'OK.' Gregg sounded hesitant. 'Why are we looking for him?'

'Because just over a month ago he was living in the flat downstairs from my place in Newington.'

39

The other three men on McLean's list were of no interest to him whatsoever. None fitted his basic profile, anyway, and it was enough to smell the roasting turkey or see the happy faces of children full of excitement to dispel any thoughts that Kate McKenzie's murderer might be among them. He was anxious to get back to the station and start trying to track down Peter Ayre anyway. The drug investigation had been stalled for months. This could be their first solid lead.

They arrived well ahead of any of the other teams. McLean sent PC Gregg to the canteen in search of an approximation of a Christmas lunch, and took himself off to Duguid's incident room, hopeful that there might be some news on the search. He was surprised to find the place almost empty, just a couple of lost-looking constables sitting behind desks and shuffling papers.

'Is the chief inspector not in today?' McLean could have sworn he heard one of the constables titter.

'On Christmas Day, sir? You've got to be kidding me. He flew out yesterday evening. Won't be back from skiing til after Hogmanay.'

'You got the info about Peter Ayre, though?'

'Aye, we got that, sir. Not sure what we can do about it right now.'

'Why the hell not? You should be tracking this guy down.'

The younger of the two constables looked sheepish, but the older – Cameron or something – obviously had more backbone.

'With respect, sir, we're not exactly working at full capacity here. You know what happens to the shift patterns at this time of year.'

It hit him like a physical blow to the stomach. As if a little bubble of excitement had grown in his brain, swelling up until it burst and took out most of his reasoning with it. Somehow McLean managed to find his way to a chair, to sink down onto it before his legs gave way. There was nothing in the constable's words that should have affected him so, but he felt like he was suddenly back there on the landing outside his flat, clasping his knees to his chest, leaning against the cold, stone wall as the night sky trundled by overhead. And he was in the flat itself, years earlier, clutching the sides of the wide open window, staring down at the pavement far below, wondering if the fall was enough to end it all, end the gnawing empty pain that was all he knew. And he was kneeling in the slow-moving, ice-cold water, slime-covered rocks hard against his uncaring knees, oblivious to the explosions of light overhead that heralded the dawn of a new millennium, conscious only of the stiff body clasped to his sodden chest.

'Are you all right, sir?'

The voice of the older constable, definitely Cameron. Martin Cameron, that was it. Solid policeman, reliable. Should have made sergeant by now.

'Sir?'

McLean looked up, took a deep breath to try and steady himself. The two constables were standing now, moving in slow motion around their desks as they came towards him. Another voice echoed their concern, only this one was behind him.

'Tony? What on earth are you doing in here?'

He looked around, vision blurring at the edges. Move more slowly. Can't quite understand what's happening. What's the chief superintendent doing in today?

'Ma'am.' McLean tried to stand up, but found his legs reluctant to comply.

'You look like death warmed over, Inspector McLean. What's going on here, constable?' The chief superintendent's focus switched away from him for only an instant. McLean tried to pull himself together and wondered idly whether this was what having a panic attack felt like.

'We were just discussing a new lead in the case, ma'am. The detective inspector has a positive ID for one of the gang growing drugs in the Newington flat.'

'Excellent, I'm sure the DCI will be delighted when he gets back from his break.' McIntyre's eyes locked on McLean's, almost ordering him to stay where he was. She didn't alter her gaze as she added, 'Constables, could you give us a moment. I'm sure the incident room won't be inundated with calls if you go and grab a bite of lunch.'

They didn't need to be told twice. The door slammed shut as two pairs of feet legged it down the corridor, hopeful for roast turkey and trimmings. McIntyre's gaze followed the sound of their departure echoing down the long wall of the incident room, then she laid a motherly hand on McLean's forehead. It felt cold and dry to him. 'What happened just now? Tony, you're burning up.'

'Just came over a little light-headed.' McLean moved

away from her touch. He was glad she'd sent the constables away, but he held little hope that his strange collapse wouldn't be common knowledge throughout the station before the day was out. 'Not sure why, really.'

'Would it have anything to do with the hour and a half you spent in your old home last night, by any chance?'

McLean looked up at the chief superintendent, astonished. 'How'd . . . ?'

'DCI Duguid has had a team watching that flat around the clock ever since the fire. It's a waste of bloody time, if you ask me, but I have to let my detectives run their own investigations. They saw you arrive and called it in. Duguid's gone to Canada for the whole festive season, and everyone else was out on the lash, so it came to me. I told them to leave you alone, only to go in if you'd not come back out again in two hours.'

McLean couldn't think of anything to say. He was recovering quickly now, the momentary dizziness passed, but McIntyre's detailed knowledge of his movements astonished him. She pulled up a chair and sat down beside him.

'I can't begin to know what you're going through, Tony. You lost everything in that fire. All your links to the past. That's got to be as bad as losing a parent.'

'I'm fine. Honestly. It was just a . . . I don't know. I just felt a little light-headed. Got up too quickly. You know how it is.'

'Now I know you're lying to me. Look, it's not a sign of weakness to be overwhelmed every once in a while. You've got a lot going on, too much really. I should never have let you take on the Audrey Carpenter case, let alone Kate McKenzie. Not now we've got the Anderson link.'

'Anderson's dead and buried. He's gone.'

'Not up here, he isn't.' McIntyre reached forward and tapped McLean gently on the forehead. 'He's still alive there. And especially so at this time of year. I don't even need Matt's interim report to tell me that. You think I haven't noticed you're always pulling the Christmas and Hogmanay shifts?'

'I'm an inspector, ma'am. I don't do shifts anymore.'

'Well what about all the detective constables and sergeants down in the canteen right now, then? Did they volunteer? And what did you think you were going to achieve, interviewing people on Christmas Day?'

'I wanted to see them at home, with their families.' It had made sense at the time. Still made sense, in a mad kind of way.

'And if any of them complain? You're not exactly flavour of the month with Professional Standards, you know.'

'I'm not going to back off just because someone thinks it's their God-given right to be offended. There's two dead women in the mortuary and their families are having a much worse Christmas than anyone I interviewed.'

'I know. But you're pushing too hard, Tony. Sooner or later something's got to give.'

McLean looked up to see the chief superintendent smiling at him, but it was a weary, exasperated smile. The sort of smile he remembered getting from his grandmother when he was a child. She'd always known when he was overdoing it. Long before he'd ever admit it to himself.

'I'll be fine, ma'am. And thanks.'

'For what?'

'For sending those two constables away.'

'You think that was for your benefit? I just didn't want them to miss out on the plum pudding.'

Joking helped, McLean found. He could laugh and for a moment that eased away the blackness. 'I think I might go and see if there's any left then,' he said, pushing himself up from his chair. His feet still seemed a very long way away. 'Would you care to join me?'

'For lunch? Why not. But then you're going home, Tony. If I have to drive you there myself.'

McLean was coaxing the fire in the library into life when the doorbell rang. He preferred this space to the more formal drawing room, and the chairs were more comfortable than in the kitchen, though at least the Aga always kept that room warm. For a moment he thought it was the chief superintendent come to check he was really at home and not off surreptitiously solving crimes.

He opened the front door to a person he didn't at first recognise. An old man with a pale, pinched face, wispy white hair and beard. He wore a long, dark overcoat and heavy black leather gloves

'Good afternoon, inspector. And a Happy Christmas,' the man said. And then the penny dropped. He'd been one of the carol singers. The one who had turned down his offer of a dram.

'Um, Happy Christmas to you, Mr . . .'

'Anton, Father Noam Anton. I'm sorry to bother you, especially on this day. I've been staying with Mary. At the manse. She mentioned that you were a detective. May I?'

'I'm sorry, please. Come in.' McLean opened the door wide to let the old man pass, not quite sure what else he could do. 'Here, come through to the kitchen. I'll put the kettle on.'

'I noticed you weren't at church this morning,' Father Anton said as McLean set about making tea.

'Actually, I was at work.' McLean switched on the kettle. 'But I wouldn't have been at church anyway.'

'And yet you welcomed us in as carol singers.'

'That's different. Couldn't really turn you away. And I like the music, even the voices. But I can do that without having to believe in the words.'

'You believe, in your own way.' Father Anton's accent was odd. It sounded foreign, but McLean couldn't place it anywhere more specific than that.

'I do?'

'The things you have seen, the things you have endured. You can't help but believe.'

'Have we met before?' McLean wracked his brain trying to remember if the old man had ever been a guest of his grandmother.

'I don't think so, no. But Mary has told me of you. And, of course, I have read Ms Dalgliesh's book.'

McLean froze in the middle of passing the sugar bowl over. 'What's this about?'

Father Anton finally unbuttoned his coat and pulled from its folds a thick wad of papers. Printed across the front page was the familiar name of a prestigious Edinburgh auctioneers and the words 'Forthcoming Sale of Antiquarian Book Collection – Draft Copy'. Scraps of yellow Post-its marked various places.

'I first met Donald Anderson in 1970,' Father Anton said. 'He came from the city to join our community. He was a nice man, quiet, thoughtful, very intelligent. We welcomed him in, even though he was quite young.'

McLean looked at the old man sitting opposite him. He'd have put him in his seventies, yes, but not a great deal older than Anderson.

'Our monastery was small,' Anton continued. 'Easily overlooked, which is exactly what we wanted. There's nothing much left of it now, not after the fire. But I'm getting ahead of myself. Do you know anything about the Order of St Herman?'

McLean shrugged. 'An anchorite sect?'

Father Anton smiled at the joke. 'Fair enough. You don't believe yourself a religious man, and there are few enough of faith who know of us. We are a small order, and our retreat was always meant to be hidden. Occasionally new members would come to join our ranks, but we never recruited. Our mission was always to be unnoticed.'

'Your mission? I thought you lot were all charged with spreading the good word across the world.' McLean twisted the catalogue around on the tabletop and opened it up at the first marker. Lot 42: an illustrated medieval bestiary. 'And what's it got to do with this?'

'Those markers, Inspector McLean, are all books Donald Anderson stole from our monastery when it burned to the ground twenty-five years ago. We had an extensive library, perhaps the most valuable collection of rare early religious works outside the Vatican. The sole purpose of our order was the protection of those books. So when the fire destroyed them, those of us who survived were distraught. We split up, went our separate ways. Travelled the world, as you say, spreading God's word to try and atone for our sins.'

'Except for Anderson. He came here, set up his bookshop and started murdering women. That doesn't sound very holy to me.'

Father Anton sighed. 'I liked Donald, truly. He was a friend for many years. I should have seen the change in him, should have realised what was going on. He knew the risks, more than any of us. But his heart was pure, that's why he was given the task in the first place.'

'What task? What is it Anderson's supposed to have done? You say he stole books from your library. Do you think he set the fire in the first place?' McLean suppressed the urge to shout. This really wasn't something he wanted to deal with right now. Not after what had happened earlier in the day.

Father Anton didn't answer straight away, so McLean let the question hang. It was a technique that worked well with criminal low-lifes, not so much with elderly ex-monks.

'This is hard for me,' Father Anton said eventually. 'I swore a vow of secrecy. I made an oath in front of God. To break that is no small thing.'

'If it helps, I can promise not to tell anyone else, unless it is absolutely necessary.' McLean wasn't sure why he was being so helpful all of a sudden.

'Understand this, inspector. Some books, like those marked there in that catalogue, are rare and beautiful things. They are filled with the devotion of the monks who inscribed them centuries ago. Some of them took decades to complete. Lifetimes. They are special. They can inspire great deeds in men.

'But there are other books that influence their readers far more directly. Not the words within them, not the meaning. For want of a better word, you might call them magic. But they don't contain spells. They *are* spells.'

McLean could see where this was going, felt the stirrings of anger as his mind connected the dots. But there was something about the old monk's voice, the sincerity in his face, that held him back.

'One such book is the *Liber animorum*,' Anton said. 'The Book of Souls. It was our greatest treasure and our greatest curse. Some say that it was dictated to a monk by the devil himself; others that it was copied from words found painted in blood on the walls of the great crypt beneath the Temple of Solomon. Whatever the truth, it is a terrible thing. Those who read it are either driven mad or blessed beyond compare. It weighs your soul, you see inspector. And if your soul's found wanting, then the book keeps it. And with each new corrupted soul, the book becomes darker, more powerful and less forgiving.'

Father Anton slumped back in his chair, as if the telling of this children's tale had exhausted him. He reached for the mug of black, unsweetened tea in front of him and took a long, noisy drink.

'And you think Anderson took this book.'

'Took it, yes. Read it, too. And he was found wanting. That's why he turned bad. It consumed his soul.'

McLean looked at the old man sitting in his kitchen; a total stranger to him. He wasn't entirely sure why he was giving him the time of day, let alone listening to his mad tales. He was tired, irritable from days of frustration, lack of sleep and the slow picking of old scabs.

'I can't do anything for you,' he said.

'But inspector—'

'I'm sorry, but you'll have to leave. I've had enough of people making excuses for Anderson. He wasn't mad, wasn't possessed by some demonic book. He was just evil, and now he's dead.'

Father Anton didn't move, just sat at the table, his hands cupped around his mug, shuddering gently as if even the warmth of the tea couldn't reach him.

'Look, if Anderson stole your books, all you need to do is contact the auctioneers. They'll pull the sale until it's all been cleared up.'

'Those books are unimportant now.' Anton nodded at the catalogue lying on the table. 'In truth, they were never that important, though their value is immeasurable. Call them camouflage, if it helps. They were there to hide what our order was charged with protecting. What we failed to protect.'

Anton picked up the catalogue and flicked it open, leafing through the typed pages far too quickly for McLean to register any of the details within.

'If something good comes of their sale, then so be it. At least the people who can afford them will know how to look after them.'

'So why did you come here then? Surely the tea's not that good.'

Anton didn't raise a smile, but he shifted his gaze, stared McLean straight in the eye.

'I've been through this list a dozen times. Donald never sold any of the books he stole from us; they're all still there. Except one. It's missing, inspector. The Book of Souls is gone.'

40

Boxing Day morning, early. Most of the country would still be in bed, sleeping off hangovers or hiding from their disappointment. McLean sat at the kitchen table, hands cupped around a mug of coffee as he stared out the window at the rising dawn; cold sunlight bouncing off the ice that had crackled onto every available surface. Mrs McCutcheon's cat lay curled on a rug in front of the Aga, purring to no one in particular. Everything else was silence.

He picked up the new mobile phone that was lying on the table in front of him. It looked surprisingly sleek, with a huge screen and too few buttons. He thumbed at it absentmindedly, flicking through the menus he only half-remembered from the demonstration in the shop all those weeks ago. What he really needed was a teenager to show him how it worked. Or failing that, Detective Constable MacBride, since he wasn't far off that age.

The contact list was pitifully small: Grumpy Bob, the station, MacBride, the mortuary. With a wry smile, he noticed that Emma's mobile number was in there; she must have put it in when they were all ogling over the new technology down the pub. Pretty forward of her, or was it justified? She'd slept in his bed, after all, even if it had been without his invitation. He'd even taken her out to dinner a couple of times, and she'd helped him rebuild his wardrobe for an afternoon, which had certainly made the chore of shopping a little more bearable. But any spark that might have been there had fizzled away under his studied indifference. Matt Hilton would say he was avoiding any deep personal relationships deliberately, and the annoying little shit would be right.

Of course it could well be someone else's number and part of an elaborate joke. He wouldn't have put that past the likes of Grumpy Bob.

Sighing, he put the phone back down on the table, then noticed that the screen had changed colour. Somehow he'd managed to hit 'dial' without realising. He snatched up the phone, searching for the off button, found it and jabbed it with his thumb. Hopefully the call wouldn't have gone through; it was really very early after all. Especially for Boxing Day.

He'd have gone to the station, waded through the ever-increasing mounds of paperwork that threatened to engulf his office, if he hadn't received graphic instructions from Chief Superintendent McIntyre as to what she would do to him if she caught him anywhere near the building. Which just meant he'd have to think of something else to do. Most likely wade through the ever-increasing mounds of paperwork that his grandmother's death had generated.

The trilling of his phone took him by surprise. Even Mrs McCutcheon's cat stopped purring and looked up with a disgusted expression. The screen said helpfully: 'Emma Baird calling', so at least he was going to find out whether it was a joke or not.

'Hello?'

'Who is this?' Not a joke. Emma, and sounding very grumpy indeed.

'Ah . . . Emma?'

'Yeah. Who is this? You any idea what time of the morning it is?'

'I'm sorry, it's Tony McLean. I didn't mean to wake you up.'

'S'OK. I was awake anyway.'

Not a good liar, McLean recalled.

'What'd you phone me for anyway?'

'Yeah, about that. Sorry, it was an accident. I thought I'd stopped it before it rang.'

'I still don't get why . . . Oh, right. I put my number in your phone, didn't I?'

'Something like that, aye.'

'Well, that kind've backfired, didn't it?' There was a muffled sound of movement in the background, a shuffling of phone from one hand to another. 'So what are you doing up at – Jesus, is that what time it is? Working on some important case, I guess.'

'Actually I've got the day off. At something of a loose end.' Even as he said the words, McLean cringed. He hadn't meant to come on to her like that, had he?

'Well in that case, inspector, there's a place not far from here that'll be open at this ungodly hour, even today. Lofty's Café, you know it?'

'Aye, I know Lofty's. Not been there in a while, mind you.'

'Well I doubt it's changed. Meet me there in half an hour and see for yourself. You can buy me breakfast at the same time.'

*

History didn't relate who the original Lofty was. Certainly not the current proprietor, who went by the name of Alphonse, and was a good six inches short of five feet tall. A third generation Scottish-Italian, Alphonse had been supplying fine coffee and simple food for as long as McLean could remember, and you had to be up pretty damned early in the morning to find the place closed, even on Boxing Day. As it was, by the time he got there forty minutes after speaking to Emma, more than half the tables were taken. None by the woman herself.

McLean ordered a coffee and a bacon buttie, then retreated to a table by the window, checking his phone as he sat down to see if there were any messages. A couple nearby held hands and looked deep into each other's eyes, oblivious to anything else going on around them and certainly unaware of the old man in a mud-splattered overcoat who was watching them with a curious intensity from the far corner. Most of the other people in the place were shift-workers by the look of them; the unlucky mob who'd lost the Christmas lottery. And there, in the far corner, two beat constables from his own station. They didn't appear to have seen him yet, but it was only a matter of time. Briefly, McLean thought about ducking out of the café there and then. Anything to avoid the inevitable comments that would follow after he was seen meeting Emma.

But then it was too late. The door clattered open with a jangle of bells and a long, heavy overcoat with a mop of spiky black hair poking from the top of it stepped inside.

On the face of it, there was no real reason to be embarrassed about meeting a work associate for breakfast, and yet McLean couldn't help cringing as Emma stamped her feet a couple of times, shucked off her coat and scarf and shouted to Alphonse: 'Bloody brass-monkeys weather out there, Al.' All eyes turned towards her; even the mooning couple broke off their love-in and looked to see what the commotion was all about.

'I like the cold,' Alphonse replied with his curious hybrid Edinburgh–Milan accent. 'It brings the beautiful ladies into my little café.'

'Flattery will get you a long way, Al, but I'm on a promise this morning. Someone owes me breakfast.' Emma looked around as she spoke. 'Ah, there you are Tony.'

If she'd waved and jumped up and down it could hardly have been more obvious. Still, he smiled, stood up and pulled out a chair for her. She slumped into it with all the grace of a dead swan.

'I thought for a moment you weren't coming,' McLean said.

'I thought for a moment I might not.' Emma pulled off a pair of fingerless gloves knitted in a riot of primary colours and shoved them into a pocket. 'It's not nice waking a girl up at this time of the morning.'

'I'm sorry, it was a mistake. New technology and all that.' McLean picked up his phone from where he had left it on the table. 'And besides, if you hadn't put your number in the address book—'

'Oh, so all of a sudden it's my fault, is it?' Emma pouted, but then broke into a big grin. 'I guess you might've been sitting here with Grumpy Bob instead of me.'

'Well, if you put it like that, then it's just as well you did.'

There was a bit of an awkward silence, broken only by Alphonse arriving with coffee and a bacon roll. Emma ordered the same, then turned back to McLean. 'So, was Santa good to you this year, then?'

It took him a while to realise what she meant. He'd long since given up on cards, and hadn't got any presents in a couple of years. There wasn't anyone left to give him any.

'Oh, the usual. How about you?'

'So so.' Emma made a non-committal gesture with one hand. That topic of conversation was pretty much exhausted.

'You didn't go home to Aberdeen for Christmas, then.' McLean realised the foolishness of the statement as he said it, and added: 'Obviously.'

'Couldn't.' Emma rummaged around in her pocket and pulled out her own mobile phone. 'On call. The curse of the childless, eh. We always get to work the anti-social shifts.'

She put the battered phone down on the table and reached across for McLean's shiny new one. 'Still, some of us get better perks than others. I guess that's the upside of being an inspector rather than a lowly technician.'

McLean was about to point out that he'd bought the phone with his own money, and perhaps add something about there being nothing lowly about being a technician, but before he could speak, his phone rang in Emma's hands. She tapped the screen and held it up to her ear.

'Hello? Detective Inspector McLean's phone.' She frowned at whatever was being said on the other end, then handed the phone over. 'It's for you. Grumpy Bob.'

'What's up, Bob?' McLean asked.

'I was going to tell you about the fire, but I guess you're

already there if Emma's with you. Why'd she answer your phone?'

McLean felt his cheeks redden, and wondered why. 'Er, what fire would this be, Bob?'

There was a moment's pause before the detective sergeant answered. Enough time for a penny to drop.

'Right you are, sir. It's over in Slateford. Old factory being turned into apartments. Started about two this morning. Fire crews have got it out now, but, well it looks like another of our mystery arsons.'

'According to the super I'm meant to be having the day off, Bob.'

'Aye, I heard about that. And I'd no' have bothered you. But I thought you'd want to know. There were a couple of casualties this time. Tramps getting out of the cold.'

'They didn't set the fire themselves?' It seemed the most likely cause, and quite different from the empty, locked-up buildings he had been investigating before.

'Not according to the fire investigator, no. I'm just heading over myself.'

'I'll meet you there then. Any ID on the dead men yet?'

'One man, one woman. And no, not yet. But we might be lucky.

'Oh aye?'

'There was a third tramp caught in the blaze, and he survived.'

41

Grumpy Bob hadn't arrived on the scene by the time McLean and Emma pulled up in her battered old Peugeot. He'd cadged a lift when her own phone had rung not long after his, demanding she get on over to a certain suspected-arson crime scene. There was a moment's awkwardness as they both sat in the car, staring through the window at the burnt-out remains of an old factory, surrounded by fire crews and squad cars.

'I suppose I still owe you breakfast, technically,' he said.

'That you do, inspector. Or possibly even dinner. I'll give you a call.' She made the universal hand-to-head signal for holding a telephone. Then she was out of the car and trotting away towards the white and rust-brown SOC van before he had a chance to say anything.

McLean found Jim Burrows, the fire investigator, over by the entrance to the old stone factory building. Its front was largely undamaged; black-soot charring to the walls above the burnt-out windows the only obvious sign of the fire. The roof was intact too, at least in the middle, where a squat tower rose above the roofline. No doubt an architectural flourish built to disguise chimneys or something. A large sign nailed to the wall was twisted and blackened, half-melted in the heat, but there was still enough of it left for McLean to make out the familiar logo of Randolph Developments. He tried to remember whether this was one of the model buildings he'd seen at the offices in Loanhead, but too much else had gone on since then.

'Morning, inspector.' Burrows greeted him with a weary grin. 'I was beginning to hope I'd seen the last of these.'

'You sure it's the same as before? I heard there were people inside.'

'Well, that's different, true. But I don't think they started this. Here.' Burrows handed him a hard hat and set off for the large steel doors that opened into the building beyond. They were pulled closed, but a smaller door set into them hung open, more black soot spilling upwards from the hole as if gravity had been reversed.

'You've checked for hidden basements, I take it?'

'Aye, we're safe enough in here.' Burrows stepped through and McLean followed. What lay beyond was a mess of blackened, fallen beams, charcoal underfoot and the horrible wet smell of a recently extinguished fire. And laid on top of it all, the faintest lingering odour of burnt wool that stuck to the back of the throat like a cheap burger and fries.

'We got in here early enough to save the roof. More or less.' Burrows looked up to the criss-cross of beams high overhead. A few slates were missing, and the skylights had all cracked, dropping their glass down into the litter on the floor below just to make life more difficult.

'Where were the bodies?' McLean asked. Burrows pointed towards the front corner of the building, where a small door led through to what probably had been offices before the factory closed down. A white overalled SOC officer appeared at the doorway carrying a heavy aluminium case.

'You moved them?'

'Thought they were still alive. One of them was, as it turns out.'

'So they weren't burned?'

'Not badly, no. Mostly superficial – face and hands. They're tramps, they were well wrapped up. No, I reckon it was the smoke did for them.'

'Where're the bodies now?' McLean looked around, expecting to see a space cleared, the dead laid out ready for the duty doctor to confirm their condition, state the time and bugger off back home.

'Ambulance out front. Survivor's gone to hospital already.'

'And you really don't think they started the fire.'

'No. They'd set themselves up back there.' Burrows pointed to the small office. 'That's where all their stuff is.'

'Stuff?'

'Bedrolls, plastic bags. One of them had an old rucksack.'

'Makes sense, I guess,' McLean said. 'So where'd the fire start, then?'

'Over here.' Burrows picked a way through the debris. McLean was careful to tread only where the fire investigator had already been. They moved deeper into the building, surrounded on all sides by sagging wooden beams and broken slates, ending up finally in a large, clear area in the centre. Looking up, he could see the ornate tower that topped the whole building, opened up to him by the collapsed ceiling. Ancient duct-work led from the four sides out into the wider building.

'From the spread of the fire, and the damage done

to these here' – Burrows pointed out several cast-iron pillars, their paint bubbled away – 'I'd have to say that the fire originated about here. What I can't tell is how it started. No obvious sign of accelerant, no electrical wires to short out. It's almost as if a flame spontaneously appeared out of nowhere.'

'Just like all the others, then.' McLean turned in a slow circle, trying to picture the place before the fire had gutted it and failing. Burrows gave an eloquent, if unhelpful, shrug of his broad shoulders.

'Just like all the others, aye.'

The Western General Hospital wasn't McLean's favourite place to be. Too many memories, and none of them good. Coming through the front doors reminded him too that he'd still not been to visit DC Robertson, stuck in traction whilst the rest of the world enjoyed their Christmas. Another thing he'd have to do. When he had the time.

There were half a dozen men in the ward, ages varying from about nineteen up to ninety. All had that sallow, sickly pallor that comes over anyone who spends too much time in a hospital, and all looked at him suspiciously as he pulled the curtains round the bed where the rescued tramp was sleeping. McLean was prepared to wait for him to wake up again, but as he pulled up a chair and sat down, the man's eyelids flickered and his hand started to twitch.

'What's your name?' McLean asked quietly.

The tramp opened his eyes, slowly at first, then wide in fear. He struggled, trying to sit up, choking as he did so. The intravenous drip in his arm flailed about, and for a moment McLean thought it would pop out of his arm.

'Calm down. You're in hospital. Remember? You're safe.'

Slowly, the man stopped thrashing around, his eyes still darting from point to point as he tried to work out where he was. His free hand went to the tube in his arm, the heart-rate monitor on his finger flapping wildly.

'You're all right.' McLean reached out and touched the man's hand lightly. Something about the contact must have worked; he immediately fixated on McLean, all other motion stopped.

'Who're you? Where'm I? Where's a' my stuff?' The tramp's voice was hoarse, though whether that was from smoke inhalation or a lifetime of substance abuse it was hard to tell. Now that he wasn't thrashing about, McLean could see his face clearly. It wasn't much to look at, really. He'd been washed, but his hair was still lank and greasy, mixed grey and white. He wore the sort of stubbly beard that comes from shaving no more than once a fortnight. It wasn't enough to hide the deep lines and folds of loose skin of a man who had once been fat, but now was not.

'What's your name?' McLean asked again.

'Who's asking?'

'Tony McLean.' There was no point telling the man he was police. Not yet, at least. He'd get nothing from him that way.

'I'm Tapper. You got a fag?' The tramp snorted, and for a moment McLean thought he was going to spit on the floor.

'This is a hospital, Mr Tapper. You can't smoke in here.'

'Tapper. Jes' Tapper. Gettin' so youse can't smoke any-where these days. How'd I get in here?'

'You were in a fire. Old factory building up in Slateford. What were you doing there, Tapper?'

'What d'ye think? Keeping warm.'

'What about your friends? Who were they?'

Tapper shrugged. 'Dunno. Jes' folk. Ain't many places a man can doss down these days. You find one, you don't complain 'bout nobody's already there.'

'So what happened? You make a campfire and sit around it with a bottle of meths?'

'Fuck off, meths. You wouldn't catch me drinkin' shite like that. Makes you go blind.'

McLean settled back in his chair and thought for a moment.

'But you did have a fire.'

'You're fuzz, aren't you?' Tapper sniffed the air as if his own odour, even after some poor nurse had washed him, were not overpowering any other smell in the ward. 'I can smell you a mile off.'

'You're right,' McLean said. 'I'm a detective inspector, if that's of any interest. But as you can see, I'm on my own. No constable taking notes, no caution. This is just an informal chat. If you help me, I'll make sure that's all it ever needs to be.'

Tapper choked back a laugh. 'That's no' how it works.'

'It is with me.' McLean caught the tramp's gaze and held it. 'Look. I know that building was empty. You weren't doing anybody any harm dossing in there. But you were trespassing, and the building you were in burned down. Your two friends died in that fire.'

'They weren't my friends,' Tapper said, but McLean could see a flicker of uncertainty in those eyes.

'Maybe, maybe not. But you're the one who survived. All that could add up to a whole heap of trouble. We start digging into your background, what're we going to find?'

McLean felt sorry for the old man. And now that was what he looked like; not a tramp, not someone hiding behind a nickname. He was old, and the life he'd lived had been hard. He slumped back against the soft white pillows as if somehow it had finally all defeated him.

'What is it you want, copper?'

'You saw what the place was like before it started. Tell me.'

'Not much to say really. Dark, wasn't it.'

'OK. How'd you get in?'

'Round the back. There was a door they'd not boarded up proper. Might've used a bit of force on it. So what if I did?'

'So you got in. You had a bit of a look round, then decided to kip down in the back. Away from the factory floor. Why not in the main hall?'

'Coz there was a fucking fireplace in there is why. That and the hall was full of all sorts of shite just waiting to go up.'

'What sort of shite?'

'I dunno. Pallets, cardboard boxes. Building stuff. I said to old Clunie at the time: "That's just an accident waiting to happen." Guess I was right there, eh?'

'So how did it all catch fire then. If it wasn't you and your friends?'

'You're the polis. You tell me. All I ken is it was cold as hell when I went oot to take a piss. Next thing the whole place is on fire. Never saw anything go up so quick. We was trapped in that wee office. Only way out was across the hall and you'd have to be mad to try that.'

'And you've no idea how it all started?'

The old tramp coughed, looked around for something to spit into, then reluctantly swallowed. 'Wasn't natural. I can tell you that much. One minute it's like a fucking freezer in there. Next it's like I've died and gone straight to hell.'

42

She's angry with herself, kicking out at the cracks in the pavement as she tries to walk off her temper. What the fuck was she thinking? The same every bloody Christmas. She knew damned well what was going to happen. His bitch of a mother coming round, poking her nose into everything, tutting at this, sneering at that. Just checking to make sure she was looking after her 'wee boy'. Wee boy like fuck. Harry hadn't ever been wee. He was a fat bastard now and if his photos were anything to go by, he'd been born a fat bastard.

Wet, lazy flakes slap into her face as she takes the hill in big strides. Snow. Just brilliant. She can't go home now, not while that two-faced cow's still there. Probably cooking up yet more food for her disgusting son. Why the fuck she agreed to marry him, she just doesn't know.

A car, struggling up the hill — change down, you idiot — sweeps her back with its headlights. Throws her shadow against the wall. Ignore it, just like all the others. Not many now. Not this late. Not today. Everyone's tucked up in bed. Back to work tomorrow. Unless they've got the whole week off. Like Harry's harpy of a mother. Why can't she just bugger off back to Glasgow and leave them alone?

Voices. No, one voice. A man calling to her. From the car. Ignore him, he'll go away. Fucking kerb-crawler.

What's he think she is, a whore? She just wants to walk around the block. Maybe make it two blocks. Clear her head and try to calm down.

'I said d'you want a lift?'

Don't turn around, don't look . . . ah, shite.

'I'm fine, OK?' She can't really see his face in the dark of the car. Is he smiling, or leering? Well, he can try something on if he likes.

'Fine. Just offering.' He winds up the window. Posh wanker with electric buttons and shite. Posh car. It's even got two exhaust pipes, spluttering steam into the night air as he pulls away. The snow swirls around a bit, then settles back into its rhythm. Christ but it's cold. She should have put a thicker coat on.

She hates the winter, and not just because Christmas always brings Harry's mum over. The short days and the freezing rain, they don't help. Makes it so you can't get out of the house and that great blob of a beached whale staring at his huge telly. What did she ever see in him? She could have done much better, surely.

A line of cars parked along the side of the road. White snow starting to settle on the tops of them. She likes the snow, really, even if she hates the winter. Maybe tomorrow she'll phone Shelley and they can go out to the park, if the sun comes out. Leave Harry and his mum behind. Maybe never bother going back.

One car, at the end of the line. No snow on it, just melted water dripping down the sides. Isn't that the one just slowed down? Oh fuck. Last thing she needs is hassle from some wanker out looking for prozzies. This isn't a red-light zone, you arsehole. And I'm nobody's whore.

She stoops to see if the man's still sitting in the driver's seat, but the car's empty. Maybe he's not an arsehole after all. Maybe he lives round here. Aye, right. Then why'd he offer her a lift? He's probably hiding in the bushes right now, jerking himself off, dirty bastard. Well, fine. She'll go home then. Just turn around and—

A man right behind her. Jesus Christ how did he . . . ? Where'd he . . . ? His hand reaches up, holding something. Spray hits her face, cold and wet like the snow. It smells of marzipan. She hates fucking marzipan.

And then the lights go out.

43

McLean always felt that winter hadn't truly arrived until there was a good dusting of snow on the ground. It soon turned to slush in the city centre, but you could always look south to the Pentlands, or across to Arthur's Seat and see the white in all its purity. And the air always tasted cleaner, too. Though maybe that was just the cold.

The city was running at half speed in the week between Christmas and Hogmanay, which suited him fine. There was plenty to be getting on with as it was. His initial interviews of the admin staff at Carstairs Weddell hadn't really come up with anything more positive than Mike Ayre and his goth girlfriend. SOC had found their prints in the shop, but not the office beyond, which suggested they'd only made it over the threshold before running. McLean couldn't blame them; the place gave him the creeps too.

He flicked through the pages of interviews that the rest of his team had carried out on Christmas Day. They all said pretty much the same thing, and he was quickly coming to the conclusion that their killer wasn't going to be found there. Likewise the staff from the auction house, though he hadn't been able to interview all of them. It was unlikely that whoever had used Anderson's basement would be so stupid as to be easily linked to the place. But then whoever it was would have had to've got hold of the keys from somewhere. None of the locks had been forced.

'You got a minute, sir?' The knock on the open door to his office came at the same time as the question. McLean looked up to see DC MacBride waiting to be invited over the threshold like some unconvincing vampire. He had a slim folder clutched to his breast. More paperwork. Brilliant.

'What is it, constable?'

'Initial fire report for the old factory over in Slateford.' MacBride took the question as permission to enter, handing over the folder as he looked quickly around the small office. If he was hoping for somewhere to sit, he'd be disappointed.

'You've read it?' McLean flicked open the file and scanned the densely typed report within. A few technical words popped out, hurting his brain.

'There's a summary at the back. Basically it's the same as the others. No obvious sign of arson, no way it could have happened by accident.'

It just caught fire, like it wanted to burn. No, that was the crazy talk of an old man gone senile. *Like I'd died and gone straight to hell;* the ramblings of a drunken tramp about to hit the DTs. McLean poked around the piles of folders on his desk until he came up with the other arson reports, neatly stacked, tucked away under a mountain of more pressing things to do. Somehow he managed to extricate them without everything toppling off onto the floor. He added the new fire report to the top and handed the whole lot back to MacBride.

'I've heard you're a whiz with the internet and stuff like that, Stuart,' he said.

The detective constable took the bundle of folders and looked at it with the expression of a man who thought he was offloading his troubles, only to find them multiplied tenfold.

'Um, I guess so, sir.'

'Well, I want you to do a bit of digging into all of these buildings.'

'It's all here already, sir. Who owns them, planning applications, the lot.'

'No, I'm not interested in what's there now. I want to know about the sites. We already know that the Woodbury building was on an old close. It's got history. Find out about the others.'

'You think that'll help?'

'I don't know, but right now I've got nothing else.' McLean wasn't sure what it was that flickered across MacBride's face; it looked a bit like incredulity. Well, the lad would have to get used to having his illusions shattered soon enough. Inspectors weren't any more infallible than constables, really. Just older, and better at covering their arses.

'It's either that or back to Dagwood's team. Unless you've got any more leads on Kate McKenzie and Audrey Carpenter?'

MacBride snapped the folders to his chest as if they were the most precious possessions he owned. 'I'll get right on it. What're you going to do, sir?'

McLean smiled. 'I'm going down to the basement. See a man about a book.'

*

McLean bumped into DS Ritchie on his way down to the evidence lockers. It was an accident; they just happened to reach the same corner at the same time, coming from different directions. He was preoccupied with thoughts about burning buildings; whatever filled her mind he had no idea. Having a head in height over her, and considerably greater bulk, he came the better off for the collision.

'Oh Christ. I'm sorry. Are you OK?' He bent down to help her up from the floor, then set to picking up the papers she had spilled everywhere. She stooped as well, and their skulls collided with a comedy thwack.

'Ow! Sorry, sir.' DS Ritchie stood up again, rubbing the top of her head, and let McLean get on with collecting paper. 'I was just coming to find you, actually.'

'Oh yes?'

'Dag— er, DCI Duguid wanted to have a word.'

'I thought he was away skiing.'

'Apparently Mrs Duguid broke her leg so they came home early. I don't think he's too happy about that. Difficult to tell, mind you. He's not exactly friendly at the best of times.'

Bloody marvellous. Not only was Dagwood back early, he was in a foul mood to boot.

'I don't suppose you know what he wanted me for,' he said.

'Something to do with the man you ID'd in the drugs case. Peter . . .' Ritchie started to shuffle through her papers, no doubt finding them in completely the wrong order.

'Ayre. Peter Ayre. Thought I'd left enough information for him to work with. The man's got form as long as my arm.'

'Well, you know that the DCI's like, sir.'

'OK.' McLean sighed. Less than a month in the station and already Ritchie had the measure of the Duguid. Self-preservation came above any other loyalty. 'I'll go and see him. But first I've my own errand to run.'

Ritchie looked at him with what might well have been pleading. 'You can't come right away?'

'No, sergeant, I can't. But if you want, you can come down to the evidence store with me. When I'm finished there we can both go and see Dagwood together.'

McLean shivered as he stepped through the heavy door to the evidence store. It was cooler in the basement than the rest of the station. Just in front of him, DS Ritchie shuddered as well.

'Bit creepy down here, isn't it?'

'Ah, you get used to it.' McLean walked up to the counter where Sergeant Needham could usually be found keeping inventory. There was no sign of him at his post, and the door to his small office was closed. He knocked, trying the handle and finding it locked.

'Not here?'

'Could be in the back, I suppose. Needy always locks his office when he's away from the front room.'

'Needy?'

'At your service, madam. Whatever your needs, Needy can service them.'

McLean and Ritchie both turned to see the sergeant in his immaculate uniform standing in the door through which they had just come. He limped across the room to where they were standing.

'You've been keeping secrets from me, inspector. Who is this delectable creature?'

'Come off it, Needy. Nothing happens in this station and you don't know about it.' McLean watched the sergeant ham a pained expression. 'All right, have it your way. Detective Sergeant Ritchie, this is Sergeant John Needham.'

Needy took Ritchie's proffered hand, enveloping it in both of his. 'Pleased to meet you at last,' he said. 'And might I add that it is a genuine delight to see such loveliness down here in my dark lair. Now, how may I help you?'

'I need to have a look at the Anderson stuff,' McLean said.

'Thought you already had it.' Needy produced a set of keys from his jacket and unlocked his office door. 'That young detective constable of yours signed it out before Christmas.'

'It wasn't the case files I was interested in,' McLean said. 'We've still got the forensic evidence, haven't we? The stuff that was needed for the trial?'

'Of course. I'll go and get it.'

Needy limped off into the depths of the evidence store, leaving McLean and Ritchie alone.

'Is he always like that?' Ritchie asked.

'Pretty much. Some people he just ignores. I think he likes you, though.'

'Aye, I got that.'

'There you go.' Needham was back, bearing a single large cardboard box. He dumped it down on the counter in front of them. 'Was there anything else?'

'No. This is fine.'

'OK. I'll leave it with you if you don't mind. I've a wee errand to run.' Needy limped off with surprising speed, leaving the two of them alone with the unopened evidence box.

'What is it you're looking for?' Ritchie asked as McLean pulled the lid off.

'Inspiration? A bit of luck? I don't know.'

Inside were a number of objects in plastic ziplock bags. The personal effects of Donald Anderson, including the clothes he had been wearing when McLean had arrested him; a rusty pair of handcuffs last seen dangling from a metal bed frame; several squares of stained cloth cut carefully from an old mattress, along with wads of horsehair padding from inside it; kitchen knives still bearing the traces of forensic examination after all these years; a long, thin rectangular strip of cloth with a repeating floral pattern on it.

McLean lifted the clear plastic bags out of the box one by one, placing them on the table in front of him. And there, filling the bottom of the box, was the old book.

The leather cover was dark and mottled, gilt tooling worn by the caress of countless fingers, the sweat of innumerable hands. He picked it up, marvelling at the weight of it. Turned it over in his hands, seeing the ragged edges of the vellum pages through the clear plastic evidence bag. The spine was cracked, but it had the title embossed on it in gold: *Codex Enterius*.

He slid the book out of its plastic cover – no longer any need to worry about contaminating evidence. The leather felt curiously warm to the touch, softer than he'd expected.

'I'll get the lights. It's like a dungeon down here.' DS

Ritchie headed for the doorway and the bank of light switches. McLean could have told her not to bother; he knew damn fine that only the two tubes worked. But he was happier with her not looking over his shoulder as he laid the book carefully down on the counter and opened it up.

Nothing happened. No demon leapt out to devour his soul. No arcane force tried to suck his soul out. The book was old, that much was plain, and the quality of the illustrations as he carefully turned the pages was undeniable. There were scribbles in the margins, too, in many different inks and hands. The content, however, was largely a mystery, written in close, archaic script with only rudimentary punctuation and appearing to be in medieval Latin. *Codex Enterius* perhaps, but not the Book of Souls. As if such a thing had ever existed.

'Damn things don't seem to work.' Ritchie flipped the switch up and down a couple of times to no effect.

'Sorry. Should've said. Saved you the bother.' McLean closed the book and his hand fell to the bag containing the thin strip of fabric. All that remained of Kirsty now that the fire had destroyed their home. Without really knowing why, he palmed the bag, slipped it into his jacket pocket. No one had seen him. No one need know.

'Found what you're looking for, sir?' Needham limped back into the room, wiping his hands on his trousers.

'Not really. I thought this might have been something else.' He struggled the *Codex* back into its evidence bag and placed it carefully into the box

'The Book of Souls perhaps? I told you not to go raking over the past, sir.' Needham whirled a finger round in

264

circles around his temple. 'It messes with your mind, that stuff. I'd've thought you of all people would remember. Those were dark times.'

'You're right, Needy. I just, you know, had to look.'

'Aye, I know Tony.' He tilted the box, peered inside, then at the items strewn over the table. For a moment McLean thought he was going to notice the one missing item, but Needham just shrugged. 'Just be careful, right?'

'Aye.' McLean turned back to DS Ritchie. 'So then. I guess it's back to reviewing those interviews.'

'Now?' Ritchie looked nervous. 'What about DCI Duguid?'

'Ah, yes. Him.' McLean looked at the items he had strewn about over the table, then started to put them all back in the box. 'I was hoping you might have forgotten about him.'

44

'I thought I made it clear this was important, sergeant.'

Detective Chief Inspector Duguid held court in the middle of the incident room, surrounded by a hubbub of uniforms and plain clothes all trying desperately to look like they were busy. Interrupted, he pretty much ignored McLean, instead fixating on DS Ritchie.

'You've been gone almost an hour. What the hell have you been doing?'

'That's my fault, sir.' McLean stepped up, trying to put himself between the DCI and the sergeant. 'I dragged DS Ritchie down to the evidence store on an errand. I wasn't aware that she'd been reassigned to this investigation. I thought the murders took precedence.'

'Don't get smart with me, McLean. It's thanks to your bloody vague descriptions that we've had to drag everyone in here. If you'd told us about Peter Ayre before—'

'If I'd known that was his name, sir, I'd have told you.' McLean looked past Duguid to the large whiteboard on the far wall. An A3 colour mugshot of the man in question had been tacked up to it, with several lines of black marker pen arrowing away to hastily scribbled questions and actions. He couldn't read much of it from this far away, but he did see the words 'Search Teams' written large and underlined above what looked like the names of every officer in the station.

'Please don't tell me you've got uniforms sweeping through Leith and Trinity.'

'That's where you said he'd be. We'll find him, then we'll get him to tell us everything he knows about the organisation he's working for.' Duguid looked absurdly pleased with himself. 'Once you confirm that he's our man, that is. We could've caught him already if you weren't so bloody hard to find.'

McLean walked over to the mugshot, studying the face with feigned intensity. Peter Ayre looked a lot worse here than he had done in the family photo on the mantelpiece back at home. Years of drug abuse had taken the promising school-leaver and shrunken his skin until it clung to his bones like dried leather on a long-dead skeleton. His eyes were black holes, his half-mad grin to the camera showing cracked, brown-stained teeth, some missing. His hair was long, but thin and greasy. Frizzy greying stubble half-hid the yellow acne that pocked his cheeks and chin.

'Well? Is it him?' Duguid barked the question from the centre of the room, and for a moment McLean thought about saying no.

'It's him all right,' he said.

Duguid turned straight away to one of his sergeants, ready to set the search in motion. McLean interrupted before he could speak.

'But if you go charging in heavy-handed, he'll disappear.'

'Don't be stupid, man. He's a junkie, not a master of disguise.'

'He'll disappear, sir. Or he'll be disappeared. Either he'll find somewhere to lie low, or the people he's working for will make sure we never find him. He'll end up in the foundations of a new building somewhere, or fed to the pigs on some Borders farm.'

'Nonsense, man. We pick up junkies all the time.'

'But you don't send the whole damned station in to find them, sir.' McLean tried his best not to emphasise the title, realising as Duguid's face reddened that he had failed.

'This is my investigation, McLean. Don't presume to tell me how to run it.'

McLean turned away from the gathering storm, casting his eyes over the lists of search teams. He spotted a few names that he recognised, hunted around for the board wiper, then deleted all of them: DS Ritchie, DC Mac-Bride, DS Laird, DC Johnson. He paused for a second, then added PCs Gregg, Houseman and Crowe to his tally.

'What the bloody hell do you think you're doing, McLean?' Duguid had relinquished his command at the centre of the room and was bearing down on him.

'These officers are on my team, sir. And in case you'd forgotten, we're investigating a double murder. I thought you said that the chief constable himself was pressuring for a quick result. You might want to consider that before you start bullying them into helping out with your little drug bust.'

Duguid looked like he was about to explode. The room had fallen silent, and McLean was all too aware that everyone was looking at him. He put hi hand in his pocket to brace himself, and felt the smooth plastic of the evidence bag. It sent a jolt of energy up his arm, or at least that was what it felt like. He no longer cared about the chain of command, about being respectful to senior officers, about obeying the rules. They really didn't matter.

'Little drug bust?' Duguid's voice was quiet, almost controlled, which was in some ways scarier than if he had been his usual shouty self. 'Little drug bust? Is that all it is to you, McLean? Just another unfortunate necessity? Would you be happier perhaps if it was all perfectly legal, shooting up on Leith Walk and mugging tourists for the money?'

McLean said nothing, but he stared Duguid down. The incident room held its breath around them, everyone waiting for the explosion like children at a fireworks display. It was the DCI who broke contact first. He turned away, spitting out reluctant words.

'Get out. Take your "team" with you. Just don't expect much sympathy when you go to pieces again.'

McLean let out a long, slow breath, feeling as if he'd been kicked in the gut. In truth, he'd never expected his behaviour over the Christmas holidays to go unremarked, but the thought that of all the senior officers, Duguid was the first one to make the dig filled him with an inexplicable anger. His fists balled without any input from his brain, and he found himself leaning forward, ready to take the older man on. A small voice of reason, sounding very much like Detective Sergeant Ritchie, broke through.

'Perhaps we'd better get on with reviewing those interviews, sir?'

McLean was almost too wrapped up in his own anger, but he saw the intent in Duguid's motion as the DCI spun around ready to tear a strip off Ritchie. He wasn't sure what the emotion was that ran through him, but it was immediate and protective.

'I think we're done here, sergeant,' he said before Duguid could speak. Ritchie said nothing but her confusion was evident as he pushed past her and strode towards the door.

45

He'd noticed the old man loitering in the street as the patrol car dropped him off, so the knock on the door was not a surprise. Since their last meeting, he'd seen Father Anton lurking nearby a few times, but he'd never actually approached the house. McLean was sure he'd seen him about the city too, walking the streets like a vagrant, always turning away to avoid meeting his eye, or pretending to be interested in a street sign, an advertising billboard, a bus timetable. A paranoid man might think he was being followed, but McLean knew that was nonsense. The old man knew where he lived, had sat at his table drinking tea, had told him a cock-and-bull story about a book that didn't exist. He didn't need to follow McLean around like some amateur private eye; he could just come and talk to him.

Which was probably what he wanted to do now, given the urgency of the knocking. Sighing, McLean put his takeaway curry on the counter by the stove and went through to the front hall to open the door.

'Have you found it yet?' Father Anton's grey face gave no hint of emotion, as if the flesh itself had been long-since paralysed. But his eyes blazed with something that could almost have been desperation.

'Come in, why don't you,' McLean said, barely able to step aside as the old man pushed past into the lobby.

'Have you got it?' Father Anton's eyes flashed with

hope, then something dead descended inside. 'No, of course you haven't. I was a fool to even think you might.'

The hall was dark; McLean still hadn't quite got the hang of all the different switches and had only managed to turn on the carriage light above the outer door. It cast long shadows through the glass skylight, picking up some of his grandmother's more eccentric furnishings in a macabre light. Father Anton stood beneath the empty shell of a giant tortoise, fixed to the wall like some bizarre trophy. He didn't move any further into the house, but shuddered with a piercing cold.

'Look, come through to the kitchen,' McLean said. 'It's warmer there. You must've frozen half to death. What were you doing, waiting around like that anyway? You could've phoned if you wanted to talk.'

He led the way, startling the cat, which had been sniffing around the bag full of curry. The large stove cost a fortune in oil to run, but he didn't care. It belted out a welcome heat and always reminded him of childhood. Shooing the cat away, he opened up one of the hobs and put the kettle on to boil before turning back to his uninvited guest. In the light, Father Anton looked even worse than he had before. His skin was white, his lips blue. He shuddered involuntarily every few moments, as if in the grip of some neurological disease. Maybe he was; it would certainly explain a thing or two.

'Sit yourself down, father. I'll make us some tea.' He set about the cupboards, looking for everything he needed, but when he turned back, the old man was still standing, watching him with hooded eyes. His coat was still buttoned up to his chin, his gloved hands shoved under his armpits.

'Look, I don't know what it is you think I can do to help you. But at least have the sense to warm yourself up a bit. I'll give the vicar a phone after you've had a cuppa. She'll come and pick you up.'

'I'm not senile, inspector.' Father Anton's voice took on a slightly annoyed edge, as if he felt patronised.

'Are you sure?' McLean looked sideways at his curry, congealing in its little metal box, so close and yet so far away. 'You certainly seem to be behaving that way.'

There was a short silence, whilst he poured boiling water into the teapot and wondered what he thought he was doing. There was beer in the cellar and whisky in the library. He'd been looking forward to some of both before an early night. Now he was stuck here drinking tea with an old lunatic ex-monk.

'I'm sorry, inspector,' Father Anton said eventually. He took his hands from his armpits, slipped off gloves to reveal white flesh and spidery blue veins, unbuttoned his coat and then sat. 'I had no right coming here.'

'Why did you come here?' McLean poured tea into mugs, added milk, found biscuits in a tin. All the while the old man said nothing. Only when they were both seated did he speak.

'I told you about the book. That was no small thing. I broke a sacred vow to do that.'

'If it's any consolation, I haven't told anyone. They'd probably think I was mad if I did.'

'You might call it madness, inspector. But you cannot begin to understand the mysteries I've seen. Nor the sacrifices I have made in my life. Oh, I'm not looking for pity. I knew what I was getting into long ago. I accepted it, embraced it even. But that doesn't make the pain any less for these tired old bones.'

McLean studied the old man as he took a sip of tea, shaking hands making the hot liquid slop against his lips. Here was a person he couldn't begin to fathom; someone with absolute faith in God; someone who had dedicated his life to religious service. It made him uncomfortable to be in the presence of such undeniable certainty, but he was even more uncomfortable with what he was about to do. He fetched a thick folder from its resting place beside his takeaway, bringing it back to the table and opening it out.

'I probably shouldn't be showing you this.' He pulled out a thin sheaf of photocopied papers and slid it across the table towards the old man.

'What is it?'

'It's the full inventory of everything that was taken from Donald Anderson's shop the day he was arrested.' McLean remembered the exasperated look on DS Ritchie's face as he'd made her go through it item by item, cross-referencing with the list from the auction house, the contents of the evidence locker and the few worthless bits and bobs that would likely turn up at the next police sale. It wasn't unheard of for valuable but portable objects to go missing, but all of Anderson's money had been in his stock, and that was all accounted for.

'I don't understand.' Father Anton ran a thin finger down the list. Most of the books were recorded by description as well as title, since in some instances that had been hard to read. 'This is everything?'

'Every single item. All checked in, all checked out. And

every single book is subsequently listed in here.' McLean pulled the auctioneer's draft catalogue from the folder. It was marked with blue biro in Ritchie's scratchy handwriting and he flicked through the pages until he found the one he was looking for. 'Even this one. The *Codex Enterius*, I think it's called.' He pulled the inventory sheet back, flipping it to the front page. 'And here, taken from Anderson's desk. Contained a strip of cloth identified as coming from . . . one of his victims.'

Father Anton took the catalogue, staring at the neatly typed pages, then back at the inventory. Back and forth, back and forth.

'You're sure of this?' he asked finally. 'This is the book you saw? The book that Anderson was reading when you caught him?'

'It was on his desk, open. He wasn't reading it when I caught him. But yes, that's the book.'

At least, McLean was fairly sure it was the book. And why shouldn't it be? It looked like the one he'd seen; same size and shape, same colouring to the leather and vellum. And at the time he'd not been too interested in the book itself so much as the marker.

Something seemed to die in Father Anton's eyes as he placed first the inventory and then the catalogue back down on the table.

'Then I have been a fool. Anderson must have hidden the book somewhere. Or passed it on to someone else.'

46

The headache wakes her up; that and the sharp pain in her stomach. She struggles out of sleep cursing her fat bastard of a husband for stealing the duvet again. And what the fuck is that smell? Has he shat himself or something? Probably got himself blootered again. She must have had a few herself, judging by the state of her head. Christ, she hopes they didn't have sex.

She tries to grope for the duvet and realises her hands are tied. How could she not notice that, strung up above her head? And how shit-faced could she possibly have got to let her slob of a husband tie her up? Fuck, she can't believe they could have made up and had sex. Not again. Not with that evil harpy in the same house.

Her arms are stiff and sore; pins and needles spring agonisingly into her flesh now that she's started moving. God, how did she get into this state? She rolls over, only half successfully, and discovers her legs tied as well. That's when the fug of sleep washes away with all the subtlety of a tsunami.

For a moment she thinks she's gone blind. There's nothing at all. Blackness so utter she can feel it crushing in on her. She moves her head slowly, wincing at the pain in her skull. It feels like her brain has shrunk in there, rattling around the walls like a dried pea in a whistle. The skin of her cheek rubs against her upper arm, but the darkness is so total she can't even see that. She moves her head some more, trying to roll over onto her side even though whatever it is that binds her arms and legs has her stretched out too far. Fear comes then; she can't remember getting this drunk before. And fat Harry wouldn't tie her up; that was never his style.

She tests the ropes, drawing her knees up as far as she can. They knock together, skin against skin, and she understands that she is naked. The pain in her head makes little stars sparkle in her eyes when she moves. A pity they don't cast any light on her prison.

Her prison.

How did she get here, wherever here is? Memories tumble through her brain: mother-in-law sneering at her; husband fat and useless on the sofa watching the *EastEnders* Christmas special; a row about nothing in particular, about everything that was wrong with her life; and then . . . what? She can't remember.

It's too quiet, now she's stopped moving. She can hear her breaths rasping in and out, hear her heart beating too fast in her chest, hear the blood pounding through her ears. But nothing else. No traffic, no sirens in the distance, no aeroplanes making their final approach to Dalhousie. No wind.

'He— Hello?' She means to say the word quietly, but it comes out as little more than a dry whisper. Her throat is parched, her tongue thick and dusty.

No one answers.

47

New Year's Day was always quiet in the station. A few overindulgent souls were sleeping it off in the cells, watched over by a skeleton staff. Most of the uniforms had put in enough overtime at the Hogmanay Street Party to justify taking time off. Even Duguid's drugs investigation was on hold. McLean liked to think that the DCI had seen sense and called off the Leith raids, but in truth it was the chief superintendent who'd talked him out of it. Unfortunately Duguid thought that someone had gone to her over his head, and he was quite happy to assume that person was McLean. There was a battle to be fought another day.

He sat at his desk and stared out the window at the grey tenements beyond. The sky was much the same colour, tinged perhaps with a tiny bit of purple that promised more snow. It was cold in his office, as usual; his fingers ached as he tapped away at the keyboard, catching up on some of the paperwork that was attracted to his little cubby-hole by some magical power. Perhaps it was because there was so much in here already. Like attracts like, and the paperwork had obviously decided this was the place to be. Maybe it was even a spawning ground for yet more paperwork. That would explain why there was so much of it. Though he'd expect to find more baby paperwork around, in little paperwork crèches. Though of course paperwork could be like aphids. He'd read somewhere that they were born pregnant.

The phone rang. McLean stared at it for a while, uncomprehending. It never rang. No one ever phoned him on his office phone; if someone wanted to talk they'd just come up and knock on the door. But it was ringing. He picked it up, noticing as he did that the little card listing the internal extensions was missing. Gone to find a suitable partner no doubt.

'McLean,' he said.

'Ah, thank Christ for that. A detective at work.' The dulcet tones of Sergeant Dundas on the front desk.

'And a happy new year to you too, Pete. What can I do for you?'

'I've got a man here says he's lost his wife.'

'Is this the beginning of some complicated joke, Pete? Only I've got a mountain of paperwork to get through.'

There was a sound of rustling and the phone muffled, as if the desk sergeant were moving. He said something that McLean didn't quite catch, presumably to the man who had lost his wife, then came back, more quietly.

'I'm sorry, sir. I wouldn't normally bother you with something like this. But, well, I can't get rid of the guy. And his mother.'

The phone muffled again, like it was being pressed against a police-issue sweater. Through the crackling, McLean thought he heard something along the lines of 'He'll be down in a minute. Just be patient, please.'

'You still there, sir?' Sergeant Dundas's voice was once more clear.

'Yes, Pete.'

'Well, could you speak to them, please. I know it's uniform work, but there's no one else more senior than a constable and this bloke keeps going on about his wife being abducted. From the look of him I'd say she more likely just walked out. But he's not going to leave until he's spoken to a detective.'

'He said that?'

'Aye. Well, actually it was his mother. But—'

'OK, Pete. I'll come down.' McLean stood, secretly grateful for an excuse to get out of his dismal office. 'But you owe me one.'

Harry Lubkin was fat; there was no other way of putting it. His face was a mess of loops that couldn't in all honesty be called cheeks or chins. More an extension of his neck, which itself was an extension of his over-large body. McLean would have put him at around five and a half feet tall and comfortably as round. His eyes were deep-set, and circled with dark bruising; his squidgy nose offset to one side. As is often the way with very fat men, he had shaved his scalp, but tufts of hair fuzzed around the edges of a couple of recent cuts. A slimmer man McLean would have taken for a brawler.

His mother, on the other hand, was whippet thin. Her thick-rimmed spectacles and pointed hairstyle made her look like something from a Gary Larson cartoon. If she'd been wearing a twinset and holding a square-edged handbag, the image would have been complete. As it was, she wore a nylon shell-suit and clutched a canvas bag that could probably hold enough for a week's holiday.

The two of them were waiting in the front lobby of the

station when McLean arrived, one sat primly on her plastic chair, the other slouched over two . . . no, three. Mrs Lubkin sprang to her feet when he arrived; Harry stayed seated.

McLean pretended to consult the sheet of paper that Sergeant Dundas had handed him for a moment, then approached with caution and introduced himself.

'And it's about time, too.' Mrs Lubkin spoke with a broad Glaswegian accent.

'I'm sorry.' McLean tried to sound it as he motioned for Mrs Lubkin to sit again and pulled the last chair out for himself. 'We're a bit short-staffed today. A lot of officers worked late last night at the Street Party. Now, you said Mrs Lubkin has gone missing?'

'Aye, the dirty wee stop-out that she is.'

'Mother, can you no' give it a rest?' Harry Lubkin's first words were something of a surprise. Unlike his mother, his accent was neutral, with perhaps the slightest hint of Edinburgh about it, and his voice was high-pitched for his bulk.

'Let's start at the beginning, shall we?' McLean glanced over his shoulder at the reception desk, hoping to give Sergeant Dundas a withering stare. He was nowhere to be seen, but the door through to the control office behind was propped slightly ajar. Pete was going to owe him big time for this.

'What's your wife's first name and when did she go missing, Mr Lubkin?' McLean asked.

Harry Lubkin looked like he was going to answer, but his mother got in there first.

'It's Trisha, and it wis Boxing Day. Wee harpy. Shouted

at me. Can you believe that? Her ain mother-in-law. I'll no' tell you what she called me. Then grabs her coat and walks out. Just gone.'

'Boxing Day? And you've only just come to us now?'

'Aye, well. We'd had a bit of a row, see.' Harry Lubkin didn't meet McLean's eye, instead finding the polished linoleum floor quite fascinating, his chubby fingers even more so.

'A row, I see. Is this a common occurrence?'

Harry looked at his mother, said nothing.

'Whit a temper that girl has!' Mrs Lubkin filled the space. 'An' strong wi' it. You can see what she did to my poor wee Harry here. Black eyes, bruises all over. She fair near broke his nose.'

'Is this true, Mr Lubkin?' McLean reappraised the injuries on Harry's face, then took out his notebook and pen, flipped through to an empty page. He didn't think he'd be needing to take any notes, but it helped with the reassuring act.

'Yes, well . . . She can be a bit headstrong, inspector. But that's what I love about her.' Harry looked at his mother. 'Mostly we get along just fine. Sometimes though, well it all gets a bit much. She usually goes off and stays with a friend. That's why I didn't think much about it. But when she'd not come back for Hogmanay, I phoned around. Nobody's seen her all week.'

Mrs Lubkin made a small 'tsch' noise which spoke far more eloquently of her true feelings on the matter than any words. McLean looked at the two of them and began to understand.

'Do you live with your son and daughter-in-law, Mrs Lubkin?' he asked. She looked at him as if he was mad.

'Me? Don't be daft. I'd sooner take my chances at the old folks' home.'

'So you're just visiting for Christmas and New Year.'

'That's right. Came over on the train Christmas Eve. I'd be heading back tomorrow morning, but if she doesn't turn up I'll have to stay and look after my wee boy.'

McLean did some counting in his head. 'So you'd been staying a couple of days before she walked out. And she shouted at you, you say. Attacked Mr Lubkin here.'

'That's right. Called me some right filthy things.'

McLean turned back to Harry. 'And you spoke to her friends, you say.'

'I spoke to her mate Shelley, aye. But she's not heard anything.'

'Does she have a mobile? Your wife, that is.'

'She left it behind.' The fat man dug into the pocket of his voluminous trousers and pulled out a tiny mobile, dwarfed by his great, fat sausage-fingers. 'Her purse too. Just took a coat and her keys.'

That all-too-familiar creeping, cold sensation began to form in the pit of his stomach. Looking down at his note-pad, McLean realised he'd started writing things down.

'Have you got a picture of your wife we could use, Mr Lubkin? Something we can run past the hospitals just in case there's been an accident.'

It was Mrs Lubkin who produced a photograph from the depths of her canvas bag. McLean took it, seeing a young, red-haired woman, not thin but neither in the same league as her husband. Trisha Lubkin. Quite what she was doing married to the Bunter sweating opposite him, he had no idea.

'I didn't get your address, Mr Lubkin.' McLean looked at the half-filled form that Sergeant Dundas had given him. Lazy sod couldn't even be bothered to process the initial contact properly.

'Liberton,' Harry Lubkin said. 'Up on the brae near the university. Usually when she's angry Trisha just walks up the hill to Mortonhall. That's where her mate Shelley lives.'

And suddenly it wasn't funny at all.

48

Snow whipped through the skeletal trees, driven sideways by a cold, lazy wind. McLean hunched his coat up around his shoulders, trying to keep what little warmth he had taken from the van to himself, rather than sharing it with the rest of Midlothian. A motley crew of grumpy looking uniforms gathered around him, stamping feet and clapping hands together in the deepening gloom.

'Right, you've all got a picture of Trisha Lubkin, and you've each got a list of addresses.'

He looked around the group for signs of assent, but wasn't surprised not to receive any. A blue-faced DC MacBride finished handing out the last of the photocopies and shoved his hands under his armpits.

'Now, we're assuming she walked up the hill. That was her preferred direction, and that's where her friend lives. Most likely destination for a woman in a light coat. I want you to split up and start knocking on doors. She was last seen around six-thirty on the evening of Boxing Day. That's the twenty-sixth for those of you who're hard of thinking. I want to know if anyone saw her, or if anyone saw anything unusual that night.'

McLean shoved his hands deeper into his pockets, as if there might be some heat down there he hadn't known about before. The constables stayed huddled around him in a small semi-circle, looking to each other for reassurance, or company.

'Come on, people. The quicker we get started, the quicker we'll be finished.'

He watched them scuttle off, knocking on doors and peering through letterboxes. DC MacBride stood beside him, shivering slightly.

'You reckon they'll get anything?' he asked.

'Chance'd be a fine thing. She's been gone a week, Stuart. The trail was probably cold an hour after she left the house.'

The sound is so alien to her that it takes long moments for her to realise what it is. Lost in her world of misery, she has withdrawn so far that she isn't even sure she's alive. But now she can hear. The tap, tap, tapping of footsteps, echoing down a corridor. And with the noise come other sensations. First the warmth, all around her like an enveloping cocoon. Then there's the pain in her ankles and wrists, where rope chafes at her flesh. And finally the emptiness in her stomach, the parched dryness in her throat. She breathes shallow, trying to avoid the foul smells that surround her. Has she pissed herself? She can't tell, her skin is so numb against the harsh mattress.

'Help, please!' she tries to shout, but it would be easier to walk on water. Her voice isn't there; just a harsh outflow of breath. And then it occurs to her that the tap, tap, tapping of feet might be whoever brought her here, undressed her, tied her up.

A line of yellow flares across stone arches overhead.

It's only the light seeping under a door, but after the end-less darkness it's bright enough to hurt her eyes. She screws them shut as the door is pushed open, flinches as more lights are switched on overhead. Their buzzing is a swarm of angry bees.

She squints against the glare, trying to see who has come. But tied to the bed, exhausted by the hours of silence and darkness, she can barely move her head enough to see the walls.

'Ah, good. You're awake.' A man's voice, familiar from somewhere. But where? She tries to remember, but it's hard to do anything as the panic rises.

'Please, help me.' It's little more than a croak.

'I was worried, you know.'

Soft, well-spoken, educated. What her mother would have called a trustworthy voice, God rest her naïve soul.

'You slept a long time. Much longer than the other ones.'

The other ones? She cracks open her eyes a bit more, wincing at the pain in her head. Her vision is blurred. Christ, she's still got her contacts in. How long can you wear them before they stick to your eyeballs? The man is standing a few yards away, quite still, watching her. She is suddenly all too aware of her nakedness and the way the ropes spread her legs.

'What do you want?' Each word rasps out of her throat as if it has been posted in a sandpaper envelope.

'What do I want?' The man seems to be considering this for a while. Then he comes closer and she can see he is carrying something. Closer still and he draws up a chair, sits down beside her. His features are indistinct, pink and blue to her dry, lens-filled eyes as he bows his head to the thing he is carrying. Opens it up. A large book.

'I want to read you a story.'

McLean didn't know the police station at Howdenhall well, but it had a canteen and that canteen had hot soup. As far as he was concerned, anything else was just window-dressing. He sat at the head of a table of uniformed officers, all tucking in, warming hands and generally looking relieved that their ordeal was over, at least for now. Beside him, DC Mac-Bride went over the results of their door-to-door enquiries.

'We've got two possible sightings on the evening of the twenty-sixth. Both around seven p.m., both people who knew her as a local but didn't know her name.' He looked down the list, making squiggles against it with a chewed biro. 'The rest is just people trying to be helpful.'

'No sightings after then?'

'None.'

'Anyone see anything else? Any cars going slowly?'

'It's the Brae, sir. They all go slowly. Uphill at least.'

McLean sighed. He knew damn well that it was too late. Trisha Lubkin had been abducted. If she wasn't dead already she would be soon. And they'd find her naked body under a bridge somewhere in the next day or two, carefully cleaned and laid out in the water.

'It's all wrong,' he said.

'Sir?' MacBride's spoon hovered in front of his mouth, soup splashing back into the bowl and over his papers.

'Anderson killed once a year. He was always in control. Never escalated. That's why we had such a hard time catching him.'

'Well, we know this isn't Anderson. He's dead. This has got to be some sick bastard copy-cat.'

'I know. But why go to all the trouble of copying Anderson and then kill twice in a month? Three times if we're being realistic about it.'

'Don't you think that's a bit premature, sir? I mean, she might just have got on a train and gone to London.'

'She had no money, no phone. She didn't get in touch with any of her close friends. It is possible she went to stay with someone else from work . . .' McLean tried to cling to that one small sliver of hope. With the holiday today and tomorrow it was almost impossible getting hold of anyone at the bank where Trisha Lubkin worked. Grumpy Bob was meant to be working on a list, but no, the hope was a waste of time. It was too much of a coincidence that she should disappear in exactly the same place as Kate McKenzie.

'I hate to admit it but I don't think we're going to find her alive.'

She feels strange. Not the oddness of being tied up for God knows how long, naked and drugged. Drifting in and out of consciousness, she can't quite understand the language the man beside her is speaking. It sounds maybe like Latin. Could be gibberish, what would she know? But the words stick in her head, swirling around in her mind, dredging up long-forgotten memories.

Like the time when she was a kid, down on the beach at Portobello, with wee Jimmy Shanks. They'd been smoking stolen cigarettes, then played 'You show me yours and I'll show you mine.' Christ, she must have been all of ten. But it wasn't that. Not her first sight of a boy's willy. It was after that, when they'd been going home and found that dog. Hit by a car, poor wee sod. Lying at the side of the road whimpering. All broken up and bloody. They'd thought it was funny, had taunted it as it tried to crawl away. Jimmy'd thrown rocks at it and she'd hit it with a stick. Why'd she done that? That wasn't her.

And then he's on top of her. How did that happen? She can still hear him reading the words from the book, but he's pressing down on her, hands kneading painfully at her breasts, trousers round his ankles, that little boy's willy angry and large now.

She tries to struggle, but his voice fills her head. The dead dog wags its tail and curls back its lips in a snarling grimace of pain. She can see its teeth, flecked with spittle and blood. Close to her head. No, not the dog, the man. She remembers him now, talking to her from his car, offering her a lift, spraying something in her face that knocked her out, raping her.

'Get off! Ah, you fucker!'

She struggles against her bonds, his mad words fading away for an instant. Long enough for her to draw her head back and then snap it forward with all the strength left in her.

'How're you getting on with that list, Bob?'

McLean stood in the doorway of the CID room, looking out over the collection of empty desks. Grumpy Bob was hunched over a print-out, lines of red ink scrawled through where he'd eliminated people from his investigation. He put down the phone and stretched back in his chair, protests coming from both spine and seat.

'Finished, near as dammit.' He dropped his pen down on the sheet of paper, rubbed at tired eyes. 'Ritchie's gone to the bank to meet up with their HR person. Said they'd go in special. But we've pretty much covered everyone she knew.'

McLean looked over in the direction of the whiteboard wall, where Grumpy Bob had nodded. The photograph of Trisha Lubkin had been tacked up alongside Kate McKenzie and Audrey Carpenter, a little further apart than the two of them. He had little doubt that soon she'd be moving much closer. They really ought to have moved everything to a proper incident room by now, if there was such a thing going spare in the station. And it wouldn't be long before top brass started making unhelpful suggestions. If they backed it up with a promise of more manpower, he'd be the last to complain.

'Well, there's really not a lot more we can do right now,' he said, glancing at his watch and wondering where the day had gone. 'CCTV on the Brae's too crap to lift number plates, and there's nothing as useful as a car stopping to pick up a pedestrian anyway. Apart from the two neighbours, no one saw anything, no one heard anything. I hate feeling so bloody useless.'

'We'll get him, sir.'

McLean looked at his old friend, noticing that what he hadn't said was 'We'll find her.' He knew how to read the signs too, and didn't like what they said either.

'Bugger this, Bob. Let's go to the pub.'

49

With hindsight, it had perhaps been a mistake drinking with Grumpy Bob. They'd not managed to persuade anyone else to come along; too many sore heads after Hogmanay. So it had been just the two of them, revisiting old haunts and falling into bad old habits. The kebab had tasted good at one in the morning; well, they always did. Now though, his mouth felt like some small creature had crawled into it, given birth to a horde of tiny demons, and then died.

The bedside clock said half-past six. Today he was meant to be having the day off, but that was before Trisha Lubkin had gone missing. Sighing, he rolled over, sitting up on the side of the bed. Rubbed at his scratchy chin. Might as well get up, then.

As he stood in the shower, letting the hot water pummel some life into him, McLean tried to massage the thickness out of his head that was more due to lack of sleep than anything else. All things considered, he didn't feel too bad. Probably because he and Grumpy Bob had only been on the beer. No late-night ramble back to the flat to murder a bottle of whisky until the wee small hours. And there was only so much of the gassy pish they tried to call ale in half of the city's pubs that you could drink in an evening before you exploded.

In the kitchen, Mrs McCutcheon's cat stared at him

from her perch on the counter beside the stove as if to say, 'What time do you think this is to be up and about?' He ignored it, making coffee as strong as he could stomach, taking his time over cornflakes and toast. If he ever remembered to actually shop for food, he might have had bacon and eggs for breakfast.

It occurred to him as he filled his mug for the second time that he should have been more hurried. A woman missing, presumed kidnapped by a copy-cat killer. Normally he'd have been at his desk within minutes of waking. Well, maybe not minutes, now he no longer lived within walking distance of the station. But niceties like coffee and breakfast had never really bothered him before. They were things to pick up on the way, consume whilst working. Now he was taking his time. Killing time. Waiting.

And when the phone rang five minutes later, he knew why.

'They've found a body, sir. Up in the hills near the A7. Place called Nettlingflat.' DS Ritchie sounded like she'd hardly had any sleep either.

'Trisha Lubkin,' McLean said.

'It's only just come in, sir. We've not had an ID yet.'

'It's her, Ritchie. I'm sorry.'

'I'm just heading out there. You want DS Laird on it too? I know it's your day off, sir.'

'No, don't bother Grumpy Bob.' Judging by the way he'd been singing just five hours earlier, the detective sergeant wouldn't be much use anyway. 'Swing past here on your way. I'll take the lead on this one.'

He hung up, placed the phone down on the kitchen

table and stared at the cat. It stared back at him, unblinking as he drank his coffee and waited.

In summer, the A7 was a wonderful road for a leisurely drive. It cut south over the Midlothian plain, bisecting the Moorfoot Hills on its way down to the Border towns. Reiver country. Large stretches of it were open to moorland on either side, barely a tree in sight to block the view. Or the wind.

In winter, when the snows came, it was a complete pig. Not aided by the fact that the pool car DS Ritchie had liberated was in dire need of a new set of front tyres. At least the heater worked, demisting the windscreen and giving them a clear view of the snowplough as it widened the single-lane track already cut through the drifts. They still missed the signpost the first time, having to turn around in Heriot and head back. A police Land Rover indicating ahead of them showed the way, and they slithered up a treacherously steep track to a collection of cottages clustered around rusty, corrugated-iron sheds and a large farmhouse.

Somehow the SOC Transit van had made it up the track, along with two squad cars. McLean showed his warrant card to the uniform who'd drawn the short straw and was busy marking out the perimeter of the crime scene with police tape.

'Where's the action, constable?' He shivered as the wind cut through his heavy coat, jacket, shirt and skin, heading straight for the bones. The constable didn't say anything in reply, perhaps reasoning that to open his mouth would mean to lose valuable body heat. Instead, he nodded in the direction of the largest of the cottages, up a short rise. At least he had a hat on, which was more than McLean had thought to bring.

The snow on the bank had been thoroughly trampled. At the top, he could see that it formed the edge of a narrow burn. Icicles hung from snow-capped rocks in the gently trickling flow, and a little way upstream, where the farm track crossed a deep-sided cutting, an old stone bridge arched over still water. A huddle of bodies clustered around the edge, keeping close for warmth. As he approached, one of them turned, revealing the be-scarfed and hooded form of Angus Cadwallader.

'Ah, Tony. I'd wish you a happy new year, but this doesn't seem the appropriate place.'

McLean nodded his agreement. 'What've we got?'

'Mrs Milner in the cottage called us about seven this morning, sir.' McLean recognised the young constable who had shown him Audrey Carpenter's body laid out just below the reservoir not five miles from here. Talk about a baptism of fire. 'She lets her dogs out every morning when she gets up. Normally they come in again after five minutes, get their breakfast. Only today they wouldn't come when she called. She found them down here. And this.'

McLean looked down at where the young constable was pointing. Ice rimed the edge of the water, pooled into a natural pond under the bridge, and through it, piercing it, a naked body was caught in a frozen moment of agony. His initial reaction was one of gut-tearing horror, even though he knew that the woman had been dead before she'd been put there. Something about being trapped under ice struck a chord of fear in him as primal as it was irrational. She lay face-upward, her hair splayed out around her head like a halo and then frozen in place as the ice re-formed around her. The rest of her body was partially obscured, but he could see that she was naked. And he didn't need a photograph to confirm her identity. He'd known all along.

50

'Can't have been in the ice more than a couple of hours. She's barely started to freeze.'

McLean stood in the clinical, clean setting of the city mortuary as Angus Cadwallader began his initial examination of the dead body. Trisha Lubkin looked even colder laid out on the stainless-steel table than she had done in the ice. Only her red hair gave her any colour, and even that looked dead. The gash that ran from ear to ear under her chin was pale, washed clean by the man who had killed her.

'Can you hazard a time of death?'

Cadwallader grimaced. 'Difficult. She'd certainly been dead enough for her internal organs to cool to ambient temperature. But that was hovering around zero anyway, so there's none of the other indicators. Might as well have put her in one of those drawers.' He nodded towards the lines of chill cabinets and their grim contents.

'But you're going to give it a shot, eh?' McLean tried a grin for his old friend, unsure whether he managed to pull it off. He certainly didn't feel all that cheerful.

'I have to hedge my bets, Tony. But between twenty-four and forty-eight hours. Unless she was kept somewhere really cold after death. You know, like in a frozen stream. But if we're working on the assumption this was the same man as killed Kate McKenzie and Audrey Carpenter, well, they'd only been dead about twelve hours when we found them.'

'Cause of death?'

'Give me time. But again, it looks like the cut to the neck. Severed pretty much everything down to the vertebrae. She'd have bled out fast, death would've been quick.'

Cadwallader continued his examination, peering closely at Trisha Lubkin's hands, her fingers. He used a slim tool to scrape away cells from under her nails, handing the samples to the silent form of his assistant, Tracy. Slowly he worked his way around the body, coming finally to her head. McLean stood still, watching and waiting for whatever tiny clues the dead woman might yield up. There was really nothing else he could do.

'This is interesting.' Cadwallader peered closely at Trisha's forehead. 'Tracy, the magnifier please. And dig out the x-ray of her skull. Frontal.'

He took the proffered glass and bent over the body, then went over to the x-ray lightbox when Tracy had sorted out the correct sheet. McLean followed, the faintest glimmer of hope in him at whatever it was the pathologist had found.

'There's very slight bruising to her forehead.' Cadwallader pointed to an indistinct area just above the point between the eye sockets on the x-ray. McLean couldn't make out anything. 'And here we can see tiny microfractures in the bone around her orbits and sinus cavities.'

'So she banged her head on something?'

'Not exactly, no.' Cadwallader went back to the body laid out on the slab, pointed a latex-gloved hand at the points as he spoke. 'There are ligature marks on her wrists and ankles. She was tied up for quite a while. If she'd fallen or been pushed over, even whilst tied up, there'd be bruising somewhere else. A hip maybe, a shoulder. I'd be surprised if her nose wasn't broken. But there's nothing.'

'So what are you suggesting?'

'You'll be familiar with the term "Glasgow Kiss".' Cadwallader smiled.

'She headbutted her assailant?'

'Not long before she died. And quite hard, too. If her own damage is anything to go by, her killer's going to be sporting a right shiner. I'd be surprised if he didn't have to see a doctor about it.'

The pathologist turned back to his subject, a warmth coming into his voice as he addressed her. 'It's a shame it didn't save you, but well done, my dear.'

'You busy, constable?'

McLean stuck his head around the door into the CID room, noticing as he did that the photograph of Trisha Lubkin had been moved on the whiteboard. Now she stood together with her fellow victims, united by their violent and untimely deaths.

'That depends on who's looking for me, sir.' DC Mac-Bride looked up from his computer and stifled a yawn.

'Don't joke about it. You might prefer to be working the drugs case right now.'

'Why, sir? What do you want done?'

'I want you to get in touch with all the hospitals and

GP surgeries in the district. If you can find any, get some uniform to help. Find out who's been in for a broken nose in the last four days.'

'Um, will they tell us that, sir? I mean, patient confidentiality and all that?'

'Probably not, no. But if you can persuade them to let you know if anyone's come to them, it might help us narrow down our location. Try the GPs first, and let them know it's a murder enquiry.'

'OK, sir.' MacBride reached for the computer mouse. 'I take it this needs doing now.'

'Or sooner. Why, what else were you working on?'

'Those fire sites. You were right, you know. Well, the ones I've managed to trace back so far. They're all linked to an outfit called the Guild of Strangers. I've not had much of a chance to work out who they were, but I'm guessing they were one of the merchants' guilds. You know, back in the sixteenth century.'

'Strangers were normally what merchants and craftsmen who weren't members of guilds were called,' McLean said. 'I've never heard of them forming their own guild.'

'Me neither. I was going to ask my uncle. He knows everything there is to know about Edinburgh history.'

'How many sites have you traced back?'

'Four so far. It's not easy getting hold of the title deeds, and even those don't always go back that far.'

Four out of twelve, few enough to just be a coincidence. And even if it wasn't a coincidence, McLean wasn't sure what he could do with the information. It wasn't as if the Guild of Strangers was still active, and even if it was, why would it be torching its old sites? And how?

'That's good work, constable. And take it up with your uncle when you see him next. But now we need to get onto those doctors. Our killer's had his nose broken since last Thursday, and I want to know where he had it fixed.'

51

The phone buzzing on his desk interrupted McLean's frustrated attempts to tame some of the paperwork in his office. Without the little slip of card that identified which internal line it was, he had no way of knowing who was calling. No doubt there was another nutter at the front desk and he'd drawn the short straw again.

'McLean.' He tried to keep the irritation from his voice, just in case.

'If you've got a moment, Tony, could you pop up to my office?' Chief Superintendent McIntyre didn't react to his grumpiness, but he could tell by her tone that it wasn't so much an invitation as an order.

'I'll be right up, ma'am.' No point in asking what it was about. He left the paperwork to go on breeding and hurried to the top floor.

McIntyre's door was always open, but she wasn't alone when he knocked on the door frame. Matt Hilton grinned up at him from one of the armchairs.

'I figured you'd forgotten your appointment, Tony,' McIntyre said. 'Matt says you're doing well, but I don't think he's ready to give you the green light just yet. And this new case . . . well.'

'I . . . I'm fine. Really.' It sounded like denial even to him, but McLean felt he had to say something.

'Then I won't have much to do, will I?' Hilton smirked.

There was no other way to describe the frog-like grin on his face.

'Do? What do you mean?'

'I think you know what I mean, Tony.' McIntyre got out of her seat, glanced at her watch and then at Hilton. 'Forty minutes enough, Matt?'

'For now, Jayne. Plenty.' The psychologist finally stood up, but instead of leaving the room, he motioned for McLean to take the other armchair.

'Just go with it, Tony,' McIntyre said. 'Matt really is here to help.' She patted him once on the shoulder, then left the room, closing the door behind her.

'Do we have to do this just now?' McLean asked. 'I'm really very busy.'

Hilton didn't answer, just settled himself back into the leather armchair. 'Please, Tony, sit.'

Unsure what else he could do, McLean complied. 'So you still think I'm going nuts,' he said.

'Well, are you?'

'No.'

'You seem very sure of that.' Hilton slumped back in his chair, crossed one leg over the other at the knee and pulled a pen out of his jacket pocket. Unlike the earlier session, he had, as far as McLean could see, nothing to write on. Instead he clicked absentmindedly at the top. Open, closed. Click, click. It was a trick McLean had used himself during interviews; he knew better than to say something just to get the man to stop.

'Let's recap, shall we? You've been under a lot of strain recently. What with Anderson's death, your house burning down. Your grandmother dying, too. Not that long ago, and she pretty much raised you since you were a bairn. Now these two . . . no, three murders. Tell me, Tony. How do you feel about these things happening to you?'

McLean shrugged. 'I don't know. Pissed off mostly. Look, I'm pretty sure we covered all this. I really haven't got the time—'

'Interesting. And that's why you argue with Detective Chief Inspector Duguid is it?'

Ah, so it was Dagwood who'd said something. No doubt to the deputy chief rather than McIntyre. Well, it made sense.

'I argue with the DCI when I think he's doing something wrong, Hilton. And when he bullies my junior officers.'

'Please, call me Matt. So you're very protective of your team then? You consider them your family?'

McLean thought of Grumpy Bob crashing on his spare bed after a heavy night. 'Not particularly. I just find that I get better results with a kind word than by shouting. Call it different man-management styles.'

Hilton smiled and resumed clicking his pen.

'You worked Christmas Day this year,' he said. 'And all the way through to today in fact. Despite being told to take Boxing Day off.'

'I was planning on having tomorrow instead.'

'I've checked the records.' Hilton continued as if McLean had not said anything. 'Apparently you always work Christmas and New Year. Why's that, Tony?'

'Someone has to. I've not got any family, as I'm sure you know. Might as well be here and let some other poor sod go home to his wife and kids.'

'That's very . . . noble. Are you sure there isn't any other reason? Something you don't want to admit to yourself, perhaps?'

'What could you possibly mean, Hilton?' McLean looked him straight in the eye, fought to keep his voice level and calm, his rising anger under control. Stress he could cope with; counselling was another matter entirely. 'Like the fact that it was Hogmanay when I found my fiancée's dead body floating naked in the Water of Leith? I told you last time: I've had more than ten years to come to terms with that, and you know what? It's not nearly enough. Call it a work-in-progress.'

The pen clicking had stopped, but Hilton held McLean's stare. 'How did it feel when you learnt of Anderson's death? I'd imagine that must have been hard to take. I mean, that's it. He's dead. You can't ever have your revenge on him.'

'Did you use this technique when you were counselling Anderson? Only it seems a little, I don't know, unorthodox?'

'I never counselled Anderson, Tony. You know that.'

'Oh? You testified in court that he was insane. You spent enough time with him to work that out, and yet you never tried to help him?'

'Anderson didn't want helping. You're very like him in that respect, you know.'

McLean ignored the barb. He'd smelled Hilton's discomfort and was enjoying the sensation. 'It doesn't say much for your professional curiosity, does it though? I mean, weren't you even interested in his motive? You must have asked him about his precious book.'

'It's not unusual for a murderer to shift the blame for his actions onto an inanimate object. Anderson's fixation on his book was notable only for the richness of his fantasy. But then he was a well-read man, he was fluent in many ancient languages. I've never met someone with such broad knowledge. And antiquarian books were his speciality, after all.'

'Sounds to me like you rather admired him.'

Hilton almost replied, then stopped himself, a slight smile playing across his thin lips. 'I believe we were talking about your revenge.'

'No, you were. But if it makes you any happier, I had my revenge when I put the bastard away.'

'And yet you still went up to Aberdeen to witness his funeral. What was that about? Wanted to make sure he was really dead?'

'I told you before, it was a burial; they're not the same thing. Like I said the last time, perhaps I was looking for closure.' McLean managed a smile.

'And did you find it?'

'Not really, no. What's done is done. I can't change the past.'

'That must be very frustrating for you.'

'Not half as frustrating as being stuck here being asked the same stupid questions over and over again when I should be trying to track down a murderer. So if you don't mind, Hilton, I really think I ought to be getting back to that.'

McLean stood up, half expecting the psychiatrist to try and stop him. They'd been talking less than ten minutes; nothing like the forty he'd been expecting to have to endure. But Hilton simply nodded, clicking his pen top and smiling that irritating, knowing smirk.

'Of course. But I want to have another chat with you soon, Tony. I'll be the one to decide when these sessions can stop. There are still unresolved issues you need to address.'

Unresolved issues, McLean thought as he slammed open the superintendent's door, scaring her secretary, Janice. Too bloody right.

52

Father Anton was waiting at the gates when McLean walked up the street to his grandmother's house, still fuming at the short counselling session with Hilton. He couldn't really blame the superintendent for the way she'd bounced him into it. He knew damned well that if she'd told him beforehand he'd have found an excuse not to be there. Well, he'd have plenty of opportunities to stand the good doctor up in the future, no doubt.

'There's been another murder,' the old man said by way of greeting. McLean wasn't surprised when he fell into step beside him, heading up the long gravel drive to the house.

'How'd you know?'

'It was on the television news. The reporter said a body had been found in a millpond. They showed Anderson's picture. He looked much older than I remember him.'

They reached the back door and McLean went in, beckoning the old man to follow him. Mrs McCutcheon's cat was sitting in its usual spot on the counter next to the stove and eyed both of them warily as they entered the kitchen.

'If you're looking for answers then I'm afraid you've come to the wrong place. I can't discuss an ongoing investigation with the public.' McLean filled the kettle then put it on the stove to boil. Father Anton meanwhile took his usual chair at the kitchen table. It seemed almost as if the old man had moved in, and McLean couldn't quite remember the number of times he'd been to visit.

'I'm not the one looking to have questions answered, inspector.'

McLean stopped mid-way from taking the teabags out of the cupboard, his hand still in the air as he turned to face the monk. 'Is there something you want to tell me? Something you know about the case?'

'I've already told you, inspector. It's the book. Someone has it. No, that's not the right way of putting it. It has someone in its grip. Just like it had Donald Anderson in its grip. Once it had taken his soul.'

Groping blindly for the tea, McLean knocked a couple of boxes out of the cupboard and had to spin around to catch them. 'Look, I know Anderson was a nasty piece of work. I know someone's mad enough and evil enough to copy what he did. And I know there's a book involved. But it's not some magical medieval text. It's a shitty little piece of tabloid journalism by a hack called Joanne Dalgliesh.'

He slammed the tea-tin down on the counter with enough force to startle the cat. It was the first time in a couple of days that he'd thought about Dalgliesh and her bloody book. But that was the cause of it, surely. That was how the man who had killed Audrey Carpenter, Kate McKenzie and Trisha Lubkin had started his sick fantasy. If Matt Hilton wanted a reason for McLean's lack of closure it was there, hardbound and with a glossy photograph of a dead murderer on its cover. Just a pity that there was a copy of it in almost every house in the country.

'And that's what you truly believe? That someone can do something as evil as this man has done, just because he's read about it in a book?'

'Isn't that what you're suggesting happened anyway?' McLean poured boiling water into the pot and wondered why he'd made tea. It was easily late enough for a beer, and after the day he'd just worked, he deserved one.

'No. That's not what I said at all, inspector. Weren't you listening?' Father Anton wrung his hands together in agitation. 'You don't read the *Liber animorum*. It reads you. It weighs up your soul, and if it finds you wanting, then it devours you. What it leaves behind is evil in its purest sense; a person without remorse. That's what happened to Donald. He let the book read him, and it seared away everything in him that was good. What was left behind had no conscience, no pity, no empathy. Nothing.'

The old monk had risen half out of his seat as he spoke, and slumped back down as if his words had drained him of energy. In the silence that followed, McLean poured tea and thought it seemed a very trite thing to do. Finally, as he pushed a mug across the table, he said: 'There is no book. I've checked the records. I told you before. One of my sergeants even went through the stores to see if we'd accidentally missed a box. It's not there. It never was. I don't know why I even listen to you going on about it, except that you knew Anderson. I hoped that maybe you'd have been able to give me a few insights into how he became what he was.'

Father Anton took a sip of his tea. 'I thought I had.'

McLean sat down at the table, drank from his own

mug. 'Why do you keep coming back here?' he asked. 'What do you want from me?'

'I've been doing a bit of investigation myself,' Father Anton said, ignoring the question. 'Been to pretty much every antique shop and antiquarian bookseller in the city. Of course none of them have even heard of the book, but that wasn't what I was looking for.'

'What were you looking for, then?'

'You'd be surprised how many of them remember Anderson. He wasn't much liked, but they respected him. He knew a lot about books. Knew a lot back when he was part of our order – that's why he ended up as our librarian. Some of the booksellers I spoke to used to deal with him. A couple of them still had some books he'd taken from the order. Books I thought had burned.'

'We know he screwed your order,' McLean said. 'You told me that before.'

'But he kept almost all of the books he stole, only sold those that weren't of great significance to us. He lived quite frugally. It was never about the money.'

'You know, if you can prove that those books belonged to you, you could stop the sale. You could start again. I'm sure some—'

'The Order of St Herman is dead, inspector. We failed in our sacred duty, the one reason for our existence. I go on because there is a terrible wrong that needs to be righted. The book was once my responsibility and I can't rest until it is either found or destroyed.'

McLean waited for Father Anton to say more, but the old monk seemed to have run out of breath.

'We're going to catch whoever killed these women. We've got clues we can follow up. Good, solid police work. If it turns out he's got some ancient biblical text hidden somewhere, we'll find it. And when we do, I'll call you in to tell us what to do with it. OK?'

'It's not enough.' The old man stood up, buttoned his coat and pulled on his gloves. Reached for his hat. 'Our order is gone. The books we collected will be spread to the four corners of the world and maybe a little good will come of that. But you will find the *Liber animorum*, inspector. I have no doubt of that. And when you do, you must destroy it.'

McLean watched the old man shuffle off down the driveway about ten minutes later. Why did he keep on coming back? And why did he put up with the priest? It wasn't as if McLean had any great respect for the Church. Maybe it was because Anton had known Donald Anderson, back before the bookseller had turned into a murdering rapist. Or maybe it was the dreams.

The house was cold and dark when he stepped back inside, the hall filled with silent shadows. There was a central heating system, but it struggled to make any great impact on such a big space. There were fireplaces in all the major rooms, too. At this time of year they should all have been lit, attended by a servant who lived in the tiny box room up in the attic. For some reason McLean found the idea of having a servant amusing, and he smiled to himself as he went back to the relative warmth of the kitchen. He could certainly afford to employ someone, but he couldn't get comfortable with the idea of having another person living under his roof with him. He'd been alone too long.

Mrs McCutcheon's cat left its favoured spot by the stove and twined itself around his legs as he wandered from cupboard to fridge in search of something to eat. There were fliers pinned to the corkboard by the telephone with numbers for local takeaways, but for the moment he couldn't make up his mind which unhealthy option he would go for. Instead, he set about the task of cleaning up the tea things, and the breakfast things that sat by the sink. And the remains of the last couple of meals he'd eaten in the library, sat by the fire. There was laundry to do too, something he'd never had a problem with back in his flat in Newington. But here, with all this space to spread out into, he realised he'd fallen into bad habits. Tomorrow he'd either have to get the iron out or head into town and buy yet more new shirts.

The doorbell rang as he was twisting the dial around on the washing machine. Non-fast coloureds, thirty degrees, forty-five minutes. McLean hit the 'On' button, hearing the whoosh of water as it flooded into the drum, then went back out through the kitchen and to the front door, wondering what the old man had forgotten to ask him this time. He got the switches right, flooding the hall with light first, then the porch and the area outside. But it wasn't Father Anton who stood expectantly in the cold night air, waiting to be invited in.

It was Emma. And she had brought pizza.

'A little birdie told me it was your day off tomorrow,' she said.

53

A creeping chill woke him slowly from dreams of nothing. McLean rolled over in the near-darkness of impending dawn, groping for the duvet and found something altogether more substantial blocking his way. Someone was lying in the bed beside him, hogging all the covers and curled up so tight that only the top of their head protruded. In the confusion of waking, it took him a long time to work out what was going on. Then the memories began to re-form, bringing with them a bitter-sweet mixture of happiness and guilt.

Emma's short hair was a mess, spiking all over the place, and her skin was so pale in the growing light as to almost merge into the soft white pillow. Despite the cold that sent occasional shivers down him, he just lay there, staring at her and listening to the soft snore of her breathing. Slowly, she opened her eyes, and without moving, looked straight at him. A smile grew on her lopsided lips and a hand snaked out from under the duvet. He shivered as it touched his side, hot for an instant, and was then hastily withdrawn.

'You're freezing,' she said, her voice hoarse and croaky with sleep. McLean didn't think he'd ever heard anything sound quite so erotic.

'That's because you've stolen the duvet.'

There was a pause, then the whole mound of bedding rose up, engulfing him in the warm scent of Emma Baird.

'You know, you really should go shopping once in a while.'

Much later. They were breakfasting on black coffee and cold pizza from the night before. There would have been enough milk, McLean thought, at least for a quick bowl of cereal. But that was before Father Anton had come round and drunk tea. He'd not been expecting Emma at all. Not that he was begrudging her unannounced visit, far from it. Black coffee and cold pizza were just fine from where he was looking.

'It was much easier when I was back in Newington,' he said. 'I could just pop out to Ali's round the corner. There's nothing near here at all.'

'That's the privilege of living in one of the city's most upmarket areas.'

'I could always get stuff delivered, I suppose. Don't the supermarkets do that nowadays?'

Emma mentioned something about squashed bananas, but McLean's attention was diverted by the clatter of mail falling through the letterbox. He padded barefoot across the hall, wishing he had slippers or at least underfloor heating for the cold, stone tiles, and rescued the pile of letters from the mat. It was unusual for him to be at home when the postman called, so it was a rather novel experience to leaf through the mail while it was still fresh.

A number of companies wished to invite him to take out credit cards; one even suggested his grandmother consolidate all her loans into one, at a particularly usurious rate. That she had been dead half a year, and in a coma for eighteen months before that, didn't seem to have registered on whatever mailing database the company was using. Which didn't speak well for any customer service they might be hoping to offer.

Hidden among the shiny plastic-wrapped catalogues and fliers, McLean found a hefty, plain, A4 envelope, with his name and address handwritten, a motley collection of Christmas stamps stuck in the top right corner. Dropping the rest of his mail on the kitchen table, he broke open the seal of this one with his thumb and ripped the paper apart.

'What is it?' Emma asked, idly leafing through the pile as if she lived here too. McLean scanned down the loose page of a letter, then handed over a series of slim brochures to her before reading out loud.

'"Dear Mr McLean. Thank you for your recent enquiry about Alfa Romeo cars."' He looked up from the letter. 'I wasn't aware that I had made a recent enquiry. Must've been Ritchie then.' McLean turned back to the letter, but not before he had seen what looked like a dark cloud pass over Emma's face.

'Ritchie?' she asked.

'Detective Sergeant Ritchie. She transferred down from Aberdeen just before Christmas. You might have met her when you were still up there.'

'Oh, that Ritchie. Yeah, I remember her.' There was something just a little too casual about the way Emma said it. 'But she was just a constable then, not long out of uniform. So she made DS already? What's she doing sending you car brochures for?'

'No idea. Probably something to do with seeing me driving around my gran's old car. She might've mentioned something about it when we were all down the pub one evening.' McLean shrugged. 'Seems there's a new show-room being opened. Today as it happens. They've invited me along to have a glass of wine and some cheese. Maybe buy a car, I'm sure.'

'Well, you do need a car. Something a bit more practical than that old banger of yours.'

'Banger? It's a classic.' McLean tried not to take offence, drank some more of his coffee. It wasn't as nice cold. 'But you're right. If I'm going to stay here, I'll have to get a car. It'll have to wait though. I've got to go to the station.'

The cloud over Emma's face darkened. 'It's your day off, Tony. '

'I know. But I'm in the middle of a case.'

'Why do I get the feeling you're always in the middle of a case? When was the last time you weren't actively inves-tigating something?'

McLean opened his mouth to answer, then shut it again when his brain failed to come up with an answer.

'What if I told you that Chief Superintendent McIn-tyre herself asked me to make sure you took some time off?' Emma asked.

McLean opened his mouth again, and once more no words came out. Instead he felt a flush of embarrassment colour his face, tinged perhaps with a bit of anger. Was that why she'd dropped round? Not because she cared, but because she was told to?

'OK, so that's not quite true.' Emma dropped the bro-chure back onto the table, stood up and walked over to where McLean was sitting. 'But she did tell me she was worried about you, Tony.' She bent over and kissed the top of his head. 'The rest was my idea.'

She smelled of soap and coffee, mothballs from one of his grandfather's old shirts which she had decided to wear. Just having her stand close to him made his heart thump louder in his chest, made him feel like a schoolboy all over again. There was no arguing with that. But there was no arguing with three dead women, either.

'Jayne McIntyre's not my mother,' he said. 'Everyone worries too much. I'm fine, honest. I don't really need a day off. Not when there's a nutter out there needs catching.'

Emma looked like she was going to explode, but the phone cut her off. She stalked out of the kitchen, trailed by Mrs McCutcheon's cat, as he answered.

'McLean.'

'Oh, good. I'm glad I got you in, sir.' MacBride won the competition for being the first of his team to phone in on his day off.

'What can I do for you, constable?'

'I was just collating the results from my phone-around of the hospitals, sir. When I got to three hundred, I thought I'd better check you still wanted me to go ahead.'

'Three hundred broken noses?' McLean pinched the bridge of his own, feeling a sympathetic ache.

'Well, they're not all broken, sir. But that's how many people have been seen with nose-related injuries since last Wednesday. Apparently they're very common at this time of year. When the pavements get all icy.'

'OK, Stuart. You'd better drop it. Not one of my better ideas, I guess.' McLean told the DC to go back to his historical analysis of the fire sites, then hung up. Emma had returned, fully dressed, and was watching him from the doorway.

'You did tell the station you were having the day off.'

'Yes, I did. But that doesn't mean they can't phone me. Your lot would call you if there was an emergency.'

Emma made a noise that sounded exactly like 'hmph'. 'What did young Stuart want anyway? Who's broken their nose?'

He explained about Trisha Lubkin and the bruising on her forehead. 'I don't know what I was thinking,' he added. 'I thought maybe there'd be a couple of dozen cases city-wide. We could probably have done something with the information. Narrowed down our search. Stupid idea, really. It's not as if doctors are going to hand us out lists of their patients' names.'

'It was worth pursuing, surely. What if there'd only been one?'

'Well, there were over three hundred before MacBride gave up counting. Seems the good citizens of Edinburgh can't stop bashing themselves in the head.' McLean nodded at Emma, trying to keep the disappointment from his voice. 'You heading out, then?'

She slumped into a chair. 'I thought we might go to town. Do a bit of shopping, maybe get some lunch. You know, spend a little time together?'

It sounded like a good plan, but the phone interrupted McLean before he could respond. Wearily he crossed the kitchen, picked up the receiver.

'McLean.'

DS Ritchie's voice sounded hollow through the

handset. 'Ah, sir. Glad I got you and not the answering machine. I didn't want to bother you on your day off, but . . .' She tailed off and McLean could hear raised voices in the background, though he couldn't make out the actual words.

'Is everything all right there, sergeant?' he asked. Ritchie didn't answer at first, but the voice in the background increased in volume enough for McLean to recognise it. Duguid, and winding himself up into a frenzy by the sound of things.

'It's DCI Duguid, sir.' Ritchie spoke in little more than a whisper and McLean had to clamp the handset to his ear to hear properly. Doing that also meant he caught the occasional word from Dagwood. 'Incompetent' was in there, along with 'lazy' and 'waste of police time'.

'He's tearing a strip off DC MacBride right now. Already sent DC Simmons back up to his incident room to help them with his bloody drugs investigation. Says if your caseload's so light you can afford to take a day off, then you don't need the manpower.'

'That's a bit bloody rich. He was on holiday until bloody Hogmanay.' McLean glanced at his watch. Late morning and Emma's talk of lunch somewhere had been really rather appealing. Trust Dagwood to bugger that up.

'OK. I'll come in and sort it out.'

In the background, Duguid's tirade began to fade away, no doubt as he chased poor DC MacBride up the corridor.

'Thanks, sir. I feel a bit of a snitch telling you, but, well, he's a DCI. I can't exactly refuse to do what he tells me.'

'It's OK. I know what he's like. I'll be with you in about an hour.'

He hung up and turned back to Emma, all ready to tell her about the conversation, and ask if she could possibly run him to the station. Her thunderous look dried the words up in his throat.

'It's supposed to be your day off.' Dry ice would have been warmer. She turned away, heading for the hallway.

'Look, Emma. It's not my fault. Dagwood's being an arse and—'

'So little miss Torry phones up and you just drop everything. Go scurrying off to save the damsel in distress.'

'It's not like that. He's jeopardising my investigation. I can't just leave—'

'But what about us?' She was at the door now, pulling it open and letting in the cold winter air. 'What about lunch? Don't you even know how to relax?'

'I won't be long. If you could just . . .'

Emma pulled her car keys from her bag and stalked across to her little blue Peugeot, parked on the gravel driveway. McLean followed, then realised that he was wearing only socks and the ground was very cold. He barely whispered the words, knowing they were futile.

'. . . maybe give me a lift?'

'Oh no, inspector.' Emma pulled open the door, threw herself behind the wheel. 'If you want to head back to your precious work, you can make your own bloody way.'

The engine roared into life, gears crunched and gravel spun. And then she was gone, leaving him shivering in the cold, grey morning.

54

McLean found an empty CID room when he finally arrived at the station, so he went in search of bodies elsewhere. A number of the smaller incident rooms were occupied by uniforms, trying hard to look like they were very busy. He hunted around for any of his team in all the usual hideouts before finally accepting the inevitable and heading up to the one place he really didn't want to go.

It was a study of desperate calm. The room DCI Duguid had commandeered for co-ordinating the drugs investigation might have been the largest available in the station, but it felt tiny. Desks had been crammed into every available inch of space; computer screens lined the window wall – God alone knew where they'd come from; and what seemed like more than the station's entire roster of uniform and plain-clothes officers busied themselves with moving bits of paper around. Standing in the doorway, unwilling to commit himself further, McLean spotted DC MacBride in discussion with DI Langley from the drugs squad over on the far side of the room beside the whiteboards. He hoped that they might notice him before anyone else did, but luck belonged to someone else that day.

'Well, well, well. Look what the cat dragged in.' DCI Duguid sauntered up the corridor from the direction of the lavatories. 'Come to help, have you? Only it's a bit late. We're narrowing in on your friend Ayre.'

McLean said nothing, trying to gauge the chief inspector's mood.

'Yes, thanks to our little series of raids, he's running out of places to hide. We'll have him by the end of the week.'

If his previous employers don't make him disappear first. Might as well have written the poor sod's death sentence.

'Then you won't mind if I take my team members back, sir. Since it's going so well. Only they're supposed to be working on the Trisha Lubkin case. It's quite important.'

'So important you had to go pestering hospitals about broken noses? So important you couldn't even be bothered coming in to work today?'

Count to ten, McLean thought. Don't rise to it. Deep breaths. Ah, bugger it.

'It might surprise you to learn, sir, that today is the first day I've taken off since before Christmas. But of course, you weren't here, so you couldn't have known. How was the skiing trip, by the way? Mrs Duguid OK?'

Duguid's face reddened at the criticism. 'If you've nothing to add to this investigation, McLean, I suggest you keep out of my way.'

'Gladly, sir. As soon as I've retrieved my team. I'd really appreciate it if you didn't keep poaching them to run your errands for you. I'd rather they didn't have their careers put in jeopardy that way.'

'What the hell do you mean by that, McLean?'

'You know damn well what I mean, sir.' McLean gestured towards the room, noticing as he did that the place had fallen even more silent than before, all eyes turned his way. 'We've got a fucking serial killer out there and you're acting like it was just a mugging or two on a Saturday night. We're short-staffed as it is, without you bullying everyone in the station into running your stupid actions for you. We're only supposed to be giving drugs logistical support anyway, not riding roughshod over months of painstaking surveillance work with your bloody raids. And you don't seem to be able to get it into that thick skull of yours that what you're doing is more likely to get our only potential witness killed than find him.'

Duguid had gone from red to white, a sure sign that he was about to blow. McLean couldn't find it in himself to care any more.

'Gentlemen! My office – now!'

Both men looked around at the same moment, shaken by how close Chief Superintendent McIntyre had managed to get to them without either noticing. McLean tried a nervous smile, Duguid started to bluster.

'Not a word, Charles. My office.' And she turned away, striding back down the corridor.

'After you, sir.' McLean stood to one side to let the chief inspector pass. Duguid glowered at him, then stalked off like an angry bear.

'Why is it that all I ever hear about these days is you two arguing with each other?'

The chief superintendent stood on the far side of her desk, using it as a barrier between herself and the two detectives. McLean noticed that she hadn't sat down, never a good sign. At least he knew a rhetorical question when he heard one. Duguid, it seemed, had benefited from a different education.

'Ma'am, I'm trying to conduct a serious investigation here, and every time I'm getting somewhere, this excuse for a detective inspector comes and takes half my team away.'

Duguid's tone was almost petulant. McLean allowed himself a silent breath of relief that the DCI was digging his own grave.

'As I understand it from last month's overtime sheets, Charles, you've actually managed to use every single officer below the rank of chief inspector, plain clothes and uniform, in this station on your investigation.' McIntyre prodded an angry finger at a sheaf of papers on her desk as she spoke. 'You've even managed to rope in half of the admin staff, which is why everything else has gone to hell in a handbasket.'

'Ma'am, I must—'

'All for one investigation, Charles. Just one. Every other DCI in Lothian and Borders is running at least six. Even the DIs are doing more.'

'I have eight other cases at the moment, ma'am. This one just needs more attention.'

'You're not even supposed to be running the bloody thing, Charles. It's meant to be a drugs-squad operation with us giving support. Tony was doing a perfectly good job of that before you ordered him off the case.'

'This poison is destroying lives. We have to get rid of it.'

McLean had been studying his shoes up to this point, but something about the DCI's words caught his attention, the way he said them with such utter conviction. There was something here he didn't know, and that put him off-guard. McIntyre did though. She finally sat down, and when she spoke again, it was with a much more reasonable tone.

'Look, Charles, no one's questioning your dedication here. But you've got to take the lead from DI Langley, not browbeat him with your seniority. He's the one who knows how to handle this kind of investigation. This isn't going to be solved by throwing lots of man-hours at it.'

McIntyre shuffled the papers on her desk for a moment, let the silence build before she turned her attention on McLean.

'As for you, Tony. I'd hoped you might have had a bit more respect for authority, and a bit more sense. What do you think it does for morale if two senior detectives start taking chunks out of each other in front of the whole station?'

McLean wanted to say that it helped to clear the air; that if no one else stood up to Duguid then the man would drive everyone to an early grave with his impossible demands and sudden mood changes. But he said nothing, knowing it wasn't a question he could answer without getting into more trouble.

'I expect my officers to behave in a manner befitting their status, gentlemen. If you can't stand the sight of each other, that's tough. You're professionals, so start acting like it. Or there'll be a report going in to the DCC.'

It wasn't an explicit dismissal, but Duguid took it for one, turning swiftly and stalking out of the office without another word. McLean pitied the poor bastard of a constable to be the first to get in his way.

'One moment, Tony.' McIntyre stopped him from leaving a safe distance behind the DCI.

'Ma'am?'

'I meant what I said. He's your superior officer. If you keep pushing at him, I can't stop the complaints from going higher up.'

'If he'd just leave me perhaps one or two detectives to work with, I wouldn't have to keep going against him.'

'I know, but just try to cut him some slack, eh? His . . . well, let's just say that hard drugs have ruined the life of someone close to him.'

So that was what this was all about. 'I didn't know.'

'Not many people do, and he'd rather keep it that way.'

McLean nodded, wondering what other secrets Duguid had locked away. Maybe if the DCI wasn't so abrasive with everyone he'd get a bit more sympathy. But then again, probably not.

'Matt said he was pleased with how your sessions are coming along,' McIntyre said after a while.

'That's nice to know, ma'am. I wouldn't want to think I was going nuts.'

'Oh don't be so bloody melodramatic about it. I can see as plainly as the next man that you're under a lot of stress. Quite frankly I can't afford to lose another detective right now, we're short enough as it is. So suck up your pride and take the help being offered.'

McLean bowed his head by way of assent. He didn't dare say anything; he owed the chief superintendent too much gratitude for that.

'There's one more thing. I know you're meant to be

having the day off, but Sergeant Hwei's been getting a lot of flak in the press-liaison office about Trisha Lubkin. We were trying to keep a lid on that, but her husband's been shooting his mouth off to anyone who'll listen.'

McLean recalled the enormous man with his quiet voice and bruised nose. It suddenly occurred to him that Trisha might have butted him and not her attacker. He'd never thought to ask exactly how she'd hit her husband. The thought put him in almost as much gloom as the chief superintendent's words. He knew what was coming next.

'We're going to have another press conference. Tomorrow morning, eleven a.m. You need to be there, and I want to see briefing notes first thing.'

He tried Emma's mobile as he trudged back from the chief superintendent's office to the CID room. It rang straight through to answering machine, so he left a message.

'Hi, Emma. It's me, Tony. Look, I'm really sorry about this morning. Maybe I can make it up to you? I should be out of here by . . .' He looked at his watch, appalled to see that it was almost one. 'Six o'clock? Give us a call if you fancy a Thai.'

He left the same message on her home phone, but somehow he felt she wasn't going to call back. Not today at least.

DS Ritchie was at her desk, two-finger typing on a laptop. She looked up when he walked in.

'Oh, afternoon, sir. Sorry I called you like that. I didn't mean for you to get into trouble with the chief superintendent.'

'It's all right, sergeant. I'm not in trouble. Well, not much anyway. Is MacBride about?'

Almost as he said the words, the detective constable backed through the door with a tray in his hands. Coffee and biscuits enough to go around everyone if Grumpy Bob didn't turn up soon and DC Simmons didn't want anything.

'Just the man,' McLean said, helping himself to a mug. 'And just what we need too. Get everyone together. We've got a press conference to prepare for.'

55

An annoying, tinny beep invaded a dream he didn't realise he was having until it started to slip away. McLean rolled over, reaching for the bedside lamp, and only then realised that it was getting light outside. The clock said eight.

Not like him to sleep through the alarm. Then he saw that it was switched off. He'd done that the morning before, after it had interrupted him and Emma. The bed was much less welcoming without her. Groaning, he snatched up the phone, still beeping and buzzing beside the clock.

'McLean.' It would be the station, wondering where he was. There was the small matter of a press conference to attend to. At least the case-files were all up to date; that was why he hadn't got to bed until three in the morning, after all.

'Hey, Tony, happy new year.'

'Phil? You back already? I mean, yeah, happy new year.' McLean climbed out of bed and went to stare out the window as he talked, shivering slightly at the cold.

'Just got in last night. I was wondering what you were up to. Fancy a pint and a blether? Usual time, usual place.'

McLean was about to say yes when an awkward thought hit him. 'I don't live in Newington any more, Phil. The Arms is a bit of a pain to get to from here.'

'Christ, yes. That was a bit thick of me, I'd forgotten all about it. Where then?'

McLean yawned, scratched at his belly. It was difficult to think straight before coffee. 'I don't know, Phil. What about the Drookit Dug? It's not far from your place, and it's on the way home for me.'

'OK, usual time.' In the background, McLean could hear shouted words, but not make out what they said. A woman's voice, most likely Rachel. Then Phil added: 'And I've to ask about everything you and Emma have been up to.'

McLean looked away from the window, back to his empty bed, remembering Emma's sudden anger the day before. 'I've got to dash, Phil. Press conference. I'll see you this evening.'

'Where the hell have you been? We've got a press conference in less than an hour.' Chief Superintendent McIntyre looked like she was about to explode.

'I left the report on your desk last night, ma'am.' At about two in the morning, to be precise, another reason for oversleeping that he didn't think would help his cause.

'I don't give a damn about the report, Tony. I need you to brief me. And the deputy chief constable as well. We don't have time to mess around with reports.' McIntyre glanced at her watch. 'The whole think kicks off in less than an hour.'

'Is the DCC here?' McLean asked, hoping for a reprieve, knowing already that it was hopeless.

'He's in my office.'

'OK, well I'll meet you in the conference room in fifteen minutes. I just need to fetch my papers.' And get a coffee, McLean didn't add.

McIntyre nodded her agreement, though she looked unhappy to be letting him out of her sight. He scurried off before she could change her mind, first heading for the CID room, where a tired-looking MacBride was staring unfocused at his computer screen.

'Morning, constable. Grumpy Bob about?'

MacBride took too long to respond, his eyes darting nervously around the room before finally settling on McLean.

'Canteen, I think. He was looking for you earlier.'

'Find him for me, can you. And track down DS Ritchie, too. I want everyone at this press conference.'

'She went off to get coffee,' MacBride said, reaching for the phone. 'Should be back any minute.'

McLean left the detective constable to track down the rest of the team and set off for his office. He wasn't even halfway there when he met Emma coming down the corridor. She was carrying a large cardboard box and looked hassled. Her expression when she saw him was difficult to judge. He decided to go for the conciliatory approach.

'Look, Emma, I'm really sorry—'

'Tony, I didn't—' She spoke at exactly the same moment. They both stopped, looked at each other.

'You go first,' McLean said.

'I didn't mean to storm off like that yesterday. I'm sorry. It was petty of me.'

McLean wanted to agree, but a tiny voice of self-preservation told him that would be the wrong thing to do. 'No, you were right,' he said. 'I shouldn't just drop everything and run back to work whenever they call. It wasn't just my day off, after all.'

Emma shifted the box, leaning it against the wall to take some of the weight off her arms.

'Here, let me take that,' McLean said.

'No, you're all right. It's evidence from the McMurdo case. I've got to take it down to the store. Anyone else so much as touches it and there'll be paperwork.' She smiled and everything was all right.

'OK. Well.' McLean paused, unsure what to say. 'Did you get my message? Messages, I should say.'

'Yeah. Didn't really feel like going out last night.'

'How about tonight then? I was going to go to the pub with Phil later. But I can cancel.'

'No, pub sounds fine. And it's always fun drinking with Phil. Get him a bit pished and he's a gold-mine of secret information. I'll see you there.' Emma hefted the box again and set off in the direction of the stairs.

'OK. Give my regards to Needy,' McLean said, but she was already gone.

'I've managed to run down a couple more of the fire sites, sir. They both have links to the Guild of Strangers.'

McLean sat on an uncomfortable chair at the white-cloth-topped table set up for the press conference. Rows of empty seats stretched away to the far end of the room and the double doors where soon the jackals would enter. The briefing could have gone better; even now DS Ritchie was closeted in an anteroom with the superintendent and the DCC discussing aspects of the case. Sergeant Hwei was sitting at the far end of the table scribbling furiously into a notepad. Of Grumpy Bob there was no sign, but that was probably for the best.

'What was that?'

'The fires, sir. You wanted historical checks on the sites?'

McLean's brain caught up. He'd been so immersed in the murder investigations he'd completely forgotten the fires. As bad as Duguid, concentrating on one case to the detriment of all his others. The thought brought a wry smile to his lips.

'And what did you find?'

'Well, it's tenuous. Just the odd mention here and there. I've been trying to get in touch with a history professor at the university. He's meant to be the expert on all the guild stuff. But he's been away in the US over Christmas. Should be back today.'

'OK. Go see him. Let's try and get something to put in the report when the investigation dies.'

MacBride nodded, but didn't leave. He looked like he wanted to ask something. McLean sat silently waiting for the DS to build up the courage.

'Um, sir?' MacBride said eventually. 'Where are you going with this link? I mean, it's not as if there's a Guild of Strangers any more. And even if there were, why would they set fire to their old sites? Jealousy? And how are they doing it? I mean, we've got no forensic evidence for arson, no sign of accidents . . .' He tailed off, run out of steam.

'I'm more interested in any sites linked to them that haven't burned yet. If we can find a pattern that allows us to predict the next fire, then we can set up surveillance. Catch whoever's doing this in the act.' Well, it was the best course of action they had, simply because it was the only one.

'You want I should get on that right away?' There was undeniable hope in the detective sergeant's eyes as he asked the question. At the same time the double doors at the far end of the hall swung open, the first of the journalists bustling in to try and get the best seats.

'Aye, might as well. No point you hanging round here.'

McLean slumped back in his seat as MacBride scuttled out; shut his eyes for a moment and tried to prepare himself for the onslaught. This was one part of the job that was definitely easier when you were lower down the greasy pole.

'Well, that wasn't as bad as it could have been.'

An hour later, McLean looked at DS Ritchie and tried to work out whether she was being sarcastic. Her expression gave nothing away, but then she had learned fast from shadowing Grumpy Bob. On balance, given the hour they had just spent with the gentlemen and ladies of the press, he was going to side with sarcasm.

'What do you think's going on back there?' He nodded in the direction of the anteroom where McIntyre had closeted herself with the DCC. Dagwood was in there with them too, which didn't bode well.

'Your guess is as good as mine, sir. We didn't have much time for the press back in Aberdeen. Not if we could work without them.'

'Yeah, well, Harry bloody Lubkin's knocked that idea for six. Moaning bastard. If he'd come to us the day his wife walked out, and not left it until almost a week later, we might've had a chance. Stirring things up with the press isn't going to bring her back now, is it?'

Ritchie said nothing, which showed she had some sense. McLean rolled his shoulders and tried to ease the tension out of his neck. It had grown increasingly stiff as the press conference had degenerated into a series of ever-wilder allegations of police incompetence. Why had it taken so long to start the search for the missing woman? Why hadn't the city been alerted about the appearance of a serial killer? What were they going to do to protect the young women of Edinburgh? Were they reopening the Anderson case to see if there'd been a miscarriage of justice? Could they find their own arses with two hands and a torch?

'Sometimes they're nice to us, you know. The press,' McLean said after a while. 'Don't know what we did to deserve that kicking. I don't much fancy Dan Hwei's job when the papers come out tomorrow morning.'

Ritchie looked like she was about to say something, but she was interrupted by the click of the anteroom door opening. Superintendent McIntyre came out first, her face dark and angry. Behind her, DCI Duguid and Deputy Chief Constable Wodehouse were sharing a joke. McLean stood up, a feeling of impending doom in his stomach.

'Ah, detective inspector, you're still here. Good.' There was little warmth left in the DCC's voice after he'd finished laughing with Dagwood.

'Sir?' McLean prepared himself for the bollocking that was the only conceivable result of the fiasco they had just been through.

'Well that was a bit of a bloody disaster, wasn't it. Have you actually got any leads to work on?'

'We're still collating a list of everyone who had access

to the keys to Anderson's shop, sir. And we're working on forensic evidence—'

'So that's a no, then. Have you any idea what you're doing at all?'

McLean suppressed his anger as best he could; there was no point in antagonising someone who could make his life even more difficult than it was already.

'We found out where the killer took his first two victims, sir. I think that's not a bad result.'

'Oh come on, McLean.' Dagwood actually guffawed. There was no other way of describing the noise he made. 'You found his lair and didn't even think to set up surveillance on the place, see who turns up?'

Because you had every single available officer running your ridiculous actions.

'I don't know about you, sir, but I was hoping to catch this bastard before he abducted someone else. Not after. And anyway, I had no way of knowing he hadn't seen us going in there. The SOC team were there long enough.'

'So what you mean is you didn't have a clue what you were doing.'

'I don't think this is really helping.' McIntyre cut into the conversation before it could descend into a brawl. 'Charles, you know as well as I do that surveillance wasn't an option here.' She turned away from the DCI before he could say anything, addressing her next remarks to McLean. 'And Tony, you have to admit that you're flying blind. We've got three dead women, I don't want to hear about a fourth.'

McLean slumped his shoulders in defeat. It looked very much like the investigation was going to be taken away from him before he'd even had a chance to get started. 'I take it you have something in mind, ma'am,' he said.

'Actually it was Terry's idea.' McIntyre nodded towards the DCC, and something in her tone suggested that she wasn't altogether happy with the intrusion. That cheered McLean up, for all of ten seconds.

'We need to profile this killer,' DCC Wodehouse said. 'We need to get a handle on his motivation so that we can predict his next move. What started him off? How does he choose his victims? Why's he following Anderson's method so closely, but killing much more frequently?'

'With respect, sir, Professor Hilton's already drawn up a profile, for what it's worth. If you'd read the case-review notes I prepared yesterday, you'd see that DS Ritchie here's been working with him on just those questions.'

'DS Ritchie?' Wodehouse said. 'I'd have thought you'd have been doing it yourself. You do have the most insight into Anderson's mind, after all.'

'We're not trying to profile Anderson, sir. He's dead.'

'I know that, McLean. You're trying to profile someone who worships Anderson, wants to be like him in every way. I'd have thought your experience of the man himself would have been essential. Isn't that why you were given the case in the first place?'

McLean glanced at McIntyre for a second before answering. 'That might have had something to do with it, sir.'

'Of course it bloody well does, man,' Wodehouse said. 'But from the way things are going right now, it looks like you're not the Anderson expert we thought you were. We need results, and fast.'

'You think I don't know that, sir?' McLean asked. 'Do you think this is easy for me?'

'That's precisely my point, man. You're too close. And anyway, this is far too important an investigation to be headed by a mere inspector. The CC's being leant on by the minister. There've been questions in Holyrood. You think that press conference was bad, just wait until the politicians get stuck in.'

Wodehouse turned his back on McLean, facing McIntyre. 'Which is why I need you to take overall charge, Jayne, with Charles directing operations. McLean will head up the team pursuing the Anderson angle, but I want separate teams on each of the individual murders.'

Dagwood's face cycled from glee, through concern, and into consternation as the ramifications of what the Deputy Chief Constable was saying slid through his mind. 'But sir, I've got—'

'No buts, Charles.' Wodehouse cut him off before he could get started. 'Results.'

56

'You seem unusually tense today, Tony.'

As if it couldn't get any worse. Kicked off his own case, having to prepare a detailed report of the entire investigation so far for Dagwood to ignore, and now this. McLean sat in one of McIntyre's 'easy' chairs and stared around the room, trying not to meet eyes with Matt Hilton. The psychologist had his favourite pen in his hand, clicking it open and closed over and over.

'Could it be that the case isn't going well? I heard there was a press conference this morning about the third victim.'

Like you don't know exactly what's going on. 'Why am I here, Hilton?'

'Why do you think you're here, Tony?'

McLean had given up rising to Hilton's bait. If these sessions were one more thing he had to endure to get the job done, then he'd just have to suffer them with as good grace as he could manage.

'I think I'm here because my commanding officer thought I needed stress counselling. Who knows, she might have been right. But we've had what, six sessions? You decided after the first that I was fit for work. So why do you insist I keep on coming back? You're not on an hourly rate, are you?'

Hilton feigned a look of indignant shock, then smiled.

'Lothian and Borders pay me a retainer. How they make use of my time is up to them. But you're right, Tony. You are fit for work. And you're also under a kind of stress that few people will ever have to cope with. The best way to deal with that is to share it. I guess I keep making you come back because I hope you'll start to share.'

McLean shifted on his seat, trying to ease the numbness that was spreading through his buttocks. 'OK then, so you want me to share with you. Fine. How about we discuss your profile of this new killer.'

'That's—' Hilton started to object, then obviously thought the better of it. 'OK. What about it?'

'Well, you focus on the background. We know we're looking for a loner, someone who's been smothered by an overbearing parent, had a traumatic experience in childhood, possibly abused, yadda yadda. You already know I don't think much about that kind of generalisation.'

Hilton nodded, but said nothing.

'What I'm more interested in is why. Why is this man obsessed with Anderson, why has he decided to copy him now?'

'Well, I'd have thought the answer to the second question was fairly obvious.'

'Anderson's death?'

'Exactly. You have to understand the nature of obsession, Tony. Our killer doesn't just worship Anderson, he wants to be him. But he can't make that final leap whilst the object of his obsession is still alive. Anderson's death gave him the permission to start killing, but I suspect he's been preparing for it for many years.'

'Which just leaves the first question. Why Anderson?

OK, there's that bloody book, but thousands of people have read that and not turned into psychopathic killers.'

'It's likely that our killer empathises with some key facet of Anderson's personality. He sees in him a reflection of his own self, his own upbringing. Anderson was an orphan, right?'

'That's what I was told.'

'So I'd be fairly confident our killer is an orphan too. Or abandoned by a parent he loved. Anderson never married, but we've nothing to suggest he was gay either. I'm guessing he had a difficult time forming close relationships. It's quite common in those abandoned at an early age.'

'So we're looking for an orphan who can't commit to close relationships.' McLean almost chuckled. 'We don't know anyone who fits that description, do we.'

Hilton gave him an odd look. 'It's not you, though. Is it?'

'That's not even remotely funny, Hilton.'

'You're right, sorry.'

'And anyway, I'm more interested in Anderson's number one fan than the man himself. How do we go about finding him?'

'Well.' Hilton clicked his pen once, then looked at it as if he'd only just noticed he was holding it. 'Our killer's looking to Anderson for guidance, and we've already established that he waited until Anderson was dead before he abducted his first victim. As I said, Anderson's death gave him permission to assume that persona. What if the killer already approached Anderson whilst he was still alive, though?'

'Does anyone in Aberdeen owe you a favour?'

DS Ritchie looked up from her desk where she had

been typing manically. The fruits of her afternoon's labours were strewn all around; case-notes being whipped into something resembling order.

'I don't know. Depends what it's for, I guess.'

McLean pulled out a chair from an empty desk and dropped into it. His backside was still numb from McIntyre's chair.

'I need to know the names of everyone who visited Anderson whilst he was in Peterhead. And everyone who wrote to him too, if that information's available. Could go through the usual channels, but you know how long that can take.'

Ritchie frowned. 'Shouldn't be a problem. DCI Reid's been in charge of the investigation into Anderson's death. That's the sort of stuff he'd insist on collecting even if we know damn well who did it.'

'Well, see what you can get by the end of today. Then I want you and MacBride to go through the list and get me as much information as possible about everyone who's on it.'

'What about the case review, sir?' Ritchie picked up a sheaf of A4 sheets and waffled them around, as if it wasn't obvious what she meant. 'Dagwood wants that on his desk by five.'

McLean looked at the clock above the door. Quarter to three already. Where had the day gone?

'He won't read it anyway, trust me. Just put all your notes in chronological order and bind the whole thing so it looks pretty. Sue in admin will do it for you if you promise her some chocolate. I need that list now. It's much more important than Dagwood's bloody filing.'

*

'Christ, what a day.'

McLean slumped into the window seat and reached for the untouched pint on the table in front of him. It was cold, wet and the first pleasurable thing that had happened to him since waking that morning. He drank deep, sinking fully a third of the beer before coming up for breath.

'Looks like you needed that.' Phil sat on the other side of the table, a half-grin on his face. His own pint was barely touched.

'God save me from journalists,' McLean said. 'A pox on all of them. And bloody profilers, too.'

'Let me guess. They've been writing unhelpful things about the police again.'

'Worse, I've got to work with them.' McLean told his friend about the press conference, the DCC and Matt Hilton. He'd spent the whole afternoon closeted in a stuffy room with the psychologist, feeling like it was him being analysed, not the man who they were trying to catch.

'I swear, if I hear someone say "conflict resolution" once more I'm going to hit them.' He took the pint down to the halfway line. 'That or "Oedipus complex". Can you believe that someone actually suggested Donald Anderson killed all those people because he was trying to come to terms with being abandoned as a child? The little tit actually said he chose women that represented some idealised notion of his mother, then raped and killed them to get his revenge. Jesus.' And the rest of the pint was gone.

'You must be stressed,' Phil said. 'I've never seen a drink disappear so fast. And you don't normally talk about your cases until they're closed.'

McLean rubbed at his face, picked up the empty glass and looked at the foamy suds in the bottom. Put it back down on the table.

'Sorry, Phil. It's just picking at the scab, you know. Everyone's gabbing away about motives and planning and the symbolic importance of this and that, and there I am thinking about Kirsty. What that bastard did to her.'

'D'you really think you should be working this case, then?' Phil reached for the glass but McLean beat him to it.

'No, my turn Phil. You know the rules.' He stood up and shuffled around the table. 'And I asked for the case. I pleaded for it. There's no way I was going to let anyone else fuck it up.'

The pub was busy, with only one harassed barmaid serving the throng of thirsty students. McLean waited his turn in a parody of a queue and tried to forget the job, just for a moment. Forget Hilton's increasingly wild speculation. Forget the frustration of waiting for Aberdeen to get back with their list. Forget that he now had to waste valuable hours writing up reports for Dagwood that would never be read. Forget . . . ah fuck it, who was he kidding?

Clutching two fresh pints and with a packet of chilli crisps between his teeth, McLean made it back to the table after what seemed like only a week or so. Phil was still nursing the first half of his beer, so maybe it hadn't been that long.

'How was your Christmas then? How's Rae?', he asked after he had split open the bag for them to share.

'Fraught,' Phil said, then after a little consideration added: 'Both of them.'

'Oh? Did she not get on with your parents, then?'

'I guess so. Sort of. But you know what my mum's like. Give her a drama and she'll make a crisis out of it. Rae's gone completely mad about the wedding anyway. Put the two of them together and, well, it's light the blue touch paper and stand back.'

'Ah well. At least they're a long way away. You only need to see them every once in a while.'

'Don't you believe it. They're talking about coming up here for a few weeks to help get things sorted out. A few weeks!' Phil took a long drink, then looked at McLean with a conspiratorial air. 'You're rattling around in that old place of your gran's, Tony. You could put them up.'

'Rattling around? Says who? I'll have you know I've had plenty of people come to see me since I moved in.'

'Aye, Grumpy Bob and that lad MacBride, I'll bet. Drinking your whisky. I know what they're like.'

'Actually they're probably the only ones who've not been round much. I had the carol singers in before Christmas. Emma's been a couple of times.'

'Oh yes?' Phil nudged McLean in the ribs. 'Tell Uncle Phil all the details.'

'In your dreams, Jenkins. A gentleman doesn't kiss and tell.'

'So there was kissing involved. Better and better. At least tell me you've asked her to the wedding. Rae's going to go mental if you haven't.'

McLean looked at his watch, then around the bar. 'She's supposed to be meeting me here tonight, as it happens. I didn't think she'd be this late. Maybe she's still mad at me.'

'Mad at you? What've you been up to, Tony?'

McLean did his best to explain, though for the life of him he couldn't see what the problem had been. 'She was in the station this morning though, delivering stuff to the evidence store. Said she'd meet here at eight. Everything seemed fine.'

'Well that's women for you. Right now she's probably sitting with her feet up on the sofa, watching a soppy movie on the telly. She's got a litre carton of ice cream and just the one spoon. And that's all the company she needs right now. Tomorrow she'll phone you with some excuse about a crap day and falling asleep in the armchair. Mark my words.'

'But she said—' McLean stopped as his brain caught up with his mouth. Phil was right, of course. This was just a little light revenge for a missed lunch.

'Mind you, she's cutting off her nose to spite her face. I mean, she could have had my delightful company, fine ale and the distinct possibility of kebabs. Instead she's got Meg Ryan, *Sleepless in Seattle* and a quart of Häagen Dazs. A poor deal, I reckon.'

McLean looked at his empty glass, then up to the bar with its line of handpumps waiting to be sampled. Thought about the shitty day that had just passed and the one that was going to come tomorrow.

'Did you say kebabs?'

57

He knows it is a dream before he even sees anything. The fear is there, lurking like an old friend in the back of his mind. Like a murderer. Like a rapist.

The fog swirls around him, thick as tar and just as black. For a moment it is difficult to breathe, and then breathing isn't important any more. Just the fear.

A lamp-post appears ahead of him, chasing away some of the darkness. It's old-fashioned, cast iron, with a heavy glass head on the top of it, sputtering as it burns the poor-quality gas. He can smell the rotten-egg sulphur of the smoke, thick like the fog. Alive.

Onwards, and the street opens up to him like a corpse on the mortuary table. Incised, peeled back to reveal the sick secrets behind each new façade. His feet are cold. The sensation causes him to look down, moist cobbles glistening like the round coils of spilled entrails. And when he looks back up again, he is here already.

No time passes between opening the door and standing in the oddly bright office, but he remembers the shop he must surely have crossed. Dark, dusty shelves, long emptied of the books that gave this place reason. All are gone save one. It lies open in front of him.

Kirsty stares up at him from the open page. Her eyes are dead, her hair splayed out around her head like a halo of dark, rippling softly as the Water of Leith tries to carry it away to the sea.

He turns the page.

Audrey Carpenter scowls at him, angry at the world, her father, her stupid death. She struggles against the bonds that tie her, then tumbles away in the flow as they snap.

He turns the page.

Kate McKenzie sobs for her lost love as she floats face-up in the cold, cold burn. Tears trickle from her eyes, sliding down the sides of her face in a never-ending stream. The water is deep now, his shoes ruined, his trousers soaked. He can feel it rising up to his chin, threatening to overwhelm him. Drowned in a sea of tears.

Grasping for a lifeline, he turns the page again.

Trisha Lubkin fights against invisible shackles, shouting and screaming silent curses. Her head snaps back and forward as she tries to head-butt an invisible, faceless foe. Then her eyes catch his and he can hear her chastising him, in the voice of the deputy chief constable. 'Why didn't you look for me sooner? Why did you let him kill me?'

Ashamed, he turns the page once more.

It is blank; plain parchment scraped smooth, ready for the next soul. But as he watches, lines start to appear, bubbling up from nowhere. They form a rectangle at the top of the page, the border of a new picture as yet indistinct. The fear grips him harder now, sinking its talons into him so that he can't escape. Can't turn the page. Can't turn his head or close his eyes. Only watch as the image slowly forms, like a photograph being developed. And like a darkroom, everything is bathed in hellish red.

He knows what he is seeing long before the image has set. A woman lies spreadeagled on a blood-stained mattress, her arms and legs chained to the metal frame of an ancient bed. She is naked, motionless, he cannot tell if she is dead or alive. He strains to see her face, knowing full well who she is. He has seen that body before.

And beneath the picture, a word begins to form, beginning with a large, drop-cap letter E.

58

The phone woke him for the second time in as many days. For a moment he was confused; he'd set the alarm, he was sure of it. Then he noticed the time: five in the morning. Never a good time to get a call.

'McLean.' He winced at the dryness of his throat. The voice on the other end was not one he recognised.

'Inspector McLean? Lothian and Borders?'

'Yes. Who is this?' A female voice, but beyond that he had no clue.

'Oh, yes. Sorry. I'm Alison, Alison Connell. I work with Emma Baird on the SOC team. I think we've probably met a few times actually. Um, is she there? Emma?'

A chill gripped McLean's body that had nothing to do with the lack of central heating. He scrabbled out of bed and went to the window, staring out at the frosty darkness beyond. 'No, she's not. I've not seen her since yesterday morning. Why?'

'We've been trying to page her for the last hour. She's meant to be on call. I tried her home number but it just went to message. And, well . . . She mentioned something about seeing you, so I thought . . . sorry.'

'No, don't be.' McLean rubbed at his eyes, trying to clear his muddled thoughts from the outside. 'When did you last see her?'

'I've been on a different shift since Monday, but I asked

around here and no one's seen her since she left yesterday morning. I had a quick check of her computer and she's not logged on since then either.'

'Listen, she's probably had to go home to Aberdeen in a hurry or something. Probably forgot to charge her mobile.'

'Yeah, you're right. Em can be a bit scatty at times. Sorry to have rung so early, only the boss can be a bit . . . well . . . I probably shouldn't say.'

'It's OK, I was awake anyway.' McLean said goodbye and hung up. Outside on the lawn, Mrs McCutcheon's cat stalked across a patch of lawn painted orange by the street light filtering through the trees. It crouched and slunk, every inch the hunter, creeping ever closer to its prey. He was about to tap on the window when the cat pounced, landing on an unsuspecting bird in an explosion of feathers. A swipe with a paw, a grab with its mouth and the whole thing was over. It padded off towards the dark bushes with its kill.

Light flickered in the stained glass of the church window as McLean slowed his car at the end of the street. He'd never really paid the place much attention; it was there, a solid centre to the local community, but his grandmother had scoffed at religion and he had learnt her scepticism at an early age. Someone was up at this early hour, and busy about their devotions. Alongside the church, the manse was as black as all the other houses nearby. People wouldn't be stirring from their warm beds for hours yet.

Not quite sure why, he pulled over. When he pushed against the heavy oak doors, it was with little expectation that they would be unlocked, but they swung open on cold and almost dark. Stepping over the threshold felt like entering a new world.

The light he had seen came from a pair of stubby red candles flickering on the altar at the far end of the nave. Rows of wooden pews flanked the aisle, a narrow red carpet partially covering the stone floor. The ceiling vaulted high overhead, supported by reassuringly heavy columns, but the shadow of the carved stone buttresses swallowed the flickering light like a hungry monster. The tall stained-glass windows were black, dead eyes. No dawn for hours yet.

McLean walked slowly down the aisle, grateful for the soft carpet that silenced his footsteps. Nothing should be allowed to spoil the echoing silence that filled the cold space. Nothing save the low susurrus of prayer rising up from a point somewhere in the darkness in front of the altar.

'You came. I knew you would.' Father Anton's voice sounded tired, as if the old monk hadn't slept in weeks. He didn't turn at first, though he clambered onto unsteady feet and bowed his head once more to the altar.

'I had a dream,' McLean said. 'About the book.'

Only then did Father Anton turn away from his prayers. 'I know.'

In the flickering half-light, he looked paler than before. Even his coat seemed faded to a slate grey. Only his eyes gleamed, catching the candle flame and reflecting it back.

'What does it mean?' McLean asked.

'Come, sit.' Anton pointed to the nearest pew and shuffled over to it, settling himself down on the hard wooden bench with a dreadful creaking of joints. 'Tell me what you saw, in your dream.'

McLean sat down beside the old man and tried to gather his thoughts. The images, feelings and half memories were swirling around in his head, not helped either by the atmosphere of this cold church with its echoing silence, or by the five pints of beer and a kebab he had consumed scant hours earlier.

'It started round about the time Anderson died,' he said after a while, then realised that this wasn't true. 'Actually, it's been going on ever since I found my fiancée's dead body in the Water of Leith. Every year, come Christmas time, I dream of her. But this year it was different. This year I started to dream of Anderson's shop, and the book. Last night I saw inside it, the dead women. They each had a page. And I saw a new one being written. I think there might be another victim. Someone I know.'

'Tell me, how did you find Donald, inspector?'

The question took McLean by surprise. 'I thought you knew the story. He had a strip of cloth, was using it as a bookmark. I recognised it as part of Kirsty's dress.'

'No, you misunderstand me. I meant how did you know to go looking in that shop? What were you doing there? You specifically. The only person who would know the significance of what you saw?'

'I . . . I don't really know. We were profiling. Anderson must have fit something.' But that didn't ring true. The profiles had been rubbish.

'You weren't on the case, though, were you. The minute your fiancée was identified as a victim, you would have been taken off the team. I'd have expected compassionate leave too.'

McLean said nothing. Anton was right. There was no

way he could have stayed on the investigating team once Kirsty was confirmed as a victim. And yet for all these years he'd been telling himself that he'd caught Anderson by chance, following up a random action spewed out by the computers.

'You went there, I think. To his shop. Before he took your fiancée. Maybe you wanted to buy a book, maybe you were just asking questions. It's not important. What is important is that you saw the book then. It read you and you survived.'

'I don't remember.' And he didn't, truly. The more he tried to focus on the events leading up to that terrible time, the less he could be sure of what was real and what was nightmare. The old monk's mad tales were getting to him, that and the setting. What had he been thinking, coming into a church in the wee small hours? Why did he even listen to this madman?

'I have to go. He has Emma.' McLean stood up, turned to leave, but Father Anton reached out to stop him. His touch was icy cold, like the Water of Leith at Hogmanay.

'I fear so. But there's still hope. In your dream the page was just beginning to be written. She is not dead yet.'

Not dead yet. But what she was, where she was, didn't bear thinking about. McLean freed his hands from the chill embrace, stood up, looked at the altar with its simple wooden cross. No silverware in a city church these days; too easy for someone to steal. He felt no compunction to mutter a short prayer for help.

'I need to go. Time's running out.'

*

Emma's flat was in a small tenement in that ill-defined area between Warriston and Broughton, a favourite with the city's ever-shifting student population. There was no answer when McLean leant on the buzzer, but the front door itself swung open when he pushed it. As he walked down the narrow entrance hall, he realised that he'd never been here before; he had no idea which of the apartments was hers. Fortunately the downstairs doors had name-plates, and these also had names. Upstairs was the same, and the one on the left held a smudged scrap of paper with 'Baird' scribbled on it in hasty biro. He knocked on the door, then paused, letting the sounds of the building come to him. It was silent at this time of the morning, but that didn't mean she hadn't already left.

He knocked again, a bit harder this time. Still nothing. He tried the door, finding it locked; pulled out a super-market loyalty card and wiggled it into the space between the doorjamb and the lock. Something clicked, he turned the handle again and the door swung open.

The hallway smelled of her and he stood still just breath-ing it in for long seconds, listening all the while for any sign that the flat was occupied. There wasn't much to it, really. An open door showed a galley kitchen with a grubby win-dow looking out the back onto the river. Another door opened on a tiny bathroom, lit only by a narrow skylight overhead; a third went through to a surprisingly large liv-ing room, deep bay window onto the street, curtains open, unmatched sofa and armchair arranged around a gas fire and small television. He half expected to find an empty ice-cream carton on the floor with a dirty spoon poking out of it, but there was nothing. Not even a wine glass. That left the fourth door. The bedroom.

It was barely big enough for the double bed and the heavy, antique wardrobe, but McLean hardly took in any details. Just that the duvet was neatly pulled up to the pillows, and that the only occupant of the bed was a large, grey, rather threadbare hippopotamus. He slid a hand under the duvet, feeling the cold sheets. No one had slept there recently.

In the kitchen, a mug lay turned upside down on the drainer. Picking it up, he ran a finger around the inside. It was dry, as were the sink and the dishcloth draped over the tap. Unused in at least twenty-four hours. The kettle was cold, too.

The bathroom was the same; no water around either the sink or bath plugholes, no drops clinging to the tiles around the shower. The towel hanging from a peg on the back of the door was soft and smelled intoxicating, but it hadn't dried anyone in a while. Toothbrush and toothpaste sat in an old mug with a broken handle, again unused, though it was always possible she had a spare for travelling.

It took a while for him to find the answering machine, hiding on the floor behind the sofa in the living room. There were two new messages from him, both left the night before; one from Alison Connell, telling Emma to check her mobile and pager. He listened to them twice, marvelling at just how awful his own voice sounded on the phone, trying not to accept the truth that Emma hadn't been home when he had recorded them.

A horn sounding in the street outside brought him back to his senses. Looking out, he could see a snarl of traffic beginning to grow around his car where he had abandoned it on a double yellow line. Time to go.

On the way back to the door, he noticed for the first time a handful of framed photographs on a low sideboard. Most were of people he didn't know, but there was one of himself, somewhere dark, probably the pub. He didn't remember it being taken. Alongside it, there was a professional portrait of Emma herself, a graduation photo.

Hoping he'd be able to give it back to her soon, he grabbed it and headed out the door.

DS Ritchie clattered into the otherwise empty CID room and dumped her bag on the chair by her desk.

'Got here as quick as I could, sir. What's the— oh shit.'

McLean stood back to let her get a better look at Emma's graduation photograph where he had taped it alongside Audrey Carpenter, Kate McKenzie and Trisha Lubkin. The door banged open again, and DC MacBride's back appeared, followed by the rest of him bearing a tray with coffee and bacon butties.

'I got your message, sir. What's so important it can't wait— oh.' To his credit, the detective constable didn't drop the tray.

'Is Grumpy Bob here yet?' McLean asked, not wanting to get down to business until the whole team was there.

'I saw him coming in the front just now, should be here any minute. But sir. Em? What's going on?'

'She's missing. She didn't go home last night, and she

didn't meet me in the pub when she was supposed to. She's not answering her mobile or pager.'

'I don't want to sound sceptical, sir, but what makes you think she's been ... well ... abducted?' DS Ritchie helped herself to one of the coffees and a brown-paper-wrapped packet.

McLean paused, unsure quite how to proceed. He wanted to say: 'He took my fiancée last time,' but somehow that wasn't going to make as much sense to anyone else as it did to him. DS MacBride would do as he was told, and Grumpy Bob had worked with him long enough to understand when not to ask those kind of questions. Ritchie, though, was perfectly right.

'At the moment it's a mixture of hunch and guesswork. She fits the profile of the other three victims closely enough and there's no other obvious reason for her disappearance. If I'm right then this is our best chance yet to catch whoever's doing this. If not and she turns up in an hour or two looking a bit sheepish, well I'll take whatever flak necessary.' He reached for a mug of coffee and bacon buttie to try and cover the shudder that ran through him.

'OK, so what do we need to eliminate? You've been to her flat, I take it?'

'Yup. And she's not out on call – that's how I found out she was missing. She could have gone up to Aberdeen, I guess. If there was a family emergency.'

'I'll make a couple of calls.' Ritchie turned to her desk and picked up her phone.

'What do you want me to do, sir?' MacBride asked.

'Go round the station, ask if anyone remembers seeing her. Speak to Needy. Last I saw her, Emma was taking some evidence down to the store. If we can get a time off the paperwork, that gives us a starting point. She might even have told him where she was going next.'

'Needy's off sick, sir. He went home early yesterday. Flu apparently.'

'Bloody marvellous. Who's in archives today then?'

'PC Jones, I think. What about her car, sir?'

McLean was momentarily puzzled. 'What about it?'

'Should I get onto traffic, see if they can find it?'

'Good thinking. You know the registration?'

'SOC should have it, if she claims mileage.' He hurried off to his desk and started making calls.

'You sure you know what you're doing, sir?'

McLean turned to see Grumpy Bob standing in the doorway, his eyes on the picture taped to the whiteboard.

'Nope.'

'You know what Dagwood's going to say about this.'

'Let's worry about that when it happens, eh?'

Grumpy Bob shrugged. 'You're the boss. Where do we go next?'

DS Ritchie dropped her phone handset back into its cradle. 'That was Emma's mother. She's not spoken to her all week. As far as she knows there's nothing unusual going on.'

'OK. So I think we can pretty much rule out an innocent explanation for Emma's disappearance. Anyone contacted the hospitals? Stuart, anything from traffic on the car?'

MacBride was still talking on the phone and held up his hand for a moment's peace. McLean stifled the urge to shout; everything was taking too long. Emma was out there somewhere and the longer it took to find her . . . He didn't want to think about it.

'Sorry, sir. Traffic's not got any record of the car being in any accidents in the last twenty-four hours. They've put out a call to all units to keep an eye out for it. They'll call me the moment they find it.'

No sooner were the words out than the phone rang on his desk. All eyes were on the young detective constable as he took the call.

'Hello, . . . yes . . . Are you sure?' He hung up. 'It's Emma's car, sir. They've found it.'

'Where?' McLean pushed himself up from the desk like he was on springs.

'Out the back, sir. In the car park.'

59

The little blue Peugeot sat in a narrow space between two battered riot vans. His own car was parked almost directly opposite. How the hell had he missed it when he'd come in that morning?

McLean peered in through the window, rubbing away at the grime of accumulated road salt and other unidentifiable muck to get a better view. On the other side of the vehicle, DS Ritchie tried the door handle.

'It's not locked, sir,' she said as the door popped open.

Inside it was just as messy as it had been the last time he had ridden in it. McLean breathed in the familiar damp smell from the carpets, casting his eyes over the back seat. There was a SOC-issue fleece, a pair of heavy walking boots and a moth-eaten old cardboard box filled with latex gloves, dead batteries and other detritus of work. The foot wells were a repository of empty sweet wrappers and crisp packets; a place where the unwanted crawled to die.

He dropped the driver's seat back into position, noticing as he did that the keys still hung in the ignition. House keys dangled from the ring, along with a beaten-up rubber gnome with a tiny tuft of bright pink synthetic hair on the top of its head. Pulling them out, he went round to the back of the car and opened the boot. Inside, a collection of coats and overalls were squashed up to either side, leaving a space just about the same size as the box he had seen Emma carrying the day before. In the middle of it sat a soft, squashy leather handbag.

'I guess she didn't mean to be gone long,' Ritchie said as she picked up the bag. McLean felt an instant of irrational jealousy, dispersing it with a quick shake of the head.

'Where the hell did she go then? Off to the shops to get some lunch?'

'Purse is still in here.' Ritchie guddled around in the bag. 'Pager too. And phone.' She pushed a couple of buttons and peered at the screen. 'You left a lot of messages.'

McLean ignored the comment, looking around the parking lot for inspiration. The back of the station loomed over on three sides, the fourth protected from the rest of the world by a high stone wall. CCTV cameras covered the whole area, as did windows, behind which were offices where police sat all day. As he stood there, a couple of squad cars came in, another one leaving on patrol. Almost all of the parking bays were taken, his elderly Alfa looking very small and frail beside a BMW 4 x 4 that meant the deputy chief constable was in again. The only spaces of any size were the yellow-hatched area in front of the workshop, and the narrow ramp that led down to the basement stores.

'Come with me,' McLean said, setting off for the back door to the station.

'What should I do with this, sir?' Ritchie held the bag aloft, and McLean realised he was still holding the car keys in his hand. He threw them to her.

'Stick it back in the boot, and lock up,' he said, waiting impatiently as she complied.

'Where are we going now?' she asked as he hurried back to the station door, but McLean was already on his mobile.

'MacBride? Get the CCTV tapes of the car park. From nine o'clock yesterday morning until the same time today. I want to know who went near Emma's car. It's in bay twenty-three, next to the ramp. And get Grumpy Bob to give Needy a call, can you. I know he's off sick, but he's the last person who'll have seen her. She might have said something about where she was headed next.'

He hung up as they stepped from the cold dry day into the warm, moist interior, Ritchie still a step behind him.

'Come on, sergeant, get a move on,' McLean said. 'Time's wasting.' And he set off down the steps into the basement.

The evidence store wasn't the same without Sergeant Needham's cheery face to welcome you. In his place, PC Jones was manning the fort, and by the look of it struggling with the computer system. He looked up as McLean and Ritchie approached, worry writ large across his broad, young face.

'Sir, ma'am.' He sprang to his feet behind the counter like a Jack-in-the-Box. McLean thought he might even salute.

'It's Tim, isn't it?' McLean asked trying to put the constable at his ease.

'Terence, sir.'

'Sorry, Terence. How are you coping? I hear Needy's off sick today.'

'It's alright, sir. Just a bit confusing, sir. Sergeant Needham has a unique filing system, sir.'

McLean tried a smile, though with each new hurdle the effort became ever greater. 'You had some evidence brought in yesterday morning, about ten. Emma Baird, the SOC officer?'

'I can check, sir. But there's something up with the system.'

'May I?' Ritchie pointed towards the computer screen. PC Jones looked a bit worried, but then nodded. Ritchie settled in the vacated chair and was soon tapping away at the keys.

'Did you see Needy ... Sergeant Needham yesterday, Terence?' McLean asked, partly to distract the constable from what Ritchie was doing. Technically neither of them should be accessing this computer without leaving a paper trail. Contaminating evidence could jeopardise a conviction, bugger up any number of cases, even his own. McLean put a guilty hand in his jacket pocket, feeling the folded strip of fabric still there.

'No, sir. He'd gone by the time I arrived.'

'What time was that?'

'About twelve, sir. I had the morning off, sir.'

'Here it is,' Ritchie said after a moment. 'Evidence pertaining to the McMurdo investigation. Logged in at ten minutes past ten yesterday morning. Emma Baird handed them over.'

'Should be a paper record, too.' McLean turned back to the constable. 'Is that all still kept in the filing cabinets?'

'I ... Yes, sir. Would you like to see it, sir?'

'Please.'

Constable Jones took a large set of keys from the desk and crossed over to one of the filing cabinets that lined the wall, returning soon afterwards with a series of sheets of paper, all stapled together neatly. The top was a form with the investigation code number and various other details filled in, Emma's loose signature at the bottom alongside Needy's more formal autograph. The other sheets were a manifest of everything that had been in the cardboard box. No different from the paperwork accompanying Anderson's things, but it proved one thing: Emma had been here at the back of ten. He glanced at his watch; twenty-two hours ago. So where had she gone?

The first thing McLean noticed when they got back to the CID room a few minutes later was that Emma's photograph had disappeared from the whiteboard. Grumpy Bob was at his desk, doing a good job of looking busy. He looked up as McLean came through the door, eyes darting to the side. Too late, he realised what was happening.

'Just what the hell are you playing at, McLean?'

Dagwood had been hiding behind the door. At least that's what it seemed like. He held Emma's photograph in one hand and slapped at it with the other like it was some unruly child needing discipline.

'I'm conducting my investigation, sir. What did you think I was doing?'

'Using half the force to search for your girlfriend, by the look of things. When you're meant to be giving me a briefing so I can take over this case. You haven't even finished the report that was supposed to be on my desk yesterday.'

Out of the corner of his eye, McLean saw DS Ritchie creep away to her desk and log into her computer. He could hardly blame her; the last thing she needed was to be caught in a row between two of her superior officers. Again.

'Something came up,' he said. 'A new development.'

'Yes, I heard. You had an argument with your precious little SOC officer and now she won't talk to you. Don't you think that launching a full manhunt is a bit over the top?'

How did he get to be a chief inspector? No, how did he even get to be in CID?

'We've got a serial killer out there, sir. He's abducted three women already. Now a fourth has gone missing. No one knows where she's gone. Her car, her handbag, her house keys: they're all here in the station car park. That sounds very much to me like she might have been, oh, I don't know . . . abducted? Forget that she's a SOC officer, or that I even know her. She's been missing for less than a day. If we can track her last movements we might just possibly be able to catch the sick bastard who took her.' And save her life.

'This is nonsense, McLean.' Duguid shook the photograph. 'You've no evidence she's been taken. It's just supposition. There's a proper procedure—'

'Sir . . . er, sirs?' DS Ritchie said. 'There's something here I think you should see.'

Dagwood turned on the hapless detective. 'What is it, sergeant? Can't you see we're busy?'

'Er . . . Well . . . It's just that I was doing some background checks on Anderson. For DI McLean? And I've just had a list of visitors he had whilst he was in Peterhead.'

'And this is relevant how?' Dagwood asked.

'Well, it's just that there's one name I wasn't really expecting to see. Went to see Anderson about once a month for the last eighteen months or so.'

'Who?' McLean peered at the partially obscured computer screen.

'Sergeant John Needham, sir.'

'Needy?' Dagwood scoffed like a professor presented with a genuinely novel idea. 'You've not been here long, missy, otherwise you'd realise what a stupid suggestion you're making. Sergeant Needham was one of the team that brought Anderson to justice. He's been a stalwart of this police force for decades. His father and grandfather were both policemen. You're not really suggesting he's our new Christmas Killer, are you?'

'I only meant to point out—' Ritchie started, but Dagwood wasn't listening.

'It's just as well the DCC asked me to take over. This whole investigation's a complete and utter farce. McLean, I want a full briefing in one hour, and then you and your team can get on with reviewing all the old Anderson cases.'

McLean's phone stopped him from striking a superior officer. It rang in his pocket, and being able to ignore the DCI by answering it was almost enough.

'McLean?'

'Um, MacBride here, sir. I've been going through those tapes like you asked. I think we might have got something.'

McLean ended the call and dropped his phone back into his pocket. 'Bob, Ritchie, with me.' Before he could move, Dagwood grabbed him by the arm.

'Where the bloody hell do you think you're going? Briefing in one hour, remember?'

McLean shrugged off Dagwood's hold. 'Oh fuck off, you pompous old twat,' he said, and stormed out the door.

Grumpy Bob was trying hard not to chuckle as they walked up the corridor towards the video viewing room, leaving an open-mouthed Dagwood standing alone in the CID room. 'Was that wise, sir? I mean, it was inspired, yes. But he's going to kick up a hell of a row.'

'You know, Bob, I really don't care. They can sack me if they like. Then I won't have to work with idiots like him any more.' McLean noticed the mobile phone clutched in the sergeant's hand. 'Did you get in touch with Needy, by the way?'

'No answer, but he could've popped out to the shops.' Or he could be raping Emma Baird, Bob didn't say, but the look on his face was enough. They had arrived at their destination, and squeezed into the darkened viewing room without another word.

'See here.' DC MacBride fiddled with the video controls and a picture appeared on the screen. 'This is the car park yesterday morning. There's two cameras, but this one shows the best angle.'

McLean squinted at the poor-quality image, watching as a pale blue Peugeot kangarooed into a parking space in a series of jerky hops. A short, dark-haired figure got out, opened the boot, took out a big box, slung something in, closed the boot and headed off towards the back door to the station, disappearing off camera soon after.

'I've been through the tapes for the next twelve hours. Admittedly quite fast, but there's no sign of her coming back.'

'This much we knew, Stuart. What did you bring me here for?'

'Ah, well.' The detective sergeant clicked another button and the image changed angle. Now the camera showed the ramp leading down into the basement loading area just off the evidence locker. It was too dark to see if the metal roller doors were open or closed, but after a few moments, a large estate car backed down the ramp and disappeared. Minutes later it came back again and drove off. McLean looked at the time-stamp on the video. Half-past ten in the morning.

'That's Needy's car, isn't it?'

'There's more, sir,' MacBride said. 'I asked around if anyone had seen him yesterday. Nobody had spoken to him, but Gladys, the canteen lady, said she saw him first thing when she was getting the stock in for the day.'

'Well we know he was here. His car's here.' McLean pointed at the screen.

MacBride pressed another button on the console and the image changed again. This time it showed someone standing by the same estate car that they had seen earlier. He zoomed in on the face, and although the resolution was bad, it was easy to see that something was badly wrong with it.

'Aye, but we all thought he had the flu. Not a broken nose and black eyes that make him look like a panda.'

60

'You really think Needy's our man?'

DS Ritchie sat beside McLean as they drove south out of town towards the bypass. The sun low over the Pentland Hills made visibility a bitch, and the early rush-hour traffic didn't help. It seemed like only a few hours ago he had been talking to Father Anton in the candlelit church that morning, and now evening was falling rapidly. McLean wished he could go faster, whilst at the same time knew more haste would ultimately mean less speed.

'Fuck, I hate to have to admit Hilton could be right, but everything's pointing to Needham at the moment.' McLean ignored the angry toot of a horn as he cut up the inside of a dawdling school-run mother. One hand off the steering wheel, he began to count out the points. 'He's a loner, dominated by his father all his life. He's been mouldering away down in the evidence store for years now, passed over for promotion God only knows how many times. He could have been a DCI by now if some toe-rag hooligan hadn't put a broken bottle in his leg. He was on the Christmas Killer team longer than anyone else. And of course he had access to the keys to Anderson's shop.'

Ritchie grabbed for the dashboard, supporting herself as the car tilted alarmingly round a roundabout. 'Look out, sir!'

McLean slammed on the brakes as a taxi swerved across

his path and to the side of the road, where it proceeded to unload an elderly gentleman. McLean wished he'd been able to get hold of a squad car, or even one of the unmarked CID pool cars. They all had sirens and hidden blue lights that could have cleared his route in no time. But as usual, all of them were out or broken, leaving a choice of the Alfa or Emma's Peugeot. And they'd really needed to leave that for forensics to check over.

Dropping down into second gear, he roared past the taxi, twin-cam Italian engine bellowing a far better expletive than anything he could have come up with. The road ahead was clear for a bit and he concentrated on driving as fast as he safely could.

'I hope Stuart's managed to get in touch with traffic. It'll be a right pain if you get pulled over.'

'It's all cameras along here,' McLean said. 'And frankly I don't care right now if I set a few of them off. Damn!'

The traffic backed up to Kaimes Junction and once more he was forced to slow down.

Ritchie laughed. 'You sound like Grumpy Bob, you know.'

McLean didn't answer, and her smile soon faded. 'We'll find her. It'll be all right,' she added.

'You knew her, back in Aberdeen?' McLean wasn't sure he wanted to talk about Emma, but anything was better than staring at the glaring brake lights of a thousand unmoving cars. 'I'd be right in saying there was a bit of history?'

Ritchie shuffled in her seat. It could almost have been called squirming

'We met on a few cases, yes.'

'And that's it? So why d'you go all stiff and formal every

time she's mentioned? More to the point, what's she got against you?'

Ritchie said nothing for a while, just staring ahead as if she, too, were willing the traffic to evaporate. When she did finally speak it was in an oddly formal voice.

'There might have been a bit of a misunderstanding. Over a certain detective constable.'

'A male detective constable, I presume.'

'As it turns out, he wasn't worth either of our attention. Little creep's a DI now, transferred down to the Met. And he shat on everyone to get there so quickly.'

'So he's long gone. Why're you two still fighting over him?'

Ritchie didn't answer, and McLean was left to ponder as the line of cars started to move. Traffic gnarled slowly along the short section of dual carriageway past Burdie-house and under the bypass, finally freeing up as McLean took the turning to Loanhead. How long was it since he'd come this way with DS Robertson? Not more than a month. It felt like years.

The headquarters of Randolph Developments was a blaze of lights as they slipped past the compound. The old stone factory buildings were surrounded by machinery, but most of the portacabins had been moved away. McLean remembered the models that William Randolph had shown him, his plans for the regeneration of the city and its suburbs. No doubt work was about to begin on turning this place into yet another luxury living ex-perience.

'Give MacBride a call, will you?' McLean said, an odd thought crossing his mind. Ritchie flipped open her phone.

'What do you want to ask him?'

'Did he ever get to speak to that professor at the university?'

The message was relayed and an answer came back: 'Yes.'

'Then ask him if the old . . .' McLean squinted in the arc-lit gloaming at the name carved in stone above the main factory entrance. 'McMerry Ironworks site in Loanhead was ever associated with the Guild.'

Again Ritchie relayed the information, before asking a question of her own. 'Guild?' she mouthed, hand covering the phone's mouthpiece. McLean didn't have time to explain before MacBride's answer came back.

'He says he doesn't know, but he can find out.'

Ritchie ended the call and put her phone away.

'What was all that about?' she asked.

'Just another hunch,' McLean said. 'It's my day for them.'

'That's a big old pile for someone on a sergeant's pay.' DS Ritchie looked up at the imposing bulk of Needy's house as the Alfa crunched over the gravel of the long driveway towards something that wouldn't have looked out of place in a period drama.

'It's been in the family a long time. The Needhams built the ironworks back there.' McLean pointed to the rear of the building, where a steep bank rose sharply up, the stone hulk of the old factory just showing through a skeletal line of winter trees. 'We all used to come out here from time to time. When we were working on the Christmas Killer case. It's looking a bit run down since then.'

Closer in, McLean could see the grey-brown render on the walls was cracked in places, the sash windows in bad need of paint. Thick ivy grew up one gable wall, threatening to strangle the chimney stack and bring it crashing down onto the garage roof. He parked the Alfa a good distance away, just in case.

The front door was locked, but then that was no surprise. The windows reflected the low sun, and behind them shutters blocked any view of the rooms inside. McLean went to press the ornate porcelain bell-push, then hesitated.

'Let's just have a wee nosey about first, shall we?'

The gravel drive continued around the back of the house, through a stone arch that connected to the garage block. Not so much parked as abandoned in front of this, the grubby off-green Jaguar estate sat with its rear facing the back door. Looking up, McLean could see no lights from the windows on this side of the house either. Shutters blocked the downstairs views of everything except the back lobby and kitchen, both empty. He tried the back door, but it was locked.

'Car's not been anywhere in a while.' DS Ritchie had her hand pressed to the bonnet. She took it off and tried the door handle. 'Locked too.'

The garages were converted from earlier coach houses, and were also locked tight. It wasn't surprising, really, with the house being so close to Loanhead. A place like this would be a magnet for all the unemployed and disaffected youth living in the schemes further down Roslin Glen. Overshadowed by the hulk of the ironworks, it almost begged to be burgled and vandalised.

'Looks like something's been dragged here, sir.' DS

Ritchie crouched down by the tailgate of Needy's car, looking at the gravel intently. McLean joined her.

'What is it?'

'See here.' She pointed at a shallow depression in the gravel. 'Looks like something heavy was dropped out of the back of the car, then dragged off in that direction.'

McLean ran his hand lightly over the surface, feeling a rough outline of two parallel tracks. Two heels carving a path to Needy's back door.

He stood up, pulled out his phone and hit speed dial as he followed the indentations to the door. DS MacBride answered on the second ring.

'I need a warrant to search Needy's house,' McLean said before the constable could get more than his name out. 'And we need to find him.'

'On it, sir,' MacBride said. 'Oh, and you were right, by the way.'

'I was? What about?'

'The McMerry Ironworks, sir. It's built on an old Guild of Strangers site. Their first site, as it happens. It's where they set up after being driven out of the city by the merchant guilds at the turn of the sixteenth century.'

'Fine, constable. You can give me the history lesson when we've found Emma. Just get me that warrant. Then get yourself over here quick as you can.'

Waiting for things to happen was never McLean's style. He paced around, peering into the window that looked onto Needy's kitchen, tried the locked door again, just in case, then looked around for any evidence of a spare key. Ritchie came over to join him.

376

'You know, I could have sworn I heard someone shout "Help" just then.'

'What?' McLean looked at her, standing by the back door.

'There it is again.' Silence filled the air, underlined by the distant hum of the bypass, the whine of a jet plane.

'D'you know, I think you're right, sergeant. It sounds very much like someone's in need of help.' McLean shrugged his hand up into his sleeve for protection, picked up a fist-sized rock lying by the back door and used it to smash one of the small windows. The key was still in the lock on the inside, so he reached carefully in and opened the door.

'Jesus! What's that smell?' Ritchie wrinkled her nose as she stepped into the back lobby. McLean sniffed and then wished he hadn't. A mixture of rotting garbage and open sewer assaulted his senses. Shallow breathing through his mouth, he pushed open the door that led to the kitchen and stepped through.

The air was slightly better in here, but still not pleasant. Most of the aroma wafted up from the large double sink, filled to overflowing with unwashed pots and crockery. The table was strewn with rubbish: empty pizza boxes; Chinese takeaway cartons, beer cans and chocolate wrappers. A bowl in the middle of the table contained several pieces of fuzzy green fruit. It was a stark contrast to the spotless tidiness of Needy's office back at the station.

'This isn't what I was expecting,' Ritchie said. McLean could only agree.

They worked their way quickly and quietly through the downstairs rooms. Most looked like they'd not been used in years, shuttered up against the light and left to moulder gently away. Patches on the walls showed where the paintings McLean recalled from earlier visits had gone, and there was far too little furniture. The smell from the kitchen subsided the further they went into the house, to be replaced with the unmistakable reek of mildew. Flicking the lights on in the large drawing room to the front of the house, McLean saw black mould creeping down the walls from the ornate plaster cornicing; brown circle stains in the ceiling and powdery, flaking paint.

Upstairs was, if anything, worse than the ground floor. The roof was obviously in dire need of repair; in places the ceiling had collapsed altogether, leaving just bare laths and daylight peeking in from the attic above. The whole place had a feel of abandonment about it, as if nobody had lived there for years. And yet the key had been in the inside of the door. Needy's car was out the back. The man himself had to be somewhere.

It was Ritchie who found the attic rooms, tucked up in the eaves at the back. The half-hidden staircase was narrow and bare wood, designed for the servants to reach their accommodation without upsetting their master. Most of the rooms were empty, damp-spotted and water stained. One had old trunks piled up in it, covered in dust and spider webs. And one was where Needy had grown his obsession.

An old pedestal desk sat in front of the dormer window, looking out across the narrow gap to the tree-lined bank and the ironworks. It was strewn with newspaper cuttings, spiral-bound notebooks filled with neat handwriting, loose paper covered in loping scrawl and crazy doodles. A well-worn copy of Jo Dalgliesh's book was half buried under a stack of police files, and several more boxes from the archives were piled in a corner. But it was the walls that sent a chill down his spine.

Needham had blown up photographs of Anderson: from the trial; from his shop; even the mugshots taken when he was arrested. And there were other photographs too: the victims, pinned to every available surface, in a disturbing parody of the whiteboard in the CID room. On top of them were Post-it notes and larger sheets of paper, stuck up with yellowing sellotape and with cryptic messages scrawled on them. 'How does he choose them?' 'Why under a bridge?' 'Where's the book?' and at least twenty that simply said 'Why?'

'How long's he been doing this?' Ritchie asked. McLean rummaged around the desk, picking up a notebook at random. Needham's handwriting was hard to decipher but the front page was dated over two years earlier.

'A long time.' He put the book down, picked up what looked like a letter. The familiar logo of Carstairs Weddell, Solicitors and Notaries Public, caught his eye.

'What you got there, sir?' Ritchie craned her neck to see, so close he caught the faintest whiff of her perfume.

'It's a letter detailing the inheritance tax due on Needy's dad's estate. This house, basically. Seems he owes the Chancellor the thick end of a million quid.'

Ritchie let out an explosive breath. 'Well, that'd tip me over the edge.'

'Oh, I think that just sped his fall.' McLean dropped the letter back onto the desk, looked around the room once more. 'Needy went over a long time ago. We just never noticed.'

61

Back downstairs, McLean poked around the large hallway, trying to remember the old house from when he'd last visited it over ten years ago. He was fairly sure they'd covered all the rooms, but a place this big and this old had to have a basement. None of the doors so far had opened up onto stairs, and in the semi-darkness of the shuttered hall, it was almost impossible to make out any detail.

'Have you got a torch, sergeant?'

A short interval, then a narrow beam of light in answer. Ritchie handed it over, and he played the torch over the area under the stairs, boxed in with more of the heavy panelling. Then he saw the turned wooden door handle and well-hidden keyhole. The door opened onto darkness, but as he peered carefully into the space, he could make out a faint glow at the bottom of a short flight of stone stairs. There was light down there somewhere.

'Do you think we should wait for back-up, sir?' Ritchie asked.

'Probably.' He set off down the stairs. They brought him to a vaulted corridor about six feet wide that appeared to run the length of the house. He killed the torch, and by the time his eyes had adjusted to the glow coming from one end, Ritchie had joined him. She was about to say something, but he lifted a finger to his lips. Straining his ears, he tried to make out any noise at all but there was nothing.

They crept along the corridor past a number of closed doors until they finally came to the end and the source of the light. More steps dropped further down, and at the bottom, a wide wooden door stood partly ajar. The light beyond it flickered, reflecting off a polished flagstone floor.

The temperature seemed to rise as he climbed slowly down the steps, the stone walls radiating heat as if he were descending into the magma layer, not just a few yards underground. Ritchie pressed in close behind him, her scent filling the enclosed space as they moved further away from the reek upstairs. As he reached the bottom, he put his hand up for her to stay behind him, and brushed gently against her arm. At least he hoped it was her arm. Keeping as much of his body behind the half-open door as possible, he peered around it into the room beyond.

It looked like a small chapel, or perhaps the undercroft of a larger church. Heavy stone pillars rose up from the floor like the petrified trunks of long-dead trees. The ceiling vaulted high overhead, shadows of ornately carved figures lurking in the eaves. The walls were adorned with heavy plaques, their inscriptions too dark to see in the flickering candlelight that spread from half a dozen sconces. The scent of burning tallow was heavy in the air, only half masking something less pleasant. It was warmer even than the tunnel, lending the place a hellish feel.

Slowly, McLean edged into the room, looking around and trying to make out detail in the semi-darkness. A low stone altar stood at one end, holding up more candles that illuminated more elaborate carvings. Beside it, a heavy wooden lectern angled towards the room, shaped like an eagle with its claws extended, wings spread wide to land.

But there were only a few old pews near the front for any congregation to sit on. The rest of the space had been cleared back to smooth flagstone floor, then piled with an odd assortment of boxes, some rolled-up carpet, an old sit-up-and-beg pushbike with a wicker basket mounted on the handlebars. A heavy, cast-iron bedstead, complete with manky, bloodstained mattress, stood to one side. From where he stood, he could only see a corner, but it was enough. A pale, small hand was chained to the head-board with a shiny new handcuff.

All thoughts of stealth forgotten, McLean ran across the dimly lit chapel to the bed. Emma lay on her back, spreadeagled and naked, bound by her hands and legs. The bare mattress stank of dried blood and piss. For too long he just stared at her, trying to work out if she was dead or alive. She looked so pale, so still; like Kirsty had looked when he had found her all those years ago. Please God, don't let it happen again.

'We have to get her out of here.' McLean dug in his pockets, looking for a set of handcuff keys. His hand found them nestling beneath the strip of cloth, still in its plastic evidence bag. Not knowing quite why he did it, he pulled both out, palmed the keys and opened the bag. The fabric was soft, thin between his fingers, a little jolt of something like electricity running through him at that first touch. Hastily he shoved it into his trouser pocket, reached over with the keys. Emma didn't stir as he undid the cuffs, one by one. She didn't stir as he gently eased her arms back down by her sides. Nor did she stir as he pulled off his jacket and laid it gently over her. And all the while DS Ritchie stood hesitantly nearby, as if unsure whether she should help or not. If she'd seen him handling the strip of cloth, she said nothing about it.

'Is she . . . Is she breathing?'

McLean knelt down, gagging at the smell coming off the mattress, and touched a finger lightly to Emma's neck. He just caught the merest motion of a pulse in the flickering light before a scream pierced the quiet.

'She's mine!' Needy came from nowhere, brandishing a heavy brass candlestick and moving faster than McLean had ever seen him. He was wearing some kind of long cloak and a gold medallion around his neck that glinted in the candlelight as it swung. Ritchie ducked to avoid the blow, but was too slow. It connected with the side of her head as she turned, and she crumpled like a discarded puppet. Needy didn't even look at her, swinging the candlestick round again as he rushed on, eyes lit with a mad fire. Kneeling down, McLean could only put up his arms for defence, trying to parry the blow rather than take it full on.

The pain was instant, and he could swear he heard bones cracking. The shock ran up his arms into his shoulders, dulling his vision. He could barely move, and yet he knew that Needy would be swinging the candlestick around for a second blow. A killing blow. He rolled onto the floor, felt the air split where his head had been a second earlier. There was a dull crash as the candlestick connected with the flagstone floor and McLean took his opportunity.

Needy was bent over, off balance as he tried to haul back his makeshift weapon. From his position on the floor, McLean swept his legs round, trying to bring Needy down. The sergeant jumped out of his way, laughing, seemingly unencumbered by his damaged leg.

'Can't get me like that.' And he brought the candlestick down again.

McLean rolled under the bed, feeling something sticky on the floor pull at his shirt. The candlestick clanged against the edge of the bed, tumbling rust and other less pleasant things onto his face. His forearms still hurt like he'd bench-pressed a train, but at least he was getting his wits together. As Needy pulled the candlestick up again, McLean rolled right under the bed and scrambled up on the other side.

'Put it down, Needy. It's over. You don't want to hurt anyone else.'

'She's mine, I tell you. Mine. It said I could have her if I read her a story.'

'John, look at yourself.' McLean kept one eye on the wavering candlestick, but he was close enough to see Needy's face. It was contorted in a grimace that was somewhere between agony and ecstasy, black eyes and swollen nose making him look like an insane ape. God only knew what he was on. Some mixture of painkillers and amphetamines by the look of him. Was there any possibility of talking him down?

'Sergeant Needham.' McLean tried to put as much authority in his voice as he could muster. 'Stand down.'

'You don't understand. It's what it wants. I have to do what it tells me.'

'What tells you? Who wants you to do this to Emma? She's your friend.'

'No friends. Only people who want things from you. Only people who hurt you. Only people who make jokes about you to your face. But it's different. It understands.'

384

'Who understands, Needy? Who are you talking about?'

'You should know. It talked to you, too. It told me all about you.' Needham's eyes had been fixed on McLean's, but as he talked they kept darting away, towards the lectern and the heavy old book lying open on it.

'The book?' The eyes flicked back again, and McLean knew he'd guessed right. 'You found Anderson's book? The Book of Souls?'

'It was there all along, only hiding.' Needham's voice steadied slightly. He sounded like he was simply giving an account of a crime he'd solved. He still held the candlestick high though, ready to swing at anyone who came near. 'Biding its time, it was. Waiting. You don't know what it's like, Tony. The voices in your head, the freedom it gives you. There's no guilt, no pain. Just joy and immortality.'

'It's not real, John. There never was a Book of Souls. I should know. I was there, remember. I found Anderson.'

Needy focused his stare on McLean and the madness was back again. 'You spurned it. You were meant to be next in line but you ignored it. How could you? How—'

'I think I've heard quite enough from you, Sergeant Needham.'

McLean and Needy both turned at the voice, each as surprised as the other. DS Ritchie stood just feet away from Needham, well within range of the candlestick and waving from side to side like a punch-drunk boxer. Blood seeped from a gash at her temple. She had a can of pepper spray in her outstretched hand, and before he could do anything she let Needham have the whole thing in the face.

62

'Cuff him to the bedpost, I don't want to take any chances.'

McLean rubbed at his wrists, wincing at the jabbing pains that ran up to the tips of his fingers. Blood stained the arms of his shirt and he hadn't dared to roll up his sleeves to see what damage Needy's candlestick had done. At least they weren't broken, he was fairly sure of that. It hurt way too much.

Ritchie scooped up one of the handcuffs that had been securing Emma to the bed and looped it round one of Needy's wrists. The sergeant didn't resist; he was too busy wheezing and puking onto the floor, his face a puffy red mess around his panda eyes. She clacked the other end onto the bedpost as instructed, then bent to pick up Emma.

'It's all right, I've got her.' McLean scooped her up, marvelling at how light she felt. She was still unconscious, and as he carried her across the empty chapel, he could see blood matting the back of her head. Needham must have hit her, but why? What had he said in his mad ravings? 'Only people who make jokes about you to your face.'

'Oh fuck. I did this.'

'I beg your pardon, sir?'

'I told her about Trisha Lubkin and the broken nose.' McLean could almost picture the scene now, down in

Needy's little empire beneath the streets. 'Emma probably made some joke about it when she saw him yesterday morning. He must have hit her to stop her telling anyone else what she'd seen.'

'Shit. If she's been out cold for twenty-four hours . . .' Ritchie didn't finish the sentence. She didn't need to. They needed to get Emma to a hospital, if it wasn't already too late.

Ritchie unbolted the front door, letting light flood the hallway as McLean staggered out into daylight with Emma in his arms. It felt like he'd been underground for hours, though in truth it had only been a few minutes. He got Emma over to his car, dismayed to see that back-up had yet to arrive.

Emma's skin was as white as the cloud-filled sky and twice as cold. He somehow managed to get the passenger door open on the Alfa, and lowered her gently onto the seat, then tilted it back as far as it would go. There was a blanket in the back – one of his grandmother's. He wrapped her up in it as much to preserve her modesty as anything, then went around to the other side and started the engine, cranked the heater up to full. DS Ritchie came over as he was closing the door to keep the heat in; she was still very unsteady on her feet; light-headed from the blow to her head. Even so, she had her phone in her hand.

'There's been a pile-up on the bypass and the traffic's fucked big time. Penicuik and Dalkeith are both on their way, and I asked for an air ambulance as soon as possible.'

'You did good, sergeant. Kirsty. Thanks.'

'All part of the job, sir,' Ritchie said, then sank to her

knees. McLean caught her before she could fall over completely, helped her into the driver's seat of his car.

'I don't think I'm fit to drive anywhere, sir,' she said.

'Just wait there in the warm. Keep an eye on Emma.' He closed the door gently. 'I'm going to go back and secure the crime scene. You can let the others know when they get here.'

The air in the basement was oppressively thick as McLean trod lightly down the stone steps to the chapel. Brushing the stone vaulting of the passageway with his hand, it was warm to the touch, not the cold dampness he would have expected. It was almost as if he were in an oven, or the stonework was just a narrow barrier between this evil place and hell itself.

He paused at the door; should he have waited for back-up? Why had he come back down here anyway? Needy wasn't going anywhere, not with a broken nose and a face full of pepper spray. And he was handcuffed to the bed, wasn't he.

McLean's hand went unbidden to his pocket, where the handcuff keys were safely stowed. He'd shoved them in there after freeing Emma, he was sure of it. And yet there was nothing but the thin strip of fabric that he'd taken from the evidence store. Kirsty's dress. A shiver ran down his back, despite the warmth, and an image coalesced in his mind of the key slipping out as he rolled under the bed. He tensed, listening for the faintest sound. It was silent, not the dull background roar of the city bypass, not even the rasping breath of a man with a broken nose and a lungful of pepper spray. Crouching low in self-preservation, McLean edged around the half-open door and into the chapel, crossing as quickly as he could to the old cast-iron bed. A shiny new handcuff hung from the bedstead, one half open, a key protruding from the lock.

Needy was nowhere to be seen.

McLean whirled around, expecting to be attacked, but he was alone. The candlestick still lay on the ground where Needy had dropped it. The smell of the pepper spray hung acrid in the air, hurting McLean's eyes and tickling the back of his throat. How could Needham have done anything with a face full of that, let alone found the key and freed himself?

A pool of vomit and blood marked where the sergeant had been lying, and sticky wet footprints led away from it. McLean followed them, though they went in the direction of the altar rather than the door. There was no junk piled up at this end of the chapel, just a few wooden pews facing the altar. The walls were lined with delicately carved plaques. Playing Ritchie's torch over the nearest, McLean could see that it was actually wooden, not the stone he had assumed. It bore an inscription to one Torquil Burroughs, and the next one was dedicated to a Septimus Needham. A particularly ornate plaque read: 'IN MEMORIAM: ANGUS CADWALLADER — GRAND MASTER OF THE GUILD OF STRANGERS' and was dated 1666. Beneath it was some Latin McLean couldn't immediately translate, but it brought a welcome smile to his face. Later, perhaps, he'd be able to point it out to his friend the pathologist, but for now there were more important things to do.

As he shone the torch back down on the floor to try and follow Needy's footprints, the light flickered once and then died. McLean shook it, but nothing happened. He crossed over to the altar, to grab one of the candles. The eagle-carved lectern was empty. He was sure there had been a book on it earlier, and stooping low he could see that the footprints led first there, then around the back of the altar. Then they disappeared.

He studied the carved panelling behind the altar as best he could in the yellow flickering candlelight, but it was hard to see anything in great detail. Then he noticed that the flame guttered as he moved it past a certain spot. There was a gap in the woodwork, and when he pushed at it, something gave. A door opened up on darkness beyond.

63

'It is the judgement of this court that you are found guilty of all charges. Namely the abduction, rape and murder of Laura Fenton, Diane Kinnear, Rosie Buckley, Jane Winston, Sarah Chalmers, Sarah Smythe, Josephine English, Henrietta Adamson, Corrine Farquhar and Kirsty Summers.'

The press are back again, filling the courtroom as if it were some cheap theatre. He sits at the front listening as the judge reads out the names, each one a stiletto in his soul. And then the last. Kirsty Summers. His Kirsty. He looks up at the guilty man. No longer the accused, no longer the slightest potential of innocence. Donald Anderson stares back with blank eyes, his face unreadable.

'There is only one sentence for the crime of murder, and that is life imprisonment. Given the evil nature of your crimes, and since you have shown no remorse for your actions, and indeed have attempted a quite preposterous plea of insanity, I am recommending that you serve a minimum of thirty years with no opportunity for parole before that time. Gentlemen, take the prisoner down.'

The bang of the gavel is a starter pistol for a thousand voices. It is all over, and now the chatter starts. He watches as two policemen lead Donald Anderson away. He is sixty-three years old; he will die in prison. Justice has been served.

It is not enough.

It can never be enough.

64

The blood and vomit footprints dried up after a half dozen steps, but there was no doubting that this was the way Needham had escaped. A gentle breeze fluttered the candle flame so that McLean had to hold his hand out in front of it to stop it going out. Enough light escaped to show a well-built arched tunnel with stone walls and floor. The silence was eerie, as was the unusual warmth of the breeze, as if it were midsummer outside, not the depths of winter. There was a slight brimstone smell, too, and the air felt oddly unsatisfactory, leaving him short of breath. The candle flame was tiny, as if it too were struggling to breathe. He moved slowly, all too aware that even the dim light would mark him out to anyone watching and waiting at the other end, yet still reluctant to extinguish it. After a short while, the passageway stopped at a spiral staircase, climbing up.

Disorientated by the twists and turns of the basement under Needham's house, McLean wasn't sure quite where this might bring him. The garage perhaps? Or were there any other outbuildings in the garden? Too late to back out now. He took a step upwards.

It was after he'd been climbing for more than a minute that McLean began to understand what was going on. The house had been built by the man who owned the iron-works; he remembered Needy telling him, years earlier, how they'd once been the wealthiest family in Midlothian.

Quite how the Guild of Strangers fitted in, he had no idea, but this tunnel, and the chapel down below, were obviously some early Victorian folly. A rich man's conceit; maybe even a way of spying on his workforce unseen.

His suspicions were confirmed moments later when he emerged into a windowless room lined with empty wooden shelves, and felt the temperature drop by several degrees. There was only one door, artfully disguised as part of a bookcase in the large office into which it opened. Shafts of light broke through gaps in the boarded-up windows. The candle cast shadows over some plain 1950s office furniture, but it was obvious from the decoration that this room had originally been the domain of the boss.

The beep, beep, beep of a truck reversing broke the silence, and with it McLean realised he could hear distant traffic again. He moved as fast as his candle flame would allow, across the office and into the next room. It, too, was boarded up, disused since the ironworks had closed down. This would have been the reception area for the administration of the business, he guessed. The door to the outside was locked, leaving only one other way that Needy could have gone. Into the great steel hall itself.

The space was huge; cast-iron pillars rising like spruce trees to support the roof high overhead. The lower windows had been boarded up, but higher up they were still clear, the light outside painting the distant ceiling and casting evil shadows. Most of the heavy machinery had long since gone, and the floor space was now taken up with piles of building materials. Scanning around, he couldn't see Needy anywhere, but there were plenty of places to hide. Only one way out, though; the big roller doors that opened onto the compound beyond. They were closed right now, so with a little luck, Needy was trapped.

McLean put the altar candle down carefully on the concrete floor, then went to get his mobile phone out. Only then did he remember that it was in his jacket pocket, draped around Emma's unconscious body. He took one step towards the roller doors, looking for help. Something whistled out of the shadows at him.

Twisting out of the way, he took most of the blow on his shoulders and back, but it was enough to drive the wind out of him and send him to his knees. Coughing and retching, he tried to stand as Needy danced into view, an old leather-bound book clasped under one arm, a length of two-by-four in the other. His face was a mess of swollen redness, his eyes puffed up so much he surely couldn't see. And yet he was grinning like an idiot.

'You came back! I knew you would. It told me you would.' Needy shrugged the arm with the book under it, then raised the two-by-four again. McLean rolled out of its way as it cracked on the floor, and felt his arm knock something over. There was no time to see what it was, Needy was coming back for another blow. He rolled away again, and again, as the blows came faster and faster. He had to get to his feet, had to find something to fight back with.

The two-by-four hit the ground inches from his head; splinters cracked off the end of it, cutting his face. For an instant it seemed that Needy had run out of breath. McLean seized his opportunity, grabbed at the length of wood, and pulled hard. He'd been hoping to catch Needy off balance, but the old sergeant yanked the stick free with surprising strength. Still, it had given McLean enough time to get to his feet. Now all he needed was a weapon of his own.

And then he saw the fire.

It was a small flame, but growing rapidly. The candle lay on its side, rolled up against a pile of sweepings that had caught and then spread to a pile of sawn timber. As he watched, tongues of blue flame licked up the walls, spreading both ways with a speed that couldn't be natural. It looked like a giant gas burner had just been turned on, and he was standing in the middle of the oven.

McLean was so transfixed by the sight that he lost track of Needham and the two-by-four. It struck him hard in the stomach, driving him to his knees. Before he could react it had whipped back the other way, clattering the side of his head and sending him back to the floor. The blood roared in his ears, he couldn't move, couldn't breathe. It was hard to focus, the edges of his vision dimming so that all he could see was Needy's legs and the fire behind them.

The two-by-four clattered to the ground, and then McLean felt hands grab him under his armpits. He tried to fight, but all the strength had gone from him. He was dragged a short way, propped up against a pillar. He managed to raise one hand, though it felt like it was encased in concrete, and touched the side of his head. Sticky wetness coated his fingers and pain exploded across his vision in a shower of sparks. When they cleared, he could see Needy, bending down and looking at him through those horrible, puffed-up eyes. He had the book in his hands, a quizzical expression on his face.

'Why do you fight it? It's nothing to be afraid of.' Needy opened the book and then held it up so that McLean could see. His vision was still blurry from the smoke and the blow to his head, but there was something about the size and shape of it that filled him with a terrible certainty. This was the book he'd found the slip of Kirsty's dress in. This was the *Liber animorum*, the Book of Souls.

'I can't read it, Needy,' McLean said, his voice cracking. The heat was rising quickly now, the fire spreading between the piles of materials stacked up against the walls nearby. Needy didn't seem to have noticed at all.

'No, no, no. You don't read it. That's the whole point. It reads you! See?' The sergeant turned the book back around, his eyes went down to the words and he started to mouth cod-Latin gibberish.

'*Itis apis potet avere bygone. Iacet summare quaelam coveris.*'

McLean saw his opportunity, lunged for the piece of two-by-four lying off to his side. The wood was heavy in his hand, too heavy maybe. He rolled over, getting his other hand to it too, ignoring the pain that shot through his head. Scrabbling to his knees, he brought the weapon round in a sweeping arc just as Needy realised what was going on. The sergeant let out a surprised squawk, jumped up and let go of the book. He took two steps backwards in an attempt to steady himself, then tripped over his cloak and toppled over into the fire.

The flames leapt on him as if they were alive and hungry. His cloak caught first, then with a horrible fizzing sound audible over the roar of everything else, Needy's hair burst alight. He struggled upright, pulling himself out of the fire with hands that were bubbling and blistered. And yet he didn't scream, just kept on mouthing unheard words. McLean staggered back, legs giving out as the last of his strength left him. A pillar of human fire limped towards the book, stretched out its weeping hands, sank to its knees and then toppled forward onto the open pages. The paper caught in an instant, wrapping Needy's head in a wreath of yellow flame. McLean could only watch as the skin bubbled away, oozing red blood and yellow pus, Needy's jaw still working away as he tried to read the words that had consumed his soul.

McLean watched the book and the man who had been his friend as they burned. A part of him, deep inside, was shouting at him to get up, get out, but he could hardly breathe now. It felt like he was at the top of Everest, every muscle in his body screaming in pain. It was too much effort. He was so tired. He had no strength left. He'd fought so long to right the wrong that Anderson had done. Perhaps now it was time to stop fighting and just give up.

With the last of his dwindling strength, he put his hand in his pocket. Pulled out the thin strip of fabric that had been torn from Kirsty's dress. Barely able to hold it between his fingers, he watched as the fire-driven wind rippled it this way and that. He remembered her wearing it, how it hugged her figure, how it twirled when she danced and the smile in her eyes.

And then she was dancing again, that last tiny fragment. Pirouetting in the air currents, up and up, around and around, closer and closer until the roaring flames took her too. Tears stung his eyes, but they could not run. The heat evaporated them before they could wet his cheeks. Thwarted even in that last lament, he slumped onto the floor and prepared to die.

65

She comes to him in his pain, like an angel of mercy. She is naked, but there is no shame in that. Her face is filled with joy, her hair tumbling over her shoulders like a deep black waterfall.

'Don't panic, Tony. It'll be over soon. One way or another.' He hasn't heard her voice in too long. He used to have a tape, but the fire took it, like it took everything else about her, left him only his memories. She bends down beside him, soothes his forehead with a hand as cool as the first good snow of winter.

'Kirsty.' He croaks the word, his throat like baked sand. It's so hot, he feels like he's burning up.

'Shhhh. I'm here. We're all here. It's going to be all right.'

And she's right, they are all here. One by one he sees them. Trisha Lubkin, Kate McKenzie, Audrey Carpenter, Laura Fenton, Diane Kinnear, Rosie Buckley, the list goes on as all the people Needy and Anderson killed walk past him, one by one, and touch his brow with cool fingers. They are all naked, but all smiling, lively, excited. All free. And there are more, too. People he doesn't know, and people he does. John Needham as he was a decade earlier, staring at nothing, an expression of terror on his face. Donald Anderson, younger, dressed in a monk's habit and wide-eyed as he sees what he has done. What the book has made him do.

'Kirsty.' His voice is little more than a whisper, and now he can hear a great roaring wind, feel it gusting on his face, searing off the skin. It sweeps up the people all around him, whipping them into the air like a tornado. They go willingly, their arms spread wide, their faces upturned and rapturous. Too late he realises that she must go too. He reaches for her arm, taking her hand. It is cool to the touch, so smooth. He'd forgotten what she felt like. He misses her so much.

'Don't go.'

'I have to go,' she answers with that slow, patient way of hers. 'You have to let me go. It's time to move on.'

Her fingers are slipping away from his. She is floating up into the air, her hair whipping round her face. She stares down at him and smiles, fading away from his sight.

'I love you, Kirsty,' he says. And then she is gone.

'What did you say, sir?'

McLean's eyes snapped open and he found himself staring up at the sweat-streaked face of DS Ritchie. He felt like someone had shoved him into an oven at gas-mark nine, and it wasn't hard to see why. All around was flame.

'We've got to get out. Now.' Ritchie stooped down and hauled McLean upright. He dimly recalled that she'd been injured herself. What was she doing coming here endangering herself? He'd tell her off later, he decided.

Everything hurt, but his legs seemed stronger than they had any right to be. Once he was up, he was able to stagger towards the nearest doorway, back into the admin block. Smoke billowed around the lower ceiling, flames eating at the wooden desks and shelving. They half walked, half fell down the spiral stone steps to the tunnel. The air was slightly better down here, a steady draft being dragged through by the fire up above. Still, it was difficult to breathe.

McLean paused as they crossed the chapel. 'We need to secure this. It's a crime scene.' His voice was little more than a croak. DS Ritchie leant against the wall by the door back to the house, panting.

'With respect, sir, fuck the crime scene. We need to get out of here before the whole place explodes.'

As if to underline her point, a dull thwump echoed from the tunnel, followed by a roar that rose in tone as it rose in volume. Brain addled by lack of oxygen, it took McLean long moments to realise what was happening. Then the hidden door in the wood panelling disintegrated in a ball of flame. Splinters stung his face and the force of the blast knocked him to the ground. He crawled over to the doorway as flames started to eat away at the wooden plaques and the eagle lectern.

'You're right, sergeant. Fuck the crime scene.'

They leant on each other for support, struggling up the stone stairs, first to the basement and then to the hall. The acrid smell of smoke was everywhere, even in the hallway. And overlaid on top of it was that horrible rotten-egg gaseous smell. McLean tried to place it, but his brain was too addled to make any sense. Marsh gas? Broken sewers?

The air outside was a blessed relief, cold and sweet and pure. The two of them struggled across the gravel to the car, still no sign of the promised back-up, or the air ambulance. They'd only gone halfway when a huge explosion shattered the calm. McLean turned, seeing a great black cloud rising from the site of the ironworks. Then there was an odd whistling noise, like a train coming out of a tunnel at full speed, and the whole front entrance to Needy's house blew open in a gout of flame. Windows shattered, firing razor shards of glass out across the driveway.

Both of them were knocked to the ground. McLean ended up face-down in the gravel, clinging on as if he were about to fall off the world. His head rang with the explosions, the heat, the onset of concussion. But slowly, as the winter chill eased his burns and the vertigo ebbed away, he began to hear the wail of distant sirens and the reassuring whup whup whup of an approaching helicopter.

66

He walks down the street the same as he did almost every day for two years. It was part of his beat, part of the regular rhythm of the job. But today is different. He hasn't worn the uniform for a while now, and in his absence this part of the city has changed. At first he's worried as he sees the new coffee bars and expensive fashion boutiques. Perhaps the shop he seeks is no longer there. So much is different now that the parliament is being built; the old order demolished to make way for the new.

But it is there still, the little shop with its neat green paint and tinted windows. Some things will always hold out against the march of progress, and that is good. He pushes open the door, hears the tinkle of the bell and glances up at the movement of it jangling on its little spring. Nods in approval; the shop has the right feel to it.

Not all the books are old, but none of them are new. He runs his fingers down their spines as he walks through the line of shelves towards the little counter at the back. The shopkeeper greets him with a friendly smile. He's an old man, with a trustworthy face.

'Can I help you, sir?' A trustworthy voice, too. Warm and relaxing.

'I'm looking for a gift, actually.' He's embarrassed a little, but the old man's smile wins him over. 'It's for my fiancée. We're getting married in the spring.'

'My congratulations, sir. And did you have anything particular in mind?'

'Well, this might seem a little stupid. But she's a junior doctor. Just graduated. And I thought maybe some old medical text. You know, something from a time when they used leeches and cupping and stuff. I thought it would be . . .' He tails off. Spoken aloud, the idea seems almost insulting. These are valuable books, after all. They need to be cherished and protected. Not the sort of thing you give on a whim.

'But what a splendid gift.' The shopkeeper's smile notches up another inch. 'And so appropriate. Of course, there are doctors today who still subscribe to both cupping and leeches. But a memento of a time when medicine was raw and experimental. Yes, splendid.'

And then everything is fine. The shopkeeper knows the very thing, and it's reasonably priced too. Not in the shop at the moment, but if he could take some details, he'll be in touch just as soon as he's retrieved it from his store.

He leaves the shop with a spring in his step. She's normally so difficult to buy presents for, but she'll love this. He just knows it.

67

It was going to take more than twenty-four hours' rest and a change of clothing to make McLean feel fully human again. For a start his face and hands felt like he'd been on holiday in the Costa del Sol for a fortnight and forgotten to pack the sun cream. And there was the nagging sense of unreality about it all, too. He'd heard about anoxia and the strange hallucinations it could bring on, but knowing that didn't make it any easier to accept.

'You were in here when it started? Jesus, inspector. What the hell happened?'

McLean snapped out of his reverie, remembering where he was, and with whom. Jim Burrows, the fire investigator, was surveying the steaming remains of what had once been the McMerry Ironworks. There wasn't much left of the vast building; the roof had burned out completely, and half of the walls had collapsed. From where they stood on the edge of the debris field, McLean could see the stumps of the great iron pillars that had held up the wooden rafters, black with soot and piled all around with rubble. To the rear of the building, a team of firemen were slowly clearing a path, searching for bodies.

'I was meant to be coming here to do a fire-risk assessment next week,' Burrows said. 'Looks like they could have done with it a bit earlier. How'd it start, did you say?'

McLean muttered something about candle flames and sweepings.

'Christ, what kind of idiot would bring a candle into a place like this?'

McLean coughed, grimacing as pain spread across his chest. He'd barely recovered from the fire at his tenement, and now all this.

'There was more to it, though. It went up way too quickly. And there were odd blue flames running up the walls. Never seen anything like it before.'

'Blue flames? Tinged with yellow?' Burrows had a thoughtful look on his face. 'And you say it was hot before it started?'

McLean nodded.

'What about a sulphur smell?'

McLean wasn't sure what there had been. His memory was a mess. He really shouldn't have been here at all; should have taken the day off. Maybe the month. Should have gone to the hospital, except that held more fears for him than this.

'Aye, I think there might have been,' he said. 'Rotting eggs.'

Burrows looked around the ruined building, then turned and walked out into the wide compound surrounding it. McLean followed as the fireman strode over to the nearest patch of scrubland and began hacking away at the soil with his heel. After a while, he pulled up a lump of shiny black rock and sniffed it.

'This whole area's been mined for coal since Roman times. Probably before.' He handed the lump to McLean. It was warm to the touch; hardly surprising given its proximity to the fire. When he lifted it to his nose, the unmistakable reek of sulphur caught his already sore throat. He dropped the rock and descended into a fit of coughing, culminating in a big wet ball of phlegm.

'Sorry, I should have thought,' Burrows said. 'Smoke inhalation's a wee bugger.'

'What's this got to do with anything?' McLean asked once he'd managed to get his voice back. He kicked the dropped lump of coal.

'Well, the ground round here's riddled with old mine workings. Shafts, tunnels, you name it. And there's a lot of coal still down there. Up Bilston way there's a great store of it, filled in half the glen. But sometimes you get other stuff mixed up. Might be an old landfill tip, might just be gas pockets. Firedamp, you know? My guess is that's what we had here. And an underground fire, too. Could have been burning for years and no one noticed. Heated everything up nicely, gas escapes up through cracks in the soil, hits the floor of the factory. The only place it can escape's where the concrete meets the walls. Something sets it off, and there you have it, sheets of pale blue flame running up the walls. Must've been like being stuck in a huge gas cooker.'

'And that would account for all the other old factory fires?' McLean knew what the answer was going to be, but he asked anyway.

'Er, no. Maybe worth having a look at the old geological maps and mine-works surveys. But . . . no. Here, I can see it. In the city? No. And we don't know what started any of those fires.'

'The tramps lit a fire in the office of that factory over in

407

Slateford,' McLean said. 'Strange you never mentioned it in your report.'

'Didn't I?' Burrows pulled off his hard hat and scratched at his forehead. 'To be honest, it could've slipped my mind. Winter's not a good time for a fire investigator, you know.'

'What, you don't like the cold?'

'No, inspector. There's a lot of fires.'

McLean managed a smile, then an odd thought popped into his head.

'It's Burrows, isn't it?' he asked. 'The way you spell your name: B-U-R-R-O-W-S?'

The fire investigator looked a little confused, then said, 'Aye, that's right.'

'Never been spelled O-U-G-H-S, you know, like Edgar Rice?'

The look on Burrows' face was a mixture of confusion and concern. 'Not as far as I know. Why?'

'Oh, nothing,' McLean said. 'Just a hunch.'

They found the remains of Sergeant John Needham about an hour later. At least, McLean suspected it was Needy; formal identification would have to be through dental records or DNA analysis of the charred bones. He was lying on his front, arms clutched around a pile of ash that was all that remained of his precious book. Most of his uniform had burned to nothing, melting into the mess that had been skin and fat and muscle. Even the gold chain he had been wearing around his neck was broken, links melted away to precious slag. But the heavy, round medallion that had been in the middle lay on the floor beside him.

Careful not to disturb the body before the pathologist arrived, McLean fished in his pockets for an evidence bag or latex gloves to pick it up with. It was then that he realised he had lost the thin strip of fabric, torn from Kirsty's dress. He cast his mind back, trying to remember. He'd had it with him in the chapel, but what had he done with it after that? He remembered holding it in his fist, wrapped around his fingers. Then it was gone. Burned up in the fire. The last piece of her. Time to let her go?

Tears burned in his dry eyes then and he was forced to look away. Shoving his hands back into his pockets, McLean pushed himself upright, stepped back from the curiously peaceful body. The medallion lay where he had left it, undisturbed. There was still no sign of the pathologist. But as he walked away from the scene, he realised that he no longer cared about the investigation. Someone else could deal with all that. He'd had enough.

'Parcel for you, sir. Courier just delivered it.'

PC Gregg stood in the doorway to McLean's office and tried not to look like she was staring. He couldn't blame her, really. He must look a state. Six stitches in a gash on his right temple, black eyes, singed hair, burnt-red cheeks like he'd been boozing all his life. And he still couldn't get rid of the horrible smell of smoke that seemed to follow him everywhere he went.

'Thank you, constable. Just put it on the desk. If you can find a space.'

She did as she was told, then hovered as if waiting to be dismissed.

'Was there something else?'

'I didn't know if you heard, sir, but that lad we were looking for just walked into the station and gave himself up.'

'Lad? What lad?'

'You know. We interviewed his brother at Christmas.'

'Peter Ayre?'

'Aye, that's his name. He's down in Interview Room 3 talking like he don't know how to stop. I've never seen Dag— er, Chief Inspector Duguid look so happy, sir.'

'I'll have to go and have a word with him.' McLean pictured the destruction done to his tenement. Saw the pale dead face of his neighbour. 'Thanks for letting me know, constable.'

PC Gregg nodded and scurried out of the room, leaving McLean with his parcel. It sloshed like a bottle of something and was about the right shape and size for a good malt. He slit the brown paper with a careful knife, and opened it up to reveal a twenty-five-year-old Springbank, nestling in a wooden display box. There was a note attached, written in surprisingly childish handwriting: 'My wee girl can rest in peace now. You have my thanks for that. I won't forget. This and the other present are a token of my gratitude.'

It wasn't signed, but McLean knew exactly who it was from. He slid the bottle out of its box and held it up to the light. Liquid gold. By rights he should take it straight to the chief superintendent; accepting gifts from a Glasgow gangster could get him into all manner of trouble. And there was also the question of how MacDougal could possibly know what had happened. On the other hand, McLean reckoned he'd earned it. And it would probably be a month before his throat was healed enough to drink it. Slipping it back into the case, he shoved the whole lot in a drawer and headed off for Interview Room 3.

Peter Ayre looked as bad as McLean felt. Quite apart from the obvious signs of withdrawal, his face was a mess of bruises and he held one arm like it might well have been broken. His right hand was wrapped up in a grubby, bloodstained bandage that looked suspiciously like it hid too few fingers. He should have been in a hospital, not an interview room, but McLean wasn't going to be the one to tell Dagwood that. Not this time.

The chief inspector had a look of insufferable glee on his face, and it wasn't hard to work out why. From the observation room, McLean could hear Ayre's dull mono-tone junkie voice listing names and addresses as if he'd had them drilled into him. Even given Dagwood's track record, the gang responsible for the cannabis farms dotted around the city were going to be finding it very hard to operate.

'Can you believe he just walked in?' DI Langley stared at the interview being carried out on the other side of the glass. 'He pretty much begged us to lock him up. He's terrified.'

'What about his information? Any good?' McLean wasn't sure why he asked. He knew what the answer would be.

'What we can tell so far. It's pretty early days. But he seems to have been a key player. He knows all the sites, all the people. And he's said he'll testify if we can help him get cleaned up. Someone's due a promotion out of this.'

Aye, and we all know who that'll be, thought McLean, and he's not standing in this room. 'So who do you think will move in on the patch. Once you've put this lot away?'

Langley looked at McLean with a quizzical expression. 'What do you mean?'

'My money's on Glasgow. East side.' McLean pulled open the observation-room door to leave. 'Those Weegie bastards have been trying to get a foothold over here for years.'

Outside the station, the cold air soothed his face, but tickled his throat. McLean put his head down against the wind and started the long walk across town. His grandmother's car was safely tucked up in its garage, away from road salt and exploding buildings. He'd give it a really good wash just as soon as the weather turned a bit warmer. Then maybe take it to that garage in Loanhead he'd heard about, get them to do some serious rust-proofing. He wondered if the electrics were up to powering an airwave set.

Despite the credit crunch, Christmas being over, most of the banks going bust and unemployment rising faster than Dagwood's blood pressure, Princes Street was as full of shoppers as ever. He dodged between teenage mothers wheeling pushchairs, old biddies with lethal umbrellas unfolded despite the clear skies, teenagers in clothes several sizes too large and a hundred and one other variations on humanity.

And then he saw him, staring into the window of a huge chain bookstore at a display of the complete works of Ian Rankin.

'Anderson!' The shout spasmed his throat and McLean

bent double, coughing and hacking like he was a sixty-a-day smoker.

'You OK, pal?'

After an eye-watering minute, McLean was able to look up. From a distance, perhaps, the man who was talking to him might have looked a bit like Donald Anderson. But now he was standing there, it was quite obviously not him. His face was rounder, for one thing, and the nose was all wrong. And Anderson would never have worn clothes like that.

'Only, I thought you were calling me.' The man's voice was all wrong too. There was warmth in it. Concern even.

'Sorry,' McLean wheezed after a while, forcing himself upright. 'I thought you were someone else.'

'No bother.' The man gave him a friendly pat on the shoulder. 'Happens all the time, y'know.'

She lay on pristine white sheets, propped up by a couple of heavy pillows. Her arms hung limp by her sides, wires and tubes disappearing into both. Monitors clustered around the bed like trainee doctors, watching her constantly, checking she was still breathing through the tube that forced its way past her lips and on down her throat.

McLean stood at the door to the intensive care ward, staring through the glass, not daring to go in. He wanted more than anything for this not to be happening.

'Oh, sir. I'm sorry. I didn't realise . . .'

He turned to see DS Ritchie approaching down the corridor. Unlike him, she wasn't carrying a bunch of cheap petrol-station flowers. Like him, her face looked like she'd been several rounds with Muhammad Ali. The cut on her temple was neatly stitched, the flesh around it a riot of swelling and colour.

'Any change?' Ritchie nodded towards the IC ward.

'I don't know. I only just got here.'

'You going in?' It wasn't as stupid a question as it sounded.

'I guess I should.' McLean took a deep breath and went inside.

It smelled of antiseptic and alcohol hand-wash. The ever-attendant machines beeped and whirred like some nightmare sci-fi computer gone mad. As he approached the bed, McLean noticed that Ritchie hung back, and he was grateful for her sensitivity. This was a terrible kind of torture, seeing Emma lying comatose, surrounded by the same apparatus that had kept his grandmother's body alive for so long. Some would have seen the technology as a reason for hope, but he'd been down that road already and knew the odds all too well.

There was no bedside table; the monitors took up all the space. The flowers hung heavy in his grasp. He couldn't think of anything to do with them now, and wondered why he'd brought them. It wasn't as if Emma could see them, and they had virtually no scent. But they were a splash of colour, he had to admit that. So he laid them on the blanket at the end of the bed.

'I should go,' Ritchie said from the other side of the room. 'I just wanted to . . . You know . . . See if there was any . . .' She shrugged.

McLean nodded. 'OK. I'll see you tomorrow. And Kirsty? Thanks.'

He didn't feel any more comfortable after she had

gone, but he did manage to find a chair. Placing it carefully down amongst the tubes and wires, he sat beside the bed and took Emma's cold hand in his own.

'She could wake up at any time.' He looked around to see a young doctor standing in the doorway through which DS Ritchie had just left. Or had he been sitting there unthinking for hours? It was difficult to tell.

'That's the thing about a blow to the head. They say recovering consciousness quickly is essential, but sometimes it's best if the patient doesn't wake up. Gives the brain time to heal itself.' The doctor crossed the room, raised a single eyebrow at the flowers, and then picked up the chart hanging from the end of the bed. McLean knew a prop when he saw one.

'There's a "but" in there somewhere, isn't there.'

The doctor tried a reassuring smile, too weary to be really effective. 'It's an amazing thing, the brain. There's so much we don't know about it. Sometimes what looks like enormous damage leaves no discernible after-effect. Sometimes the smallest injury can kill. We've done all the scans and tests we can, but until she wakes up, we just don't know. You need to prepare yourself. There's every possibility that she might have suffered irreparable damage.'

Irreparable. McLean tried not to dwell on the word as he stared at Emma's face. Her eyes were sunken, rounded with dark bruising. Her once-spiky black hair now hung around her ears in rat-tails. Her skin was sallow, her lips pale. It was hard to think of her as the woman he'd woken up with just three days ago. One more person's life destroyed because he'd let them get too close.

'Erm, technically visiting hours are over for today,' the doctor said. 'But seeing as you're a police officer . . .'

'It's all right.' McLean released Emma's hand and stood up. She didn't move, didn't protest, didn't do anything to make him stay. 'I'll come back tomorrow.'

And the day after that, he thought as he pushed his way out into the corridor. And the day after that.

Epilogue

The ceilidh band was in full swing, the party warming up nicely. On the dance floor, Mr and Mrs Jenkins whirled and jigged their way through an eightsome reel to much whooping and cheering. Drink flowed freely, and everyone was filled with fine food. Nobody noticed the best man slip out through the back door of the hotel and climb into his shiny red car.

The speech had gone OK, McLean thought as he pulled slowly out of the car park. It was debatable whether or not Phil would ever talk to him again, but then that was the nature of these things. He should never have confided so drunkenly in his flatmate if he didn't want the world told all on his wedding day. Maybe one day Phil would get to return the favour. Maybe.

Skye in June was sunny, the evenings long. He'd wanted to do this a couple of days earlier, but as was inevitable, wedding preparations had conspired with a particularly unpleasant investigation to mean he'd only arrived at the hotel late last night. At least he had the map that DC MacBride had printed off for him. With luck he might just find the place.

The road turned to track, and then finally ended at a rickety wooden gate in a dry stone wall. McLean stopped the engine and stared through the windscreen out to sea for a while. It was certainly a beautiful place, a perfect retreat.

But bleak. Outside the car, the wind whipped at his kilt and tugged his hair. Now it was warm, but in the winter it wouldn't be half so accommodating. He clambered over the gate and followed the slight indentation in the grass that suggested where once the track had continued, heading towards the cliff edge where the gulls soared and screamed.

A pair of gnarled and ancient rowans marked the edge of the old monastery compound. It had taken nature very little time indeed to reclaim the place after it had burned down. A few sheep eyed him suspiciously as he peered into the rubble-remains of old buildings, finally ending up at the hulk of the church.

Its roof was long gone, along with the east wall and most of the south. The north and west walls still stood against the battering weather of the Atlantic Ocean, but they probably wouldn't last long. McLean tried to imagine the place still intact, with a dozen elderly monks going about their daily worship. There were times, he felt, particularly in the last six months, when the idea of giving it all up and coming somewhere like this was very tempting. There was something about having a simple routine to fill each day, unchanging and reliable. But he knew that he would only get bored after a month or so. Itchy feet would drive him away. And there was the whole God thing, too.

Leaving the ruined church, he walked through the graveyard. Headstones tilted this way and that, as if the monks buried beneath them were struggling to rise up and take back what had once been theirs. Some were old, their inscriptions worn away to illegibility; others still bore the names of those they commemorated. They were simple inscriptions, no flowery sentiment here. Just a name, a date, a prayer. A few told of what part the dead had played in the tiny community – beekeeper, fisherman, herbsman. The last one caught McLean's attention, though not in surprise. More it was as if everything finally made sense.

Fr Noam Anton
1897–1979
Librarian

He stood in front of the grave for long minutes, just staring as the breeze whistled past. Then he turned and walked away. He could be back at the wedding reception in half an hour.

With luck, nobody would notice he'd been gone.

Detective Inspector McLean will return soon in:

The Hangman's Song

Available from Penguin in 2014

The following short story was first published on my blog, sirbenfro.blogspot.com, back in June 2005. I'd been juggling a few ideas around for a while, looking for a hook to hang them all on. Back then in the innocent days of blogging, I found myself following a group of people who would set themselves an occasional challenge – to write a short story, each based on a simple theme. A lurker rather than participator, I was never invited to join the party – not that I particularly expected to be or minded that I was not. Something about the theme for this particular round – a police auction – clicked in my mind and all the pieces fell together. I wrote the story very quickly after that. It was my first ever attempt at crime fiction.

This and five other McLean short stories can be downloaded for free at www.devildog.co.uk. You can find my work in other genres there too.

The Final Reel

Monday

'What've you got for me, Bob?'

McLean ducked under the police tape and entered the dingy apartment. A dying fly battered itself against a grimy window, and there was a damp smell about the place, old mould and unemptied garbage. Something worse. He followed his nose into the smallest room. It wasn't much wider than the ancient cludgie it held, but three men had managed to squeeze in there. DS 'Grumpy' Bob Laird, a SOC photographer and the deceased.

'I'd say he died a few days ago. Massive trauma to the head,' Bob said. McLean peered closer, wished he hadn't.

'Pulled the chain and the whole cistern came off the wall,' Bob continued. 'It had to weigh a good hundred pounds.'

'A tragic accident then.' McLean stepped back to let Bob out of the room. The photographer's flash popped a couple more times and then he too backed out.

Cleared, McLean could see the whole scene now. The cistern was still attached to the pan by its thick lead pipe. The brackets had come out of the wall and the whole thing had tipped forward, smashed into the victim's head. Death would have been instant.

'RIP Shuggy Brown,' McLean said.

'You know him?'

'Small-time cat burglar. Used to go through the death notices in the papers and do over the empty houses.'

'Oh, aye, the Obituary Man. I remember,' Bob said.

McLean looked at the dead figure in front of him, the cistern flopped to one side, its brackets still fixed to it. The bare wooden floorboards were dark with damp, but not soaked.

'Who turned the water off?' He stepped forwards into the room, stared up at the pipe. It had sheared off neatly where it would have entered the cistern.

'No one, as far as I know,' Bob said. 'Neighbours complained of a smell. We forced entry. Called in as soon as we found him.'

'Hm.' McLean leant over the recumbent corpse, trying hard not to breathe. There were four small holes in the wall above his head, where the cistern had been attached. A century of thick paint had left two bracket-shaped marks. Looking down, he saw the old brass screws lying behind the pan, two to each side. Their heads were also glossed with a thick coat of paint. Slots a distant memory.

'Maybe not an accident then.'

Tuesday

The actress Shauna Zapata, who died last month at the age of 102, was cremated today in a private ceremony at Mortonhall Crematorium. Shauna, best known for her Hollywood career in the inter-war period, returned to her home-town of Edinburgh in the mid-sixties. A recluse, it's understood that she spent her latter years, and the fortunes of her three late husbands, on tracking down all original prints of her roles. Film historians had hoped that she would bequeath this invaluable archive to the nation, but it was revealed today that her entire body of work was cremated with her.

McLean flicked off the radio and peered through the rain-smeared windscreen at the line of traffic snaking along Clerk Street. Edinburgh was its usual grey, a vicious wind throwing the moisture around the square-cut buildings like a child in a tantrum. Cocooned from it by his metal box, and with the heater working for a change, he was happy just to crawl along. Dan McFeely wasn't going anywhere in a hurry.

The apartment was in Newington, respectable enough without being too ostentatious. A uniform let him in the front door and he climbed four flights of stone stairs worn smooth by countless passing feet. Gloss green walls peeled with damp, stained by a hundred years of salts leaching from the sandstone. On the top landing, a rusty old bicycle frame was padlocked to the railings, its wheels and saddle long gone. Everything smelled faintly of cat piss.

'He's this way, sir. In the bath.' Another uniform showed McLean into the apartment. Inside it was a different world, neat and tidy, ordered. Expensive works of art hung on the walls and everywhere there were shelves of pottery figurines, silver figures, collectibles.

The bathroom was small, with a skylight high in the roof. Dan McFeely lay in a pool of scummy red water, one arm dangling over the tub, the other resting on his pale, hairy chest. He head tilted back as if he were staring at the sky through the little square porthole. A neat gash ran under his pointy chin from one ear to the other.

'He's been here awhile,' the uniform said.

'Let me guess, the neighbours complained about the smell?' McLean could almost taste the tang of iron in the air.

'No, sir,' the uniform said. 'I was going house to house, asking about the schoolyard muggings. I knocked and the door swung open.'

'And you came looking for him in the bathroom?'

'That door was open too, sir. I think he might have left them like that on purpose. To be found.'

'What d'you mean?' McLean asked. Then he noticed it, red and shiny in the blood-stained hand. A cut-throat razor.

'Shite.'

'Sir?'

'This is Dan McFeely, sergeant,' McLean said. 'Feely

the Fence. See all that stuff out there? That's stolen goods, only he knows we've no way of proving it. The dodgy stuff he's always kept hidden, but he's a cocky bastard who likes to show off how much cleverer he is than us. If he committed suicide, then I'm in line to be the next Pope.'

'Death would appear to have been caused by heart failure due to acute loss of blood.'

McLean stood silently, watching as the pathologist poked and prodded the white body on the slab.

'Loss of blood would appear to be a result of the severing of the carotid artery with a sharp blade. A cut-throat razor such as that found in the subject's left hand. However, appearances would be deceiving in this matter. Whilst a great deal of blood has been lost, there is more still in the body than would be consistent with such a death.'

'What?' McLean asked.

'I'm saying,' the pathologist fixed him with a withering glare, 'that he didn't die from this wound. He was as good as dead already when it was inflicted on him. What's more, the cut goes from left to right, and the blade was found in his left hand.'

'What did kill him then?'

'I can't be sure, but he's got some interesting bruising on his neck around the incisions. I'll have to do some tests to be sure, but he could've been strangled first.'

Wednesday

Half-past four and it was already dark. Sometimes McLean hated Edinburgh and mostly that was during the winter months. Dark when you got up, dark long before the working day was over. If his working day could ever be said to be over.

The house stood back from the road, screened from the traffic by a high wall and mature trees. It was a substantial building; three storeys of blackened sandstone and tall windows. Grumpy Bob met him at the door and they stepped inside.

'Gabriel Squire,' Bob said.

'The art collector, I know. What's the story?'

'His housekeeper found him.' Bob pointed to a slight woman, sitting on the other side of an entrance hall.

'Mrs Davey, this is Detective Inspector McLean,' Bob said as the housekeeper looked up. Her eyes were red with crying, her cheeks drained of colour. 'Could you tell him what you told me.'

'I was just cleaning the house, like I do every Thursday,' the woman said. 'Mr Squire was in his study. I don't go in there. But I heard voices, you see. Mr Squire shouting at someone. I . . . I . . . was listening at the door. I know I shouldn't, but Mr Squire, he's ever so nice a gentleman. I couldn't bear it if he was . . . Well then I heard a woman scream, "It's mine, give it to me." And then there was this terrible crash.' Mrs Davey stopped, the tears welling in her eyes.

'Perhaps I'd better have a look,' McLean said to Bob.

A huge fireplace dominated one end of the study and a large desk sat under the window, strewn with odd items. Most of the walls were lined with bookcases and cabinets filled with curios. A body lay sprawled across the hearth.

Gabriel Squire had been in his late fifties, fit, with a full head of greying hair. He wore a velvet smoking jacket, a silk cravat around his neck. Rather incongruously, McLean thought, he sported a pair of fading tartan baffies on his feet. And a large bloody mess where his left temple ought to have been.

'Looks like he tripped over the rug. Hit his head on the fireplace.' Bob pointed to a skin-and-hair bloodstain on the carved stone.

'What a way to go,' McLean said. 'Killed by an Adam. But what about this woman?'

'Don't know about that, sir,' Bob said. 'Mrs Davey . . . Well, I don't think she's playing the full team, if you know what I mean. She says she knocked, and when she didn't get an answer, she came in. Found him dead. Called us straight away.'

McLean crossed over the room to the window. It was latched, a thick layer of paint gumming up the works. He doubted it had been opened in years. There was only the one door. His eyes fell on the desk and its collection of curios; jewellery mostly, small stuff but expensive. McLean was no great expert, but he knew diamonds when he saw them. And craftsmanship. An intricately carved silver figurine instantly put him in mind of Dan McFeely's apartment.

And in the midst of it all sat a shallow round tin, perhaps ten inches across and an inch deep. There was something about it that was almost mesmeric. Perhaps because it looked so out of place. Only years of instinct stopped him from picking it up. Instead, he went back into the hall where Mrs Davey was being comforted by a WPC.

'Mrs Daley, has Mr Squire had any unusual visitors recently? Say in the last week?' he asked.

The housekeeper made a strange face, as if thinking about things didn't come naturally to her. She started to shake her head, then stopped.

'There was a gentleman. Last Thursday it would have been. He didn't stay long.'

'Wait here a moment.' McLean went back to his car. On the back seat the Dan McFeely case file sat amidst a mound of other paperwork and detritus. He fished a picture out of it. Mortuary shot of just the head.

'Was that him?' he asked Mrs Davey back in the house. She looked at it nervously.

'Yes, I think so. Only he doesn't look at all well there. He wasn't nearly so pale.'

'You'd think he died from the blow to the temple,' the pathologist said. 'But in actual fact he was dead before he hit the fireplace. I understand it was an Adam?'

'Stolen from Auchencruive,' McLean said. 'It turns out that Mr Squire was quite the collector of other people's antiques. So what killed him then, heart attack?'

'No. He was throttled. Quite violently. His windpipe's been crushed and there's severe bruising to his neck. The odd thing is that his cravat was still perfectly tied.'

Thursday

'This piece is exquisite. Nineteenth century. Made by ourselves, of course.'

McLean sat in a small office at the back of Douglas and Foote, Jewellers to Her Majesty the Queen. Across a tiny desk, an elderly man was peering through an eyeglass at one of the silver figurines found at Gabriel Squire's house.

'Do you know who it was sold to?'

'It was part of a set of nine, commissioned by the seventh Marquess of Queensberry. See, it has a number on the base? That was your stick number for the day's shooting. It came back to us in the seventies, part of an auction to raise funds to pay death duties. My predecessor, Mr Mayfield, liked to buy back our more exceptional work whenever he could.'

'So it was stolen from you?' McLean asked.

'Stolen? Heavens no,' the old man said. 'We sold this piece to Mrs McLeod not more than a year ago.'

'Mrs McLeod?'

'You'd probably know her better by her stage name, Shauna Zapata. Such a shame she died. She was one of our best customers. Had a good eye. No, this piece belongs to her estate.'

Friday

It took McLean only five minutes to decide he didn't like Kiernan McTavish. The solicitor was executor for the will of the late Shauna McLeod. He was also shifty, never letting his eyes settle anywhere. He fidgeted constantly. And he was evasive.

'Mrs McLeod's worldly goods have all been accounted for,' he said, barely looking at the small silver figurine. 'They're to be auctioned at Sotheby's at the end of the month. All proceeds will go to the Children's Hospital.'

'So you're sure there was no burglary? Nothing's gone missing. None of these items?' He laid out a number of pictures on the desk. McTavish pounced on them like a clumsy cat. Anything was better than having to look McLean in the eye. He watched as the lawyer peered at each photo, hoping for a spark of recognition. Nothing.

'Or this?' he asked, finally, placing a photograph of the circular tin in front of the lawyer. 'It's a roll of eight-mill film. But it's so old and rotten no one can tell what's on it.'

'Nope,' McTavish said, just a little too quickly. Something like fear flitted across his face and all of a sudden he stopped fidgeting, looked straight at McLean. 'Do you know anything about Mrs McLeod?' he asked.

'Only what I read in the papers. And I've seen a couple of her movies on the telly.'

'Shauna McLeod was a troubled woman,' McTavish

said, his voice suddenly formal, as if he were summing up before the jury. 'After her third husband died, she began to believe she was cursed. She thought that every film she'd made had taken a little piece of her soul. So she set about trying to get them back. She tracked down and bought every original printing of every movie she ever appeared in. Every screen test. Every gag reel. Even the cuttings that had found their way into the hands of collectors. She found them all, and she bought them all.'

'And then she had them all cremated alongside her. I heard it on the radio. They had to close Mortonhall down for the day.' McLean said.

'Quite, inspector,' McTavish said. 'And she was a meticulous woman. Everything was catalogued. Everything. It was stipulated in her will that if her wishes were not carried out, then I – that is to say, we – would not receive our fee. It was a not inconsiderable sum, which is why, inspector, I am perfectly certain that none of these items belonged to Mrs McLeod at the time of her death.'

McLean took back the photographs. 'Well, thank you for your time, Mr McTavish,' he said.

'I'm glad I could be of help. Tell me, inspector, what happens to those?'

'These? Technically they belong to the estate of Gabriel Squire, but since they were among other items identified as stolen they'll be treated as the same.'

'And?' McTavish was fidgeting again.

'We'll hang onto them for a couple of months and if no one's claimed them they'll be put up for auction.'

'I see. Well, thank you, inspector. Goodbye.'

A Couple of Months Later

It was an expensive car; a 1960s Bristol still as shiny and polished as the day it rolled out of the factory. McLean looked through the windscreen at the body of Kiernan McTavish. His face had turned blue.

'Not something you see much of these days,' said Grumpy Bob. 'It doesn't work with modern cars. You just get a nasty headache.'

'Quite.' McLean looked up at the house and then back to the car. How long was it since he had spoken to McTavish? He knelt down by the open door, reached in and turned the key. It was dead, no juice in the battery. But it was in the 'On' position. He looked at McTavish. The lawyer was relaxed, as if he had fallen asleep, but there was a livid bruise around his neck.

'How'd we find out about him?'

'Neighbour called. Said the car had been left running all night. Uniform came round to have a quiet chat about being more considerate.'

McLean looked around the interior of the car, all leather and polished walnut, shiny chrome and Bakelite switches. A piece of paper was scrumpled into a ball in the footwell by the pedals. He unravelled it. An auction receipt for £500, paid for Lot 786, plus 15 per cent commission. Cash sale. Dated yesterday.

'Anyone had a look in the house?' McLean asked.

'Not yet, why?'

'Because this man was murdered, then put in here to make it look like suicide. Sound like a familiar MO to you?'

'Gabriel Squire?' Bob asked.

'And Dan McFeely, and I'm thinking Shuggy Brown too. The burglar, the fence, the client and the lawyer. But who? And why? Get a SOC team down here, Bob. I'm going to have a quick nosey inside.'

Outside, the house was classic Edinburgh West End Georgian. Inside it had been stripped down to a white-painted minimalist shell. The floors were dark polished wood, the doors the same. The hallway held nothing but a tall metal hat stand. McLean slipped on a pair of latex gloves, then pushed open the nearest door.

It led into the sitting room, which looked out onto the driveway in front through a tall bay window. There were no curtains, just the flimsiest of white canvas blinds, rolled up to the ceiling. A gas fire flickered in a brutal square stone fireplace beneath a wall-mounted plasma television as big as a cinema screen. A white leather sofa faced both. The only other furniture in the room was a desk made from a sheet of glass suspended between two metal trestles. Lying on top of this was Lot 786: the tin.

McLean prised the lid off with his thumb, eyes watering at the smell of decomposing celluloid. There wasn't much left of the film, just a vaguely spiral gooey black mess. He touched it lightly with one finger and it slid towards the edge of the tin, revealing a corner of stained paper label underneath. Flipping the tin over delicately, he tried to get the sticky goo to drop into the lid. It oozed out in great strings, then suddenly dropped with a noise like a dying trifle. He held the tin up to the light, peering at the indistinct words on the darkened paper.

Shauna and Morag. Summer 1919. Balnakiel.

'It's mine! Give it to me now!'

McLean tried to whirl around, but all he could feel was hands at his throat. Powerful fingers cut off his breathing in an instant, choked him so that he couldn't even shout for help. Instinctively he dropped the tin and reached up for his attacker. His vision was already narrowing, stars popping in his eyes.

'Mine I tell you! Mine!' A woman's voice, mid-Atlantic accent, familiar.

His hands were at his throat now, but he couldn't find her hands, even though he could feel them squeezing the life out of him. Then he saw her, reflected in the glass tabletop.

Long blonde hair tumbling over her shoulders, she looked like some dame from a detective movie. She was dressed for the part, too. Thirties chic, all the rage once again, and she had her hands around his throat. She was choking the life out of him. He'd seen her before. In black and white.

But she wasn't there. She couldn't be there.

McLean reached out blindly for the lid of the tin. The remnants of celluloid lay inside it, oozing out into a sticky black puddle. He could feel his strength fading as his fingers grasped at the edge.

And then he had it. With a last effort, he flung it as hard as he could in the direction of the fireplace.

*

'The attacker must've left the gas fire on without lighting it. Reckoned it'd go bang and cover up any evidence.' McLean stared up at the smiling face of Grumpy Bob from his hospital bed. The sergeant had brought a big bag of grapes and was slowly eating his way through the lot of them. 'The SOC boys were well pissed that you torched their crime scene,' he added. 'And the chief wants to know what you were doing in there in the first place. But it could be worse.'

'How so?' McLean asked, then wished he hadn't. His throat hurt even when he thought about swallowing and his face felt like he'd been asleep in the sun for a week. No one had let him near a mirror so he had no idea how much hair he still had left.

'Well now.' Grumpy Bob popped the last grape into his mouth, scrumpled up the bag and threw it in the vicinity of the bin. 'You could be dead.'

Without whom . . .

Like *Natural Causes* before it, *The Book of Souls* was first published as an ebook, under my own publishing imprint, DevilDog Publishing. It's impossible to spot all your own mistakes, so I am indebted to Heather Bain and Keir Allen for pre-publication proof-reading, and to Lisa McShine, Ellen Grogan, John Burrell, Scott M. Ryan and Malcolm Gray for pointing out errors further down the line. Any mistakes are mine; their lack entirely due to the keen eyes of others.

Many thanks to Alex Clarke and the rest of the team at Michael Joseph, for taking me on and for honing these books into even better shape. Thanks, too, to my agent, the irrepressible Juliet Mushens.

Observant readers may have noticed a certain Detective Constable Stuart MacBride gracing these stories. This is no coincidence; Stuart has been a good friend and given me support for many years. His in-depth critique of early drafts of both *Natural Causes* and *The Book of Souls* played no small part in them being short-listed for the CWA Debut Dagger, I am sure. If you haven't read Stuart's books, then you must. No, right now.

An honourable mention goes to Sandra Ruttan (pronounced Roo Tan) and all the crew at Spinetingler Magazine, for publishing my stories long before anyone else took me seriously. Thanks also to Phillip Patterson and Dorothy Lumley.

There are innumerable others who've given me support and deserve a thank you; the Harrogate Irregulars and my Twitter and Facebook friends in particular. I know if I try to list them individually I'll forget someone, so best to avoid that embarrassment and give you all a collective hug. You know who you are.

And finally, because you should always keep the best for last, there's Barbara, whose surname I stole for my hero, and who has put up with me for too many years to admit.